CROMWELL'S BLESSING

ALSO BY PETER RANSLEY

Plague Child

PETER RANSLEY

CROMWELL'S BLESSING

Harper
Press

Harper*Press*
An imprint of HarperCollins*Publishers*
77–85 Fulham Palace Road,
Hammersmith, London W6 8JB
www.harpercollins.co.uk

Published by Harper*Press* in 2012

1

A catalogue record for this book
is available from the British Library

ISBN 978-0-00-731239-9

Typeset in Minion with Medici Script display by
G&M Designs Limited, Raunds, Northamptonshire
Printed and bound in Great Britain by
Clays Ltd, St Ives plc

For Finlay

Acknowledgements

Thanks to my editors: Clare Smith, who encouraged me from the book's conception, Essie Cousins who saw it through its final stages and copyeditor Helen Day, who had an unerring eye for my inconsistencies; to my researcher, Deborah Rosario, for digging out everything from the origins of early shorthand to the intricacies of seventeenth century bowls; and above all to my wife Cynthia for her help and patience during my frequent absences in the seventeenth century.

Acknowledgements are usually to the living, but I want to salute George Joyce, the real character who was instrumental in kidnapping the King. He lit the fuse that ignited the very English revolution in 1647, which, although it petered out, was an inspiration for the American and French revolutions that followed. He remained a revolutionary all his life. In a sense he never died. After the Restoration he was hunted down and was last heard of in Rotterdam in 1670, where he vanished. I like to think he is haunting these pages.

1647
Charles I:
the final
journeys

Scots sell
Charles I
to English

Newcastle

King kidnapped
with 'Cromwell's
blessing':
Tom's freedom
march

Charles held
by Cromwell's
enemies

Holdenby
House

Cambridge

London

Hampton Court:
Charles held by
Cromwell

Putney debates

Charles' attempted
escape to France

PART ONE

A Silver Spoon

Spring 1647

I

I could not stop shivering. That February morning in 1647 was the coldest, bleakest morning of the whole winter, but it was going to be far colder, far bleaker for Trooper Scogman when I told him he was going to be hanged.

Most mornings I woke up and knew exactly who I was: Major Thomas Stonehouse, heir to the great estate of Highpoint near Oxford, if my grandfather, Lord Stonehouse, was to be believed. Now the Civil War was over, sometimes, in that first moment of waking, I woke up as Tom Neave, one-time bastard, usurper and scurrilous pamphleteer.

That morning was one of them.

I should have left it up to Sergeant Potter to tell Scogman, but he would have relished it: taunted Scogman, left him in suspense. At least I would tell him straight out.

My regiment was billeted at a farm near Dutton's End, Essex, part of an estate seized by Parliament from a Royalist who had fled the country. The pail outside was solid ice. The dog opened one eye before curling back into a tight ball. Straw, frosted over in the yard, snapped under my boots like icicles. A crow seemed scarcely able to lift its wings as it drifted over the soldiers' tents.

More soldiers in their red uniforms were snoring in the barns, where horses were also stabled. We were a cavalry unit, the justification for calling Cromwell's New Model Army both new and a model for the future. Whereas the foot soldiers were pressed men, who would desert as soon as you turned your back, the cavalry were volunteers. They were the sons of yeomen or tradesmen, who brought to war the discipline of their Guilds. They joined not just for the better pay – and the horse which would carry their packs – but because they were God-fearing and believed in Parliament.

Except for Scogman.

I approached the wooden shed which was the camp's makeshift prison. I half-hoped Scogman had escaped, but I could see the padlock, still intact, and the guard asleep, huddled in blankets.

Scogman on the loose would have been worse. The countryside would have been up in arms. Villagers resented us enough when we were fighting the war. Now it was over, and we were still here, they hated us.

Six months had passed since the Royalist defeat at the battle of Naseby. Yet the King was in the hands of the Scots. We were supposed to be on the same side – but the Scots would not leave England until they were paid and there were rumours they were doing a secret deal with the King. In spite of the stone in his bladder, his piles and his liver, Lord Stonehouse was in Newcastle, negotiating for the release of the King.

'We could not govern with him,' he wrote tersely to me. 'But we cannot govern without him.'

The guard, Kenwick, was a stationer's son from Holborn – I knew them all by their trades. I prodded him gently with my boot. 'Still there, is he?'

Kenwick shot up, turning with a look of terror towards the shed, as if expecting to see the padlock broken, the door yawning open. He saluted, found the key and made up for being asleep on duty by bringing the butt of his musket down on a bundle of straw rising and falling in the corner. The bundle groaned but scarcely moved. Kenwick brought the butt down more viciously. The bundle swore at him and began to part. Somehow, I thought resentfully, even in these unpromising conditions, Scogman managed to build up a fug of heat not found anywhere else on camp.

I waved Kenwick away as, with a rattle of chains, Scogman stumbled to his feet. His hair was the colour of the dirty straw he emerged from, the broken nose on his cherub-like face giving him a look of injured innocence. Trade: farrier, although sometimes I thought all he knew about horses was how to steal them.

'At ease, Scogman.'

He shuffled his leg irons. 'If you remove these, sir, I will be able to obey your order. Major Stonehouse. Sir.' He brought up his cuffed hands in a clumsy salute.

Kenwick bit back a smile. I stared at Scogman coldly.

He was about my age, twenty-two, but looked younger, thin as a rake, although he ate with a voracious appetite. Scoggy was the regiment's scrounger. He stole for the hell of it, for the challenge. In normal life he would have been hanged long ago. But when a regiment lived off the land he became an asset.

It only took one person to point out a plump hen, and not only would chicken be on the menu that night, but a pot in which to cook it would mysteriously appear. There were many who looked the other way in the regiment, except for strict Presbyterians like Sergeant Potter and Colonel Greaves, but in war the odds had been on Scoggy's side. In this uneasy peace his luck had run out. Scoggy had been caught stealing not just cheese, but a silver spoon. Not only that. He had stolen it from Sir Lewis Challoner, the local magistrate.

I chewed on an empty pipe, knocked it against my boot and cleared my throat. Scogman could read my reluctance and in his eyes was a look of hope. I cursed myself for coming. I should have sent Sergeant Potter. Scoggy would have known, however Potter taunted him, there was no hope. I struggled to find the words. In my mouth was the taste of the roast suckling pig Scoggy had somehow conjured up after Naseby. Even Cromwell had eaten it, praising the Lord for providing such fare to match a great victory. Cromwell believed in the virtue of his cavalry to the point of naivety, but when they sinned, he was merciless. I must follow my mentor's lead.

'You know the penalty for stealing silver, Scogman?'

'Yes, sir. Permission to speak, sir.'

'Go on,' I said wearily.

'Wife and children in London, sir. Starving.'

He knew I had a son. We had talked over many a camp fire about children we had never or rarely seen. 'You should have waited for your wages like everyone else.'

'We're three months behind, sir. There's talk we're never going to be paid what we're owed.'

It was true Parliament was dragging its feet over the money the troops were owed, and a host of other problems, like indemnity and injury benefits. Meanwhile soldiers scraped by on meagre savings, borrowed or stole.

'That's nonsense. Of course you'll be paid. Eventually. You should tighten your belt like everyone else.'

Scogman glanced down at his belt, taut over the narrow waist of his red uniform. Again Kenwick repressed a smile. I took the spoon from my pocket. My breath fogged it over. It looked a miserable object to be hanged for. 'Why the hell did you steal a silver spoon?'

He couldn't resist it. 'Because I never had one in my mouth, sir.'

Kenwick showed no sign of laughing, after looking at my expression.

'You will go before the magistrate.'

Even then he didn't believe me. 'I'd rather be tried by you, sir.'

'I'll bet you would. Sir Lewis may be lenient. Lock him up, Kenwick.'

I turned away, but not before I caught Scogman's cockiness, his bravado, shrivel like a pricked bladder. Outside, while the crows flapped lazily away, I tried to do what Cromwell did when he ordered a man's death. He prayed for his soul; it was not his order, he told himself, but God's will. Then he would unclasp his hands and go on to his next business. Rising over the thud of the door and the rattle of the padlock came Scogman's voice.

'Lenient? Sir Lewis Challoner, sir? He's a hanging magistrate! Major Stonehouse!'

I put my hands together but could not find the words to form a prayer.

2

Sir Lewis was also the local MP. He was, Lord Stonehouse had warned me, one of the more amenable Presbyterian MPs and a man I must be careful to cultivate.

There were now two parties. The Presbyterians were conservative, strict in religion, and softer in the line they pursued with the King. The Independents, led by Cromwell, were tolerant to the various religious sects that had sprung up during the war, such as Baptists and Quakers. They wanted to make sure the absolute power of the King, who had plunged the country into five years of devastating war, was removed.

That, at least, was how I saw it. My burning ambition was to be one of the Independent MPs who reached that settlement. I was Cromwell's adjutant when Lord Stonehouse suggested I was sent here to quell the unrest. He did not say so, but I was sure it was a test – handle the delicate relationship between soldiers and villagers and I would be on my way to Parliament. It was all the more important because the New Model Army was Cromwell's power base. Discredit the army, and you discredited him.

Word about Scogman got round quickly. Troopers saluted me, but averted their eyes and muttered in corners. I retired to the farm kitchen where Daisy, the kitchen maid, brought me bread and cheese and small beer. Her eyes were red. She sniffed and wiped her nose with the corner of her apron. Scogman not only stole chickens, pigs and silver spoons; he stole hearts. She kept poking the fire, scrubbing an already scrubbed pot and sniffing, until she turned to me, blurting out the words.

'It's my fault, sir.'

'Your fault, Daisy?'

'He stole the silver spoon for me, sir.'

'Why on earth would he do that?'

'It's, it's … a sign of love, sir.' She scrubbed the scrubbed pot and went as red as the fire. 'Is it true, sir … you're going to hang Scoggy?'

'No, Daisy.' Her eyes brightened. I gulped down the remaining beer. 'He's going before the magistrate.'

She burst into tears and fled.

Worst of all was Sergeant Potter who congratulated me for getting rid of that evil, thieving bastard. That would send a message to the other God-forsaken backsliders! The regiment was getting out of control and Dutton's End was up in arms. Had I marked the minister's sermon, echoing other sermons throughout Essex calling for a petition to Parliament to disband the army, which from being a blessing had become a curse, a leech, sucking the life-blood from village and country?

I winced when he said his only regret was that he could not tie the neckweed himself and retreated to the outhouse where I had my office. I wrote the letter to Sir Lewis, handing Scogman over to his jurisdiction and asking him for a leniency I knew he would not grant. I sent for Lieutenant Gage to deliver it. Instead I got Captain Will Ormonde.

Of all the delicate situations at Dutton's End Will was the most sensitive. We had rioted together in the uprising for Parliament, the riots that had driven the King from London. We had fought in the first battles of the war together. When this regiment's Colonel, Greaves, had fallen ill, Will had expected promotion. Instead, I had been sent to take temporary charge. He was right to think bitterly that it was because of Lord Stonehouse he had been passed over. But it was only partly that. He was too hot-headed and radical. Before I got here, he had made a bad situation worse.

Will was in his early twenties but, like all of us, looked older. He wore his hair long to cover an ear mutilated by a sabre slash.

'You can't send Scoggy to that bastard, Tom. We've all eaten his meat.'

'This isn't meat. It's a felony.'

'He's denied it.'

'Will, he was seen at the robbery! I searched his pack and found the spoon there. I've given him warning after warning.'

'I know,' he conceded. 'But Scoggy.'

That was his best argument. But Scoggy. Scoggy was more than a scrounger. A thief. A womaniser. He was a joke at the end of a day of despair. The man who could always find a beer, whose flint was dry when everyone else's was wet.

Will stared at the letter I had written, sealed and ready for Lieutenant Gage to deliver. 'Try him here.'

'Parliament wants felonies passed to the civil authority.'

'*Parliament.*' There was disappointment, frustration, impatience in his voice.

'It's what we fought for.'

His answer was to pull out a sheet of paper. 'Have you seen this?'

I knew what it was before he handed it to me. There was a rebellion in Ireland and the army was trying to raise volunteers. The paper contained the names of the men in the regiment. Only a few had ticks by them. They were rootless men like Bennet, a gunsmith, who had developed a taste for war and was the regiment's crack marksman. The last thing the vast majority wanted was to go to Ireland. They wanted, above everything else, what I wanted – to go home.

'The men believe they won't be paid unless they agree to go to Ireland.'

'That's nonsense.'

'That's what Potter's saying.'

'I'll speak to him.' I picked up the letter.

'Tom. If you send that letter to Sir Lewis the soldiers will riot.'

My mouth was suddenly dry. I got up, opened the door and shouted for Lieutenant Gage. I waited until I was sure of controlling my voice. 'There is to be no riot, Will. You are to keep order.'

His fists were clenched, his face a dull red. I could see Lieutenant Gage approaching. Will brought his hand up in a salute and barked savagely: 'Very good, sir.' He almost cannoned into Gage on his way out. I handed Gage the letter and gave him instructions for delivery.

It was a few minutes before I could stop shaking.

There was a lane with high hedgerows not far from the shed where Scogman was kept. It twisted away from the camp towards Dutton's End and I hoped that, if the bailiff took Scogman that route, any disturbance could be kept to a minimum. The last thing I expected was for Sir Lewis Challoner to come for his prey himself.

He had been a Royalist at the beginning of the war but when he had seen which way the wind was blowing had changed sides, bringing a vital artillery train to Parliament. He rode into the farm-yard followed by his bailiff Stalker. He looked as if he had lunched well, spots of grease gleaming on his ample chins as he smiled affably down at me from his horse.

'Well, well, Major. We are returned to the rule of law, are we?'

'We never left it, Sir Lewis,' I said, returning his smile.

There was a cheer from somewhere nearby, and the smile went from Sir Lewis's face. Soldiers had appeared from the barn and the stables. Daisy was at the kitchen window, dabbing her face with her apron. Bennet, the marksman, was cleaning his musket. The dog that followed him on his poaching expeditions was at his heels.

I could smell the wine on Sir Lewis's breath as I went close to him. 'Better do this as quietly and quickly as possible.'

He gave me a fat, innocent, smile. 'You can control your men, can't you, Major?'

'You are provoking them, Sir Lewis,' I said coldly. 'I will not have it. If you want him, take him.'

He glared down at me. 'Very well. The felon, Stalker.'

Stalker did not smile. He was a devout Puritan and gave the soldiers a gloomy but satisfied look, as if the world, which had been upside down, had righted itself again and he was back in control. He nodded to several of them, as if to say – *I know you. You stole a ham. And you, you fornicator. She's with child. Don't worry. I have you all on my list.* Some of the men slipped away under his gaze. Others muttered angrily. Only Bennet returned his gaze with interest, and patted the growling dog gently.

I got my horse and led the two of them across the fields. Sir Lewis still seemed eager to pursue an argument. He jerked his thumb back at the soldiers. 'Some of those fellows, I believe, think the final authority rests not with the King, nor the Commons, but the people.'

I shook my head. 'They might in a London alehouse. Not here.'

His pale eyes narrowed. 'Is that so?'

'Most are not interested in politics, Sir Lewis. All they want is to be paid what they're owed, go home to their families, work and no longer be a burden to the countryside.'

'They are pagans,' Stalker said. 'They declare themselves preachers. Spread false doctrine.'

'They only pray here, Mr Stalker, because you will not allow them in your church.'

'Because they are rabble, sir.'

'They preach because they have no minister available. Is it not better that they try to reach God, than not try at all?'

Sir Lewis pursed his lips. 'Dangerous, sir, dangerous.' But he was mollified by the sight of Scogman in chains being bundled into a cart by Sergeant Potter. Stalker rode off towards them, and Sir Lewis thawed even further, to the extent he said he could see why Lord

Stonehouse put such an extraordinary amount of trust in so young a man. He gave me a prodigious wink and began to rhapsodise about the beauty of the countryside around us. It was neglected, but the soil was rich and it was well watered. He gave me another wink, a slap on the back and said perhaps we could meet again to talk about country affairs. I was somewhat bemused by this abrupt change of heart, but put it down to the wine at lunch and – perhaps a little – to my diplomacy.

'My regards to Lord Stonehouse,' he said, and made as if to leave.

I turned away, expecting Sir Lewis and Stalker to ride off immediately, escorting the cart and its prisoner down the lane to avoid the soldiers. But I heard Scogman give a yell of pain.

I ran back to see the cart had come to a stop at the beginning of the lane. Scogman was being manhandled from it by Stalker and Sergeant Potter. They were threading a rope through his chains with the intention of tying it to Stalker's saddle. I hurried back to them.

'Sir Lewis, for pity's sake take him in the cart! You will rouse my soldiers!'

He put on a puzzled look, belied by his quivering jowls. 'The New Model Army? It is a model of discipline, Major, is it not?'

Scogman pulled away, tripping and falling. His britches were torn and his legs bleeding where the chains had cut into them.

'Release him. Take him in the cart, or you do not take him at all.' I struggled to keep my voice even.

Stalker hesitated. Sir Lewis lifted his head. I could see why they called him a hanging magistrate as he gave me a look of unflinching hostility. But he kept his voice friendly, even jovial, taking out the letter I had sent him.

'This is your signature, sir? Your seal, is it not? You have released him to me and I will have him as I will. Good day to you, sir. Get on with it, Stalker! What are you waiting for, man?'

Stalker yanked Scogman towards his horse and tied him to his saddle. I stood impotently. What a stupid, naive fool I was to think a man like Challoner would ever be in a mood for compromise. He wanted to drag his prisoner through the town to demonstrate his power. Stones, rotting vegetables and shit would be hurled at him. He would be lucky to enter prison alive.

Diplomacy? Far from helping to heal the wounds between town and soldiers, releasing Scogman would inflame them.

At least if God had made me eternally hopeful – or hopelessly naive – he had given me the quick wit to get out of the mire I found myself in. Or perhaps, as some had held, ever since I was born, it was the Devil.

And mire it was. Crows rose and flapped as soldiers, aroused by Scogman's screaming, streamed from the farm. Will was keeping them half-heartedly under control, but I saw the barrel of a musket poking through the hedge. Stalker was riding slowly, Scogman stumbling after, almost under the hooves of Challoner's following horse. As they saw the soldiers, Stalker urged his horse into a trot. Scogman stumbled and fell. He made no sound as he was dragged from the ditch into the lane and back again. Perhaps he would not cry out in front of his fellow soldiers. More likely he was barely conscious.

I pushed through the hedge but could not see the musketeer. It must be Bennet. If it was, Sir Lewis was as good as dead. We would no longer just have a problem of unrest but a major crisis that the Presbyterian majority in Parliament would seize on against Cromwell. I heard the click of the dog lock, releasing the musket's trigger.

'Wait!' I shouted to Sir Lewis. 'You have forgot the evidence!'

I pulled the spoon from my pocket. The ridiculous-looking spoon, slightly bent. A man's life. Sir Lewis, a stickler for correctness in his court, checked his horse.

'Get down from your horse unless you want to be shot,' I said.

'Go to hell.'

'Get down, man, or I cannot guarantee your life!'

He saw the barrel of the musket. He had courage, I'll grant him that. He tried to ride forward, his horse's hooves an inch from

Scogman's face, but at that same moment I made a grab for his horse's reins and Stalker, catching sight of the musket, slid from his saddle. Sir Lewis lurched and fell clumsily to the ground. A cheer rose from the watching soldiers before Will quietened them.

I tried to help Sir Lewis up, but he shoved me away, lips, jowls shaking in a face so puce with rage I thought he had had a stroke. I apologised to him and said I thought a mistake had been made.

For a moment he could not trust himself to speak. Then his face gradually resumed its normal dull red colour and he found his chilling, courtroom voice. 'A mistake! Sir, you have made the mistake of your life! I will have you in the same cell as him,' and he pointed at Scogman, who was coming round, staring up at us in bewilderment.

'He may not have committed a felony.'

'May not …? May not …? He stole silver, sir!'

'Blake!' I shouted across the field. 'Where is Trooper Blake?'

Blake pushed his way through the soldiers, who had by now spilled into the lane ahead of us. He was an odd man, prematurely bald, slightly hunchbacked, but the soldiers respected him because he could fix almost anything, from a leaking pot to a broken flintlock.

'Trade?' I said.

'Journeyman silversmith, sir,' Blake said with a salute. 'City of London, Goldsmiths' Guild.'

He straightened, losing some of his stoop, and his eyes gleamed with pride, a pride that began to be reflected in many of the sullen, punch-drunk faces around him. These were men who had almost forgotten they had trades, and another life, and were beginning to wonder, in this purgatory of waiting, whether they would ever return to them. They began to grin as I handed the spoon to Blake.

'What do you think this is, Blake?'

'A – it's a spoon, sir.'

There was a volley of laughter from the men until Sergeant Potter shouted them into some kind of order.

'No, man! I mean, is it silver?'

Challoner snarled at me for what he called my equivocation but then, in spite of himself, watched as Blake bit the spoon, polished it and bent it. Finally he peered short-sightedly at the leopard's head on the back of the handle. There was complete silence, except for the rattle of chains as Scogman stumbled to his feet. Blake seemed wholly concerned with making as honest and accurate a judgement as he could, no matter that a man's life was at stake.

'Mmm. It's difficult to say, sir.'

'Your opinion, man!'

Blake caught the sharpness of my tone and slowly it dawned on him that I wanted him to perjure his craftsman's judgement. 'Well … the leopard's head mark is very crude … I would say it's a fake.'

Someone held Scogman up as he almost collapsed. Challoner tried to grab the silver spoon before it disappeared into my pocket again. 'Give it to me! I'll have it assayed!'

'Lieutenant Gage!' I shouted.

Gage cottoned on much more quickly than Blake. Stepping forward into my makeshift court, he declared himself to be from Gray's Inn, giving the impression of a lawyer, rather than the clerk he was. Blake valued the spoon at a few pence. Thefts above a shilling were a hanging offence. Whether a soldier might be punished by the army or the civil courts for a lesser offence was a grey area. I told Challoner I would punish Scogman myself. By this time he was almost incoherent with rage.

'Justice? You call this New Model Justice? I'll give you justice!'

On one side I had Challoner threatening me. On the other, the grinning soldiers and Will whispering in my ear that I had the judgement of Solomon. I could not stand either of them. I could not stand myself. I had fondly imagined I would bring both sides closer with my diplomacy. Now they were so far apart there would be open warfare between town and soldiers. I was filled with a cold ferocious anger which I could scarcely keep under control. Stalker was helping Challoner back on his horse when I stopped him.

'Justice? I will show you justice!'

I snatched the whip from Stalker's saddle and told Sergeant Potter to unchain Scogman.

'Strip him.'

There was not much to strip. His britches were in shreds from being dragged along the lane and his jerkin came off in two pieces. His fair hair was dark with matted blood and weals stood out on his ankles and wrists. He stumbled groggily as Sergeant Potter spread-eagled him against a fence. Still he grinned at his mates and, when he saw Daisy peering from the edge of the crowd, waggled his sex at her. Cheers rose when she fled into the farmhouse.

Challoner watched from his horse, his curled lip indicating he believed this to be as much a masquerade as the spoon.

I tossed the whip to Bennet, the man I believed had held the musket, which had disappeared. 'Twenty lashes.'

In spite of his bravado, Scogman would scarcely have been able to stand without the ropes that tied his hands to the fence. His knees buckled. Blood ran from a fresh head wound and trickled slowly down his back. Ben, the surgeon, took a step towards me, but turned away when he saw my expression. He knew this mood of mine.

Bennet smoothed the lash between his fingers. He measured his stance. The crowd fell silent. The whip cracked. Scogman winced and his eyes jerked shut, although the tip of the whip barely touched his flesh. Bennet's natural love of violence was held in check by the feeling of his watching colleagues. Perhaps, instead, he gained a perverse pleasure from taunting Stalker and Challoner by not drawing blood. The whip cracked harmlessly again, and this time there was no doubt about it, Scogman joined in the masquerade, jerking and writhing theatrically.

Challoner turned his horse away in contempt and disgust.

I wrenched the whip from Bennet's hand and lashed out clumsily at Scogman's back. He gave one startled cry and then fell silent. I wanted him to cry out, to scream, but where he had performed for Bennet, he would not perform for me. After the first line of blood the watching faces disappeared and I saw nothing and heard nothing, until my arm was gripped and Ben pulled me away. I stared at him blankly, then at the whip, then at what I at first took to be a piece of raw meat in front of me. It was all I could do to swallow back the vomit that rose in my throat.

I flung the whip back at Challoner.

'Satisfied?'

3

Over the next few days Challoner continued hounding me to hand Scogman over, but I refused. Ben told me he was not expected to live. The least I could do was let him die under Daisy's care for, while there was a shred of life left in him, Challoner would certainly hang him.

Ben wanted to purge me, saying my humours were severely out of balance, but I would have none of it. I had a curt letter from Lord Stonehouse in Newcastle, ordering me to go home. Colonel Greaves had recovered, and was returning to the regiment.

I rode alone from Essex to London. The countryside was bare, many fields overgrown with weeds, while all the troop movements had left the roads looking as though a giant plough had been taken to them. In a world upside down, even the seasons had not escaped. Spring was not merely late; it looked as if it would never appear. Most of the trees had been chopped down for firewood, during the Royalist blockade of Newcastle that had stopped coal ships coming to London.

All I could see was Scogman's raw, bleeding back and the sullen resentful faces of my men. No – no longer my men. I had lost them. Lost myself. By the time I arrived in London, those memories had left me in total darkness. My wife Anne knew the mood, the strange blackness that came over me, and saw it in my face when I half-fell from my horse into her arms. Her embrace was more soothing than any physic, blotting out the memory of that bleeding back.

For days I slept or wandered in the garden of our house in Drury Lane, where Anne's green fingers had planted an apple tree. The one in Half Moon Court where we had played as children, then snatched our first kisses, had been chopped down in the last bitter winter of the war. I felt the first, tight swelling of the buds on the young tree, still black, waiting for the warmth of the sun. There would be spring in this little garden; perhaps the tree would bear its first fruit.

Cromwell lived in the same lane and I screwed up my courage to go and see him, but was told he was ill, with an abscess in the head which would not clear. The news made me even more disconsolate.

'You are not yourself, sir,' said Jane, the housekeeper.

I tried to laugh it off. 'Exactly, Jane! I am not myself. I must find myself! Where am I?'

Was I with the sullen resentful men, or was I, could I ever be, with people like Challoner?

'Where am I?' I said to my son Luke, who, when I had arrived, had stared in wonder at this strange man tumbling from a horse into his mother's arms. 'Am I under the chair, Luke? No! The table?'

Luke ran to Jane, covering his face in her skirts. 'Come, sir!' she laughed. 'Tom is your father!'

'Fath-er?'

It grieved me that I had spent half my life finding out who my father was, and now Luke did not know his. He had dark curls, in which I fancied there was a trace of red, and the Stonehouse nose; what in my plebeian days I called hooked, but Lord Stonehouse called aquiline. Although Luke's grandfather doted on him, he treated the boy very sternly. Perhaps because of that, Luke often ran to him, as he did to the ostler, Adams, who would level a bitten fingernail at him and order him to keep clear of his horses, or he would not answer for the consequences. Luke would run away yelling, then creep quietly back for another levelled nail before at last Adams would snatch him up screaming and plonk him in the saddle. I felt a stab of petty resentment he would not play these games with me, and went upstairs to the nursery to find my daughter Elizabeth.

She was a few months old. Anne had been bitterly disappointed she was not a boy. It was a rare week which did not see at least one child buried in our old church of St Mark's and Anne wanted as many male heirs as possible to reinforce Lord Stonehouse's promise I should inherit.

Lord Stonehouse's first son, Richard, had gone over to the Royalists, and when Lord Stonehouse had declared I would inherit I had fondly imagined it was because of my own merit. In part, perhaps it was. But it was also because he had been discovered helping Richard escape to France. Declaring me as his heir not only saved Lord Stonehouse's skin. It enabled him to back both horses: whoever ruled, it was the estate that mattered, keeping and expanding the magnificent seat at Highpoint and preserving the Stonehouse name at the centre of power.

Elizabeth, little Liz, did not look a Stonehouse. In my present, rebellious mood, she was my secret companion. Or was it weapon?

'Liz Neave,' I whispered to her, giving her the name I had grown up with when I was a bastard in Poplar, and knew nothing of the Stonehouses. She had scraps of hair, still black, but I fancied I could see a reddish tinge. Her nose was not aquiline, or hooked, but a delicious little snub. Anne called her fractious, but her crying reminded me of my own wildness.

When I held out my finger she stopped crying, gripping it with her hand so tightly, I could not stop laughing. Her lips, blowing little bubbles of spit, formed their first laugh. I swept her up, and hugged her and kissed her. Fractious? She was not fractious! I rocked her in my arms until she fell asleep.

I went to our old church, St Mark's, to see the minister, Mr Tooley, about Liz's baptism. Anne wanted it done in the old way, with water from the font in which she had been baptised, and godparents. Mr Tooley still did it, although the Presbyterians, who were tightening their grip on the Church, frowned on both.

The church was empty, apart from an old man in a front pew, his clasped hands trembling in some private grief. The familiar pew drew out of me my first prayer for a long time. I feared Scogman was dead. I prayed for forgiveness for my evil temper. For Scogman's soul. He was a thief, but he stole for others, as much, if not more than for himself. There was much good in him, he was kind and cheered others – by the time I had finished he was near sainthood and I was the devil incarnate. One thing came to me. I determined to find Scogman's wife and children and do what I could for them. I swore I would never again let my black temper gain control of me.

The man rose at the same time as I did. It was my old master, Mr Black, Anne's father. I had never before seen tears on his face. He drew his sleeve over his face when he saw me.

'Tom … my lord …'

I wore a black velvet cloak edged with silver. My short sword had a silver pommel and my favourite plumed hat was set at a rakish angle.

'No, no, master … not lord yet … and always Tom to thee.'

I embraced him and asked him what was the matter. He told me he might be suspended from the Lord's Table.

'Thrown out of the Church? Why?'

He told me the Presbyterians were setting up a council of lay elders. The most virulent of the elders, who morosely policed moral discipline in the parish, was none other than Mr Black's previous journeyman printer, my old enemy Gloomy George.

I could not believe it. We had fought a long, bloody war for freedom and tolerance, and what we had at the end of it was Gloomy George. I began to laugh at the absurdity of it, but stopped when I saw what distress Mr Black was in. The Mr Black I knew would have laughed too, but this one trembled in bewilderment so much that I sat him down.

I could see how the church had changed. Mr Tooley had allowed a few images, like a picture of the Trinity, because they comforted older members of the congregation. Now it was stripped so bare and stark even the light seemed afraid to enter. Mr Black said that when Mr Tooley used to preach, stern as he was, you left counting your blessings. Now, with the Presbyterians breathing down his neck, his sermons left you counting your sins.

'But what sin could he possibly find in you?' I cried.

'Nehemiah.'

'Your apprentice? He is as devout as you are.'

'More so. But he has become a Baptist, and refuses to come here.'

'If he refuses you, he has broken his bond. You could dismiss him.'

Mr Black's watery eyes flashed with some of his old fire. 'He is a good apprentice. And he is devout. I will not dismiss a man for his beliefs.'

We sat in silence for a while. He stared at the blank wall where the Trinity had been. All his life he had been a staunch member of the congregation and the community. He was as responsible for Nehemiah as a father for his children. But the Presbyterians condemned all sects like Baptists as heresies and unless Mr Black brought Nehemiah back into the fold, he would be refused the sacraments. Friends and business would melt away. Even threatened with hell, he stuck stubbornly to his old beliefs in loyalty and duty.

'How long has Nehemiah's indenture to run?'

'Nine months.'

I pretended to calculate, then frowned. 'You are surely mistaken, master. It ends next week.' I stared at him, keeping my face straight. 'Once he's indentured he can leave. Get another job.'

He returned my stare with interest. He needed no abacus or record where figures were concerned. 'I don't know what you're suggesting,' he snapped, 'but I know when he's indentured. To the day.' He picked up his stick and I flinched, an apprentice again, fearing a beating. He limped out of the church and stood among the gravestones as if he was gazing into the pit.

'The Stationery Office has his full record,' he said.

'Records can be lost. Once he has completed his apprenticeship he is not your responsibility. Is he good enough to be indentured?'

'Better than most journeymen.'

'Well then. When he is indentured I can help him get work elsewhere and you can take on another apprentice.'

'It is most irregular,' he muttered.

'If everything had been regular, master, we would not have won the war. There were not half enough qualified armourers and black-smiths to make all the arms we needed.'

He still looked troubled but said: 'Well, well, if that is the way the world is now … But I would not know what to say to him.'

'I will do it. We got on well, and he will listen to me.'

Elated with what I hoped would be a better attempt at diplomacy, I went to see Mr Tooley about Liz's baptism. He was engaged in a room across the corridor. I waited in a small anteroom. A cupboard, I remembered, contained books I might occupy myself with. It was locked, but I knew where the key was hidden for I used to borrow books to improve my reading. When I opened it, out spilled a number of objects that had once been part of the church.

There were old, mouldering copies of the Book of Common Prayer which the Presbyterians had banned, brass candlesticks spotted with green mildew, the picture of the Trinity I had missed in the church, cracked and torn, and a rolled-up linen surplice. Everything that had once brought light and colour into the church had been buried here. An ineffable sense of sadness crept over me as I opened a prayer book and the musty smell brought back to me the light and comfort of the old church.

A nearby door opened and a chill ran through me as I heard the unmistakable voice of the man who had beaten me so often as a child – for the good of my soul, as he put it. I put the prayer book down on a chair and went to the door, beginning to open it so they would know I was there. But they were too intent on their argument to see me.

George was in the doorway of Mr Tooley's study, his back to me. He was almost bald, his head gleaming as though polished.

'You must name Nehemiah a heretic in church on Sunday, Mr Tooley.'

George used to address Mr Tooley with wheedling deference. I was amazed at his hectoring tone. Even more so by Mr Tooley accepting it, although his face was flushed and he struggled to keep his voice even. 'I will see Mr Black again.'

'He is obdurate. Stiffnecked. As the Proverbs have it, Mr Tooley: "Comes want, comes shame from warnings unheeded."'

The years dropped away. He could have been talking to me when I was an apprentice. My nails bit into my palms and my cheeks were burning.

'What irks a man more than vinegar on his tooth? A lingering messenger,' Mr Tooley responded. 'As the Proverbs have it.'

I gave a silent cheer. As George turned to go, I saw I had left the cupboard door wide open. Mr Tooley's old surplice lay unrolled on the floor. Hastily, I crammed things back into the cupboard, shut the door and hid the key. During this, George fired his parting shot. It was couched more in sorrow than in anger.

'The warning is not just for the sheep, Mr Tooley, but for the shepherd.'

'Don't you dare talk to me like that!'

Mr Tooley was livid with anger. George, seeing his point had struck home, twisted the knife. 'Oh, it is not me, a humble sinner, talking. I am but the poor messenger of the council of elders, which by the 1646 ordinance ...'

Ordinance! As well as proverbs, George was stuffed with ordinances, which listed the scandalous offences of renouncers of the true Protestant faith. Mr Tooley took a step towards George. His fist was clenched and a pulse in his forehead was beating. George did not move away. He cocked his head with a look of sorrow on his face, almost as if he was inviting a blow.

Afraid Mr Tooley would strike him – and afraid, for some reason, that this was exactly what George wanted – I stepped out into the corridor.

The effect on the two men could not have been more different. Mr Tooley plainly saw me as he had always seen me.

'The prodigal son,' he said, with a wry smile, holding out his hand.

George bowed. 'My lord, congratulations on your good fortune. I beg to hope that your lordship realises that, in a small measure, it is due to me not sparing the rod, however much that grieved me.'

There was more of this, but I took the unction as I used to take the blows. I had promised God I would not lose my temper. There were to be no more Scogmans. Diplomacy, not confrontation. I told them there was now no need to name Nehemiah a heretic in church.

'He has recanted?' George said.

'He will be leaving Mr Black.'

'He's been dismissed?'

I bowed almost as deeply as he did. 'I believe people should worship according to their conscience, but the law is the law. Nehemiah will be replaced by another apprentice who will attend church in a proper manner.'

I winced as he clasped his hands and lifted his eyes. 'God be praised! I shrank from putting Mr Black through so much distress, as I did when I applied the rod to you, but it was for the good of both your souls.'

He put out his hand. It felt as cold and slippery as the skin of a toad. I arranged the baptism with Mr Tooley in two weeks' time. When I left I still had the clammy feeling of George's grip. Matthew, the cunning man who had brought me up, would say I had been touched. It was a stupid superstition, but all the same I wiped my hand on the grass.

My spirits rose again when I rode into Half Moon Court. The apple tree was a sad, withered stump, but from the shop came the familiar thump and sigh of the printing press. Sarah, the servant, came out to greet me. She walked with a limp now, but her banter had not changed since she used to rub pig's fat into my aching bruises.

'What has tha' done to master, Tom?'

'Done?' I cried in alarm.

'He's had a face like a wet Monday for weeks. Now he's skipped off like a two-year-old with mistress to buy her a new hat for the baptism.'

'I only talked to him about his problems,' I said modestly.

'I wish you could talk to my rheumatism. My knee's giving me gyp.'

'Which knee?' I said, stretching out my hand.

'Getaway! I know you. Think you can cure the world one minute, and need curing yourself the next.'

She hugged me just as she did when I was a child, then walked back into the house quite normally, before stopping to stare at me. 'Why, Tom! Tha's cured my knee!'

I stared at her, my heart beating faster. Perhaps it was something to do with my prayers that morning.

Sarah laughed, then winced at the effort she had made to walk normally. She flexed her knee and rubbed it ruefully, before limping back into the house. 'Oh, Tom, dear Tom. If tha believes that, tha'll believe anything.'

Nehemiah was as good as any journeyman, I could see that. He was too absorbed in what had once been my daily task, to see me watching from the door. He was taller than me, and would have been handsome but for spots that erupted round his mouth and neck. It was a hard task for one man to feed the paper in the press and bring down the platen, but he did it with ease.

I wondered why he did not put the sheets out to dry, as he should have done. Instead, he interleaved them with more absorbent paper before putting them carefully in an old knapsack. I gave a cry of surprise when I saw it was my old army knapsack. Nehemiah whirled round, dropping a printed sheet, and grabbed hold of me. I thought I was strong and fit but he twisted my arms into a lock and bent me double. His strong smell of sweat and ink was overpowering. I yelled out who I was. Only then did he release me with a confused apology.

'I – I did not recognise you. I thought you were a spy, sir,' he muttered.

I laughed. The Half Moon printed the most boring of government ordinances. 'A spy. What has Mr Black got to hide?'

I bent to pick up the sheet he had dropped but he snatched it up and put it in the knapsack. I shrugged. While his master was out he was doing some printing of his own. I thought him none the worse for that. Most apprentices of any enterprise did so. When I was going to be a great poet I had secretly printed my poems to Anne on that very press.

I gazed fondly at the battered knapsack, which I thought had been thrown away.

'You do not want it, sir?'

I shook my head, and he thanked me so profusely for it my heart went out to him, for I remembered when, in my crazy wanderings, it once contained everything I had in the world.

'How would you like to be a journeyman, Nehemiah?'

'Very much, sir. I have dreamed of it long enough.'

'Well then, you shall be. In a few days' time.'

I smiled at his look of astonishment.

'But my indentures are not over for –'

'Nine months.'

'And twenty days,' he said, looking at the base of the press, where for the past year he had carved and crossed through each passing day before his release.

I told him he was as skilled as he ever would be and the paperwork was a mere formality. I would arrange it. As a journeyman, his religion would then be a matter for his own conscience. I began to go into practical details, but he interrupted me. He had a stammer, which he had gradually mastered, but it returned now.

'Has my m-master agreed?'

'Yes.'

'It is ...' His face reddened, intensifying the pale blue of his eyes. 'D-dishonest.'

I told him the rules were dishonest for apprentices – medieval rules, designed to give Guild Masters free labour for as long as possible.

'What about George?'

'There'll be no trouble there. I've told him you were leaving.'

'With-without telling me?'

He began to make me feel uncomfortable, particularly as I thought he was right. I had been high-handed. 'I'm sorry, but the opportunity arose. And I was worried about Mr Black being thrown out of church.'

'That would be a good thing,' he said fervently.

'A good thing?'

'He could join the Baptists and see Heaven in this life.'

The idea was absurd. But he elaborated on it with a burning intensity until I stopped him. 'Nehemiah, Mr Black is old and he's been in St Mark's all his life. I'm sorry, but you have to leave. Or go to your master's church.'

'Obeying G-George? Like you did?'

He knew the story of how I had struck George and might have killed him if Mr Black had not intervened. Then I had run off. I sighed. Helping him was not as easy as I blithely imagined, particularly when he brought up how I had acted like him – or even more violently – in the past. I walked outside to untether my horse. He followed me, saying he h-hoped he did not sound un-g-grateful – I detected a note of sarcasm in his stammer – but e-even with his journeyman papers he had no position to go to.

I mounted my horse. 'I will take care of that.' I told him of a printer who, at my recommendation, would pay him twenty-eight pound a year.

He gazed up at me, open-mouthed. 'All f-found?'

There was no sarcasm in his stammer now. Money. Everything came down to money. I was a fool not to mention that at first. 'All found.'

'Twenty-eight pound!' he muttered to himself. 'All found!' He caught the saddle of my horse. 'He is one of Lord Stonehouse's printers. I would be beholden to Lord Stonehouse.'

'We are all beholden to someone, Nehemiah.'

'No!' he cried, with such violence my horse reared. 'We are not! We are beholden to ourselves!' He gave me that look of intensity again, then abruptly bowed his head. 'I-I am sorry. I know I have been churlish, but I have not slept since this business began. I was a fool to think Mr Black would become a Baptist.' He gave me a wry wincing grin and I warmed to him, for he brought back to me all the torments I went through at his age. 'I must consult my brethren. And pray.'

'And sleep,' I smiled, telling him to give his answer to Mr Black in the morning.

Who would have thought peace was such hard work? It was easier to face cavalry across open fields than try to bring conflicting minds together. But I felt a surge of optimism as I rode past Smithfield on the route I used to take as a printer's runner. I may have made a great hash of the Challoner business, but I was learning.

* * *

Next morning a letter came from Mr Black. Nehemiah had gone. He had scrupulously broken up the last forme, distributed the type and cleaned the press. In the night he had woken Sarah, apologising for taking a piece of bread, which he promised to repay. He put the bread in the old knapsack, with his Bible and a pamphlet whose title she knew, for he had read it to her interminably. It was called *England's Lamentable Slaverie*. There was no printer's mark. It was from a group naming themselves the Levellers. It declared the Commons as the supreme authority over which the King and the Lords had no veto. Also found in Nehemiah's room was a copy of a petition to Parliament circulating round the army. It asked simply to be paid, to guarantee indemnity for acts committed during the war, and no compulsion to serve in Ireland.

Nehemiah went off at first light, breaking his bond as I had done, years before.

4

It preyed on my mind. What Nehemiah had done was completely stupid. He could have been a journeyman, earning far more than most people of his age, free to practise his religion – what more did he want? And why did it trouble me so much?

'I would be beholden to Lord Stonehouse.'

That was the problem, of course. He reminded me I was beholden to Lord Stonehouse. Nehemiah was like a piece of grit in bread that sets off a bad tooth. However much I told myself it was nonsense – he could be a liberated slave and see how far that got him – the ache persisted.

Anne knew, as she always did, there was something on my mind, but I refused to talk about it. She would laugh at me, just as she had when I was like Nehemiah. So I whispered it to little Liz and she put everything into proportion. I was beholden to Lord Stonehouse because I was beholden to Liz, to my whole family, to peace.

'That's it, isn't it?' I whispered.

She gurgled and put out her hand, exploring my face. I laughed with delight, held her up, kissed her and rocked her to sleep. I crept away, stopping with a start when I saw Anne watching me.

'You never kiss me like that now.'

I bowed. 'Your doctor has warned me against passion, madam.'

It was true. Liz had been a difficult birth. Anne had lost a lot of blood, and had been bled even more by Dr Latchford, Lord Stonehouse's doctor. That was one of the things I hated most about being a Stonehouse. I felt like a stallion, not a lover, only allowed to cover the mare in season.

'Dr Latchford,' I said, giving her the doctor's dry, confidential cough, 'says it is too soon to have another child.'

'Dr Latchford, fiddle!' She picked up the mockery in my manner and drew close to me. 'You're back,' she whispered.

Perhaps it was Nehemiah, that ache in the tooth, which made me say 'Tom Neave's himself again.'

'Oh, Tom Neave! Tom Neave! I hate Tom Neave! He is nasty and uncouth and has big feet.'

I choked with laughter. This was exactly the sort of game we used to play as children after I had arrived without boots and she had mocked my monkey feet. 'How can it be? Tom Neave or Thomas Stonehouse, my feet are exactly the same size, madam!'

'They are not! Look at you!'

In a sense she was right. I was not really conscious of it until that moment, but since seeing Nehemiah I had taken to wearing my old army boots, cracked and swollen at the toes, but much more comfortable than Thomas Stonehouse's elegant bucket boots. I slopped about in a jerkin with half the buttons missing and affected indifference to changing my linen.

I loved her in that kind of mood, half genuine anger, half part of our game, teased her all the more and tried to kiss her.

'Go away! You stink, sir!'

I pulled her to me and kissed her. She shoved me away. I collided into the crib, almost knocking it over. Now really angry, she went to the door. Contrite, I followed to appease her, but the baby was giving startled, terrified cries and I returned to soothe her.

The encounter with Anne roused me. We had not slept together since I returned, but I resolved not to go to her room. Although I mocked Dr Latchford, I could see that, even when she had been out in the garden, her skin did not colour. Her blue eyes had lost some of their sparkle. She loved rushing round with Luke, but she left him more and more with Jane and Adams.

I was asleep when she came into my room and climbed into bed beside me.

'Are you sure?' I mumbled.

'Sssshhh!'

'Dr Latchford –'

'Do you want me? Or do you want Dr Latchford?' She leaned over me and kissed me on the mouth.

There was a violence, a hunger in that kiss that swept away the dry old doctor and all our arguments and fears, swept them away in the wonderful rediscovery of the touching of skin, bringing every feeling crackling back to life until her cheeks coloured and her eyes sparkled. We laughed at the absurdity of our arguments, at the sheer joy of being together.

We were side by side. I began to climb on top of her.

'No!'

'No?'

She twisted away and wriggled on top, which seemed unnatural, outlandish to me. I had heard some of the men, in their cups, talking of whores having them like men. I had reproved them, not just for the whores, but saying did they want to wear skirts, like cuckolded husbands shamed in a Skimmington? But, before I could utter a word, she had clumsily but effectively put me inside her. I was on the brink and could not stop, until she gave a cry of pain and pulled back. I checked myself but her nails dug into my back as she thrust me back into her and we came together in a confusion of pain and pleasure. She instantly rolled away and lay panting with her back towards me.

'Are you all right?'

She nodded and curled up to sleep.

'What was all that?'

'Did you not like it, sir?' she murmured. 'It's called world upside down.'

It was a well-worn phrase describing the chaos after the war, vividly illustrated in a pamphlet by a man wearing his britches on his head and his boots on his hands. Now it seemed to have entered the bedroom.

'World – world –? Who on earth told you that?'

'Lucy.'

I was outraged. 'You talk about *our* love-making with *that* woman?'

Lucy Hay, the Countess of Carlisle, had been the mistress of John Pym, leader of the opposition to the King. Since he had died, there had been great speculation about who was now sharing her bed.

Anne sat up, fully awake, her gown half off. Her belly was slacker, her breasts full, but her neck was thinner, her cheeks pinched. 'We talk about how a woman should keep a man when she has just had a child. About what to do when – when it is difficult to, to make love … That's all.'

'All!'

She hid her face on my neck and I held her to me. I could feel her heart pounding. 'We should wait,' I said half-heartedly. 'You know what the doctor –'

She pulled away. 'Wait? I want another child in my belly before you go off again!'

She spoke so loudly and ferociously I clamped my hand over her mouth. There was silence for a moment, then a cry from Liz, broken off by a stuttering cough.

'I will not be going away again.'

'You will. I *know*.'

Liz gave a long, piercing wail. 'She's hungry. Could you not go to her?'

'Women who are in milk can't conceive. The wet-nurse fed her. Don't you *want* another child?'

'Yes, but when you are well.'

'I *am* well.'

I put my hand over her mouth again as footsteps stumbled past the door. I listened to Jane's soothing, sleepy voice, the clink of a spoon against a pot of some syrup, until the coughing eventually ceased. Anne ran her finger gently down my nose and along my lips. She dropped her gaze demurely. 'I'm sorry,' she whispered. 'I will not do that again, sir, if it displeases you.'

I swallowed. I could not get out of my head the vision of her being above me and began to be aroused again. She laughed out loud at my expression. 'You're like a small boy who's just been told he can't have a pie!' As I moved to her, she stopped me with a raised finger. 'Wait, wait, wait! Promise me you are Thomas Stonehouse, and not that stupid Tom Neave.'

I put on my deepest gentleman's voice. I enjoyed being a gentleman when it was a game. 'I am Thomas Stonehouse –'

'I mean it!' She clenched her fists. 'Why do you put on that stupid voice? Why do you quarrel with Lord Stonehouse? You can get on with him so well when you want to!'

'When I do what he wants.'

'*Please*, Tom!'

'All right.'

'Promise? Promise you will not quarrel with him when he gets back from Newcastle.'

'I promise.'

'Touch the bed.'

When we were children we made solemn vows by touching the apple tree. Now we touched our marriage bed. Being a great lady was as much a game for her as being a gentleman was for me. But for her it was a deadly serious game. I looked at her knotted hands, her earnest, determined face, even lovelier in its fragile, faded pallor.

I felt a deep, swelling surge of love for her. Being a gentleman at that moment seemed a most desirable thing to be. No more fighting. Sleeping in my own bed. Or hers. I touched the bed-head.

'I promise.'

When the letter arrived next morning it felt like too much of a coincidence. I could not believe she had not known, before coming to my room, that Lord Stonehouse was on his way back. But she looked so shocked that I could ever think she would dissemble like that, and said it so charmingly, and was so full of excitement, and fussed so much over my linen and over a button on my blue velvet suit – in short, it was so much as if we had just been married all over again that I was completely disarmed and able to read the letter, if not with equanimity, with more composure than otherwise. Lord Stonehouse, as frugal with words as he was with money, presented his compliments and would appreciate me calling at Queen Street at noon sharp.

5

Only in Queen Street, from where Lord Stonehouse ran the
Committee of Acquisition and Intelligence, was it business as usual.
The title was a euphemism for plunder, but since everything had
been plundered, spying had become its main occupation. Lord
Stonehouse looked much the same, although there were more medi-
cines on his desk along with the wine he habitually drank while
signing papers. The fire burned brightly; there was never any shortage
of coal in Queen Street.

He did not ask me to sit, but waved me to the same spot on the
carpet where I had stood as a bastard apprentice, long before he had
declared me his heir. He wasted no time on preliminaries. I had
been sent to that part of Essex to improve relations. They were now
at their worst since the end of the war. I had made a most dangerous
enemy in Challoner. Why had I not let him hang the wretch?

I winced inwardly, seeing again that raw, bleeding flesh. But I said
nothing, determined to keep my promise to Anne. It was the price
I paid for the house she loved, for the children, for my fine bucket
boots, the fall of my exquisite lace collar, and the thought of more
nights in a world upside down. I came out of my reverie as he
brought his fist down on the desk.

'Lost your voice? That's new. That's something, at least! You have
lost that part of Essex to us as well.' He banged his fist on a bundle

of papers. 'Nothing but petitions from the people there. Disband the army. Cromwell's only bargaining point. Holles will do it. His Presbyterians are in control of Parliament. Or have you become such a fool you do not realise that?'

I hung my head, murmuring that I did. Denzil Holles, who led the Presbyterians in Parliament, hated Cromwell. He had sued for peace during the war, eager to reach a settlement with the King at almost any price.

'Not only do you not hand the thief over to justice, he's now deserted!'

He was flinging the Essex petitions into a tray as I came out of my torpor.

'Scogman?'

'What?'

'He's alive?'

'Of course the wretch is alive. Very much alive, unfortunately. Why do you think I've sent for you?'

Lord Stonehouse pulled out a pamphlet from the jumble of petitions, and flung it at me. It had a neat play on the New Model Army in its headline, which I had to admire: *New Model Thieves Let Robber Escape*. The pamphleteer had had a field day. In his lurid prose, Scogman became the most wanted man in Essex, the silver spoon a priceless collection of plate. A woodblock depicted him with one tooth and a devil's tail.

Scogman alive! I felt a lift of spirits that no lace collar could give me. The most wanted man in Essex! I could not keep a smile from my face when I thought of Challoner's puce-faced reaction.

'You find it amusing, sir, do you?'

I straightened my face hastily. 'No, no, no, my lord. I am, er, concerned about the inaccuracy of the report.'

'Standards were higher in your day as a pamphleteer, were they?'

Sometimes I could not make him out. Was there an edge of mockery in his voice, a sign that the worst of the storm was over? 'It was a spoon, my lord, not plate. Not even silver.'

'Thirty pieces of silver,' he murmured, staring into space.

'I beg your pardon, my lord?'

He gave me a baleful look and stared into the fire. There was a silence apart from the click of the coals and the drumming of his fingers on his old leather desk. He broke it abruptly.

'For your ears only. We have the King.'

I went forward impulsively. 'Congratulations, my lord.'

He waved me away, a frown forming. 'Well, well, there's more to it. Unfortunately. I'll come to that.' But he could not contain his exuberance, and his face lit up again.

'D'you know how we got His Majesty? We bought him! As good as. He was going to do a deal with the Scots but had to accept their religion. Charles loves the warmth of his Anglican ritual, and they chilled him to the bloody marrow with their damp kirks and bored him senseless with their gloomy hairsplitting.'

He took up his wine and then – it was unheard of – poured me one. He sprang up, animated, almost young again.

'Warwick sat there. Moneybags Bedford there – what are you standing like a loon for, boy? Sit down! Sit down! Oh, of course we were paying for the Scottish army to leave. On the face of it. For services rendered – coming to our aid. You don't buy a King, do you?'

He put on a shocked look, then laughed. 'The grasping Scottish tinkers wanted nearly a million and a half pounds! For a King. Beaten. We knocked them down to four hundred thousand. Four hundred thousand.' Lord Stonehouse relished the figure, as he savoured the taste of wine on his tongue. 'In two instalments.'

I had never seen him so lively. He finished his glass and stood over the fire. 'Newcastle fishwives threw rotting herring at the Scots as they left, crying "Judas!", and I bought a shipload of coal. Warmest coal I've ever burned.'

He kicked at the fire, oblivious of the smouldering coals which singed his boot. Flames lit his face, throwing into sharp relief his aquiline nose, which was reflected in the family symbol of the falcon. For a moment the shadows took his years away and he stood there, proud, full of belief in himself, as he must have been when he first built his great house, Highpoint. But as the fire burned higher, the lines returned to his face and the stoop to his back.

'Now we've lost him.'

'The King? The King has escaped?'

'No, no, no. But almost as bad. Holles and his Presbyterians have him. He's in the middle of England under house arrest. Holdenby House, Northamptonshire, guarded by one of Holles's Presbyterian regiments.'

'Any settlement with the King will have to be ratified by Parliament!'

He gave me a bleak look. 'Who controls Parliament?'

I swallowed my wine. 'We must win the debate. It's what we fought for. Parliament.'

'Majority opinion?'

'Yes.'

'All well and good.' He went back to his desk. 'When it's on your side.' He opened a drawer that was double-locked, the one I had nicknamed his dirty tricks drawer. 'What matters is not the debate, but what you can dig out beforehand. I must find out what Holles is up to. I had an informant high up in his inner circle I was hoping to catch. Unfortunately, I've lost him. I think you are the man to reel him back in.'

This was going far better than I had feared. But I looked at him warily as he drew out a fat bundle of papers. What exactly did 'reel him back in' mean? The last thing I wanted was to be drawn into Lord Stonehouse's shady network of spies and informers. I wanted to defeat, perhaps even convince Holles, but by argument, not dirty tricks.

'I will do all I can to help, my lord, but …' I groped for a diplomatic way of putting it.

'But?'

'After the battle of Naseby,' I said, 'I accepted the sword of the Royalist Jacob Astley.'

'Lord Astley. Did you now.'

'Astley said: "You have done your work, and may go and play, unless you fall out among yourselves."'

He leaned back in his chair, rubbing his chin. 'A good aphorism. I must remember it. Meaning we should not quarrel, but reach agreement?'

I beamed at him. The wine put a rosy glow on everything. The firelight gleamed on the old oak furniture that smelt of polish, and on the jewelled falcon perched on his signet ring. This was the moment. I was on the verge of suggesting he put me up as an MP to fight Holles in Parliament when he struck like the bird on the ring, his voice acid with contempt.

'I would as soon reach agreement with Holles as I would with a poisonous snake. Don't you understand? He has the King! The English Presbyterians are not like the dreary Scots! They hold him at a fine house, where Charles practises his religion, and holds his court. Holles will push through all the concessions the King wants, just to have him back on the throne. In a year or two the King will have his own army, dismiss Parliament –'

'Cromwell will never agree to such concessions!'

'Cromwell has given up.'

This was too much. Lord Stonehouse had sat here throughout the war, his arse warmed by his coals. He had no idea what Cromwell and his army had been through. 'Cromwell is ill, my lord,' I said coldly.

'Ill? Cromwell ill? He should have my years. My bladder. My stone. Ill? A grateful Parliament has conferred on him £2,500 a year. From estates *I* confiscated from the Marquis of Winchester.

Cromwell ill, sir? He has drawn his pension, that's the only thing wrong with Cromwell. Meanwhile we are in danger of losing all we fought for.'

'Holles has no soldiers to launch a coup.'

'He has Poyntz's northern army.'

That at least was true. Major-General Poyntz's soldiers had been recruited from strict Presbyterians. 'They are no match for the New Model.'

'Yet.' He pointed to the petitions heaped up on his desk. 'Holles is seeking to disband half the New Model and send the rest to Ireland.'

'Nobody wants to go to Ireland. Cromwell will never let him disband –'

'Cromwell, Cromwell.' The name seemed to stick in his throat and he began to cough. 'Cromwell is counting his pension and waiting for God to tell him what to do. Until God speaks or someone puts a keg of gunpowder under his arse in the form of solid proof of what Holles is up to, he won't budge. I was on the verge of getting that proof from my informant but –'

He burst into an explosion of coughing. I picked up his wine.

'Not wine … Cupboard … Not that one! Cordial …'

I opened the cupboard. In it was a miniature of a strikingly beautiful woman with greenish eyes. With it was a partly folded letter in which I caught only the opening line: *This is a true likeness of …*

'Quick!'

I pulled out a flask and poured him a greenish liquid which smelt pleasantly of cinnamon. He swallowed some, spurted it out, mopped his face and took another sip or two, until the coughing gradually stopped. I moved to return the flask, but he stopped me and did so himself. I had disturbed the miniature so it was on the edge of the cupboard shelf. When he moved away, the miniature was no longer there. It was a clumsy surreptitious movement, and for a moment he did not meet my eyes. He looked almost human for a moment. Surely, I thought, he's not fallen in love. At his age! The idea brought a smile to my face. It was wiped off immediately when he rounded on me.

'I don't know what you have to smile about. You have no idea what you've done! The informant who was going to tell me what Holles is up to is Sir Lewis Challoner.'

It was a world upside down in this room too, where nothing was as it seemed.

'You sent me there to keep the army under control,' I protested. 'How could I know there was anything else going on!'

'Just so, just so,' he conceded. 'I should have told you. But I could not afford to trust you. You and your damned scruples. Your radical views. You might have told anybody! I thought that your desire to be an MP would keep you in check. But now – now, I can't afford *not* to trust you.'

He began coughing again and drank more cordial before he told me that Challoner had been planning to meet him, until the incident with Scogman.

'Challoner knows Holles's plans. He should do. He's part of them. Why do you think there is so much trouble between the people and the army in Essex? Challoner is fomenting it.'

'Why should he tell you Holles's plans? He hates Cromwell.'

'He loves land more.'

Everything fell into place. I remembered Challoner's sudden burst of friendliness, his winks and slaps on the back as he rhapsodised about the beauty of the countryside.

'The farm, you mean.'

'Oh, more than that. The estate Parliament seized. I was negotiating to sell it on favourable terms if he came over to us.'

I winced. 'And I thought his friendliness was because of my diplomacy.'

'Diplomacy?' He laughed. He patted the bundle of papers he had taken from the drawer. 'This is the real diplomacy, Tom. Forget all this nonsense about being an MP. MPs are rhetorical froth. I want you to actually *do* something. You must apologise.'

I did not think I was hearing him correctly. 'Apologise?'

'To Sir Lewis. You made him a laughing stock.'

'You expect me to crawl to that man?'

'It is a matter of honour to him.'

'It is a matter of honour to *me*! Or do you think I have no honour because of where I come from?'

He locked his hands together, rested his chin on them and gave me a long stare before opening the file. Whether he got it by money or extortion I had no idea. A creeping sense of unease began to fill me as he read some reports and showed me others, concealing names. There were greasy scraps of paper about secret meetings between Holles and the Governor of the Tower, details of armouries and the strength of soldiers guarding them, which, Lord Stonehouse claimed, had been seized from a spy of Holles. How much was true, how much fabrication, and how much distorted by his own fears, I did not know. But, in a voice growing hoarse with speaking, it was what he said next, in a dead, tired, matter-of-fact tone, that chilled me.

'If there is a coup, Cromwell will be removed. I will be in the Tower. So will you. At the right time there will probably be trumped-up charges. We will be lucky to escape execution. What would happen to your little son, Luke, my grandson, I do not know.'

His voice petered out. He looked as exhausted as he had been lively earlier, his eyes half-hooded. It was so quiet I could hear a distant hawker cry, and the crackling of the coals in the fireplace. He put the papers away, the keys rattling as he double-locked the drawer, a faint echo of the gloomy litany of sound in the corridors of the Tower where I had once visited a pamphleteer imprisoned for sedition. If there was any chance he was right, what did my honour matter? But then the rattle of those keys he always carried brought back Scogman, in chains, dragged by Stalker's horse, stumbling, falling, dragged from lane to ditch and back again.

'I will not apologise to that man.'

'You will do as I say!'

I said nothing.

'Get out.'

He began coughing again, knocking the glass of cordial over. I went to help him, but he reacted so violently and was so red in the face that, fearing I was doing more harm than good, I went for Mr Cole.

6

Anne's reaction was almost as violent as Lord Stonehouse's – I had promised to remain on good terms, what if Lord Stonehouse was right, what would happen to us? I told her about the miniature he had concealed, to divert her from fears about the coup, but it only added fresh ones. Who was this woman? *This is a true likeness.* Wasn't that the sort of language people used when they were setting up a meeting with a view to marriage. What would happen to us if …

I got no sleep that night. Lord Stonehouse was old, cantankerous, suspicious to the point of madness, but what if he *was* right about the coup?

The fears gradually receded with daylight. I was reassured when I learned a week later that Cromwell had recovered and returned to the House. I wrote to him, in the hope that he might offer me some position. To prepare for an interview, I saw my tailor, Mr Pepys.

It is humiliating to discover from your tailor you have no money. I was careful with my allowance from Lord Stonehouse, and realised he had stopped it. I could feel myself going a deep red. Mr Pepys was very delicate about it. No doubt Queen Street had made some error? He would happily have made me the new suit I craved for, but I knew he had a large family to support, including the expenses of his son Samuel at St Paul's, and I would not go into debt with him.

It was even worse telling Anne.

'And what do we live on?' she said.

'My army pay.'

'And when do we get that?'

I did not know. Negotiations were dragging on in Parliament. I had read that Cromwell, still too busy to see me, said the New Model Army would lay down its arms when Parliament commanded it to do so. That did not sound like a political crisis.

What upset me most was that Adams, our ostler, was taken back to Queen Street by Lord Stonehouse. Luke moped for the loss of his old friend. But he had a habit of inventing creatures of fancy, sometimes talking to Adams as if he was still there. One day Luke cried that he liked the new ostler, a handsome soldier who had let him ride and said he was a fine horseman. He told me after I discovered he had taken the horse from the stable on his own, which I had strictly forbidden. When I told him he must not invent stories to cover up the truth, it upset me even more when he refused to confess but cried: 'It's true. It's true. There was a man!'

Although it was May, there was frost at night with cold north winds driving sharp showers of rain. The emerging buds in the apple tree seemed to shrink back in themselves. We all got colds and Liz's persisted, so we put off the baptism with Mr Tooley until the weather was better. Anne and I scarcely spoke to one another until the letter arrived.

It was from Lord Stonehouse's eldest son, Richard, in Paris. Despite my discovery that he was my real father, Richard had never acknowledged me as his son. I had not seen or heard from him since the battle of Edgehill five years ago, when we had fought on opposite sides and he had almost killed me. His hand, as he admitted, was as bad as ever:

Dear Thomas,

I am no better at this riting game and have throwne this away or its brothers more times than I can Rembere over the years. But nowe the war is over and Wee are at peace I must write to say I no you can never see me as your Father. Howe can you when I have done such Base & Bad things. But the Warre has changed me. I needed to be away from my Father to find myself, that at anye rate is what a Priest here says. We are on differant sides but I believe I have done mye Duty to mye King & from what I heare you are a Man of Honoure and a brave soldier who has done youre Duty to what you believe.

I doe not deserve nor expect a replye but if you finde it in your hearte to forgive me a letter left with Jean de Monteuril, the French envoy in London will find your father,

Richard Stonehouse

His signature was unreadable. The letter was so totally unexpected and so difficult to decipher, with myriads of blots and crossings out, that the first time I read it I sat bemused, still, as shocked as it it was a letter from the dead.

I read it again. If the first shock was that he had written at all, the second was that he had asked me to forgive him. Was he genuine, or was he dissembling?

The third shock was to find I had feelings for the man I knew to be my father. He was dissolute and violent, but how much was that a reaction to his father and his perception of me as a usurper? Lord Stonehouse had brought me up in secret, but had once shown Richard my writing to shame him about his own hand. Was it any wonder that when he found out who I was, he had come to hate me? I knew what he had gone through at the hands of his father, for was I not having the same whip cracked at me? It was the effort Richard had clearly put into writing it himself which began to persuade me he was sincere. He despised writing: scrivener's work as he put it. But I now felt his childish struggles had left him ashamed of his scrawl.

I was in my study. It was but a poky little room, with no fire, but it was the place I would most miss if we were forced to leave Drury Lane. On the small table, which I had in lieu of a desk, I had written some ideas for my interview with Cromwell. I wrote a good Italian hand, in sharp contrast to my father's chaotic script. The third time I read his letter, I read not the words, but the effort that had gone into making them. I felt the painful determination to form letters, the sudden bursts of irritation as words tumbled illegibly into one another, and the anger in slashed loops and crossed 't's. Anger at me, or at himself? Whole sentences had been crossed out. Other men would have made a fair copy, but he was incapable of that. Or they would have got a scrivener to do it. But he had wanted to write to me himself. He did not know, he could not imagine, that it was that effort, as much or more than the words themselves, that moved me.

Perhaps he had changed. I was afraid of believing it, but could not help myself. I suppose it is always there, in an abandoned child, that hope for reconciliation. I told myself I was being stupid as I felt the onset of tears.

Anne touched my shoulder. I had no idea how long she had been in the room. There was a sympathy in her touch which had been missing since I had refused to work with Lord Stonehouse. I blinked back the tears and handed her the letter.

'What a hypocrite.'

'You do not think he is sincere?'

'Do you?'

'I don't know.'

'You don't *know*? He tried to kill you!'

There was a knock at the door. I stared at the letter, half-hearing Jane tell Anne that Liz had had another bad night and been unable to keep her milk down. Anne began to follow Jane, but turned back.

'What are you going to do?'

'Invite him to supper?'

'Please don't joke. What are you going to do?'

'I have no idea, Anne.' I picked up a quill, drew my fingers down the feather and felt the point. I did not intend to write a letter. It was an automatic reaction, to help me think. I was still dazed by the father I had all but forgotten, suddenly taking on human shape.

'You're not going to answer it, are you?'

'Of course I'm going to answer it.'

'What are you going to say?'

I was conscious of Jane hovering on the stairs. 'That is my affair,' I said coldly.

She told Jane she would be up shortly, then closed the door. She was trembling, and her cold had left her voice raw and hoarse. 'It is as much my affair as yours, sir.'

'This is the world upside down, is it? When a woman tells a man what to do?'

'Has her say, sir, has her say. While you have been fighting I have built this place up. I have flattered Lord Stonehouse, sympathised with his illnesses, suffered his moods, his suspicions, his rages, his belches, his farts, smiling while I wanted to scream. When Luke was born I felt as if I was being torn apart. I thought I would not live.'

I got up and wanted to hold her but she pushed me away, telling me with a concentrated fury what she had been through while I was away. Things I never realised. I knew Lord Stonehouse had acknowledged me as his heir only out of expediency, when Parliament suspected his loyalty, but did I have any idea how shallow that acknowledgement was? He wrote secretly to Richard. She knew that from Mr Cole. Oh, she flattered him too. Promised him preferment when I inherited. Did I not know that? Did I really think it was a world upside down? It was the same old world, greased and oiled by favours – or the promise of favours when the King came back. Everyone was jostling for position except me, she said, who believed the world was changing into a different, a better, place.

Surely I realised, she went on, I was still a whim as far as Lord Stonehouse was concerned. It rarely happened that a bastard inherited such a great estate. It was almost unheard of that his wife was a commoner – a commoner with no dowry, no lands to bring to the estate. If Lord Stonehouse was planning to marry again, it was not for love, as I saw it, but for another Stonehouse. Another male. We were a fall-back, a second string, if there was no other Stonehouse blood left to inherit. When she said this, I felt I had known it all the time, but never put it into words. What I really cared about was the attainable – becoming an MP. Even that he had brushed to one side.

My anger mounted as she told me how she was treated, rebuffed when she did not conceive at first. Lord Stonehouse was not at home. Or he was in meetings. There was no coal. Only straw on the floor. Why on earth did she not tell me all this? Because I would not have grovelled. I would have ruined everything. Only men had the luxury of pride, she said bitterly.

In my brief, snatched visits during the war, what for me had been love, for her had been desperation, followed by the continual, gnawing fear of being barren, and of further rejection from Lord Stonehouse's favour. Had I not seen the straw on the floor, or realised they were burning chopped-up furniture for me?

She had tried to find out if the entail on Lord Stonehouse's will had been removed. The entail was the contract by which the landed classes double-locked and bolted the estate to the eldest son. Mr Cole knew most things, but that was a secret only Lord Stonehouse and his lawyer knew.

Her voice grew hoarser. I could not stop her. I did not want to. It was like a boil being lanced. She had not slept much because of Liz. She wore no paint. Lines I had barely noticed before cracked her beautiful skin. Her hair hung lifeless. She was so thin she looked as though she would break. Only her blue eyes crackled with furious, burning energy.

'Luke furnished this place. When Lord Stonehouse thought Liz was going to be another boy the stables were built. Those fine horses arrived. Stallions.' She put some of her old mockery into the word. 'I do not want to go through having another child, but I will go on and on until we have what we want. I have done all that and I am not allowed my say?'

Her voice had shredded to a croaking echo. I held her tightly, stroking her, feeling her bones protruding from her skin.

'What we want? That's what matters. I want you, I want you,' I whispered.

'Do you?'

I kissed her. 'Nothing else matters. We don't have to have another child. Not yet. I will stay away.'

'But I want – I want you near me.' She kissed me passionately.

'I'll be careful.'

She half-smiled. 'You never are.' She stroked the scar on my cheek with a sudden tenderness. 'Scar-face.'

'Bag of bones.'

She buried her head in my chest and we held each other close, until the rasping of her breath slowed and I could feel our hearts beating together. 'We don't need all this,' I said, gesturing the house away.

She said – ferocious again – she couldn't bear to lose it. Not now. It would be like showing a child a magnificent meal, then snatching it from her. 'And you need it. To be an MP. Change the world.' If that was half-mocking, half-serious, her next words were in earnest. 'And you need Lord Stonehouse.'

'No. I won't crawl to him. Particularly after what he did to you.'

She clenched her fists in frustration. 'I knew I shouldn't have told you all this!'

I unpeeled her fingers and smoothed them between my hands. 'Better we do things our own way.' I remembered Nehemiah's words. 'Be beholden to no one.'

'How?'

'Cromwell will help me.'

'Are you sure?'

'Sure?' I laughed. 'He's the most powerful man in Britain.'

I told her I must go to the House and see him, and got my papers together. Still she lingered, staring at Richard's letter. 'You know why he's written to you, don't you?'

I smiled at her expression of absolute certainty. Sometimes she had the air of an astrologer predicting the future. 'No. Do you?'

'Because he knows about your quarrel with Lord Stonehouse.'

Since the Royalists were based in Paris, where Queen Henrietta held court, letters were censored and delayed, if they arrived at all. 'Unlikely. That was over a fortnight ago. The news would hardly have reached him in Paris.'

'It would reach him here.'

I laughed. 'He'd never come here! It's too dangerous.' Unlike many Royalists, Richard had never surrendered. He was close to Queen Henrietta, a Catholic, and Cromwell had intercepted papers that proved his involvement in the present Irish rebellion. 'If he was caught here, he'd be in the Tower. Not even Lord Stonehouse could save him.'

The French envoy's address had suggested Paris. But there were no French markings. It was not dated or sealed. The only mark was a posthorn, such as might have been used in any London alehouse. 'It's a coincidence. The letter and the quarrel.'

'Do you think so?'

'No.'

I shivered suddenly, violently. The thick, smeared scrawl, with the savage sword-like crossing of every 't', brought memories flooding back of when he had hired people to kill me, when I used to check every alehouse before I entered, jump at every sound in the street. I crumpled it up.

'I'll burn it,' I said.

'No,' she said. 'Take it to Cromwell.'

7

You could hear the noise in Whitehall, sense the tension in the shops and stalls of Westminster Hall. Cromwell was back. There were rumours that he and the Presbyterian leader, Denzil Holles, had come to blows. That the army was in revolt.

A coin to the Sergeant got me into the lobby. I waited for an opportunity to see Cromwell, my father's letter burning a hole in my pocket. The debate grew in intensity. I could hear Cromwell's voice, rising over shouts of derision. There is no more thrilling place than the House when you are part of it, and no worse, confusing place when you are out of it. I was even jealous of the printers' runners. Reporting was forbidden and they smuggled out speeches, as I did years before.

When the debate was adjourned I saw one runner, illegal copy stuffed in his britches, wriggling his way through a crowd of arguing MPs. He was as snot-nosed and eel-slippery as I used to be, but a coin from my pocket stopped him. I deciphered the scrivener's scrawl. The debate was about the army petition I had seen in Nehemiah's room, for pay and indemnities. 'H,' I read. That must be Holles. I could not believe what he was quoted as saying: 'The soldiers who have signed this petition are enemies of the state ...'

Enemies of the state? The army that won the war? And was simply asking for its pay?

There was a shout. The boy snatched the papers and ran.

'Seize him.'

The MP who gave chase was young and would have the legs on the boy. I felt responsible for having stopping him. And I was a runner at heart. It was instinctive. I stuck out my foot. The MP went flying, arms flailing. I just managed to catch him to break the worst of his fall and help him up.

'I'm terribly sorry.'

He glared at me angrily, but my suit, if old, was of the finest silk, and I spoke with such concern, in my best Stonehouse, that he stopped short of accusing me. Someone else drew him away, telling him they had a motion to draw up. I recognised the sharp, vinegary tones immediately. I had tripped up Denzil Holles's bag carrier.

It was stupid, but I could not resist it. I was longing for action, and if I could not debate Holles in the House, this was second best.

I bowed. 'Lord Holles.'

He spoke through me, to the bag carrier. 'Stonehouse. Comes from the same filth as that pamphleteer.'

I bowed again. 'The same filth, my lord, who won the war, and whom you are calling enemies of the state.'

He whirled round. He was about fifty, and had eyes as sharp and vinegary as his voice. 'Are you one of the men behind this wretched petition?'

I was about to answer when a hand clamped over my shoulder and I found myself staring into Cromwell's eyes. He always seemed to look not at you, but into your very soul with his piercing eyes, somewhere between grey and green. His face was almost the colour of his buff uniform: he had not bothered to change before coming into the House. A wart above his left eyebrow quivered as he steered me away.

'Don't make it worse,' he said. 'We are losing the debate.'

'Keep your puppies away from me, Cromwell!' Holles shouted.

Cromwell did not respond, going towards the corridor that led to his office with another MP, Ireton. Mortified, I plunged after him, asking to see him, bumping into various people as I tried to catch his attention. Either Cromwell did not hear me, or he chose not to.

'Make an appointment,' Ireton said curtly.

I hated Ireton at that moment. In fact I hated Ireton at any moment. I hated him because he was thirty-six against my twenty-two, because with his sunken, hollow eyes he was broodingly serious and never laughed, because he was cold and rational where I was impulsive and, most of all, because he was Cromwell's son-in-law and always at his elbow.

I stood dejected, watching them walk away. Then Cromwell turned and beckoned. If you had ridden with Cromwell in close combat you were one of his soldiers. Whatever your rank he knew your name. Whatever your weaknesses, if you struggled to overcome them he would stand by you. He never bragged, putting his victories down to God's grace. When he talked to a regiment every single soldier felt he was talking to him. However tired he was, and I could see how drained he was after his illness, he had time, however little, for one of his soldiers. I shot over the lobby as if I was still a runner, then managed to control myself.

'You'll have to wait.' Ireton scowled. 'In there.'

I walked where he had pointed, into an anteroom so stuffed with drafts of speeches and yellowing parliamentary papers the door would not close properly. I sat squashed between a pile of ordinances and some old papers about the draining of the East Anglian fens, while Cromwell had meeting after meeting.

Boots clattered, voices droned. Cromwell was making arrangements to ride to Essex next day to hear the soldiers' demands. In that stuffy, cramped space I nodded off. It was Ireton's words that woke me with a start.

'… French boat. They captured one of the sailors, but the man they were landing got away.'

Over a pile of papers, through the partly open door, I could see Cromwell reacting sharply. 'When was this?'

'A month ago.'

'Who was he?'

'I think you can guess. He was an excellent swordsman. He killed two of the customs men. He's somewhere in the City – he's been spotted at the Exchange. I have men out looking for him.'

A month ago. The dates fitted with Richard's letter. So did the swordsmanship. I felt again the prick of the sword he held at my throat after Edgehill, touched the scar on my cheek where it had been cut open by one of his men. A surge of excitement ran through me. At one stroke I could have everything. It was my ticket to working with Cromwell, to becoming an MP. But it would have to be done so Lord Stonehouse did not know I was involved

Clever, clever Anne, who had put this idea into my mind. But she was wrong in one thing. She thought I had swallowed Lord Stonehouse speaking of me as his heir. I was a fool, but not that much of a fool. I had gloried in the possibility, but in my heart of hearts I knew it would never happen. A bastard and a printer's daughter? That was why I kept my feet in Thomas Neave's boots, while wearing Thomas Stonehouse's plumed hat. Because I was determined to be my own man. But this changed everything.

With Richard out of the way, I would be the sole male heir. From that moment, hemmed in by a cage of musty papers, I could afford the luxury of belief. All this ran through my mind as Cromwell closed the door on Ireton and returned to his desk, eyes half-lidded in weariness.

Reflecting this sudden expansion of my inner world, I tilted my chair backwards, knocking over a pile of ordinances.

Cromwell pushed the door fully open. 'Why, Tom! I forgot you were there.'

I scrambled up in confusion, picking up the papers.

'Leave them, leave them. That is the Blasphemy Ordinance. Hanging people for denying the Trinity? The Presbyterians will never get that through.'

He unearthed the letter I had sent, asking to work with him. 'Work with me, Tom?' he laughed. 'I hope not. We are at peace. Disbanding.'

'I mean here.'

'Here? In this Tower of Babel? Trying to bring all these contentious voices together? You would be bored to death.'

'Not working with you.'

I meant it. As soon as I sat opposite him I realised how much I missed working with him. He made men not only believe in what they were doing, but believe in themselves. His brooding self-criticism, constantly questioning his own ability and his own frailty, led people to be much more open to his criticism of them. And so everyone worked with a common purpose, knowing that he drove no one more relentlessly than he drove himself.

I drew out Richard's letter and opened it, glimpsing the words 'forgive me … your father.' Once again, the effort of that laboured scrawl brought a rush of feeling that caught me unawares. My eyes pricked and I was unable to speak. Suppose Richard was genuine? What if he had changed? I dismissed it. A man like that, who sent people to kill me?

'What have you got there, Tom?'

'I …'

It was not so much that I believed Richard was genuine; more that I knew I would never forgive myself if I did not at least try to find out before giving him away.

'What is it, Tom?' Cromwell said, more sharply, reaching out for the letter.

I pulled it away. 'It – it is from a gentleman supporting me to be an MP.'

'Lord Stonehouse will support you.'

'He has refused to.'

'And you expect me to?'

His refusal was implicit in the question. His manner became brusque. I had seen him reject people asking for favours many times before in this abrupt way, but it was humiliating when it happened to me. I stuffed my father's letter in my bag and went to the door.

'Wait. You have quarrelled with Lord Stonehouse? He has cut your allowance?'

He knew everything. Probably, I thought bitterly, Lord Stonehouse had told him, blocking any chance of him putting me forward as an MP. What happened next was even more humiliating, although he did it with the best of intentions, in the manner of a helping hand for an old army colleague down on his luck. He took me down the corridor to an office where a clerk was transcribing his last speech. A warrant made out to Thomas Stonehouse for army pay had the amount already filled in. Cromwell signed an army warrant in his large, rolling script, clapped me on the shoulders, and went.

The clerk checked the amount of pay I was owed in a ledger and completed the army warrant. He wore a fine linen shirt, rolled back at the wrists to protect it from ink splashes. It was the splashes, rather than the man, that I recognised.

'Mr Ink,' I cried, flinging my arms round the man whom I had known as a humble scrivener at Westminster, when he had smuggled out Mr Pym's speeches for me to run with them to the printer, speeches which had begun the great rebellion against the King.

'I am Mr Clarke,' he said. 'William.' There was a hint of reproof in his bow. His dark grey doublet was severe, but fashionably unbuttoned at the waist to show the quality of his linen.

'You have a new name and fine new clothes,' I said.

He told me Clarke had always been his name. It was I, as a child, who had christened him Mr Ink, but now he had risen in the world he would appreciate being called William Clarke, Esq. It was said with a wink to show that somewhere inside those new clothes was my old friend Mr Ink, but it added to my feeling that everyone was rising in the world but me.

When I left that feeling stayed with me, and the army warrant in my pocket only reminded me of my humiliation. I walked slowly but reached Drury Lane all too soon. As I went through the passage, I thought of my father, wanting to answer his letter.

Anne looked at me expectantly as I was going into my study.

'I did not tell Cromwell,' I said. 'Whatever he's done, Richard is my father. I'll write to him. See if he is sincere.'

I went to close the door but still she stood there. 'Is that all?'

Silently I gave her the army warrant. She stared at Mr Ink's elegant hand, and the rolling loops of Cromwell's signature. For four months' back pay I had been awarded eleven pounds, six shillings and threepence.

'You fool,' she said.

I thought she was going to tear it up. I snatched it from her so it did tear. There was a rush of blood to my head. A roaring in my ears. I gripped her by the shoulders and God knows what I would have done to her if I had not seen Luke staring from the hall.

Anne turned away and, without a word, took Luke by the hand and led him upstairs.

8

My power with words deserted me when it came to answering Richard's letter. I balked at the first hurdle. Dear Richard? Dear Father? Dear Sir Richard? The coldly formal Sir?

In the end, I opted for the last. I wrote:

Sir,

I do not know what to write (true). After what you have done to me in the past you will forgive me for feeling suspicious (to put it mildly). I believe you are in London. I should report you to the authorities. I have not given you away (at the moment) because I would like to meet to find if you are writing ab imo pectore (the Stonehouse motto: from the heart). I shall be at the Exchange, at the sign of the Bull, tomorrow, Thursday and the following day, at noon.

I remain, Sir, yr humble servant,
Thomas Stonehouse

I waited at the Exchange on those two days with a strange, growing eagerness which gradually turned into disappointment and disillusion. When mail came my heart beat a little faster; but there was no reply. Perhaps Richard had returned to France. Or feared a trap. On one of the visits to the Exchange, being near London Bridge,

I remembered my promise to take money to Scogman's wife and children. My prayers for his survival had been answered and he had become a kind of folk hero to me. I crossed the river to Bankside and went to the address from the regiment list. It was a brothel.

When I was woken that night by Liz's coughing I could still see the whores wiping their eyes as they laughed.

'Scogman? Married? Give the money to me, dear. I'll see she gets it! Kids? He scarpers too quickly to give his name to any kids. Scoggy? Give him my undying love, darling.'

I winced as I remembered how, previously, I had lent him an angel, which he still owed me, to send to this starving family.

I tried to forget my humiliation by helping Jane to nurse Liz and, since Dr Latchford seemed at a loss, the next morning rode to Spitall Fields to get a herbal syrup from Matthew, the cunning man who had brought me up. Late in life he had had a stroke of good fortune. Unwilling to disappoint anyone, he had always promised a cure for everything, from the plague to a broken heart. Too erratic to be trusted, his business was on the point of failure when he met an apothecary, Nicholas Culpepper, who separated those remedies of Matthew's which worked, from those which didn't. And he put his finger on Matthew's unique ability. While his remedies were unreliable, his knowledge and collection of herbs, from aloe to vervain, were unrivalled.

Together they produced simple herbal remedies for the poor. Culpepper infuriated doctors like Latchford by setting himself up as a doctor in Spitall Fields, outside the City, where the College of Physicians had no jurisdiction. Matthew had a room in the apothecary's house, which, on a gloomy day, was like walking into summer, the air smelling of rosemary, lavender and sage.

When I arrived, Matthew was chopping herbs on a bench. One of his eyes was milky blue, and he stooped like a goblin, but he was as lively as ever, and his optimism unquenched.

'Little Liz! The poor mite! I know exactly what will cure her. It drew three infants back from the grave last week.' He caught Culpepper's eyes staring sternly over his spectacles, swallowed and toned down his promises. 'It will soothe the cough so she can eat more easily and sleep.'

I put the jar of syrup in my saddle pouch and rode back through the City. Crowds were building up, and it was increasingly difficult to get through. They were thickest round the bookstalls and hawkers: there were more pamphlets sold that day than hot pies.

From one pamphlet I learned how badly Cromwell had lost the debate. Half the army was to be disbanded, receiving a miserable six weeks' money in lieu of their long arrears of pay. Another gave an ominous response from the soldiers: not a petition this time, but a set of demands. One called for an apology from Holles for the soldiers being called enemies of the state they had fought for. Another was for full pay. It was signed not by the soldiers, but by men who called themselves agents, or agitators. Levellers. One of the signatories was Nehemiah.

Going down Cornhill, there was such a press of people I found it difficult to control my horse and was forced to dismount. The trouble came from a bookshop displaying the sign of the Bible. More people came to it to argue than to buy books. A Presbyterian minister called Edwards was haranguing the crowd. He had written a series of books called *Gangraena*, the latest an attack on the sins of Cromwell's army. The gangrene lay in the heresies the army was supposed to spread.

Edwards, a tall cadaverous man who wore his hair long, was railing against 'sectaries' who broke away from the true Presbyterian Church. A severe-looking Puritan holding a copy of *Gangraena*, a tome as thick as the Bible, stared directly at me, his expression saying he knew I was one of the heretics.

'Such people believe in liberty of conscience!' Edwards cried, as if liberty was worse than the plague. 'I tell you this. Liberty of conscience leads to thought, thought to error and error to hell.'

I could not stand there silent. 'So we are not to think for ourselves?'

'Not in religion, sir.' People stood aside as he pushed towards me. 'A farmer does not expect a weaver to plant his corn, nor a weaver allow a farmer to weave his cloth.'

'But if the farmer, or his corn, is bad – what is a man to do? Starve? Can he not plant his own corn?'

'Plant his own corn! You heard him. Here is another of your damned sectaries.' He pushed his face into mine. 'Because, sir, your corn would come up as tares and weeds – heresies and blasphemies.'

Once I had started I would not give way. The Puritan holding *Gangraena* with all the reverence of the Bible shook his head despairingly at me. From angry mutterings, the crowd began to jostle and abuse me. It was an astonishing reversal of the mood of the crowds before the war, who had all been for liberty and their rights, whether for religion, a patch of ground or a loaf of bread. Perhaps they now linked liberty to the pillaging soldiers in five years of chaos and war. There was such an aching desire for normality, for order at any price, that people were willing to give away their very thoughts to this narrow-minded churchman. Another voice came from the back of the crowd.

'I know him! He is a bastard, a devil who pretends to be a lord!'

George's manner suggested he knew about my rift with Lord Stonehouse. His voice chilled me even more than it had as a child, for at least then I could believe he was the only one who was mad. Now that madness seemed to have infected half London. George pushed his way through the crowd, his face flushed with religious zeal. He had shaken my hand only a few weeks before, but now he levelled a finger at me.

'I accuse him. He denies he has a soul,' he cried.

There was an abrupt silence. People near me drew away. Others craned forward, breaths stilled, eyes staring. A gob of food slipped unnoticed from the mouth of a man eating a pie. The shop sign creaked as a kite perching on it swooped to snatch the pie the man was holding. Almost nobody laughed, all of them giving way to the minister, his long hair drifting round his face in the wind, his voice soft with disbelief.

'Do you deny the immortality of the soul, my son?'

In a sense, George's accusation was true. Every time he beat me he said it was for the good of my soul, until one day I told him that, as I did not have one, he could stop wasting his time. That same perversity brought the words from my mouth.

'I did when he beat me.'

The Puritan holding Edwards's book looked at me in horror. Moses when he saw the golden calf could not have acted with more anger than the outraged minister after I uttered those words. 'He has condemned himself out of his own mouth!'

'Blasphemy.'

'Heresy.'

'Arrest him!'

A stone hit me. I ducked another and tried to draw my sword, but hands seized me. Two cutpurses, under the guise of holding my horse and quietening it, were gradually edging it away. They called it the penny horse lay: if the cutpurses were caught, they demanded a penny for holding it. If they got away, they sold the horse at a farrier outside the walls. I drew my sword, scattering people in front of me, but my sword arm was caught from behind.

George grabbed me triumphantly. The minister was shouting for constables. George was about to march me off when something struck his head. A book fell at his feet as he slowly released me and sank to the cobbles. *Gangraena*. A man came towards me and in my groggy state I thought the Puritan who had been holding the book wanted to claim me as his own arrest, until I looked into his eyes under the stovepipe hat and heard Richard's cultured, measured, unhurried voice in my ear.

'I think we should be going. Unless you prefer to lose your horse, rather than your argument?'

He threw my sword at me and stopped the cutpurses at a narrow opening known as Pissing Alley. The stench caused even hardened Londoners to recoil. Another moment and my horse would have been lost in the warren of streets round Leadenhall Market.

'My friend's horse, I believe,' Richard said.

One of the cutpurses put his hand on his dagger. The other, looking into Richard's cold eyes, at odds with his pleasant voice, had more sense. 'We were only holding it for the gentleman,' he whined.

'That'll be a groat,' said the man with a dagger sullenly.

Two constables were pushing their way through the crowd. Richard drew out a handful of coins and flung them in the air. The cutpurses, half the crowd and one of the constables dived after the rolling coins.

Richard grinned as I helped him on the back of my horse. 'They'll hang the devil, but take his money.'

The alley was so narrow and twisting we could barely squeeze through. I reined in the horse. Silhouetted at the end were three men. They were not constables who would run after a few coins. Nor did they have on the uniform of the City Trained Band. They were armed and had the tense, edgy watchfulness of people hunting, wearing the buff army jerkin I had worn for so long, and their faces were as tough and seasoned as the leather from which it was made. They were Cromwell's men. Their voices echoed down the alley.

'That's him.'

'Sure?'

'Positive.'

I glanced back. Richard had changed. Five years had lined his face, pouching his eyes and cutting deeper grooves into the corners of his mouth. It was not just the absence of a beard and fine clothes that made him unrecognisable. It was the absence of arrogance. Even the aquiline Stonehouse nose seemed to lose its prominence in this exiled, hunted face. But when he drew his sword I recognised him well enough. I recognised the look in his eyes, sharp and cold. This was the face of the man who had tried to kill me.

'Drop your sword,' shouted one of the soldiers.

The click of the dog lock on the man's pistol echoed down the alley. Richard kicked savagely at my horse and it leapt forward. There was a blinding, echoing flash and a stink of sulphur. For a moment I could neither see nor hear. The horse plunged. I lost the reins, then grabbed them again. Richard's fingers dug into me, half-slewing round my jerkin as he scrabbled to cling on. I ducked as the empty pistol was thrown at me and saw another soldier taking aim. We were only just emerging from the alley, a perfect target. The pistol grew very large, then jerked upwards, firing harmlessly in the air as Richard's sword went through the soldier.

9

Partly because the bolting horse took us in that direction, and partly because, when I had her under control, I wanted a place where few questions would be asked, I rode through the back streets to The Pot, where I used to drink as an apprentice. Neither of us spoke. It was that time in the afternoon when people have just eaten, and are reluctant to get up from the table or the fireside. The stable yard was empty. Not even a dog appeared.

He slid from the horse first, holding up his hand for the reins. I did not give them to him, nor look at him.

'He would have killed you,' he said.

I could scarcely get the words out. 'Only because you wouldn't stop!'

He spread out his hands. He looked far more vulnerable than I remembered. 'You would have given me up.'

'Yes. Yes. I would,' I shouted.

There was no sign of a stable boy. While I tethered the horse, Richard drifted aimlessly over to a neglected bowling alley at the corner of the yard. I remembered once losing my boots in a bet there. The Presbyterians, who condemned gambling, had closed it, along with shutting down the theatres. The wooden box with the bowls and jack had been broken into. Richard tossed the jack on to the green. It bumped through the overgrown grass to rest against a stone. He half-knelt and sent a bowl after it, curving it to knock away the stone and rest against the jack. He tossed a bowl to me. Dazed by what had happened, and the incongruity of the green, I flung the bowl down. It bounced crazily, before finishing up in the ditch. Richard pursed his lips and shook his head. In a burst of irritation I seized another bowl, adjusting the bias so it swung in, knocking away his bowl and rolling back nearer to the jack.

He raised his eyebrows. 'Not bad.' He picked up another bowl. 'I shall never get one like it,' he said. 'My sword, I mean. The balance was perfect. It was made in Bologna by Fabris himself –'

Suddenly overwhelmed by the enormity of what had happened, I knocked the bowl from his hand. 'You killed him. Cromwell's soldier. You killed him. I work for Cromwell. Worked. Wanted to –'

The words choked in my throat. All my hopes, all my ambitions, my future had disappeared with that one thrust of his sword.

'No one would have recognised you. Not in that dark alley. The confusion.'

I became incoherent, one word jamming into another. 'They know who you are. You left your sword in him. They'll work out I was with you. You killed him. You –'

He put out a hand in a comforting, reassuring gesture. 'He was one of the rabble, Tom.'

I grabbed him by the doublet, tearing his collar, and drove him across the yard against the stable door. It was not just the speed of my attack that shocked him. Five years of war, including a period in the infantry, had given me a ferocity in hand-to-hand combat that he could not match. He was half the man without his sword. I was at the height of my strength, while he was in decline. I saw the realisation of this in his face, and the fear in his eyes when he found he could not release my grip as I held him with one hand and reached for my knife.

I brought back the knife. '*I* am one of the rabble!'

'Behind you,' Richard said frantically.

I almost laughed at him thinking I would fall for that one but, to be sure, kneed him in the groin and glanced round. A stable boy, knuckling his eyes, straw still sticking to his hair from where he had been sleeping, was gazing at us open-mouthed. When I had lived on coins given to me by gentlemen, a penny would buy a good loaf and my silence. Now it was nearer twopence. I held out sixpence.

'You heard nothing.'

His eyes bulged. He cupped his hand round his ear. 'What, sir? I bin deaf as a post since birth, sir.'

The coin disappeared into his pocket. Whistling, he took the horse to water. I pushed my dagger back into its scabbard, went to the pump and sluiced water over my face.

Slowly, painfully, Richard straightened himself up. His right cheek was streaked with blood. 'You fight like one of the rabble.'

I pumped water over my handkerchief and walked across the yard towards him. Stone chips from the wall had scoured his cheek. One was still embedded in his lip. In the stable the boy murmured to the horse as he rubbed her down. Richard kept his eye on my dagger as I approached, and jumped as I held out the dripping handkerchief. He hesitated before taking, it, then wiped his face, watching me all the time, wincing as he dislodged the stone fragment from his lip.

By some silent agreement, we said nothing more as we walked through the yard. Richard went into the inn first and I followed close at his heels, afraid he might make a bolt for it.

The Pot was now patronised by a mixture of market traders, scriveners and pamphleteers who traded gossip over lamb pies at tables shut off from one another by high wooden stalls. It was as gloomy as night. What little light crept through the narrow windows was snuffed out by the smoke from ill-swept chimneys.

We found a table cluttered with dirty plates and I bought sack for him and a small beer for myself. He looked disparagingly at the beer.

'Keeping your wits about you?'

I said nothing. Under the banter, when he ate a piece of fat from one of the dirty plates, I saw again the fear in his eyes when I had rammed him against the stable door. As he flirted with the serving maid, saying that if the lean of her mutton was as good as her fat he must have a leg of it, I scarcely took in how charming he was with women. I was still seeing the shock on his face when I drew the knife and he realised I was stronger than him. I would have been a fool to kill him. I had done something far better. I had killed the nightmare of my late childhood, the man who had hired men to kill me, terrifying me because they came out of the darkness, for no reason, like bad dreams. It was as if I had awoken from a long, disturbed sleep to see the nightmare had a paunch, with skin beginning to slacken into jowls, and that, although he was kissing the serving maid's hand, she was looking at me.

I could not believe I had been moved to tears by his letter. Anne was right. All I had to do was hand him over. What had happened made no difference. I had been colluding with him only to find out what his plans were. To take those plans to Cromwell would put Ireton's nose out of joint and be a great feather in my cap. The maid served him his leg of mutton. As he tried to grab her again I gave her a smile of sympathy, which she returned with interest. He saw our glance. Again there was that moment of disorientation, of seeing himself in the mirror of other people's eyes. Recovering, he fell on his mutton, declaring it the best he had ever tasted. And the raisin and gooseberry sauce!

He swallowed half of a second glass of sack. 'Come. Our first meal together and you are not eating?'

I told him my only appetite was to know what he was doing in London. All the false joviality left him. He jumped up, glancing at the nearby stalls. The only diner in sight was asleep, and the maid was throwing scraps from his plate to a dog. 'Serving my King,' he said. 'Cromwell is planning to take the King from the Presbyterians and exile him.'

I laughed. 'Rubbish. Disobey Parliament? Cromwell would never do that.'

We spoke across one another in an increasingly heated argument, laying bare our feelings about politics in a way we could not do about each other. I said passionately that Cromwell did not want to exile the King. The people wanted both King and Parliament. Richard thought Cromwell a great ogre, but I was as fervent about Cromwell as he was about the King. The arguments got nowhere, petering out into an exhausted silence. Neither of us had talked in any depth before to someone on the opposite side and, in spite of our violently different opinions, they drew us closer in a way I would never have anticipated.

Richard painted a rueful, witty picture of what he called the charms of exile. The hospitable French spared nothing, he said, to encourage their guests to leave as soon as possible. They had given their poor relations lodgings at the wrong end of the Chateau de St Germain, damp and draught-ridden, where Queen Henrietta's court bickered, fought duels to allay boredom, and dreamed of home. The Queen, desperate to return and impatient with Charles's religious scruples, was arguing for Charles to settle with Parliament, in impassioned letters of which Richard was the entrusted messenger.

'You have the letters with you?'

'I'm not such a fool.'

Nevertheless his hand went to a bulge under his shirt. He had become so animated, a number of people had entered the inn without us being aware of it. Two men passing stared at Richard, making him jumpy, until one joked that if Puritans were drinking there was hope for them all. A tinge of malice went through me as he glanced nervously towards the door every time it opened, just as I had done when I was on the run. He went to the bar to pay the maid, fumbling under his shirt for a bulging purse. I glimpsed not letters, but money, before he concealed it again. A lot of money. Gold unites and angels. It was growing darker, and the maid was lighting candles.

'What are you doing in London?'

'Keep your voice down. I told you. I have messages for the King.'

'The King's in the north. What are you doing here? With all that money?'

'I came to see you.'

'Why?'

'Because you are my son.'

I would have treated that with the same distrust I had given his letter, had not a flickering candle thrown light fully on his face. His mask of arrogant certainty had slipped. He seemed at a loss; surprised he had said the words. He gave me a cautious look, ready to flee behind some flippancy. Perhaps he expected rejection. Derision. Instead I was struck dumb by the same conflict of feelings that had run through me when I opened his letter. The door opened and the draught plunged us back into shadow. When the silence continued to lengthen he ordered more wine and poured me a glass. I shook my head.

'You will drink with me, damn you, sir, or I will say no more.'

I took the glass. 'If you wanted to see me, why didn't you reply to my letter?'

'Because when it came to it, I was afraid it was a trap. Was it?'

'No. But I nearly took your letter to Cromwell.'

'Nearly? Did you?'

'No.'

He moved further down the bar so he was out of the light and I in it. He told me that when he had landed a month ago on the Kentish beach, one of the customs officers he killed had wounded him slightly. The wound had turned infectious. He was too ill to ride but could not entrust the letters to anyone else. The first day he was up he heard at the Exchange that Lord Stonehouse had thrown me out. He celebrated with two bottles of sack. That perfect boy, whom Lord Stonehouse had treated as if he was his own son, had turned out to have feet of clay! But that night the priest came back to haunt him, robbing him of sleep.

Priest? He told his story in fits and starts, in no kind of order, staring not at me, but at the candle. With the pools of light, and the high wooden stalls like pews, it was as if we were in church. He crossed himself even while he swore that, in St Germain, it was impossible to get away from the bloody papists. Half drunk one night, he took a wager from Prince Rupert he would go into confession. He knew enough about the damned breed from the Queen, who was brought up one, to fool his way into the box. Box?

'Box of tricks, I thought. A grille. A voice. I could scarcely keep my face straight! Peccavit. Holy Father, I have sinned. I started to talk about you. Well. I had to say something.'

He shivered. He glanced round one way, then another, at the jumping shadows.

'Went in there without a problem in the world. Came out in hell.' He laughed, but his face glistened and he licked his lips compulsively. 'Much healthier for the soul in England. No bloody priests. After celebrating when my father threw you out, I had a nightmare – bloody priest threatening me with hellfire. That's when I wrote you that letter.'

'I replied. I waited at the Exchange. Twice!'

'First time I feared a trap. Had to check it out.'

'And the second time?'

He fiddled with his glass. 'When you turned up at the 'Change I didn't know what to say. Didn't know what the hell I was doing there. Followed you. Curious, I suppose, that's all. Curious.'

He moved to pick up his glass, but made a face as if the wine had gone sour. For the first time he looked at me directly.

'I saw your face when you came out of your tailor's empty-handed. How many times have I been through that when my skinflint of a father cut my allowance!' He slapped his thigh and laughed until the tears shone. 'I almost went up to you then.'

He had stood on the same patch of carpet. Suffered the same torrents of abuse, the same unexpected grunts of praise, which led only to dashed hopes and even more savage recrimination. Gradually, it was impossible not to wince, laugh, warm to him. I took several glasses of the wine, while he no longer touched it.

'When he picks up the seal, do you duck?'

'Never!'

He nodded approvingly. 'Sign of weakness.'

He wiped his eyes. 'Followed you to your house.' I stiffened. He shook his head. 'Very mean. A merchant would do better for a poor relation.' He was disapproving, but at the same time expressed a measure of satisfaction that I was living in such modest circumstances. 'No ostler, even. Your son mistook me for the new one.'

I went very still, pushing my glass away and gripping the edge of the table to control myself as he went on.

'Chatted away. Fellow has spirit. Good on a horse. Got on famously —'

He saw my expression. I kept my voice low only with an effort. 'Touch my son and I will have you in the Tower, whatever happens to me. I should do so now. I'm a fool to talk to you.'

'Not so much a fool as me.' His tone was as savage as a moment before it had been affable. 'You're supposed to be so clever, but you don't understand, do you?'

'I understand when someone is spying on me.'

'Spying? The boy is my grandson. Do you think I'd harm him?'

That he could say that with a straight face took my breath away. 'You tried to kill me.'

'That was different.'

'How different?'

'I don't know. Different. I was young. Thought I knew everything. Now I think I know nothing, except that one day the King will have his own again. That's all that matters. All I hang on to. You're like that damn priest. Cornering me like a fox.' His voice took on a new edge of bitterness. 'All right. I can understand why you think I will harm your son. But I would be a damn fool to do so. I know my father thinks the sun shines out of his little arse.'

He had a knack of saying something that was reassuring and disturbing at the same time. 'Does Lord Stonehouse know you're here?'

'No! For God's sake don't tell him. He risked everything to get me out of the country years ago. I don't want to get the old sod in any more trouble.'

In spite of their turbulent relationship, and their violently opposed views, Richard seemed to genuinely care for his father. Like the aquiline Stonehouse nose, some of that ambiguity of feeling seemed to have been transmitted to Richard and me. We stared across the table at one another like two fighters who no longer have the energy to aim a blow, but are too apprehensive to turn their backs. Unless he was a very good actor, the effort he had made to write the letter struck me as true. I could not reject him. I could not. Apart from anything else, he had killed the soldier and, whether or not I had been identified, he could implicate me.

He picked up his glass and put it down untasted. 'Can we work together?'

He read the suspicion that leapt into my face and spoke with a passion I had not suspected. He was seeing the King. Knew what was in the Queen's mind. I knew what was in Cromwell's. In however small a way we could influence what was put on the table, bring people closer together, just as his letter had brought us together. After all, we were both Stonehouses.

I felt the scar that one of his men had left on my cheek. 'You think I can trust you?'

'As much as I trust you,' he said.

'Touché,' I muttered.

My heart suddenly began to pound. It was what was needed – talking, instead of endless fighting. What was there to lose? If he was sincere, I might have a hand, however small, in influencing the negotiations between the King and Cromwell. If he was not, it was a chance to get my hand on those letters.

I began talking. Cautiously – not giving away the weaknesses of the New Model, but telling him about those regiments solid for Cromwell, so the King would not have any illusions about the forces against him. I never knew what he might have told me in exchange for, in a patch of light, I glimpsed an agitated face which disappeared into the shadows like the will 'o the wisps on the marsh in my childhood. Jane, my housekeeper? In an alehouse? I believed I had drunk too much, or she was a trick of the light, but then I saw her again, weaving in and out of the chattering, laughing drinkers, who cursed when their drinks were jostled. I called her and she ran towards me.

'Master. I've been looking everywhere for you. It's Liz, little Liz.'

Jane kept saying there was no time, no time. She had a Hackney outside and I scrambled into it with her, leaving Richard at The Pot. We travelled down Fleet Street, and were in Newgate before I pieced together what had happened. Jane told me Anne had called Dr Latchford when Liz's breathing had become more and more laboured. What little milk Liz took from the wet-nurse, she vomited up. Before the doctor arrived the baby was in such distress that Anne put her on her breast even though she could not suckle. This seemed to revive her, but the doctor said he could do nothing more for her and advised Anne to send for the minister to baptise her.

'Mr Tooley baptised her?'

'No, no. Mr Tooley has gone.'

'Gone?'

'Lost his living. George broke into a cupboard, found his old surplice, prayer books and pictures, and accused him of practising the old religion.'

A chill ran through me. I was sure I had locked everything back in the cupboard. Then I thought of the old prayer book I had taken out to read. Had I put it back? I could not remember.

'What is going to happen to her?' Jane sobbed. 'No one to baptise her. What will happen to her poor little soul?'

'Where is she? Where are we going?'

'Anne took her to your old church to find the new minister. I tried to tell her Liz was too ill, but she is half crazy. She got it in her head she must have Liz baptised, and in that church.'

It was almost dark when we got to the church. No candles were lit. I could just pick out the figures of a small congregation in the gloom. I stumbled a few steps before I picked out Anne at the font. She was as still as the stone it was carved from. She neither acknowledged me nor spoke. Her whole being was concentrated on the baby, folded in swaddling clothes at her breast.

'Is she ...?'

Anne did not answer. The only movement came from the rise and fall of her breast. The bundle stirred and the smallest, driest cough echoed round the dank church. Anne kissed her and rocked her gently. All the love she had never given Liz after the disappointment of her not being a boy was lavished on her now. Luke ran to me. I took him by the hand, motioned him to be quiet, and asked Jane what was happening.

'The minister has been sent for,' Jane whispered.

'Mr Tooley?'

'The new Presbyterian minister, Samuel Burke.'

Anne shivered, it seemed as much from the name as from the cold seeping into her from the damp stones. Her shawl had slipped from her shoulders and I wrapped it round her, alarmed at her ghost-like pallor.

'Is there nowhere warmer you can wait?' I asked. She did not answer me. 'Anne?'

'She will not leave the font,' Jane said.

I begged Anne to let me take her somewhere warm. She turned to me for the first time, as if she was she was staring at a stranger. Luke seemed to appear from nowhere and went to tug at his mother's skirts. I snatched him up in my arms. He struggled for a moment, protesting, then twisted round to gaze down at his sister with black, darting eyes, deep-set aside the sharp aquiline crescent of the Stonehouse nose. He rammed a thumb in his mouth. He had sensed from the moment he was born he was special, with the undivided love from Anne and the visits and presents from Lord Stonehouse. His manner suggested he could not understand why this insignificant scrap, who had been nothing but a nuisance from the moment she arrived, was getting all the attention.

'She will go to hell if she is not baptised,' he said, with a mixture of awe and satisfaction.

Anne rounded on him furiously. 'Go to your place!'

Luke burst into tears at the unexpected ferocity of her attack. I struggled to comfort him but he wriggled and jumped away. My eyes were more accustomed to the dimness now and I saw Mr Black, holding out his arms to Luke. Before Luke reached them, he turned, his voice ringing with injustice.

'He said so. He said she would go to hell.'

'Who did?'

'He did.'

Luke pointed to a figure crouched in a pew, before flinging himself into his grandfather's arms in a fresh burst of sobs.

'Who?' I repeated, reluctant to approach the man, who was deep in prayers.

'Who does tha' think?' Sarah's voice came from the shadows of a pillar, cast by moonlight beginning to filter through the windows. 'George won't waste a candle until he's sure minister will do a service.'

I walked up the aisle where George was on his knees. His mumbled prayers became louder as I approached. 'God deliver this evil back into the pit from whence it came.'

I touched his shoulder. 'Light the candles.'

He drew away with a shudder, his face bowed into his clasped hands. 'Protect us, and protect us even now from this evil he has sired —'

His bones seemed to grind together as I dragged him up from the pew. He was as grey and pallid as the moonlight, except for his eyes. They had a strange, greenish hue, glittering at me with a mixture of fear and hatred.

'Would you strike me even here?' he said, shaking his head with a kind of resigned sadness.

I had tried. I could never make peace with him. It may have started from jealousy, when Mr Black took me, a strange, unlikely child, as an apprentice, but it had become an obsession, a belief that I was evil. He believed I was evil as much, perhaps more, than he believed in God. Perhaps he was right. I no longer cared. All I cared about was the tiny choked-off cough behind me, the murmur of Anne comforting Liz, the desperate need for God's blessing before – no, I could not, would not, think of that.

I released George. 'For pity's sake, George! Where is the minister?'

'I have sent for him. I can do no more.'

At the same time I heard an approaching horse, and glimpsed a light in the vestry. A single candle was burning. I lit others as a tall man entered. Drops of rain gleamed on his riding cloak and in his bushy eyebrows as he gazed round with eyes as black and small as currants. He had either lunched late or dined early, for his stomach rumbled and I smelt food on his breath as he was introduced to me by George, with a stream of obsequious apologies for disturbing him, as the Reverend Samuel Burke.

I pleaded with him to carry out the ceremony straightaway, but he said with a belch that there were certain formalities that could not be dispensed with, whatever the urgency. He had to be sure who we were, and whether we were married, whether we had been properly instructed.

'Please! Please. She is very ill! Can you not understand?'

Anne's voice, ringing round the church, would have moved a stone pillar. Burke moved towards Anne, saying with a small bow to me as he did so, 'You are Lord Stonehouse's grandson?'

From his manner, I judged that was the only reason he had allowed himself to be disturbed from his meal. I did not care. 'Yes. Yes. We wish her to be baptised Elizabeth –' The Stonehouse name stuck in my throat. I said the name I had always whispered to her. 'Elizabeth Neave.'

'No!' Anne cried.

Burke gave a rich, fruity laugh and declared he had had many a dispute over given names, but never over the surname.

'All right, all right,' I said to Anne. 'What you wish.'

During this, George had taken Burke by the elbow and drawn him to one side. I heard him mention Edwards and the bookshop in Cornhill, whispering, 'He declared he has no soul.' Burke's manner changed. He gave me a long, cold stare. But a burst of coughing from inside the swaddled bundle cut through all arguments.

It was a cough of stops and starts, beginning with a wheezing and ending in a strangulated whoop before beginning again. We went through every stop, every start; all her strength seemed to be in that cough; we willed her with every gasping breath to fight on. I put out my little finger and she grasped it with her hand. I felt as if I was fighting for my own life as I must have done when, after just being born, I was left out on a cold wet field to die. I even fancied I saw, in the dim shadows of the church, Kate Beaumann who had put me there and Matthew, who after flinging me in the plague cart, rescued me after I cried and kicked and struggled my way back to life.

The cough, the struggling, even broke through the barrier of Burke's stony formalities. He beckoned Anne forward into the church. She did not understand until he rapped out that he would baptise the child, but not at the font as that was not part of the Presbyterian Directory of Worship.

She went forward falteringly, the shawl slipping from her. I followed her, keeping it round her shivering shoulders. She hesitated, her teeth chattering as she spoke. 'Will you give her the sign of the cross?'

George shook his head sadly. 'Ah, Mr Burke, there you have it – how Mr Tooley tainted his flock with Romish heresies.'

'I will not perform such papist ceremonies,' Burke said. 'I feared this. No signing, no font and no godparents.'

'No godparents?' Anne said falteringly.

I saw then that Matthew and Kate were not fantasies, but part of the small congregation.

'Do you wish the child to be baptised or not?'

'I want Mr Tooley to baptise her,' Anne cried.

'Mr Tooley has been dismissed,' Burke snapped.

My voice shook, however much I tried to keep it level. 'I am sorry we disturbed you. We no longer need your services. Please go.'

His eyebrows knotted together. 'It is you who must leave *my* church.'

I wanted to tell him it was not his church, it belonged to the people, but Liz began to cough again. That stuttering, feeble cough was the end of diplomacy for me. What was the use of diplomacy when people would not listen?

I went up to him. 'Get out.'

He looked as though he might stand his ground, but George said, 'Have a care, Reverend. He tried to kill me once.'

All the violence that had built up in me when George had the tender care of my soul returned. But it was now hardened and tempered with the discipline of a soldier.

'The next time I will make a better job of it, George.'

George was in such a hurry to get down the aisle that he knocked over a pile of newly delivered copies of the Presbyterian Directory of Worship.

Burke retreated more slowly. 'Your connections will not protect you from God or Justice, sir, I promise you that.' A fanatical light shone in those small, currant-like eyes. He had seen the enemy and would not rest until he was destroyed. He stared round the congregation, his voice stern and inflexible. 'Evidently, it is God's will to take this child from such a family.'

I went for him then, but a hand stopped me. Matthew was old, but he still had the grip of the shipyard worker he once was. He did not release his grip until the porch door banged. 'Kill him outside,' he said. 'When God's not looking.'

I pulled away. 'I must find Mr Tooley.'

'Mr Black's gone for him.'

Mr Tooley was hiding at the pewterer's in Half Moon Court. Hiding! It had come to this. He entered wearing a surplice, holding the old prayer book. Liz coughed at intervals but more quietly, as if the peace that had entered the church had entered her. More candles were lit, brought in by the candle-maker, Mr Fellowes; not tallow, but his best candles. Mr Tooley stood before the font in the old way.

'Dearly beloved, I beseech you to call on God … to grant this child that thing which by nature she cannot have; that she may be baptised with water and the Holy Ghost …'

During the service other people crept in. There was Mr Reynolds, the pewterer, Mr Fellowes and his wife, a bookbinder I could not put a name to, and Gibson, the butcher, who was so frail he clutched at each pew as he went along. They were mostly old, and had all been married here by Mr Tooley and had their children baptised by him.

By the time Mr Tooley had sprinkled water and made the sign of the cross, christening the baby Elizabeth Neave Stonehouse, she was not coughing or moving, but Anne swore she could feel Liz's heart beating and Mr Tooley said he felt her breath on his hand.

Sarah built up the fire at Half Moon Court, which revived Anne, who was chilled to the bone, but nothing could revive little Liz. When Anne's eyes jerked closed I took the baby and whispered to her as I used to do, chafing her limbs and kissing her, feeling sure that I saw a finger unclench, or the tiny eyelids tremble, until I felt overcome and Anne took her. I scarcely noticed people passing or heard what they said, but I did see that Kate had brought the simnel cake that she used to make for my birthday. She had made it for a happier baptism and tried to conceal it. But Mr Tooley told her to cut it and divide it with a piece for everyone, for it was a resurrection cake.

It was still dark when Matthew stirred us. From one of the parishioners he had found the wood to make a small coffin. Mr Tooley roused the gravediggers early to prepare a grave on the patch of ground that Mr Black had bought for his family. The tears came then and I kept feeling Liz was alive, and would not let them have her until, as the first glimmers of light appeared in the sky, Mr Tooley warned me the Presbyterians would not let him carry out the ceremony if we left it too late.

More like grave robbers than mourners, we hurried to the churchyard. A thin, mean wind whipped around us. It was still more night than day and we could scarcely see to pick up soil to throw. It took only a few handfuls to cover the coffin.

But, as the earth rattled on the lid, grief was followed by lacerating guilt. I could never forgive myself for my delay in returning home with the syrup. It might have made a difference. I might have found Mr Tooley, might have prevented Anne in her distraught state from taking Liz into that cold, damp church. Might, might, might.

Guilt was overcome by anger. If Mr Tooley had never been driven from the church in the first place, Liz might have lived. At least she would have had a more peaceful end and we could have mourned her loss. I had too much anger to mourn. More than Liz was buried that cold morning. For me, peace was buried with her.

What peace could there be with intolerant men like George, Sir Lewis Challoner and Burke? As we left the churchyard, Mr Tooley was being taken by the pewterer to a safe house in another parish. Did it never occur to the Presbyterians that the rising discord and unrest among Baptists and other sects came, not so much from them, as from the Presbyterians' intolerance to them?

What if Lord Stonehouse was right and the Presbyterians took control? If they put Charles back on the throne without safeguards or a strong man like Cromwell to keep him in check? Lord Stonehouse's bleak words rang in my head.

'I would be executed. So would you. What would happen to Luke, I do not know.'

I stopped at the lych gate, turning to see Luke struggling to keep up as he held on to his mother's hand. I held out my arms to him and he ran towards me, hurling himself into them. Anne gave me an eloquent look, a mixture of approval and surprise that he had run to me so readily, and I realised that, as much as anything, it was my aloofness that had kept him away.

He wriggled, pulling at a lock of my red hair as if he did not believe it was real. He had black hair, like a proper Stonehouse. 'Is Liz in heaven?'

'Yes.'

'Then why did the man say she was going to hell?'

'Because he's a bad man.'

'Are you going to kill him?'

I hushed him, pulling him close as he snuggled against me, wrapping my cloak round him against the biting wind.

PART TWO

Cromwell's Blessing

Summer 1647

11

Lord Stonehouse was as unpredictable as the weather which, cruelly, two days after the funeral, became not just spring but summer, so warm that the front doors of the house in Queen Street were wide open. I thought I had missed him, for his carriage shot out of the yard as I approached, but he was not in it. The sole occupant was a lady. Her face was veiled so I could see none of her features, except the greenish glitter of her eyes.

When Mr Cole showed me in, Lord Stonehouse's whole stance at the window, a slight smile on his face as he stared in the direction the carriage had taken, suggested to me, improbable as it may seem, that he was in love.

Love, however, had not made him notice summer. The windows were shut and the coal fire burning as usual. It was so stifling that sweat trickled down my back as I stood on the patch of carpet. When he eventually turned to acknowledge my existence there was no smile on his face. He gave me the same cold look of distaste as he gave the flask of cordial, which had replaced the usual wine on his desk.

'Come to your senses?'

I felt I had no senses to come to. They had been buried with Liz. I wanted to mourn, to weep, to pray, but I could not. Once, when I went up to the nursery where her crib was, and rocked it, just for a moment, I saw her turn and it was so real I found myself holding out my finger for her to grasp before she vanished. But I could not weep. Curiously, it was Anne, who had never seemed to care for her while she was alive, who wept and mourned. At least I could meet Lord Stonehouse's gaze with a look as dead and cold as his.

'I will do the job you want me to do, my lord.'

'Oh, you will, will you. Just as you kept the peace with Sir Lewis Challoner in Essex? An artillery train has been stolen near Oxford – by Presbyterians, Independents? I do not know. You will do what I want? You think you can walk in here and say that, do you? Short of money, are you, or frightened of arrest?'

He opened a drawer, the third one down. My drawer. Richard's was the first. He pulled out a document with a City seal, which I recognised as an arrest warrant.

'It is fortunate for you the magistrate is a friend of mine. Well, not so much a friend – more importantly, he owes me money.' He tapped the warrant. 'You threatened a minister and drove him and his elder out of his own church. Is there any reason I should plead for you not to be arrested?'

When I first stood on that stretch of carpet I would passionately have said there was every reason. It was Mr Tooley's church. More than that, it was the people's church. Those feelings were still there, more strongly than before after what had happened to Liz, but they were now focused on action, not on argument. I said, indifferently, 'None, my lord.'

He rarely looked away from my gaze, but he did so then. 'Were you in Cornhill two days ago, around noon?'

'Yes.'

'There was a murder there. One of Cromwell's soldiers. Do you know anything about that?'

'I did not kill him.'

His voice scraped out of his throat, high-pitched and shrill. 'I said, do you know anything about it?'

I stared back at him, saying nothing. Richard. My father. His son. Did he know? Or at least suspect? Again he looked away first. He stretched out his hand to where his wine usually stood, saw the cordial, and pounded his fist on the desk. 'Damn the stuff. I will take no more of that disgusting dog's piss. Get me some wine. No, no, no wine. No wine. Damn Dr Latchford. Damn you. Damn –'

Leaving the last consignment to hell unfinished, he rested his head on his clenched hands until his breathing returned to normal. He picked up the arrest warrant for assaulting a minister. Safer ground.

'You returned the day after the funeral and threatened this minister … Burke.'

'I returned to make sure they did not disturb my daughter's grave.'

'You half-drew your sword.'

'Not true. It is true that I looked at him and, if he had tried to interfere, I would have killed him.' I touched the sword at my waist.

He began to cough and, with a grimace, took a swallow of the cordial. He looked at the sword, then at me, as if he had just realised I was not dressed as a gentleman. I wore the buff jerkin and high riding boots that I had thrown into the cupboard when I returned home. Luke, who had never seen the clothes before, had helped me dress in great excitement, marching round and putting on my belt. Anne had tried to pull him away, for he was not yet in britches, but I stopped her and explained what everything was. He was instantly quiet, staring up at me with his large, liquid eyes. I taught him as Lord Stonehouse's steward Eaton had taught me, on our ride to Highpoint, lessons not from a manual, but lessons of survival.

I favoured a short sword, which I took from a dead mercenary at Naseby. With it was a matching *main-gauche*, or left-handed dagger, to parry blows. Their only ornaments were the scars and nicks on the blades. With short cross-pieces, a simple guard and hilt, and perfectly balanced, it was the sword of a man who earned his living by killing.

Lord Stonehouse digested these weapons with another swallow of cordial. 'I was sorry to hear about …' He hesitated. He had forgotten her name. 'Your daughter …'

'Elizabeth.'

'Elizabeth. Yes. Still, not as if you've lost a son, mmm?'

I said nothing, although anger at this casual dismissal of Liz surged through me. But it was cold anger, anger with a purpose I did not want to waste on him.

He brought his fist down on the warrant. 'Have you nothing to say in your defence?'

'No.'

'I will never get to the bottom of you! Never. Not in this world. You expect to work for me?'

'I am prepared to.'

'Prepared to! Oh! *Prepared* to. Very generous of you.' He walked round me, inspecting me as if I was on parade, pushing his face into mine as he used to, except there was the sickly smell of cordial on his breath instead of the sour tang of wine. 'Perhaps you would be good enough, sir, to explain to me why you have had this sudden change of heart?'

'Because I think you are right, my lord. If the Presbyterians return to power with the King they will kill my son just as they killed my daughter's soul. She will not rest in peace until we are rid of them and neither will I.'

He stood in silence, staring at me, walked away and whirled back, staring once more, seeming to scrutinise every pore of my face. 'You are prepared to serve me?'

'Yes, my lord.'

'Do all the things your fine moral sense previously despised: spy, lie, cheat, dissemble?'

'Yes.'

He picked up the greasy, well-thumbed file he had shown me before. 'You will work with any of my informants, and prospective informants, however repellent you may find them, to get the information we need?'

'Yes.'

'You will apologise to Challoner and do what is necessary to get the information from him?'

'Yes.'

It was in his nature to suspect some trick, some subterfuge. He kept pacing the room and turning, waiting for me to speak, but I said nothing more. I was not seeing him, but the churchyard as it took shape at the end of that long night, silhouettes beginning to become faces, Mr Tooley urging us to hurry, for if it got much lighter they would not let him bury her.

Mr Cole brought in a letter for me to sign. It was carefully crafted, begging Sir Lewis to accept my humble apologies for a moment of hotheaded behaviour I deeply regretted. It had all the diplomacy I lacked; it even made me smile, containing as it did the loftiness, the condescension of someone with prospects of a peerage, however remote, to a mere gentleman, turning the apology into granting a favour, in a way someone like Sir Lewis Challoner would be too unsubtle to notice. Mr Cole held out an inked quill.

'There is one condition,' I said.

Mr Cole quivered. A drop of ink threatened to fall from the quill. Lord Stonehouse's eyes narrowed and his lips tightened.

'While I was away my wife suffered from shortages of coal in winter. Her allowance has been inadequate.'

A pulse beat in Lord Stonehouse's forehead. 'Everyone had to suffer during the war. Coal was blockaded.'

I stared meaningly at the fire, crackling merrily up the chimney. 'All I am asking, my lord, is that you do not punish my wife for what you may perceive as my shortcomings.'

Lord Stonehouse's pulse looked as though it would burst out of his skin. The drop of ink fell from the quill and Mr Cole, in terror of it going on the carpet, only just managed to catch it in his other hand.

'I will review your wife's allowance,' Lord Stonehouse said, each word drawn from him like a tooth.

He kept his eyes on me all the time as I took the pen. Without his protection I could do nothing. Even so I hesitated. It was just a matter of words, that was all, I told myself, only these were not the words I had run with through the streets, words which I believed would change the world, but words of double-meaning and deceit.

Then I heard the rattle of soil thrown hurriedly on Liz's coffin before the light broke, and felt Luke snuggling against me under my cloak as we slipped like graverobbers from the churchyard.

I signed.

Thomas Stonehouse.

The name had an air of finality about it. It was a scribble of ink, that was all, but I felt I was taking a step into another country, from which I might not return. Lord Stonehouse expelled his breath in a long sigh, then took the letter to sand it himself, as though I might snatch it back.

'Here. You can get anything you want with this – providing you sign for it.' He gave me a signet ring, a smaller version of his own, with the falcon standing proud. Its claws seemed to grip my finger as I slipped it on. I bowed and began to go.

'Wait!'

I might have foreseen it. He was like an angler casting a lure on to water. Once you swallowed it, you were hooked, reeled in, little by little.

'You will deliver this letter in person.'

'To Sir Lewis?'

He gave me a wintry smile. 'That is to whom it is addressed, Thomas.'

Thomas now. Welcome back to the Stonehouse fold. This was to be the punishment for my transgressions. Not just the letter, but crawling before Challoner. I could see that in Lord Stonehouse's eyes – the cruel streak that had once sent me to the plague pit, with that very same falcon seal drying on the letter. I bit back words of protest. For the sake of my family I would endure it. I was bonded to him now as tightly as any apprentice to his master, but I resolved he would not break me, any more than the cane had broken me when I was Tom Neave. I took the letter and gave him another bow.

'Wait!'

He ordered Mr Cole to hand me some papers from the pile of petitions. They included the pamphlet on Scogman. Lord Stonehouse was now in a very genial mood. 'You will use your best endeavours, as the lawyers say, to track down this wretched thief and hand him over to Sir Lewis.'

It would have been politic to agree and then not to find Scogman. But I was yet new to being completely Thomas, and Tom got the words out of my mouth before I could stop him. 'I cannot do that.'

Like registering the change of wind before a storm, Mr Cole backed away, trying to disappear in the tapestries. Lord Stonehouse, already into next business, did not even lift his eyes from the document he was reading. Scogman was of so little importance to him that he completely misinterpreted what I said. 'Nonsense. Of course you can do it. A man of your resources? Sir Lewis will not see you until Scogman is brought to him in chains. I'll wager you know where he is. Eh? Or your friends in the army do.'

Arrest Scogman? Hand him over to that brute!

When I did not reply he looked up, his smile tightening. By his elbow was the warrant for my arrest. He would have no compunction in using it. A pulse, a second cousin to his, thudded in my temple. As his hand hovered over his bell to summon his servants, mine crept towards my sword. I stilled it. In prison I could do nothing. What had Scogman ever done for me, except take me for a fool? Even his starving wife and family, with whom he had played on my emotions, had turned out not to exist.

I gave a deep, final, bow. 'I am grateful for your lordship's confidence in me.'

12

In The Cart Overthrown, at Dutton's End, I stared at the figures Will gave me in dismay. About a third of the regiment had agreed to go to Ireland. A third was prepared to accept the paltry back pay offered, which Parliament had grudgingly raised to eight weeks. The rest were split between men who were undecided and a hard core who were holding out for what I thought was a proper settlement.

'This is how the men voted?' I said to Will.

He nodded. I was stunned. All the grievances – the protestations of men who said they would resist such unjust treatment to the last – had withered to less than a page of names.

'All these men have agreed to go to Ireland?'

'That's the list Colonel Wallace gave to the Parliamentary Commissioners.'

He went up to the bar to get me another drink. I needed it. When I left London Holles had persuaded the City, with its part-time force of 20,000 men, to go over to the Presbyterians. Parliament had voted to disband the New Model Infantry, Cromwell's power base, in two weeks' time, in the middle of June.

If cavalry regiments like this one were dismembered, Cromwell was finished. The Presbyterians would be in total control. The King would be back without the strictures that Cromwell would put on him. I stared at the list. Every night I awoke with the same nightmare. I was in that damp, dark church, unable to move, hearing that Presbyterian minister argue while Liz coughed her life away.

The one hope was to get Cromwell to act. He would not do so unless I could prove that, although so far everything Holles had done was through Parliament, he was planning a coup.

Two labourers came in while Will was bringing back the drinks. One spat in the straw, narrowly missing Will's boot. 'The beer's not that bad,' Will said with a smile. The man gave him a sour look. The other ignored him. They joined a group at the other end of the inn. There were occasional shouts of laughter, which dwindled into sullen mutterings when they glanced towards us. A man with a yellowing black eye got up drunkenly, held back by his companions.

'I know he,' he said, pointing at Will. 'He cursed my cow.'

'Friendly as ever,' I said.

'He blames us for the death of his cow. Me in particular because I refused his claim. We're banned from this inn. I'm surprised you're able to stay here.'

I said nothing, pretending to concentrate on the names. It was Challoner's influence that got me a bed at the inn. I had expected to stay at his seat, Byford Hall, but my letter of apology had not been enough. He refused to see me until I produced Scogman. In desperation I had contacted Will, hoping to tap him for information about Scogman. After our difficulties over my promotion, I was unprepared for the warmth of Will's greeting.

He had always known I was a radical at heart, he said. He confessed he had been jealous of the way the men looked up to me.

'Looked up to me? I thought they hated me for lashing Scogman.'

'They respected you for turning the tables on that shit Challoner. You have Cromwell's ear. They'll listen to you.' His eyes gleamed.

'You know what this feels like? When we first started … in The Pot. Do you remember … when you were on the run …'

'Like Scogman. The most wanted man in Essex.'

'The rubbish Challoner puts out about him! It's because you made a fool of him. Scogman's a changed man. He's walking in the way of the Lord.'

'Scogman? He'd steal a baby's milk!'

'Not any more.'

'Where is he?'

He stared at me with sudden suspicion. 'Why do you want to know?'

I felt as if I had been infected by those greasy bits of paper in Lord Stonehouse's file. I shifted uncomfortably.

'I'd like to see this walking miracle.'

'So would Sir Lewis. But he'll never find him.'

I returned to the lists. Bennet, the marksman who had aimed his musket at Stalker. Whether he would actually have fired the shot I did not know, but he killed for sport. I was not surprised he had put his hand up to go to Ireland. But Knowles? Knowles was a shoemaker for whom I had written a letter telling his wife and children he would be home soon. I remembered his wife was ill and he had enclosed a little money for her, which he said he had earned by soling boots.

'He borrowed the money for his sick wife from Jenkins,' Will said.

I groaned. Jenkins ran an unsavoury alehouse always on the edge of losing its licence. It was one of the few places that would serve soldiers. Jenkins operated a little usury on the side.

'Sergeant Potter got Jenkins to call in his debt, then threatened Knowles with arrest unless he went to Ireland. Come on, Knowlesey, he said. What's another few months? With plenty of loot.'

I went down the list. 'Bromley? He said he'd never go to Ireland!'

'Wasn't at the meeting. If you weren't there, Sergeant Potter spoke for you.' Will gave an excellent, stiff-necked imitation of Sergeant

Potter, saluting to Colonel Wallace. 'Sir, discretion to use personal knowledge of soldier's wishes. Bromley keen to go to Ireland and wreak the Lord's vengeance on those murdering papists!'

'Maddox?' A weaver with his apprenticeship in Shoreditch to return to, who would gamble on anything, which frequently got him into trouble.

'Accused of stealing. Hauled before the Colonel. Charges to be waived if he agreed to go on the boat to Ireland.'

'Gough?'

'Always goes where Knowlesey goes.'

'Kenwick?'

'Wasn't at the meeting. Sick. He'll be even sicker when he knows he's on the boat.'

I grew angrier and angrier as we went down the list. If this was happening in other regiments where Presbyterian officers had control, then the figures Parliament had voted on were lies and falsehoods. The labourers gaped at us as we drew a map in the sawdust on the floor, showing where the regiments with Presbyterian officers were stationed. Roughly half the rest, we reckoned, would be loyal to Cromwell. At the moment. But he was taking no action. He believed in Parliament. Holles believed only in manipulating it to get the King back, at any price.

Will whispered he had a link with a group in another cavalry regiment, which planned to seize the artillery train near Oxford. Sporadic mutinies would be worse than useless, I thought, playing into Holles's hand, but I said nothing.

I destroyed the map with my boot and we finished our drinks in silence. Two weeks and Holles would be in control.

The man with a black eye rose groggily to his feet and began to slur his way through a ballad. 'I … will beat a plough into a sword … and become a thieving soldier!'

He fell back in his seat. The labourers applauded and thumped the table.

'There's a muster in two days' time,' Will said. 'Men are being paid before they march to embark to Ireland.' He looked at me expectantly. 'That's when you should walk in.'

'Walk in?'

He clapped me on the back. 'Come on, Tom. You can tell me what Cromwell's planning.'

I looked away. No wonder he had greeted me so warmly. It was not me he welcomed, so much as the bearer of Cromwell's instructions. A word from Cromwell would stop the men from leaving. But I knew he would never give it. I shook my head. 'Cromwell can't *afford* to go against Parliament. He *serves* Parliament, don't you understand?'

'No. I don't. And I don't understand why you've come.'

'To stop the troops from leaving.'

'How?'

Will was staring at me, suspicion narrowing his eyes. I would have to take a chance and tell him about Challoner. 'Go outside. I'll get another drink.'

Will stopped at the door while I went to the bar. The man with a black eye got there at the same time, pushing against me. He stank of beer and cow clap as he slammed his pot in front of the ones I had already put down. The landlord, when I had arrived, had been perfectly civil but cold, making it clear he did not want me there. He had smiled indulgently during the singing, but now his voice carried a sharp, warning edge.

'This gentleman was in first, Billy.'

'Oh, gentleman, is he?' Billy said. 'I thought he was a soldier.'

The labourers laughed and thumped the table except one, more sober than the rest, who caught the landlord's expression and took Billy by the arm.

'Come on, Billy. You've had enough.'

'Aye. You're right. Enough of them. Cursing my cow.'

He was a man at the end of his tether. Nobody believed in magic more than these countrymen to whom the death of a cow meant poverty. He shook off the other labourer. There was a sudden tightening of his lips, a shifting of balance, a moment before his fist flew at me. I ducked, taking the blow on my shoulder, before grabbing his left arm and twisting it round his back. He kicked and struggled until the landlord said, 'He be a guest of Sir Lewis, Billy.'

The name stopped Billy struggling instantly. The other labourer led him away. Will was staring at me bleakly from the door. I followed him as he left, going towards the stables.

'Will … listen. You don't understand.'

'Oh, I understand, all right. A guest of Sir Lewis. You've come to persuade the soldiers to *go* to Ireland.' He called the boy to get his horse.

'The reverse! I've come because Sir Lewis will tell me what the Presbyterians are planning.'

'Nice of him. Why would he do that?'

I told him what Lord Stonehouse had told me. Will was dismissive. Anyone with half a brain knew the Presbyterians were plotting something.

'It's proof we need! If I can get proof Cromwell will act. Without Cromwell we're nothing.'

Will tossed the boy a coin and took his horse, but did not mount it, taking it under a sycamore tree where it cropped the grass. The sky had the milky softness of evening. There was not a breath of wind to stir the fields of wheat and barley, green with the hope they always showed in May, only to be dashed in recent harvests by too much rain or too little. Billy lurched out of the inn between two labourers. He tore a branch from the hawthorn hedge and twisted it in our direction, muttering under his breath. We were used to being cursed. They believed God would strike the unjust as firmly as they believed if it rained on St Paul's day, in mid-June, then corn would be dear.

Will folded the regimental list into his saddle bag. 'What do you want me to do?'

'Tell me where Scogman is.'

'Why?'

'Because he's a liar and a thief. Because I should have let him hang. And because Sir Lewis won't help me unless I hand him over.'

He could scarcely get the words out. 'You want me to betray Scogman?'

'Yes. What's his life against stopping the Presbyterians?'

There was the creak of a gate. Billy's fellow labourers tried to stop him but he stumbled into the yard, muttering imprecations.

'I told you. Scogman's changed.' Will lowered his voice, laced with contempt. 'But even if he had robbed me blind, I wouldn't turn him in. He's our link.'

'Link?'

'With the other regiments.'

'Mutiny?'

'We have no choice.'

I did not know whether to laugh or cry. 'And your organiser is Scoggy?'

He pushed his face into mine. 'Judas,' he said softly, before walking to his horse.

'Will, listen –'

'We've done enough listening.'

'You're doing exactly what Holles wants! He'll say you're what you are. An undisciplined mob –'

Will lashed out. The blow caught me full in the face. I staggered and almost fell, the yard swaying round me, cheers from Billy and the labourers ringing in my ears. I could taste the salty blood on my lips. I made a dazed, conciliatory move towards him. Will hit me in the stomach and brought his elbow up into my face. I struck the cobbles to shouts and applause from the labourers as Will galloped away.

Vaguely aware of the sharp smell of torn leaves, I opened my eyes to see Billy twirling the hawthorn branch round and round above my head. 'God has struck him,' he said.

But, just to make sure, he brought his boot into my ribs.

13

It was the stable boy who brought me round, squeezing water over me from the cloth he used to rub down horses. Every breath was an excruciating pain but my ribs felt bruised, not broken. There wcrc long shadows across the yard.

I took a few, testing steps, asked the boy for directions to Byford Hall and told him to saddle my horse. There was no time to think about Scogman. I had to get to Sir Lewis and pray that his greed for the land Lord Stonehouse promised him would overcome pride and I would get the evidence I needed. First, from my room, I had to get a letter Lord Stonehouse had written to Sir Lewis.

The room overlooked the yard. Glancing upwards, I glimpsed a movement from it and caught a brief flash of metal in the low evening sun.

Fear is a wonderful antidote to pain. I forgot my aching ribs as I went upstairs. My door was slightly ajar. I was certain I had locked it. A maid? I could see one through the open door of a nearby room, turning back the bed. I loosened my dagger and went softly up to the door of my room. I kicked it open. A man was lying on the bed, partly obscured by the tester. As he scrambled up I held the knife at his throat. With his twisted nose he looked more like a dirty, battered cherub than ever.

Scogman. 'Sorry, sir. I couldn't help trying out the bed.' He brushed flakes of mud hastily away from the coverlet. 'Beg your pardon, sir.'

Scogman. Slightly filled out, buff jerkin and britches brightened by linen and a flash of red boot-hose, no doubt stolen. Ditto the boots that looked as if they had once belonged to a cavalier, tops turned rakishly down to show off the silk hose. And ditto the useful-looking cavalry sword in his belt.

Scogman. If God had put Billy's boot into my ribs, he had also delivered me Scogman. At first, that was all my bewildered mind could fathom.

'Will told me you were coming to help us and I wanted to thank you.'

Not God, but Will, before he knew what I was planning to do, had put Scogman into my hands.

'Thank me?'

'For saving my life.'

Saving his life? All I could remember was beating his back into a raw, bloody pulp.

'From Sir Lewis, sir.'

Dazed from his reply, as much as from the shock of seeing him, I slumped down on the bed while the words poured out of him. He did not just tell me what he had felt like when he had been dragged in chains by Stalker's horse, he lived it. His frame jerked as if his limbs were being pulled from his body. I could almost hear the tearing of skin, the crack of cartilage.

He told me he had been convinced he was going to die. Die? He thought he was dead. Hell was a ditch of thorns ripping his skin, of stones and dirt filling his mouth and nose as he gasped for breath. Sweat poured from his contorted face.

If it was a performance, it was an extraordinary one. He was like one of those visionaries which the war had thrown up in abundance, making Messianic prophecies that this was the end time. But Scogman's revelation had a twist. He saw not God, for what use was

God if you were not one of the elect, chosen by God from birth, as the Presbyterians had it?

He saw not the end of the earth, but a fresh beginning. His eyes gleamed and his lips shone with spittle. He told me that when I rescued him and lashed him, the soil in his mouth became the earth of Eden. He did not spit it out. He chewed it and swallowed it, stones and all, for the earth belonged to everyone.

His body sagged, his eyes blinked and closed, as if he was being pulled off the fence where I had beaten him. I continued to stare at him, until the birds' evening calls penetrated through the open window, marvelling at how he had been transformed from a common thief into a visionary. Or, perhaps, how he had dressed up his old tricks in new clothes. There seemed only one way I could bring him out of his trance.

'Trooper Scogman. Attention!'

He shot up with a start, his eyes still glazed, his hand moving towards his sword. I brought up my dagger.

'You might fool Will with your visions, but you don't fool me.'

'I am far from perfect, sir.'

'Far from perfect? You're a liar and a thief.'

He nodded abjectly. I now saw there was a hole in his hose and the sole of his boot was coming away from the upper.

'You remember I lent you money to send to your wife and starving children in London?'

He nodded again, his tongue passing nervously over his lips. 'An angel, ten shillings exactly, I do remember that, sir, yes.'

'When I thrashed you, I thought I had killed you. You are going to wish I had.' He became still, his eyes fixed on the knife. 'Thinking you were dead, I was so full of remorse I went to look for your poor, starving family on Bankside. You remember them, do you?'

His head could not possibly have dropped lower on his chest. I could scarcely hear his voice. 'Those lies have been very much on my conscience, sir.'

On his conscience! My cheeks burned as I remembered what a fool I had felt before the jeering whores. This was going to be easier than I thought. Easier? I was amazed I had any qualms at all about handing over the snivelling wretch to Sir Lewis.

'Turn round.'

'Permission to –'

'Not granted. I'm going to do what I should have done in the first place.' I prodded him with the knife. 'Turn round. Hands behind your back.'

When he did so, I lifted his sword belt by the buckle, sliding off the sword in its scabbard. Following it was a purse. Coins rattled as it hit the floor.

'That's for you, sir,' Scogman said.

'D'you think you can bribe me?' I yanked the belt tight round his wrists.

He winced as the buckle bit into his skin. 'It's the money you lent me, sir.'

'Don't give me any more lies,' I said wearily, shoving him towards the door.

He rounded on me so rapidly I dropped the knife. 'It's true! That's why I came. To thank you. And to pay my debt. It's all there. Count it. An angel. Ten shillings. Count it.' He spoke with the despairing injured vehemence of someone who has lied too often to expect to be believed. Then his tone changed, becoming quiet, matter-of-fact. 'You not only saved my life, sir. You changed it. I would do anything for you, sir, anything.'

I walked right up to him. He looked me straight in the eye. Not a muscle in his face moved. I would be a fool several times over if I believed him. I could not afford to believe him. The sun was going down, the room full of shadows. I had to deliver him to Sir Lewis before nightfall.

He spoke so quietly I could scarce hear the words. 'Count it, sir, please.'

I flung it on the bed. Money rolled out on the coverlet. Nine, ten eleven shillings.

'One for interest, sir,' he said.

He gave me an injured look as I began to laugh. 'Do you take me for a complete idiot? You're wanted all over Essex for your thieving! You stole this, just as you stole from me!'

He tugged angrily at his bound hands and advanced on me. I picked up the knife but he kept coming forward. 'I earned that money. Every penny of it. I earned it by selling meat. Coneys I trapped. Once a deer. They were all on Kingsnorton Common. You know where I mean, sir?'

I nodded. It was land Challoner had enclosed during the war, following bitter disputes with the villagers.

'They still calls it that. Kingsnorton Common. Villagers got the old manor rolls on it. Kingsnorton Common. I thought common meant common to all but perhaps they changed the meaning of the word as well? I earned that money.'

The knife had gone through his doublet and was pricking his skin. I let the knife fall. I remembered responding with the very same anger to Lord Stonehouse when I was a pamphleteer wearing gentleman's clothes that he thought I could not possibly afford. Did I not use the very same words? I *earned* that money from my pamphlets, I said with the same vehemence. It felt like a lifetime ago. More than that. It was another life. I suddenly felt very tired.

'Are you all right, sir?'

I dropped on the bed. All I wanted to do was to curl up and go to sleep. He turned his back to the door and opened it with his tied hands. I forced myself up, thinking he was escaping, but he had called the maid.

'Major Stonehouse is not very well. Could you bring some hot water, Mary, and one of your revivers?'

At least that was normal. That was how he had got into my room. He had not lost his charm with women. He told Mary he had got into a bit of a tangle with his belt. She giggled and had a little game with him, pretending it was too difficult, before eventually releasing him. She brought hot water and, as I had still not moved, sponged my face to make it more presentable. The reviver turned out to be a large Dutch brandy with strong spices. One swallow did not so much revive me as make me feel more than ever like sleep. I pushed it away and stared outside. Mary had brought candles, which made the fields disappear and etched trees deep black against a sky streaked with red.

'Mary,' I said. 'Do you know Byford Hall?'

'Yes, sir. My sister works there. Kitchen maid. Up at the crack to light the fire. Bit different from this is Byford Hall.' She giggled. She told me the way, and the name of a footman, Murray, her sister was walking out with.

I forced myself to get up. 'Scogman … you said you would do anything for me?'

He looked up from chafing his wrists where the belt had bit into them. 'Anything in the world, sir.'

14

For a market town which, in Sir Lewis's words, was determined to have law and order, pursuing the ungodly, from murderers and thieves to drunkards and sabbath breakers, at whatever cost, Dutton's End spent very little on its gaols. The Blindhouse was the lockup for drunks, one of whom had recently burned it down. The House of Correction was a cross between a workhouse and a prison where vagrants, unwed mothers and masterless men like runaway apprentices were corrected by beating hemp or being beaten themselves. A child could have broken out of it. The County Gaol was secure enough, holding people on trial for the Assizes, but that was twenty miles away.

That was why, that evening, I stopped my horse outside the third prison in Dutton's End: Stalker's house. Thrown over the back of my horse was Scogman, in a very sorry condition: hands bound, a gag thrust into his mouth.

The house was a more substantial one than I expected. Unlike its thatched neighbours, it had a tiled roof and walls in a herringbone brick pattern. Only the barred windows on the ground floor gave any sign of its use as a prison. It normally held debtors and petty criminals, but serious cases were held overnight before being transferred to the County Gaol. Stalker regularly complained to the bench about the lack of a suitable prison but, since he made his money

out of prisoners, I suspected that the complaints paid for the bricks
that built his house.

The house was dim and silent, like many others in this Puritan
town, giving the impression that its inhabitants were at prayer or
asleep. I rang the bell. At the sound Scogman struggled, a strangled
whimper coming from his gagged mouth. But I thought of the
country being reduced to the huddled grimness of this little town
if Holles and his Presbyterians took over, and remembered little Liz
with her hurried burial. I steeled myself and rang the bell again.

It sounded like a prison then, with the double unlocking of the
door and the drawing back of a bolt. A grumbling maid held up a
tallow to inspect me, saying her master was 'at the Bible' and I
should take the prisoner to the House of Correction. At the end of
a passage behind her there was a glimmer of light at the edge of a
thick fustian curtain. I hesitated. There was a murmur of voices,
which I took to be prayer, until I heard a different litany: 'Fifteen
for two, three for a flush and one for his Nob. Would you believe
it. Up again!'

I pushed past the maid and pulled back the curtain. Stalker and
a gentleman whose face was as crumpled as his linen were playing
cribbage. Stalker scooped up the money from the table in guilty
confusion, curtly ordering the gentleman to his room and sweeping
the cards out of sight.

'I have Scogman for you.'

'Scogman!'

Stalker's winning streak was nothing to this. He hurried outside,
yanked up Scogman's head by his hair, in order, he said, to identify
the prisoner, and drew back his other hand.

'You are to treat him humanely,' I said.

'Humanely? Very good, sir.' He released Scogman's head, which
slammed against the saddle.

I insisted on him writing and sealing a note of safe receipt that
I could show to Sir Lewis. As he wrote it he disturbed the cards he

had tried to conceal, one of which fell to the floor. It was the Queen of Spades. Spades are a bad omen, and the Queen is the worst. Stalker coughed and licked his lips nervously. He asked me not to mention the playing cards to Sir Lewis. He had discovered them on the gentleman, who was imprisoned for debt, and was confiscating them, but Sir Lewis, who had a particular antipathy towards gambling, might misinterpret the situation.

'By playing cards with the debtor,' I said, 'and taking his money, you were merely demonstrating to him the error of his ways?'

He beamed, impervious to sarcasm. 'Exactly, sir! Exactly. The error of his ways. Oh, very good, very good. We are in accord, sir.' He shook hands and signed the receipt with a flourish. 'I will certainly show this wretch the error of his ways.'

He checked the rope binding Scogman's hands tightly in front of him, told him he had another fine piece of hemp waiting for him, and carried him into the house like a sack of potatoes. Stalker opened the door of the cell, which, he said, had been kept warm by the last prisoner. Scogman cannoned into the piss-pot, which had not been emptied, its contents spilling on to the filthy straw as he collapsed into a corner.

'You see what animals these people are, sir,' Stalker said.

Scogman stared up at me in mute reproach. A thin smear of blood was trickling from his lip. I was at the door when I heard a metallic rattle. Stalker was in a small office. From a row of hooks he was taking down a key and leg-irons.

I only just managed to keep control of my voice. 'At least let him sleep. He does not need irons until you take him to the gaol.'

'He is not secure, sir.'

'Dammit, man, his hands are tied, the windows are barred and you have a heavy lock on the door!'

'Leg-irons is the rule, sir. To make him double secure.'

I walked up to him. 'Mr Stalker, he is as secure as I am in the knowledge that you were confiscating those cards, not gambling.'

He gnawed his lips, absorbing the threat, before replacing the leg-irons on their hook.

It was now dark, but with the unrest at the regiment I could not delay seeing Sir Lewis and rode to Byford Hall. There was a fork from the main driveway, used recently by a number of horses. Thinking that this would lead directly to the stables, I took it. On the edge of a copse I checked my horse. I was some distance from the main driveway where there was the glimmer of light in the lodge.

'Who's that?'

A figure came out of the lodge. I was about to answer when another man came out of the shadow of some bushes. The moon glinted on his half-drawn sword.

'Fox,' he said. 'After Sir Lewis's coneys.'

'The men are all here?' asked the lodge-keeper.

I did not hear the reply as they went back in the lodge. To state my business there would mean further delay. The men all here? Was there some kind of a meeting? I urged my horse gently forward over the grass. At least Sir Lewis would be up.

Candles flickered in many of the bay windows of an older, Tudor wing. The main building was much more imposing, crowned with lead-capped stair turrets and Dutch gables. In what looked like a long gallery on the first floor there was the shadowy movement of servants picking up dishes. I knew the Parliamentary Commissioners who supported Holles stayed here when they investigated the army claims. I moved into the shadows of a tree, quietening my horse. My career as a spy would not last very long if I walked into a meeting between Sir Lewis and the very people Lord Stonehouse hoped he would betray.

The moon lit up a courtyard on the end of the wing from which came the sound of a number of horses. I edged my horse away from it, into the shadow of a clump of trees, and tethered it there. I hesitated over leaving my sword, but they would take it away from me anyway. Sliding it into the saddle holster, I walked towards the house.

If there were Commissioners present, it was too risky to give my name as Stonehouse. I said I was Thomas Neave. Sir Lewis would know who I was when he saw the prison receipt for Scogman. The footman did not seem surprised at such a late call. The tiled floor was scored with muddy bootmarks. It was a house of creaks and shuffles and lowered voices, of doors softly opening and closing. My heart began to thump alarmingly. To be seen by one of Holles's ministers would be a disaster.

Fortunately, unlike the Tudor wing where I had glimpsed some light and life, the main wing was the darkest, gloomiest building I ever entered. I stood in the shadows until the footman showed me into an austere, oak-panelled chamber which served part as waiting room, part cloakroom. It was damp, ill-lit and still smelt of winter. I hung my cloak next to one with a velvet collar which put mine to shame, torn and bedraggled from the fight with Will.

On a mahogany side-table a copy of the Bible was dwarfed by two folio volumes of Foxe's *Book of Martyrs*, full of woodcuts of Protestants burned at the stake by Catholics. Like many strict Puritans Sir Lewis expected his visitors not to waste a moment, but to contemplate the forces of Antichrist they were battling with – not only Catholics but ministers like Tooley who preached toleration. There were so many illustrations, the books seemed to reek of burned flesh.

I turned to the title page. There was a written inscription, dated 1610: 'To Lewis. Read a martyr a day to remind you the staires to Heavene are paved with peril, toile and pain. Fugit ora. James Challoner Bt.'

Presumably this was Sir Lewis's father. *Fugit ora* – time flew. A birthday present when he was five, or six? I shuddered. It did not give me a greater liking for Sir Lewis, but I felt I understood him a little more. I shut the book. A sudden eerie silence had fallen on the house. I opened the door a fraction. Further along the gloomy hall a door was open. I picked out Sir Lewis's bulky shape, but the figure with him was in shadow. He made a move towards the front door, but Sir Lewis stopped him.

'My cloak …'

'Not that way.'

It sounded as though Sir Lewis was as apprehensive as I was of being seen. His visitor's voice sounded vaguely familiar, but I could not place it. I closed the door. A servant came to fetch the cloak, returning a short time later to show me into a room that the candles fought a losing battle to light. The furniture was dark oak, with not a carving to relieve its severity. The few portraits were blackened with age and smoke. One might have been Sir Lewis's father, a stern-looking man with a Bible in his hand. The other rested on a skull. Sir Lewis was pacing behind a desk on which were some papers weighed down with a seal.

'You have a nerve to come here – Mr Neave.'

'I apologise –'

'Another apology! Apologies are cheap.'

He flung the letter of apology I had sent from London on the desk. It had been squeezed out of me by Lord Stonehouse, he said. It was all round the 'Change that I had written it under the duress of being cut off, of being reduced to nothing, worse than nothing – returned to being the bastard I was. It was as sincere as a whore's prayers. My lips tightened and my cheeks burned. I had forgotten how much I loathed him.

Only an instinct that he was deliberately trying very hard to provoke me, though I could not understand why, enabled me to keep any kind of grip on my temper. That, and the urgency of getting Holles's plans from him.

'Lord Stonehouse has told me everything about your agreement with him,' I said.

The tirade stopped abruptly. He moved away from me, as if I was contagious. 'Agreement? What agreement? With Lord Stonehouse? I don't know what you're talking about.'

I brought out the letter Lord Stonehouse had given to me to hand him in person. The effect on him when he saw the falcon seal was astonishing. His cheeks, which had become almost purple when berating me, turned sallow white. The clatter of a horse in the courtyard, which I suppose was his visitor leaving, made him jump. His eyes darted from me to the seal, to the sound of the receding horse, in a mixture of fear and greed. Greed won.

He checked the seal, broke it, and took the letter into the light of the candelabra over his desk. There was no sound, apart from his rusty, laboured breathing.

'The estate contracts are ready to be signed,' I said. 'As soon as you let me have the information you promised.'

'You took a risk coming here with this.'

'I had to. Lord Stonehouse believes Holles is about to act –'

'Keep your voice down, will you!' He turned away to read the letter again, picking over every word of it like a lawyer. 'So, his lordship is finally prepared to give me everything I want,' he muttered, half to himself. He went to an old, browning map on the wall. 'The forest ... the mill ... if only he had agreed to these terms sooner!'

'What do you mean?'

He whirled round as if he had forgotten I was there. 'How did you catch Scogman?'

I cursed my stupidity. I had rehearsed my apology but not how I had caught Scogman. I could scarcely tell him the truth. I plunged into a story any self-respecting pamphleteer would have been ashamed to give to his printer. How I trapped Scogman and his band. They were desperate men. I shot one; wounded another. The fight I described with Scogman was the most vivid part of it, because I took it from the fight I had with Will, the only difference being that I won. It had the verisimilitude of matching exactly the state I was in; my bruised face and my torn and dirty clothes.

I came to an abrupt stop. I had told my story at the pace of a trickster who keeps both hands moving swiftly while he deals marked cards, or palms a weighted dice; so much so that I had scarce noticed the effect it had on Sir Lewis. He believed the gibberish I had told him. He leaned forward, his eyes bulging, small globules of sweat gleaming in his thick eyebrows. He wanted to hear more about how I had beaten Scogman. He dwelt on it, and remembered how I had lashed him in such detail that I felt sick.

Not having been brought up a gentleman, I had the advantage of having no sense of honour. For the first time I realised how much I had insulted him over Scogman, and made him a laughing stock throughout the county. It was more than that. I had not understood how Puritans suffered for their faith. Scogman had become his penance.

'Penance, sir?'

'When I failed in a task my father made me perform a penance until I succeeded. His favourite was the candle.'

'Candle?'

In reply he took a candle from a sconce on the wall and held his finger in it. Not a muscle in his face moved. He did not withdraw his finger from the flame until the skin blackened and there was a smell of scorched flesh. When he did so it was more with a look of exultation than pain. His other fingers were scarred and reddened from such a practice. One carried a blister. The practice, he told me, demonstrated to a child what the Protestant martyrs had endured for the faith.

I indicated the picture of the man with a skull. 'Your father, sir?'

'My grandfather, sir. He was burned at the stake by that papist bitch, Mary Tudor.'

I looked again at Sir Lewis's burned fingers. I had thought mortifying the flesh was more a Catholic practice, sacrificing the body so

Culcheth Library - Tel. 01925 763 293

Customer name: Metcalfe, Peter
Customer ID: *********1817

Items that you have checked out

Title: Dark tides /
ID: 34143110689112
Due: 18 February 2023

Title: The red queen :
ID: 34143100431632
Due: 18 February 2023

Total items: 2
Account balance: £0.42
28/01/2023 11.11
Checked out: 6
Overdue: 0
Hold requests: 0
Ready for collection: 0
Messages:
Greetings from Koha. -- Patron owes 0.42

Items that you already have on loan

Title: The Babylon rite
ID: 34143100959640
Due: 02 February 2023

Title: Cromwell's blessing
ID: 34143101002648
Due: 10 February 2023

Title: Enemy of God :
ID: 34143110459037
Due: 10 February 2023

Title: The Judas gate
ID: 34143100698008
Due: 10 February 2023

Thank you for using the bibl.otheca SelfCheck
System.
Thank you for using Culcheth Library.

that the soul should live, but it seemed these Puritans, too, tortured themselves as well as others. The pain he had inflicted on himself released some kind of euphoria. He became almost genial, saying he was a bad host indeed for not offering me food and a bed. I said that was very civil of him, but I had no time for either. Neither did he, if he wanted to acquire the land from Lord Stonehouse. Colonel Wallace was splitting up my regiment in two days' time. I must have the information and go.

He stared at the map, then at the falcon seal. 'I have to trust you. I'll give you some of the information now. In strict confidence, you understand?'

He steered me away from his martyred grandfather, and whispered, as if the portrait was listening. 'Colonel Wallace favours Holles. That is true. But he has not the money to pay the troops. Denzil – Holles – is raising it in the City, but those tightfisted East India merchants drive as hard a bargain as, as – well, as Lord Stonehouse.'

He laughed and clapped me on the back. I knew the soldiers would not move a step without money. He rang for a servant, ordering food and a room to be prepared. Feeling it would be churlish to reject both and wishing to capitalise on his change of mood, I agreed to eat: while I did so he could give me the information and I need not trouble him with the bed.

'No trouble, Tom. There is no greater pleasure than coming together, after such a difference of opinion, eh?'

I nodded, smelling the odour of singed flesh that seemed to linger in the oily flicker of the candles, and vowing I would not stay in that place a moment longer than I had to.

He led me to a long, dark room, gloomily lit by candelabras on an equally long table. At the far end of the room high windows were draped with a murky-coloured velvet, a smoke-blackened version of what had once clearly been a rich crimson. I hesitated before sitting. There were so many chairs, and such a long table, and only the two of us dining. I felt a reluctance to sit too near the man, his burned finger even now wafting the odour of singed flesh in my direction, yet could not sit at too great a distance. But he settled the matter in a courtly fashion, gesturing to a chair at a short distance from his own, and I was glad to sit down.

Determined to keep my wits about me, I did not touch the wine. But a large slice of cold venison pie found me unexpectedly hungry, and I swallowed too quickly. A mouthful of congealed fat, and the sight of Sir Lewis picking the blister on his finger, made me retch and cough. Before I knew it I had taken a gulp of the wine, then another. He refilled my glass and raised his to our working together. I drank to that and told him that if he would give me the information, I would go. He told me there were three problems with that, tapping them out on his blackened finger.

Item one, he found my company unexpectedly agreeable and was loath to lose it.

Item two, the information was extremely sensitive and it would be most imprudent for me to travel with it, alone, so late at night.

He paced the room, his hands folded behind his back, like a wise father counselling his son. He appeared to have entirely lost the agitation he had shown when I first produced Lord Stonehouse's letter.

Item three – his finger took on a strange shape like a blackened sausage – a letter was a letter and not a contract, even if it was from someone whom one could trust as implicitly as Lord Stonehouse. He smiled, as if Lord Stonehouse was the last possible person on earth whom he would trust.

'He told me it was urgent! There is no time to –'

I jumped up. Or rather I tried to. My legs seemed to be going in different directions. Sir Lewis gripped my arm, his voice full of concern. He knew it. I was in no fit state to travel.

Yet, curiously, it seemed I was going to travel. There was cold air on my face, and the rattle and stink of a cart. It was the plague cart into which I had been thrown when I was born. I saw my father

Richard's angry, distorted face, and smelt the sickening stench of lime-soaked straw, before I kicked and struggled out of the nightmare

Sir Lewis's face swam back into my vision. The stairs were swaying around me. I was being helped up, step by step, by two servants, except one did not seem to be a servant. He wore no livery, but the buff jerkin of a soldier. From some war wound his nose had been split, the nostrils hideously twisted, the air rasping through them into my ear. Somewhere behind me Sir Lewis's voice floated.

Tomorrow we would ride together to London, he said, to see Lord Stonehouse. After he had renewed acquaintance with his old friend, Scogman, of course.

Scogman! I tried to turn but was snatched up by the man with the split nose, and though I struggled to speak found I could not form words. I was in a room full of moonlight and red hangings, all of it pitching and tossing about me like a rough sea into which, after a brief struggle, I sank.

15

The noises penetrated my thick, sluggish sleep. Sharp, daylight noises: a fire being raked, the ring of hooves on cobbles. I opened my eyes a fraction. And shut them. Even the dim light was unbearable. I badly needed to return to sleep but my last coherent thought cut into my head, sharp as a knife. Scogman. I forced my eyes open and dragged myself up.

The room was clad with red tapestries of the seasons, musty and faded. I drew the hangings at the bay window. Whatever Sir Lewis had put in the wine had left my tongue feeling like a lump of thick cloth and my head singing.

I opened the casement and sucked in air. I was at the top of the house, looking out over the Tudor wing. The sun had barely risen. There was not a breath of wind and the light had a shimmering, luminescent quality that glittered in the dewed grass and promised a hot day.

This peaceful scene was disturbed by a distant shouting, followed by a group of men coming out of the wing, pushing and jostling one another. They wore the buff hats and clothes of soldiers. I glimpsed a hard-lined face, and caught the nasal twang of a Dutch accent when one shouted. They were mercenaries. One was wearing what I had not seen since the end of the war: the red scarf of the Royalists. They pissed in the bushes. One shoved another so he wet his britches. What began as hilarity and joking became a fight until a voice rang out. It came from the porch of the wing. I could not see the man, or hear what he said, but it had an instant effect. They finished relieving themselves in silence. The mercenary with the red scarf removed it. The man who had silenced them came further out of the porch so his boots were visible.

'Remember who you are fighting for,' he said quietly.

I leaned out of the window, gripping for support the edge of the entablature, which ran above the larger window below.

'See to your horses,' the man said.

Obediently, they went towards a group of trees, where I could now see a group of horses tethered. I had recognised my father's voice, but when he came out of the porch I barely recognised him, for he was so different from the hunted, run-down, rather pathetic figure I had seen at The Pot. He wore a plain, buff uniform with no favours or badges of rank. He did not need them. His whole manner, when he spoke, was that of a man expecting to be obeyed. Absurdly, at that moment, I felt a surge of pride for him.

As he disappeared into the wing, that pride was overtaken by a violent rush of other feelings. Anger at his duplicity. Rage at my stupidity, at being fooled by him: *If you find it in your heart to forgive me ...* And I felt fear, too, as I thought of him coming to my house and talking with Luke. Fear above all. Fear of the mercenaries' faces. Fear that something was happening that was beyond my control. I went to try the door. It was locked. I was about to shake it, kick it impotently, when I heard a rasping sound outside. I bent down to the keyhole.

A man, sleeping on a chair in the corridor, was lifting his head, air hissing through his ruptured nose. I crept away from the door. *Think. Think. Knife.* They had taken it and my belt. *Think.*

A soft breeze came from the window, carrying with it the sound of men's voices. They were giving water to the horses. Some were splashing it on their faces; although it was early, it was already warm.

There were about twenty of them. One, who must have been the second-in-command, saluted Richard, who walked towards the house. He took off his hat and fanned his head. His hair was thinning into the beginning of a bald patch. He scratched it, teasing hair over the patch. After he passed underneath my window, he disappeared into the house without ceremony. There were a number of comings and goings. The door must be open. *Think.*

Below me was a sheer drop to a flagstone path. My head spun as I looked down. I searched the room, finding only a heavy candlestick which might be of use to me, and which I stuffed down my jerkin.

I wriggled through the casement window backwards, gripping the edge of it while my feet flailed for the stone ledge. The cornice was depressed like a shallow balcony and I switched my grip to an elaborate stone carving. More in hope than belief, I had imagined I could reach the next window on the same floor. But, being smaller than mine, which occupied a Dutch gable, it had just a tiny ledge. I stretched out my foot. My muscles were at breaking point, but I could only touch it with the toe of my boot.

As I drew back, panting, I glimpsed the flagstones beneath me. Last night's meal, and the taste of congealed fat, rose in my throat. I shut my eyes and pressed my forehead against the stone. I stretched out as far as I could towards the smaller window, then jumped.

My left foot landed on the ledge. The right foot scrabbled uselessly at the wall while my hands grabbed at the column at the side of the window. A nail broke. I clung on, wriggling my left boot along the narrow ledge, so I would be in a position to swing my right boot on to it.

Before I could complete the manoeuvre footsteps rang on the flags below me. Richard's second-in-command strolled along, whistling cheerfully. My arms felt as if they were being pulled out of their sockets. The soldier stopped to answer a greeting from the ostler coming out of the stable yard, who called him Jan. The candlestick I had taken began slipping slowly down my jerkin, wriggling like a snake against the leather. I released my grip on the column, snatching out for the column on the other side of the window, lost it, clutched it lower down and swung my right foot on the ledge, trapping the candlestick with a grating clatter against the wall. Jan stopped whistling. My breath sounded so loud I was certain he must hear it. The man stared all around, scratching his flaxen hair. Finally, he walked towards the house, taking a sealed message from his pocket.

I waited until I had heard him enter the hall. I wrapped my handkerchief round the candlestick and broke the window. Finding the catch, I eased back the casement and wriggled through, dropping to the floor, sweating and retching. I must have thrown up what remained of the foul stuff Challoner had given me, for my mind cleared and sharpened. The room was much like the other, except the hangings were green and depicted hunting scenes. From the corridor came a familiar sound: a rasping, strangulated breath, punctuated by snoring.

He was sprawled in the chair between me and the landing. He gave a whistling sigh and shifted his position. I gripped the candlestick, ready to strike, but his eyes remained closed as I stepped over him and hurried across to the landing.

I slipped down one flight of stairs. On the next I almost cannoned into a maid carrying sheets. She stared at me, startled. I picked up a sheet she had dropped, smiled sympathetically and said, 'We're giving you a lot more work, I'm afraid.'

She took the sheet and gave me a small curtsey. On the next landing a soft breeze freshened the damp, stale air. The front door was enticingly open. From Sir Lewis's study came the murmur of voices. I crept down the stairs. Another second, and I would have been out of the house, but my father had a mesmerising, rich voice which carried.

'Dangerous? My son?'

'You acknowledge him? You call him that?' Sir Lewis said.

'My father does. He uses him. He's used him against me since he plucked him out of that rat-hole.'

A servant approached. I ducked down in the stairway. The servant knocked at Challoner's door and took in a tray of small beer. Challoner was wiping his red, sweating face. When the servant left, Challoner told him to leave the door open to let some fresh air in. Challoner was facing the hall. I dare not move. If he looked up, he would see me.

'I'll deal with my son when this business is settled,' my father said.

'No, sir,' Challoner responded. '*I* have him. And a considerably increased offer from Lord Stonehouse to cooperate with him.'

'You can rely on me to match that offer when we have the King, and I am sitting where my father is. In three days our forces will be raised and we will have the King.' My father smiled. 'And who holds the King, holds the country.'

Sir Lewis was drawn in by my father's eloquence as much as I had been. It was supported by something even more potent than his voice. Money. Real money. Not figures on paper, warrants or promises, but coins, rattling, jingling, pronouncing their solid worth as my father stacked them on the table. At first I thought it was for Sir Lewis but it became clear it had another purpose. It was soldiers' pay. This – my father's hand corralled a section of coins – was for Colonel Wallace's regiment.

This for Colonel Floyd's regiment … This for … Some of the coins must have been the ones I had seen in his belt at The Pot. What had he called himself? A humble messenger for His Majesty? Humble messenger! He was the King's Paymaster. His mission was to extract money from reluctant City merchants who supported the King, to speed the break-up of the New Model Army so Holles could seize power.

I was so hypnotised by the sight of the money and my father's voice that I failed to hear the man who had been guarding me until his breath was rasping in my ear.

* * *

I was trussed up like a chicken and a dirty rag thrust in my mouth. Sir Lewis wanted to kill me. I had heard too much. My father stopped him, not from any affection, I gathered, but for fear of Lord Stonehouse, who knew I was here. I heard it in my father's voice, that quiver of fear shooting through his words, as once again the mercenary carried me upstairs. That fear, my only protection, would not leave my father, I thought, until the King was back on his throne and Lord Stonehouse in the Tower.

16

Three days. Three days and they would have the King. The figure echoed in my head as I was punched almost insensible by the mercenary before he flung me on the bed in the red room. This time he sat with me, smoking a clay pipe. Bitter thoughts lacerated me, along with the ropes cutting into my wrists and ankles. I winced as I remembered boasting to my father about the strengths of the New Model Regiments. By giving away the strengths, I had exposed the weaknesses. He had learned which regiments could be broken up most easily, by persuading troops to go to Ireland – including mine. It was what I used to drum into every junior officer. Never talk. Whenever you open your mouth, you give something away. I groaned, which brought me another punch from the mercenary.

When I came round it was even hotter. A fly buzzed, then crawled over my cheek, greasy with sweat and drying blood. The fly kept returning, and I was so tightly bound I could not get rid of it. Another joined it. The mercenary yelled to a passing servant to bring food and drink. Later, he shouted from the window to the other mercenaries who were riding off. The house became silent. The mercenary grew tired of abusing me and sucked at his clay, adding a bubbling sound to his grating breath.

I could work out my father's route precisely. Like my father did, I held the maps in my head. Middle England. It was ground we had both fought over for five years. And now Richard was paying off regiments that might stand in the way of his snatching the King. After going to Colonel Wallace at Dutton's End, he would ride through Hertfordshire, crossing the Great North Road near Sandy. Colonel Floyd's regiment was based at Bedford, less than a day's march from the King. The Colonel was not a Presbyterian and did not sympathise with Holles, but the money would split Floyd's men and reduce the capability of his fighting force. I did not know what Richard planned to do then, but I could guess.

He had letters from the Queen. She would certainly have raised support with the French, and through them with the Scots. Charles was held at Holdenby nominally by Parliament, but the commander of the small garrison, Major-General Browne, was a strict Presbyterian who had never fought in the New Model and was believed to openly defy it. Whether Richard planned to take the King to Poyntz's northern army, controlled by Holles or the Scots, I did not know. Holles would throw up his hands in horror and say he knew nothing about it, but, on top of his Parliamentary majority, he would have the King; and, as my father put it, those who had the King, had the country.

This gloomy conclusion made me twist and writhe in fury at my stupidity. I succeeded only in cutting the rope deeper into my raw and bleeding wrists. There was a knock at the door and a maid said, in a trembling voice, she had brought the food. The mercenary was taking no chances of losing me a second time. He told her to put it outside, then waited until her footsteps retreated before unlocking the door and bending to pick up the tray.

There was a whirl of movement. The tray went over. Something hit the mercenary like a cannonball, knocking him to the floor. I rolled over on the bed, twisting up my head, and saw it was Scogman. In hurling himself at the mercenary he had dropped his knife. The mercenary kicked it away, grabbed Scogman and pulled him to the floor. He had a bull-like, tenacious strength, squeezing

Scogman to him while he drew closer to get the knife. I watched helplessly. His breath was like a saw, rasping louder and louder with the effort. Another moment and he would have the knife. I rolled myself to the edge of the bed. The toe of my boot caught in the coverlet. I thrashed frantically, hung suspended for a moment, then fell.

It was as much the surprise as the force with which I hit the mercenary that allowed Scogman to pull himself away, snatch the knife and bring it up into the mercenary's throat. I rolled away as the blood jumped from him. There was a gasp from the doorway, as the returning maid gaped at the scene. Scogman clapped his hand over the maid's mouth, choking off her scream, turning her face away from the mercenary's pulsing blood. I could see why he was good with women. Even with his hand clamped round her face, he was gentle, his voice soothing.

'You saw nothing. You heard nothing. Do you understand, Jane?'

She stood mute, nodding mechanically. She had a marked resemblance to Mary, the chambermaid at The Cart Overthrown. A voice shouted from downstairs.

'Is Sir Lewis there? Jane?' Scogman shook her, but even then gently, as if she might break.

'Gone to the prison. To see you.'

'Ah, yes. He would have. To see me. Of course.'

The voice shouted Jane's name again, coming closer, up the stairs.

'Tell him you upset the tray. That's all. Quick!'

She did so, mechanically, and the voice retreated, grumbling. Scogman helped her pick up the pieces and put the tray in her hands. Only then did he take the knife to the rope round my wrists.

'You were supposed to rescue me, sir,' he said reproachfully.

We had banked on Stalker believing that, since I had delivered Scogman so tightly gagged and bound, it would be superfluous to untie and search him. We had not anticipated the leg-irons. Scogman told me I had scarcely been gone an hour when Stalker opened the cell door.

'He couldn't stand me without leg-irons, sir. Against regulations. Scarce had time to get to the knife you had hidden on me,' Scogman said in aggrieved tones. 'It was close. But I left him in the leg-irons he's so fond of, in his own cell with his playing cards for company, for Sir Lewis to find.' He pulled out a bunch of keys and threw them in a hedge. 'Take a blacksmith to release him.'

Impossible not to laugh with Scogman. Impossible not to feel a lift of the heart as we put Byford Hall behind us and rode down a lane walled by high hedges, frothing with white May blossom. But my gloomy thoughts soon overwhelmed me. My first impulse was to ride to London. But even if I could convince Cromwell, by that time the cavalry he could normally rely on would be nullified. Richard would have snatched the King.

We reached a crossroads. One road would take us to London, the other to Dutton's End. The May flowers had a cloying smell. The only sounds were from the bees buzzing between them and my horse cropping grass in the ditch.

'Permission to speak, sir?' I had forgotten Scogman was there. He was looking at the sun. 'Regiment musters at one to pick the party for Ireland.'

It was noon, or just after. Better to do something than nothing, and at least try to prevent one small part of the army from breaking up. I nodded and got on my horse.

'You seem out of sorts, sir.'

I was tempted to unburden myself, but what was the point? He would not understand. Whether he was a rogue or not, I could not decide. He was certainly ingenious and resourceful, but it was confined to the narrow world of breaking into people's confidences (particularly if they were women) and thereafter into their houses. Beyond that he had no thoughts. Parliament? If he thought about it at all, it was as one more body to outwit, rather than another. But as we rode on, and he kept giving me darting, inquiring glances, I outlined the situation in as simple a way as possible, expecting him to shrug indifferently.

Instead he reined in his horse. 'You mean Parliament's lost, sir?'

'Yes.'

'I thought Parliament had won?'

'Yes.'

I knew he would not understand – understand that Holles, who, since the first battle at Edgehill, had wanted peace at almost any price, would give too much power back to the King; that the King would eventually return to dismissing Parliament as and when he pleased. Scogman checked his horse. He had a battered, decrepit, wide-brimmed leather hat which had once belonged to a dead Cavalier. He took it off and scratched his head.

'You mean all this was a waste of time, sir?'

I followed his gaze. 'All this' was a ruined castle, whose bricks littered the countryside. Wheat was growing, and animals grazing, but everywhere you looked the scene was pockmarked with the scars of war: a burned barn, a shattered cannon, trees chopped down by soldiers living off the land, and a pile of bones bleached in the sun from a dead horse they had eaten.

'I lost some good friends,' he said.

I thought of my best friend Luke, dying in my arms at Edgehill. I had named my son in memory of him. So many others had died I had grown inured to it. We were on the brow of a hill from which we could see down into Dutton's End. What was left of the regiment was filing into the church hall. I could just pick out Will, near to the tall figure of Sergeant Potter, chivvying the men into the hall, like animals driven into market, to be bartered, sold, slaughtered.

'Is there nothing we can do, sir?'

'It's the way of the world, Scoggy.'

'Is it?' He was punching his plundered hat as if the head of the Cavalier was still inside it. He found the slots in the hat where the dead Cavalier would have once inserted an ostrich plume, and put there a sprig of green laurel. I had no idea then it had any significance, and thought he was merely fooling about.

'Come on,' I said irritably. 'At least we might save the regiment.'

'Oh, we might be able to do more than that, sir.'

'I told you! I can't ride to Cromwell, gather soldiers together and get to Holdenby in time!'

'George has a troop not far from there, sir.'

Something in his voice made me check my horse. 'George? Who the hell is George?'

'George Joyce,' Scogman said. 'He's a cornet in Fairfax's cavalry regiment. Knows Holles. Best way one man can know another, he says – he's measured him. He was 'prenticed to Holles's tailor. Nasty piece of work, Holles, George says. Temper as sharp and knobbly as his knees.'

I turned away. A tailor. A cornet – the lowest-ranking officer in the army.

'He worked with Major Rainborough to secure the army's train of artillery at Oxford in case Parliament – Holles – ordered them north.'

I grew very still. That tallied exactly with the information Lord Stonehouse had given me, except he did not identify who had seized the train.

'George has five hundred horse drawn from the same regiments chosen to guard the King – because they had Presbyterian Colonels. But these men are for Cromwell.'

I swallowed as my voice came out as a kind of croak. 'Where – where are these men?'

'Bedfordshire, Northants borders. About fifty miles from Holdenby. Waiting for Joyce to join them.' He had put on his hat, and the shiny deep-green laurel leaves caught the sun.

It was possible. Just possible. To get to London. Cromwell. Ride back. Two days. Just possible. 'Who is giving Joyce orders?'

'He is.'

'He is?'

'And his men. They vote.'

'Vote?'

'It's what they do in Parliament, sir, I believe. They all decide what they want to do.'

I stared at him suspiciously. Not a muscle in his face moved. The surge of hope gave way to scepticism and the scepticism to anger. I had been made a fool of too often: by my father, by Scogman. I winced as I remembered the whores shrieking with laughter when I took money to Scogman's starving family.

'Are you lying?' I said curtly.

'No, sir.'

He stared back at me defiantly, without a trace of his shifty, hangdog air. Outside the church hall Sergeant Potter was looking around for stragglers. Probably there was something in Scogman's story – a few men who had some religious fervour, mixed with many more deserters, who were seeking plunder they had hidden during the war. A tailor. Votes. I kneed my horse forward. Scogman rode in front of me, blocking my way. His hand went halfway to his hat in an act of deference, but returned to his saddle without completing it. The leaves in his hat glinted like metal in the sun. His voice shook, but only slightly. He never raised it.

'You think I'm a rogue. Quite right. And why shouldn't I be? I was pressed into the army, like most of the foot. Scum, as Sergeant Potter reminds us. In other words, the poor. Anyone with goods worth less than five pounds was pressed. I had five pounds eight shillings, but I had stolen it. If I'd declared it, I would have been hanged. The army or the hangman – some choice. After one battle I deserted, but it was worse being a civilian than a soldier. I took a dead cavalry man's name, trade and horse and enlisted. At least I didn't have to carry my bloody pack.'

He gazed round at the wheat growing near the splintered trees, and the bleached bones.

'Before the war I never knew anything but the whorehouses of Bankside. Now I've seen all this. I never heard anything before but thieves' cant. Now I've heard people like you talk of a better world. We're not clever, sir, like you. But we're not fools. Ireland, troop movements: we knew something was going on. We didn't know what but we've seen enough, these five years, not just to sit on our arses and wait until we were pressed again.'

He clicked at his horse and began to ride downhill. I caught up with him. 'You said the five hundred men are waiting for George Joyce. Where is Joyce?'

He studied me for a moment. 'Not far away. Waiting for Will and what's left of the men when the regiment has been culled.'

Listed as a deserter, Scogman had no desire to get too close to Sergeant Potter and turned away before we reached the town. He shouted after me.

'I nearly forgot.'

He pressed a paper into my hand. I knew what the setting meant immediately, for I had printed enough of them in my days with Mr Black. It was an ordinance, one indemnifying troops from normally illegal acts they had carried out during the war.

'Where did you get this?'

'Sir Lewis's study. I thought it might be useful.'

'Why? What does it say?'

He shrugged. 'I thought it looked important enough, with enough big words to contain some really big lies. You tell me.'

He rode away, but not before I caught a hungry look, part awed, part angry, at the document, staring at something he could not steal. I had been so taken aback by his fluency on the hill that a fact I would normally have assumed came as a shock to me. He could not read.

17

Colonel Wallace was calling upon God to bless their enterprise against the Irish rebels when I squeezed between the troopers standing at the back of the hall. The sight of me checked him in the reading of a psalm and he glanced towards Sergeant Potter. Will, who was sitting at the front, twisted round. From the look on his face he could not decide whether I was friend or enemy.

Colonel Wallace recovered quickly. He had a sonorous voice. His illness had left him with skin the colour of a tallow candle and this, with his long, whitening hair, gave him the look of a prophet.

'The Irish papists have strung their bows – but your weapons will rain down burning coals upon these forces of Antichrist, brimstone and scorching winds. Such is the draught the Lord brews for them. Amen.'

The amens rippled round the dingy hall with varying degrees of fervour. Bennet, the marksman, was louder than the rest. Knowles, the shoemaker, had his eyes tightly shut, his hands clasped in fervour. I knew, from the letters I had written for him, that he was desperate to get home to his sick wife and children, but at that moment his mind looked full of burning coals and brimstone. Most muttered routinely, heads bowed.

Colonel Wallace was sitting at a table, on which were several leather bags. His black riding cloak, edged with fur, was hanging on the wall behind him. I remembered it from Sir Lewis's waiting room. Colonel Wallace was the visitor he had not wished me to see. He was effusive in his greeting.

'Major Stonehouse, welcome back. You are volunteering for Ireland?'

'No, sir. I wish to speak against it.'

Sergeant Potter sat up, ramrod straight. 'Beg pardon, sir. Point of order. Matter closed, as per last meeting. Sir.'

The Colonel nodded. 'Quite. Thank you, Sergeant. I regret, Major, there can be no further discussion.'

'I fear there were irregularities in the voting, Colonel.'

Wallace frowned. 'Irregularities?'

'I have a list of them!' Will rose to his feet, holding up the paper he had shown me.

'I am sorry. The matter is closed. Please sit down.'

Neither of us moved. A man was coughing, struggling to stop. The paper shook in Will's hand. It was the only movement in the hall. Dull red spots formed on Colonel Wallace's sallow cheeks. He spoke very quietly.

'Sit down, gentlemen. That is an order.'

Sergeant Potter moved down the aisle. He looked as if he had been waiting all his life to lay his hands on me.

Nearby, Knowles gazed at the paper trembling in Will's hand. He knew his name was on it. He was the man in debt, Sergeant Potter having threatened he would face prison unless he agreed to go to Ireland, although, probably, the debt was covered by his overdue pay. His stare shifted from the paper to me, a confused mixture of hope and despair on his face, which strengthened my resolve.

'If you prefer it, Colonel, I am happy to refer the complaints to the Army Council,' I said.

The Council was at Saffron Walden, less than an hour's ride away. Wallace looked not so much at me as at the falcon on my signet ring. It was not my words that made Colonel Wallace hesitate. Lord

Stonehouse, with his direct link to Cromwell, still had influence with the Army Council. But it was a measure of how tenuous that influence had become that Wallace deliberated for so long before answering. Just as before the start of the war, people agonised over which side they were on – or over which side would win. At last, curtly, he told me to speak.

'Sir, Parliament decided every man who has fought for it should be free to choose whether or no to go to Ireland?'

'Yes.'

'Some here have been pressed.'

'Name them.'

Knowles looked terrified that I would name him and he would be hauled before the Colonel for debt.

'Would it not be quicker and fairer, sir, to take the vote again?'

'Name one man, Major, who has been pressed.'

Gunpowder Bromley rose to his feet, shaking. He got his curious name because, in civilian life, he was a Saltpetre Man, scraping off the top layer of dung-soaked soil from pigeon-houses and stables, rich in the nitre used to make gunpowder.

'I was ill, not present at the vote, sir,' he said.

'Questioned after – put down his mark and took the shilling, sir,' Potter said.

It was the age-old device for pressing men – getting them drunk and pressing a shilling in their hands as payment to agree to serve.

'Is this your mark, Bromley?' Colonel Wallace held up a list of names, by the side of which were scrawled signatures and crosses. Bromley first denied it, then, under Sergeant Potter's wrathful gaze, conceded it might be.

Colonel Wallace sighed. He held up a pamphlet that contained pictures of the Irish washing their hands in the blood of Protestant women and killing their children. I knew it well, for I had had a hand in it. It came from the earlier rebellion before the war, when

Parliament believed the King had a secret deal with the Irish Catholics. I believed it then, but after five years of war I knew how little such pictures had to do with the truth.

'Put it this way, Bromley,' Colonel Wallace said. 'Do you want the murderous papists to continue sticking innocent Protestant babies on the end of their pikes?'

'No, sir,' said Bromley.

'Good. Sit down.'

Bromley dropped back into his seat. Bennet slapped him on the back. 'Good lad! You're coming with me to kill the Irish sods.'

Nobody else moved. Colonel Wallace had opened one of the leather bags. The men were fixated by the gleam and rattle of money on the table. It was their pay, long overdue. But Colonel Wallace handled it as if it was his largesse. The money my father had raised was about to do its job. Over half the men would march for the port to Ireland. The rest would shortly join streams of other soldiers going home. In a matter of weeks the New Model Army, which Cromwell had built up to be the most powerful war machine in Europe, would be broken up.

Will and I looked helplessly at one another. My anger turned on the men. Scogman had said they were not fools, but that was exactly what I felt they were. He was the exception. They would never speak up for themselves. They were dumb. Dumb animals prepared to be driven to the slaughter. I pushed my way towards the door.

'Sir.'

Kenwick, the son of a stationer, as quiet as he was stubborn, stood up. He was not down for Ireland, but for discharge. Wallace paused in putting down a small pile of coins. 'What is it?'

'I don't want the money –'

'Well, I daresay somebody else will have it,' said Wallace genially.

There was a burst of laughter. 'I don't want it if it means I will end up in court.'

'Court? Have you committed a crime?'

Kenwick told him that with two other soldiers he had been ordered to break into a house where a wanted Royalist was thought to be hiding. They had not found the Royalist, but had injured the house-holder, who was threatening to charge them with assault and burglary. There was a murmur round the room. Many soldiers were in the same position and, even greater than the desire for money, was the fear of being imprisoned, or even hanged, following similar accusations.

I remembered the paper Scogman had taken from Sir Lewis's study and pulled it out while Colonel Wallace reassured Kenwick that Parliament, in its wisdom, had declared an indemnity on such acts.

I found the paper on indemnities. 'The ordinance has not yet become law, Colonel.'

'It will be law. Before these men leave.'

I looked at the dates. He was right. The men's eyes were returning to the money again when, as I was sitting, folding the ordinance away, my eye was caught by a Latin phrase. Parliamentary draughtsmen always put something in Latin when they wished to bury it. For the first time in my life I blessed the teacher who had beaten Latin into me. The Colonel was dividing up the money, very amiable now, and Bennet declaring it was time for a drink, the time-honoured celebration of pay day, when I rose to my feet again.

'With your permission, Colonel ...'

Colonel Wallace gave me a weary, indulgent smile. 'What is it now, Major?'

'May I ask Kenwick a question?'

'If you must,' the Colonel said drily. 'I do not wish to be reported to the Army Council.'

More laughter and drumming of the feet as I turned to Kenwick. 'When were you ordered to break into this house?'

'March, sir.'

'March this year?'

'Yes, sir.'

'This was long after the King had given himself up and the war was over?'

'Yes, sir, but some Royalists went on fighting and –'

'All right, Kenwick,' Colonel Wallace interjected, beginning to lose patience again. 'Is there a point in all this, Major?'

'You will find it at the bottom of page two, Colonel. This ordinance only indemnifies soldiers committing illegal acts *in tempore et loco belli*.'

The soldiers became still again. Many of them saw something supernatural in these pages of hieroglyphics; they were right, in the sense that such incomprehensible ordinances often determined their fates. And this was magic on an even higher plane – words they not only could not read, but could not hear.

'Under conditions of war,' I said. 'This indemnity does not cover Kenwick and the others, for they broke into the house in what the law will call peace.'

The soldiers understood that all right. To a man, they wanted their money, but they feared the lack of indemnity more. Living off the land, hated by the country people who had been forced to give free quarter, almost every soldier in that hall had either stolen or been wrongly accused of it. Some of the accusations, like horse theft, were felonies that could see them hanged.

I saw something else, or the lack of it, in the ordinance. It had been shabbily drafted in haste, not so much to protect the soldiers but to get rid of them so Holles could take over the country. There was no provision for the King to sign it. What happened if he was enthroned again, with the right to veto, and dismissed it? I said as much, finding my voice, full of bitterness that these men who had fought for so long for Parliament could be so cheated by it. They were not getting their full pay. There was nothing for the injured. This indemnity was not worth the paper it was written on.

It was astonishing how the men, so compliant one moment, were so full of anger the next. Someone tried to snatch the ordinance from my hand. Another spat on it.

Colonel Wallace said something to Sergeant Potter, but it was drowned in the uproar of voices. Potter plunged towards me, but he was stopped by men firing questions.

Men were pressing round the table, where Colonel Wallace stumbled and almost fell. Money rolled on to the floor, soldiers scrambling after it. I shouted to them to stop but they grabbed at it like starving men after food.

'See to the Colonel,' I snapped at Sergeant Potter. 'Bennet … Maddox … put that money back. If you take that money you are accepting the conditions of the indemnity.' They dropped the coins as if they were tainted by plague. 'May I suggest, Colonel, the men for Ireland stay in the hall and I remove the rest.'

'You are inciting these men to mutiny, Major.'

'I am trying to prevent disorder.'

'Mutiny is a capital offence.'

'So is consorting with wanted Royalists like my father.'

He went white and snatched up his cane. I thought he was going to strike me. A band of men surrounded Sergeant Potter. He pushed one away but another picked up a chair.

'Sergeant Potter!' The Colonel rapped his cane repeatedly on the floor. 'Assemble the men for Ireland in this hall. All the rest line up outside with Major Stonehouse.'

'Out!' I shouted. 'Kenwick … Harvey. At the double.'

Bromley, the Saltpetre Man whom Sergeant Potter had pressed into going to Ireland, was wandering about looking dazed, not knowing which group to join.

'You want to be back in London, don't you, Bromley, scraping shit off the pigeon lofts?'

His face lit up. 'Yes, sir. I miss my pigeons.'

'Outside.'

I ushered him and a stream of other men through the door. The ones I knew were legitimately on the Irish list I sent back. Most would desert after what they had heard. Holles's strategy for demolishing the New Model, at least so far as this regiment was concerned, was in tatters.

'I will not forget this.' Colonel Wallace's voice sounded in my ear. 'Neither will he.'

I followed his gaze. Halfway down the hill, where they had stopped their horses, looking down on the assembling soldiers, were Stalker and Sir Lewis Challoner. Even at that distance, I could feel the malevolence in his gaze.

I turned away, almost bumping into Bennet on his way out. 'You're Ireland,' I said. 'You want to kill some murdering papists.'

'I want indemnity,' he said. I could believe it, from some of the things I suspected him to have done. 'And it looks as if it will be more interesting serving you.' There was a gleam in his eye I did not like.

'You are not serving me,' I said coldly. 'Colonel Wallace is in charge of this regiment.'

He looked past me at the assembling soldiers. 'Is he?'

I looked round. Dressing the soldiers smartly into line was a fresh-faced man with round, chubby cheeks who turned out to be older than me, but who looked as if he had barely left school. From his cornet's insignia, I took him to be George Joyce. With him was Scogman, his hat at a jaunty angle. Wearing a dark brown fustian jacket, walking restlessly up and down, hands clasped behind his back as if he was about to review the troops, was the apprentice who had succeeded me at Mr Black's, Nehemiah.

18

Ever since I had left London, even when I had been trussed up like a chicken at Byford Hall, I had felt responsible for my actions. Now I had the curious feeling of being handled like a puppet. I could sense the strings, although I had no idea who the puppet master might be.

'What are you doing here?' I said to Nehemiah.

He looked put out to see me. 'I might say the same of you.'

'This is my regiment.'

'Ah. I had forgotten,' he said, with an eloquent glance at my signet ring.

As well as printing pamphlets for the London Levellers, he produced some of the soldiers' petitions. It was during the delivery of these that the crisis had developed, and he was coordinating action between the soldiers and the Levellers.

'Then we are on the same side,' I said.

His lips quivered. His stammer was returning. 'I … h-hope so,' he replied. It was only months since he had run away from Mr Black's, but it seemed like years. It was like looking at myself when I had broken my bond. He was of the streets, sharp, cautious, suspicious; even here looking behind his back.

I put out my hand to him. After a moment he put out his, and the sight of that ink-begrimed hand flooded me with so many memories of our working together that I gripped it warmly.

The soldiers returned to their billets. I went with Will, Scogman, Joyce and Nehemiah up the hill to a barrow, an old burial ground with stones, once upright, which served as a convenient table. Put Scogman in a desert, and he would find food and drink. He produced rye bread, hard as the stones we ate from, and curious strips of dried, salted meat which he said was beef, but I suspected was horse. We scooped up water from a stream to wash it down.

I told them what I had heard at Byford Hall. George Joyce was as eager and impulsive as the schoolboy he looked. He jumped up so quickly he almost choked on the meat he was chewing. 'Then we must ride to my troops near Holdenby!'

'To do what?' Will, normally as impulsive as Joyce, seemed to resent losing that role to him.

'Prevent them taking the King.'

'Then what do we do?' I said.

'Take him prisoner,' Nehemiah said matter-of-factly.

He sat on a stone, above the rest of us, an alien presence in his brown fustian. Pollen drifting in the air made his nose run and he wiped it with the back of his hand.

'On whose authority?' I questioned.

'Our authority,' he said. 'That of the … p-people.'

He sneezed as he said it, turning what might have been impressive into something comic and absurd. I struggled not to smile. Nehemiah gave me a furious look. 'I told you,' he blazed at Joyce, giving me a venomous look. 'He works for Lord Stonehouse.'

'Oh, come on, Nemmy,' Joyce said. 'He's with us.'

'Is he? London says –'

'Oh, London! This is nothing to do with Leveller talk, or people's rights. It's about soldiers' grievances.'

'Of course it's about people's rights! You have these grievances because you have *no* r ...' We looked away while he tried for the word. '... *rights.*'

'We're not in The Bull and Mouth. We're on top of a hill in the middle of bloody nowhere. Without you and the Levellers we wouldn't have got anywhere. But now we must *do* something. Look.' He pointed to the sun, which seemed to be creeping down the sky even as we shielded our eyes against it. Joyce put his arm round Nehemiah with real affection, and drew him back into the circle.

'What do you think we should do?' he said to me.

'Go to Cromwell.'

'Cromwell!' Nehemiah spat the word out.

Joyce held up his hand before Nehemiah could go on. He spoke quietly. He pointed out that the commander-in-chief of the army was Fairfax, not Cromwell. He had carried the standard in Fairfax's own cavalry regiment and he knew Fairfax would have nothing to do with us. He went strictly by the rules.

'Cromwell does not,' I said. 'He is the man people respect.'

'F-fear,' interjected Nehemiah. '*Fear.*'

Joyce chewed on his salted meat and turned to me. 'What will your father do?'

'Take the King to Poyntz's northern army under the pretext he's in danger because we're rebelling. Poyntz backs Holles. The City is already under his control. If Cromwell's army breaks up, there's nothing to stop Holles. He will let the King have what he wants.'

I wished I had not put it so baldly. It deflated everyone, including me. It put us too sharply into perspective: an insignificant group, washing down horse meat with spring water, in a small corner of a remote hillside. How could we possibly affect these momentous events? They had been, were, and always would be a matter for King and Parliament – not even Parliament, I thought bitterly, but a small clique of it, controlled by the great nobles: Warwick, Bedford, Saye and Stonehouse.

Swifts called shrilly, scything through the air over the stream in search of insects, a sign evening was approaching, but it was still oppressively hot. Our clothes stuck to us and the shimmering haze blurred the town below. Pollen reddened Nehemiah's eyes. We were so still that a rabbit, a few feet away, was staring fixedly at us. Scogman gave us warning looks. Whatever the situation, his mind was never far from food. What mattered was not the thought of these great events, but that night's supper. His hands crept silently over the grass to grab it. Nehemiah's nose twitched. He struggled, but exploded in a violent sneeze. The rabbit shot away, his white bob vanishing into the hillside. Scogman swore in disgust, and said we could all catch our own supper.

'What can Cromwell do?' Nehemiah's thickening, nasal tones dismissed the question as he uttered it.

'Give us authority. A leader.'

'Authority. A leader. That is *exactly* what we are trying to get away from. Cromwell is in the hands of the nobles. He wants to be a *n-noble* himself.'

'That's true. But I know what Tom means.'

George Joyce's youthful looks gave him a pretended innocence, behind which was a shrewd and calculating mind. Tom – a sop to me, but also one to Nehemiah, for he did not defer to my seniority. A prickle of resentment and envy ran through me. He did not lose his temper. He had a knack, which I lacked, of agreeing with both sides, or at least taking part of the argument of each, then turning it in the direction he wanted it to go; he managed to deny the need for a leader while becoming one. And he had a soldier's grasp of essentials; he separated what people would like to do from what they could do.

He picked up a pebble and put it on the slab we were eating from. 'We are here.' A large stone became London; another pebble in the middle of the slab, Holdenby. 'We are sixty, seventy miles from Cromwell in London. It is the same distance from here to Holdenby.

Even if Cromwell agreed we should act with our troops, we would have to ride nearly two hundred miles in less than two days. Your horse may be Pegasus, but mine is not.'

'All right. You take the King. What then?' I seized a small number of pebbles. 'How many men are you? Five hundred near Holdenby. Will's men – others you might raise?'

'A thousand?'

I picked up a handful of pebbles, then another, heaping them on to the slab until they fell back on the grass. 'There are seventeen thousand men in the opposing army. A thousand against sixteen thousand.'

Nehemiah spoke. 'Regiments are breaking up, people will come to us!'

'Most will listen to Fairfax and Cromwell. My father will let you take the King. You will have mutinied. You will have Holles, Cromwell, Fairfax *and* Parliament against you.'

'Then what the hell do we do?' Joyce cried. 'Let the Presbyterians take him to Poyntz?'

'Ride to Cromwell.'

'It's impossible!'

'Not with fresh horses.'

'Horses are like gold!'

'I can get them.'

'How?'

I held out my hand with the signet ring on my finger. You can get anything you want with that, my grandfather had said laconically – as laconically as he had once sealed my death warrant with his ring to have me thrown in the plague pit.

'I told you,' Nehemiah said. 'He works for Lord *S-tonehouse*. Don't trust him.'

Joyce said, 'Where can you get horses?'

'Inns. He has people up and down the country.'

'Part of his spy network.' Nehemiah said. 'We know them.'

Joyce looked at the sun, then at the stones, whose shadows were lengthening. 'We must move. One way or the other. Let's take a vote.'

'A *vote?*' I said incredulously.

'We all have a say.' Joyce spoke as if it was the most natural thing in the world. He put up his hand. 'I vote for Holdenby.'

So did Nehemiah. Will and I voted for London and Cromwell. We all turned to Scogman, whom we had forgotten about. Since losing the rabbit, he had lain in the grass, tipped his hat over his eyes and appeared to be asleep. But he declared that, while doing the important business of looking for his supper, he had been listening, on and off, and said he feared and distrusted Cromwell, but he would much rather Cromwell was for us than against us.

'I would like to ask Major Tom,' he said – being Scogman, he hedged his bets between the deferential and the egalitarian – 'the question no one has asked.' I had been scornful of the vote, and frustrated by the length of the discussion, and now this. What could someone like Scogman contribute? Once again he confounded me, shielding his eyes against the sun, looking at me directly and speaking very softly.

'You know Cromwell. Not the pictures. Not the stories. You know him as a man. Will he be with us?'

It was the one question I could not answer. It was impossible to predict how Cromwell would react. He might imprison us on the spot. The only thing you could be sure of was that when the doubt, and the questioning, was over, Cromwell would act with a swiftness and certainty that made it feel there had only ever been one solution. And that was what we needed more than anything else. Decision. Action.

I betrayed none of this as I answered, without hesitation, that Cromwell would be with us.

'Then God go with you,' said Scogman, 'to London.'

19

We reached Aldgate as the sun was setting. There was an extra guard at the gate, suspicious of people entering as night was falling. Among a group of them I saw the old banner, under which I had fought at Edgehill: a red cross lettered with FOR GOD AND PARLIAMENT. But which Parliament? The Trained Bands were all Presbyterian now. Holles held the City. The great merchants, trade ruptured by war, and knowing that Holles, not Cromwell, would compromise with the King, were switching their allegiance to him. The signet ring, as it had got us horses, saw us through without real hindrance, but I could feel from the surly looks we received that its power was waning.

The heat was still locked into the City streets and the stench unbearable, until we left Temple Bar and breathed the cooler air of Drury Lane. But there was heat here of a different kind. We felt it in the number of messengers hurrying in and out of Cromwell's house, in the hum of conversation from the garden as we stabled our horses, in the tension in Mrs Cromwell's normally unflustered voice: 'Not *more* visitors! Is there enough bread?'

She kept a frugal household. The servants were hurrying out to the garden with bread and butter and small beer. My house was at the top of the lane, and I sent one of the servants to warn Anne we would be staying the night.

The conversation began to die down as we entered the garden. At first glance it might have looked like a social gathering. The air was sweet. The last of the blossom had fallen around the cherry and apple trees, picked up in the fading light. But it was no garden party. It was a council of war. There were a few MPs and army officers that Cromwell trusted. He was sitting at a table littered with despatches. Next to him as usual was Ireton, who smiled. I never liked it when Ireton smiled. He smiled with his mouth, his sunken eyes remaining black and watchful. I introduced George Joyce but there were no other introductions. No formalities. I told Cromwell what I knew, then George began to speak. Cromwell cut him short. He picked up a crumpled despatch.

'You have five hundred troops near Holdenby?'

George, overawed and stunned by the details Cromwell knew, nodded.

'Why come to me and not your commander-in-chief?'

George, looking like a frightened cherub in the half-light, swallowed. I had told him that nothing less than the truth would do. 'Because General Fairfax would order me back to camp, sir.'

'What makes you think I won't do the same? Or send you to the Tower? If we still have the Tower,' he muttered to Ireton. He turned to me. 'When do you think they will move the King?'

'In the next forty-eight hours.'

Cromwell turned away so abruptly, he almost knocked over Mr Ink who had moved closer to make notes. Cromwell shouted for candles. Maids came scurrying out with them as Cromwell paced the length of the garden and back. He had caught the sun and his face was as reddish-brown as his jerkin, making the warts above his left eye and below his lip stand out in pale relief. Although I was taller than his five foot six or so, he seemed to tower over me, gripping the edge of a chair with hands as broad and coarse as a labourer's.

'Did you see the letters your father was carrying to the King?'

'No, sir.'

'Did you see your father before you rode to Essex?'

While I hesitated, Ireton spoke for the first time. He was consulting some notes. 'May twelfth. Near the 'Change. Richard Stonehouse was seen with another man. They killed one of my soldiers. The other person was you?'

'Yes. My father killed the soldier.'

Cromwell sat down heavily. Mr Ink stopped writing. A moth hovered round the candle near him. I could hear Mrs Cromwell telling a maid to try to borrow some more bread from a neighbour. Ireton's voice was flat and monotonous.

'Did you try to stop Richard Stonehouse?'

'No.'

'What did you do?'

'I went with him. To an inn.'

Somebody laughed, choking it off immediately when Cromwell glared round. Ireton gave his father-in-law an eloquent look: he had made his case.

'To an inn.' Cromwell raked his fingers through his long hair. 'Why didn't you bring him to us? We could have got hold of the letters. Stopped him raising money. Soldiers.'

'I had no idea he was doing that. He – he wrote to me asking me to forgive him. I didn't know whether to trust him or not, but … I had to find out. He – he is my father,' I ended lamely.

Cromwell sighed so heavily a candle flickered and went out.

'Are you working for him?' Ireton's voice was flat and emotionless.

I could not speak for a moment. 'No!'

'How do we know?'

It was Ireton's lawyer tone, dry, disbelieving, colourless, as much as the accusation, that made me move to him, hands clenched. George gripped my arm.

'How do you know? Because I came here! Because I told you what he was plotting when I knew it.'

'Sit down!'

Cromwell waved me towards a bench outside the circle of lights. I was dismissed. In Cromwell's eyes I was either a traitor or a fool. I had seen it all before. Once you lost Cromwell's trust, you lost it for ever. Cromwell called George forward. I sat with my head in my hands, hearing nothing, until Cromwell sprang up. I had seen those signs before too, many times. Cromwell moved as if he had thrown off a heavy burden. His voice, always harsh, was injected with a kind of joviality. He had reached a decision.

'Your troops are from Fairfax's regiment?'

'Yes, sir.'

'The same regiment that is guarding the King – although they are Presbyterians under Colonel Graves?'

'Yes, sir.'

I twisted my hands together, burning with envy, as Cromwell walked right up to him and asked him if he could be trusted. George stood ramrod-straight and saluted. If he had not been under Cromwell's spell before, he was now. Cromwell began giving his instructions, stopping only to put his hand over Mr Ink's quill.

'No notes!' A blob of ink smeared his cuff but he seemed unaware of it as he turned to George. 'Avoid bloodshed. Some of the soldiers, Presbyterian or nay, will be old comrades. Use that. You are there to change the guard. Nothing else. Do you understand?'

'Yes, sir. We change it from Holles's guard to your guard.'

'Not my guard! I know nothing of this. This is your initiative.'

'My initiative, yes, sir.' George swallowed. 'What do I do when I have … taken my own initiative?'

'You await my instructions.'

'Yes, sir. It's my initiative – but I await your instructions.' His tone underlined the incongruity of the two orders, while his face kept a look of cherubic innocence.

Cromwell stared suspiciously at him, before giving him the barest ghost of a smile. 'Above all … you must not touch a hair of the King's head. Is that clear?'

George looked as if it was as clear as a complex cipher, but he saluted. Cromwell wished him Godspeed and turned away, picking up the despatches. 'Nothing from Holles's reception at Derby House tonight?'

Ireton shook his head. 'Lord Stonehouse's informer was taken.'

George continued to stand there. 'I would like Major Stonehouse with me, sir,' George said.

At first I thought Cromwell had not heard him. Then he whirled round, looking as if he had no idea who George was talking about. No one remembered his men and what they had done better than Cromwell. And no one could forget them more quickly when he had dismissed them from his mind. I winced when I saw the blank look on Cromwell's face. Before he could speak, George told him how I had interrupted the muster with Colonel Wallace and kept the regiment together. Cromwell waved him away. Still George plunged on. I had made mistakes because of the feelings I had for my father, but it was precisely *because* of those feelings he needed me. I knew my father's tactics, what he would do.

'Will you be quiet!' Cromwell roared.

A maid dropped a platter of more bread and butter that Mrs Cromwell must have conjured up from somewhere. George stared at the ground as she scrambled to retrieve the loaf. Cromwell picked up some crumpled despatches, and wadded them into a ball. He tossed it from hand to hand. There was the rattle of a coach, the cry of the coachman slowing the horses, the squeal of brakes. Everyone was immediately on edge, still, staring towards the sound. Cromwell squeezed the paper ball, his other hand going to his side. For the first time I realised he wore a sword – strange, in his own house and garden.

Only when the coach had passed did people turn to one another again, talking in low tones. Cromwell flung the paper ball into the bushes and beckoned to me.

'How do you feel now about your father?'

'I want to kill him as he once tried to kill me.' I only realised how savage and violent my words had been when I saw the shocked faces around me.

'I want your father,' Cromwell said. 'I want what he knows. His contacts. I want him alive. Do you understand?'

20

We went to the stables to take our horses to my house, further up the lane where we intended to stay the night. George cut off my flood of thanks. He said he needed me to get him out of the mess he was in. He wished he hadn't come to Cromwell – it had made a difficult task impossible. Avoid bloodshed. Don't touch a hair of the King's head. Nor Richard Stonehouse's!

I had not realised how heavily my secret meetings with my father had weighed down on me until that moment. I felt so lightheaded that I had confessed to Cromwell and been given this chance to redeem myself I was prepared to eat any amount of humble pie.

'At least we have Cromwell's blessing,' I said.

George exploded. 'Is that what you call it! If we seize the King, Cromwell gets the glory. If we fail, we're mutineers and hanged. Cromwell's blessing!'

At my house we gave our horses to Jed, whom I had appointed ostler before I went to Essex. He had lost his arm at Edgehill, but was using his hook adroitly to rub down the horses of a carriage – the carriage that had put Cromwell and his guests so much on edge.

It belonged to Lucy Hay, Countess of Carlisle, a close friend of Anne's. It was a measure of the unrest in the City, which she had experienced returning from a reception, that she had called so late to warn Anne to be extra vigilant. There was something else, I could feel it. With the Countess, there was always something else.

Lucy Hay was close to the Queen but, before the war, had been even closer to John Pym, leader of the opposition. She shared political secrets with Pym, by which he and Cromwell drove the King from London. Whether she shared John Pym's bed or not I did not know, but when Pym died during the war, she said she had given up love.

The war marked everyone else, but it had scarcely touched the Countess. Her skin had the same translucent quality that transfixed me when I first saw her. Her dark ringlets framed shrewd blue eyes, sparkling with belladonna. It was close on eleven but she had the whole house up. I scarcely had time to kiss a bewildered Anne before Lucy was ordering a cup of chocolate. George entered the house exhausted, knowing we had to be up at dawn, but as soon as he saw her he lost all desire for sleep.

Lucy knew how to manage people. Even when she mistook George for my batman, she recovered quickly.

'You are a cornet – you wave the flag?'

'Standard, madam,' he said coldly.

'Standard bearer, exactly. The most important job in the army.'

George smiled and bowed, looking as if he had been made a general.

Anne had told her we had been at Cromwell's. 'It can't have been much of a party if Betsy Cromwell was only giving her guests bread.'

I really believed it was witchcraft that she knew such a small detail, until Jane came in to serve the hot chocolate, and it turned out she was the source of the extra bread Mrs Cromwell had borrowed.

'Betsy served butter with it at least, I suppose?' said Lucy.

'And excellent butter it was too,' said George, coming to the rescue of Mrs Cromwell's hospitality with such gallantry that everyone burst out laughing. Beaming at the unexpected success of this, he was inspired to cap it. 'And it was something rather more important than a party.'

'Really?' Lucy set down her chocolate with a little click. The blue irises filled her eyes. 'What can be more important than a party?'

George's chest swelled. 'We are here –'

'To discuss indemnities. Pay,' I cut in, giving George a warning glance.

'Cromwell's made sure of his pay, hasn't he? Well, he deserves it,' Lucy conceded. 'He should return to the fens. A great soldier, but a disastrous politician.'

'Cromwell is our best hope for the future,' I said coldly.

'God help us then,' she said. 'For Cromwell is finished.'

George looked at her, startled. She said it in her usual throwaway tone but there was an edge to it which suggested it was more than the usual piece of gossip which she enjoyed taking her time to reveal. Anne intensified that feeling by avoiding my eyes, picking the skin of milk from her chocolate. George, unused to Lucy's bombshells, leaned forward, mouth slightly open: the sort of audience Lucy enjoyed. I took a perverse pleasure from the crash of a door and the sound of running feet that robbed her of her moment.

Luke burst into the room, crying. Jane tried to hold him but he pushed away from her, arms flailing, and ran towards Anne. A torrent of incomprehensible words came out of him before Anne managed to calm him.

'He was there again,' he sobbed.

Anne soothed him. 'It's all right. I won't let him take you away.'

'Who's he talking about?' I said.

Luke twisted round in his mother's arms. 'Daddy, Daddy, Daddy.' As I moved to take him, he pulled back. 'You are here, aren't you?'

I laughed. 'Yes. I'm here.'

He wriggled into my arms, still warm and fusty from sleep. 'I thought I heard you. But then I thought you were in my dream, but you are here, aren't you?'

'I'm here. Yes, yes. Ssshh.'

'Have you killed him?'

'Who?'

'He keeps dreaming about Gloomy George,' Anne said. 'At the funeral. He thinks Gloomy George took his sister Liz away and will come back for him.'

Luke jerked upright, almost falling from my arms. 'Have you killed him?'

I walked him round, holding him tight. 'I won't let him harm you. I promise you. Ssshh. Go back to sleep.'

But at that moment he saw Lucy. 'Aunty Lucy! Have you come for us? Are we coming to live in your house now?'

I laughed. 'You don't want to leave Jed, and Jane, and your horse, do you?'

Then I saw the expressions of complicity on Lucy and Anne's faces. 'What is going on?'

'Lucy has kindly offered to let us stay at her house. We will be safer there,' Anne said.

'Safer? What are you talking about?'

'Lord Stonehouse is too close to Cromwell,' Lucy said.

'Cromwell!' Luke said sleepily, bringing up his hand as if he was brandishing a sword.

Anne looked meaningly towards George who was gaping at us all as if he was watching a play. I gave Luke to Jane to take back to bed and showed George up to my dressing room, where there was a truckle bed. Then I left him to sleep and returned to Anne and Lucy.

Downstairs the garden doors were open and for the first time that day I felt cool. For once, Lucy began without preamble.

'Cromwell is fleeing from London.'

Deprived of her usual sense of timing, the words came out so flatly, so baldly, that I laughed. 'He has a funny way of fleeing. Drinking beer with his friends.'

She turned to Jane. 'Tell him what you heard.'

'It's servants' gossip, madam.'

'Tell him.'

It was the bread. Jane had it from the kitchen maid who had come to our house for more loaves, who had it from Mrs Cromwell's personal maid, that her chest was packed. So were Mr Cromwell's papers. He had personally burned a large quantity of papers that day. The kitchen maid had that from the scullery girl, who did the fires. The horses were kept ready. Whether they planned to go to the country, or abroad, nobody knew. Even Massachusetts was whispered. I groped for a chair and sat down stunned. Cromwell had seemed all-powerful, immovable, barking orders, but you could never keep anything from the servants.

I remembered the swords at the guests' belts, and Cromwell's hand going to his at the approach of the carriage. The despatches Cromwell wadded in his hand, and Cromwell asking Ireton if there was a message about Holles's reception at Derby House that evening. Ireton had replied that Lord Stonehouse's informer had been taken. Killed? Or in the Tower, being questioned?

'You were at Derby House this evening, Lucy?'

'Of course. I like to keep myself informed.'

'What did you learn that brought you here?'

'Tom! You are trying to pump me. You'll have to do it more subtly than that.'

Anne put a hand on my arm, but I shook it off and stood over the Countess. 'What did you learn, Lucy?'

She looked back at me steadily. 'Only that things are bad and going to get worse. I was concerned enough to offer my hospitality to Anne and Luke. Now. I must not linger. I know you have to be up at the crack of dawn.'

She knew that. She knew about our meeting with Cromwell. She was probably able to put the pieces together better than anyone else in London. But to whom was she giving her conclusions? Had she come here to help us – or to find things out?

She finished her chocolate, pronouncing it very good in the circumstances, but when things were back to normal, which she hoped would be very soon, the best cocoa would be on sale at their favourite shop in the 'Change.

Jane was waiting to put on Lucy's cloak, and I broke in on her and Anne's leaving chatter.

'How soon is soon, Lucy?'

Her look told me I had become a bore. So, I saw with a stab of anger, did Anne's. For the first time Lucy betrayed a flash of irritation. 'How do I know, Tom? I can only tell you what I hope. That the King is soon back, and we have decency and order in this City.'

Anne nodded fervently. It was heartfelt. I knew what she and Luke had been through. But as I watched Jane help Lucy into her cloak, the red silk lining rippling, I was shocked to see how completely Anne had come under Lucy's spell. When the King had been in power Lucy had been the mistress of the man closest to the royal ear, the Earl of Strafford. When Mr Pym engineered Strafford's execution and was on his way to power, she began her relationship with him. I had never thought about it, but I suppose his death had left a vacancy.

The Countess adjusted the diamond clasp on her cloak to her satisfaction.

'Decency and order,' I said. 'And good cocoa.'

She smiled. 'Exactly,'

It was the complacency of that smile that did it. The words were out of my mouth before I could stop them. 'Whose bed are you sharing tonight, Lucy?'

Her smile froze, but only for a moment before she said, 'My gloves, Jane? Thank you.'

When Lucy had gone and Anne had retired, I knocked at her door. It was locked. She had never done that before. Only when I knocked on it so loudly that she was afraid I would wake Luke again did she open it.

'You are as foul-mouthed as your pamphlets, sir.'

Everything about her seemed to be in violent movement: her lips, her eyes, her tossing hair. She had begun to undress and pulled her shift back into place to cover her breasts. The movement both inflamed and enraged me. When I would not go, she put on her dressing gown, which made me want her even more. Worst of all was that look of contempt on her face, the look she gave me when I arrived as an apprentice, without boots.

'Please don't wake Luke again.'

I sat down on the bed and put my head in my hands. 'I'm sorry. I should not have said that. But if you knew what was happening …'

I told her. At least, as much as I thought I could tell her. About Richard. About Cromwell ordering me to bring him back to London. He was giving me a second chance.

'Second chance?' she exclaimed, bewildered.

I sighed. I thought this would reassure her, bring us closer, but I had forgotten what I had told her, and what I had not. I stumbled on, growing more and more tired, more and more confused.

'You mean – you didn't give Richard's letter to Cromwell?'

I was not sure what had happened when. 'There was Liz … the funeral …'

'Is that why we couldn't find you that day? You were with *him*?'

I closed my eyes. Or perhaps they shut themselves. All I wanted to do was sleep. I may even have nodded off, but the sound of horses roused me. Cromwell's last guests were leaving.

'Is there anything else you haven't told me?'

'No. No. Well …'

I told her that the man Luke thought was the new ostler was no fantasy, but Richard. We were wrong to accuse Luke of lying when he said he did not take the horse out of the stable himself.

'That man came *here*? He could have taken Luke?'

She could not look at me. She got into bed. The coverlet was shaking. She was as remote, as unattainable, as when I had first met her.

'Don't say any of this to Lucy,' I said. 'She's working for Holles.'

She flung back the coverlet. 'Don't be ridiculous.'

'She came to find out what I was doing at Cromwell's.'

'She came because she is concerned about me and Luke, which is more than you are. You heard what she said about Lord Stonehouse. Cromwell is leaving. You go in a few hours. She was my friend. The only person I could rely on and after tonight I can never look her in the face again. Now will you please go away and let me get some sleep.'

To get to my bedroom I had to go through my dressing room. I blundered through, then stopped, startled by a figure at my clothes chest. I had forgotten about George. Guiltily, he dropped back a pair of my best britches, muttering that he could not sleep with the row going on. Surely he was not going through my pockets? I did not care. I cared about nothing at that moment. All I wanted was oblivion. I dropped on my bed and it seemed only minutes later that George was shaking me by the shoulder.

A pale morning light was dispelling the shadows in Anne's room. She had let the candle burn out and the acrid smell lingered. Sleep coloured her cheeks and her warmth drew out the smell of rosemary from the pomade she always kept under her pillow. One foot poked out and it seemed to me a miracle of a foot, small and perfectly formed. I could not believe I had once cursed it, in my misery at her laughing at my large, clumsy, monkey-like feet. I covered it, and kissed her gently.

'I care for you and Luke more than anything else in the world,' I whispered softly.

Her eyes remained closed and I was getting up to leave when she said, 'Write an apology to Lucy and I will take it to her.'

'No. I'm sorry. You must not go there. Lord Stonehouse will see that as a betrayal if she is with Holles.' She tried to interrupt but I stopped her. 'I must ask you to obey me in that. Anne. Do you hear?'

'Yes.'

'You will obey me?'

'Yes. Yes!'

I sighed, feeling the prickle of sweat inside my shirt. I had never talked to her like that in my life before. 'If anything happens and it is not safe here you will go to your father. Or better still, to Matthew and Kate in Spitall Fields.'

'Spitall Fields?' The word enraged her. She sprang up. 'Spitall Fields *Without*?' Outside the walls of the City was, to her, the end of civilisation. Beyond it. She had never been to Poplar, where Matthew had brought me up; nor would she let me take Luke there. 'Half Moon Court?' She looked round at the comfortable room, at the view of the orchard over the lane, at silver candlesticks, a Dutch vase containing roses from a bush she had planted, at a tapestry glinting with gold thread which I saw for the first time in the morning light, one Lord Stonehouse must have given her when I agreed to serve him. 'I have what I have, and I will keep it. Half Moon Court? I left there five years ago, but you still seem to be living there.'

I left her without another word and, with a silent, puffy-eyed George, supped yesterday's pottage, which Jane had warmed for us. She apologised for having no bread, the last of it having gone to Mrs Cromwell.

Jed was the only cheerful figure, whistling as he secured the packs to our horses, and gave us the old rallying cry he had shouted at Edgehill: 'Recover your pikes and charge, lads!'

The words almost choked in my throat as I said goodbye to the old pikemaster. 'Take care of them, Jed.'

'Take care of them? I'd like to see who would touch a hair of their sweet heads when I'm around!' He held me in a grip that nearly squeezed every breath out of my body. 'My arm is worth two – not to mention my portable pike.'

He swept his hook round, almost decapitating George who began to slip from his horse, until Jed dexterously slipped the hook into his belt and pulled him back. 'Steady on, lad. You're not even in battle yet.'

There was a sound of running feet and a shout. My heart leapt. Whatever our quarrels before parting, Anne always appeared at the last moment and everything righted itself. She could go to Lucy. She could do anything. I did not care, so long as she was in my arms.

It was Jane, chasing after Luke, still in his nightclothes. She lifted him, warm into my arms, smelling of sleep.

'Daddy, Daddy, Daddy! Are you going to kill him?'

I held him tightly. 'Yes. There's nothing to be frightened of any more.'

'Kill who?' said George, when we reached the top of the lane.

I made no answer, as we turned into the road north.

21

We scarcely spoke to one another until we changed horses at an inn near Bedford. From there we reckoned it was a two-hour ride to Holdenby House, where the King was held. The innkeeper, who was part of Lord Stonehouse's network, warned us not to go near the next inn in the chain, The Green Man in Northampton. The county was strongly Puritan, and the landlord had gone over to Holles. The innkeeper added that he had served a group of mercenaries earlier that day. Their leader's hooked nose bore a striking resemblance to mine.

'Aquiline,' I muttered automatically. George looked at me questioningly. 'The Stonehouse nose. Richard is just ahead of us.'

George groaned and was for riding off immediately, but we were famished and the smell of the innkeeper's boiled mutton was too much for us. Unwisely, we washed it down with his best barley beer, which he claimed was the strongest in England. I never used money to pay for our meals, but showed the ring and signed for what we had. For fear of thieves, I normally kept it in the knife holster in my boot. It was not there. I searched my pockets with increasing alarm. It was not just the doors that the ring opened for us; it was the worst possible omen to lose it. Or have it stolen.

'Is this what you're looking for?' George was holding out the ring to me. I almost snatched it from him in relief. 'I picked it up from the last inn where you left it and forgot to give it to you.'

'You are an honest fellow after all.'

'After all? What's that mean?'

The beer made it easier to be blunt about it. 'Well … I saw you going through my clothes last night …'

'And you thought I was a thief?'

He jumped up in a rage and said he might be a tailor but he had as much honour as any gentleman, and demanded satisfaction. It would have been easier to sleep in a bear pit than my house, he said. To calm himself down last night he had been looking at my clothes in a purely professional way.

'And, to be as blunt as you, sir, or my lord, or whatever you are, they do not serve.'

'Do not serve?'

'Mr Pepys was a good tailor, but, judging by the whip stitching, his eyes are gone. And the wine-red mockado suit –'

'Mockado! That is the very best grade of silk!'

'You may have paid silk, sir, but you got mockado.'

By this time we were outside in the yard, to prevent disturbing the inn, our hands trembling over the tops of our swords. The stable boy gaped at us. His feet were bare, as mine had been at his age, and in that instant I saw us as he did, as I had stared at gentlemen in the dockyard, arguing over the design or payment of a ship, and I began to laugh.

George drew his sword. 'You laugh at me, sir!'

'No, no, George, I am laughing at myself. Oh, George, I am in such a terrible muddle.'

And I told him what had led to the arguments in my house, and that I might have jumped to conclusions about Lucy just as I had about him being a thief, and he said, rather sheepishly sheathing his sword, that he had much the same fault. He had thought me an arrogant tongue-padder, which had coloured his remarks about my clothing. The quality was not in doubt, although he must be allowed to criticise the cut. He thought I was right in what I had said to my wife, for if a man could not control his wife, how could he control anything else? I told him he had the wisest head on the youngest shoulders I had ever come across. By this time we were the living proof of the landlord's claim that his beer was the strongest in England, and were convinced that misunderstanding others was the root of all evils.

A man on a fine dappled grey horse was leaving the stables and tipped his hat to us with a smile, seeming to agree with our conclusions, and we wished him goodbye. Even finding one of our fresh horses lame did not cloud our mood, although it delayed us until another was found.

It was mid-afternoon when we set off again. A heat haze clung over the road and the surrounding fields. We were less than half an hour from Holdenby, George reckoned, when he stopped to look for a scout whom Scogman had arranged to be here. There were signs of a tethered horse, but no scout. George said it was because we were late, but it made me feel uneasy. I wanted to stick to the main road because it was open country.

'And be seen?'

He rode down the forest path. Reluctantly, I followed him. The glare of the sun was cut off. Dazzling flashes of light were interspersed with shade. Eaton, Lord Stonehouse's one-time steward, had known forests. He had lived in them as a rejected, wild child. *Don't think,* he used to say. *Listen, look carefully, like an animal would. No one can move in the forest without leaving traces.* I beckoned to George to stop. He reined in impatiently. The path was still wide but ahead it narrowed, passing through a valley where trees climbed steeply on either side. Rising above one of the tallest, a number of crows were circling, crying harshly to one another.

'They don't like something,' I whispered.

'Us,' said George, in exasperation, but my unease got to him and he picked his way at a slow trot.

The crows began to settle, but I could see they did so some distance from their nests. A track ran upwards from the path, half overgrown with brambles and spindly saplings struggling to get up to the light. A couple were freshly broken, drawing my eyes along the path, where a breeze higher up the valley made a pattern of light and shade under the tree where the birds had their nests.

I pulled my pistol from the saddle holster and cocked it. The sound made George whirl round.

'The man at the last inn. On a dappled grey.'

I pointed up the slope with the pistol. It was well concealed and, unless you were looking for it, no one would spot the horse's flank.

'He lamed our horse at the inn. I should have realised. Richard Stonehouse knows his father's network. He must have learned of my escape. His mercenaries have been following us.'

George motioned me to silence. There was the sound of another horse approaching. The path we were on led into a clearing where there was a woodsman's hut and a pile of freshly chopped wood. From there it widened, the trees gradually thinning out. The mercenary could not have chosen a better spot for an ambush: high cover, looking straight down on open space.

George frowned as we listened to the approaching hoofbeats. 'Not a soldier,' he whispered.

The hoofbeats were not the regular drumming produced by a soldier who was at one with his horse. They were the jerky, spasmodic sounds of someone who did not ride with the horse but constantly urged it on then checked it. Yet he was in a hurry. The woodman? No, a civilian: there was the flicker of a brown coat before the path wound behind some trees.

George gripped my arm. Above us, nearer than I expected, the mercenary had appeared from behind a tree. He must have been distracted from hearing us by the approaching horse. He was close enough for me to see the dog lock and the engraved plate on his pistol, which he held loosely. He began to raise his pistol at the same time as I saw who the civilian was.

Nehemiah.

He had lost his hat. He was almost losing his reins, slipping from one side of the horse to the other. Before the pistol was trained I kicked my horse forward. Nehemiah galloped into the clearing. I kept two lines in my head: the line of the shot and Nehemiah's line across the clearing – inasmuch as you could call his erratic progress a line. I yelled – one long, screaming, ear-splitting yell.

A combination of the scream and my riding low on my horse across the clearing caused Nehemiah's horse to rear and throw its rider. In trying to control mine, I lost my pistol. I jumped from my horse to retrieve it, falling clumsily. In the confusion and the dust kicked up by the thrashing hooves the mercenary would have had to be very good to hit his target. He was better than that. He held his fire. Nehemiah, thrown on to a soft bank of leaves, was staggering about shouting incoherently.

Spitting dirt from my mouth, I began to scramble up to reach my pistol. My ankle gave way and I fell back. I heard the click of the dog lock. The mercenary had come further down the slope and I could see the rifling on the long barrel. Then it was obscured as Nehemiah moved into the line of sight, yelling furiously at me.

'Idiot! I-I came to warn you –'

I flung myself at him, knocking him down as the pistol went off. He went limp. His eyes were closed. A crashing, snapping of branches drew my eyes back to the slope. George had seized the pistol and wrestled the mercenary to the ground, gripping his wrists to hold him down.

Nehemiah sat up, looking blankly at the fighting men, his eyes staring, his face white. He was like a raw recruit: before battle cock-a-hoop, but turned by the first shots, noise and confusion into a rigid statue.

The mercenary was slowly twisting free from George's grip. I took a couple of limping steps and reached my pistol, but dare not risk a shot into the jerking, writhing bodies.

'Go and help him!' I cried to Nehemiah.

He looked vacantly at me. The mercenary had a hand free. George grabbed it but the mercenary was stronger, dragging his hand down towards the knife at his belt, inch by inch.

'Help him!' I screamed, yanking Nehemiah up and pushing him towards the slope. I hobbled after him as he ran up obediently enough. But when he reached them, he stood there impotently, shifting from one foot to another, with that same trance-like look. The mercenary pulled his hand free and snatched the knife. Only then did Nehemiah move. The mercenary slashed at him, catching him in the hand. The blow once again paralysed Nehemiah, but the distraction was enough for George to break free and kick the knife away.

By this time I had reached them and had the pistol trained on the mercenary. There was a silence, broken only by the raucous cries of the crows, wheeling slowly above us.

Nehemiah gazed at the blood oozing from his hand. 'He cut me.'

With his blond hair and pale blue eyes, the mercenary might have been German. Before he had recovered his breath, George had taken off the man's belt and secured his wrists.

'Where is Richard Stonehouse?'

The man smiled – the same affable smile he had given us at the inn near Bedford. 'Far from here. He has the King.'

'Liar!' I said. 'If he has the King, why are you here?'

'He *c-cut* me,' Nehemiah repeated softly, incredulously. He seemed to be in a world of his own, watching the blood drip from his hand. Suddenly he gave a cry, seized the knife and stabbed the mercenary viciously. If the man had not twisted away, the blow would have killed him. It ripped into his jerkin. Nehemiah aimed another blow and it took both George and I to pull him off. The mercenary spat towards Nehemiah. 'Madman!'

I cocked the pistol, levelled it at the mercenary, and asked him again where Richard was. Again he gave me that smile. During the war both sides used torture. It was routine but I never had the stomach for it. Perhaps that was why the mercenary smiled. He sensed it.

'Kill him,' said Nehemiah. He was gazing at the mercenary, pressing a handkerchief against his wound.

The mercenary's smile became fixed.

'We're wasting time!' George said. 'Holdenby is half an hour from here.'

I returned the pistol to my belt, picked up the knife and gave it to Nehemiah. The smile vanished from the mercenary's face. He was a handsome man, vain, careful and lucky enough to show few marks of his profession. There was a scar on his neck, but his face was unblemished.

'Take his eye out,' I said.

Nehemiah stared at me, then at the mercenary. It became so quiet we could hear the horses cropping grass below us. The crows settled in a nearby tree. Until Nehemiah moved, I never believed he would do it. When I saw his set expression, the curious, dislocated look in his eyes, I knew he would. He seemed to hypnotise the mercenary. George turned away.

'Leave him one eye,' I said. 'If he tells us what he knows.'

The mercenary lashed out and struggled. I jumped on him, sat on his legs, and held down his thrashing arms until gradually he weakened. Nehemiah approached him with the dedicated concentration of a surgeon. I looked away.

The mercenary screamed as Nehemiah brought the knife down. A trickle of blood ran down the mercenary's cheek, from a cut by the side of his eye. The crows rose, in a fluttering, barking chorus.

'I'll tell you, I'll tell you, I'll tell you!'

I pulled Nehemiah from him.

'The King is at Althorp.'

'Althorp?'

'Lord Spencer's seat,' George said. 'Twenty minutes away.'

The words poured out of the mercenary in a garbled stream. The King had been allowed to visit Althorp with a skeleton guard. Richard was there, waiting to take him north. His mercenaries were near Holdenby, prepared to engage and distract us.

'Waiting?' I said. 'You mean the King is still at Althorp?'

The mercenary rolled his eyes, staring up at the sky and the tops of the trees, round which the crows were still uneasily circling. Nehemiah made a move towards him.

'Keep him away,' the mercenary screamed.

'Leave him.' I snarled at Nehemiah so savagely he stumbled backwards. 'The King's still there?' I repeated to the mercenary.

'The last I hear. The King wished to finish his game of bowls, and Sir Richard Stonehouse deferred to His Majesty's pleasure. The English.'

He spat contemptuously.

22

Althorp lay calm and peaceful in the late afternoon sun that broke through clouds like beaten pewter. Lord Spencer had amassed farms, cottages, meadows and woods to create one of the greatest estates in the country. We saw more sheep than soldiers. Scogman licked his lips.

'Permission to speak, sir.'

'No. Touch one of those and –'

'You'll eat it?' he grinned.

I silenced him. We were scouts for our main party and had reached the top of rising ground to look down on an enormous park dotted with trees. It looked a timeless, idyllic setting for the largely Tudor mansion, with its red brick and tall twisted chimneys.

'Used to be a village down there,' Scogman said.

'How do you know?'

'Fought with a Northants man whose great-grandfather used to live there. Cleared to raise those sheep. All that's left is the village's name. Althorp.'

I signalled to George. Of his several hundred troops, he had left most below the rise, so they were not visible from the house. Now, he left two men at the top of the hill to watch our progress, and gave them instructions. He, Scogman and I then rode towards the house.

As we approached the lodge gate we were ordered to stop. When the guard saw that George was a member of Fairfax's cavalry, part of his own regiment, he was civil enough. But when George could not give a password, and refused to state his business without seeing an officer, the mood changed. Two more soldiers appeared, one with a pistol in his belt, the other with a pike. We were ordered to give up our swords. Scogman was reluctant, but George told him to undo his belt.

'Avoid bloodshed,' he muttered bitterly, echoing Cromwell's words.

The guard was sending for an officer when George saw a man crossing a window in the lodge house.

'Samuel,' he called. 'Sam.'

A fat, slow-moving man in a captain's uniform came out of the house, gaping at him in astonishment. 'George! What are you doing here?'

'Changing the guard, Sam.'

The captain stared at us. 'The devil you are.'

'Listen, Sam.'

George took him to one side. They walked up and down outside the lodge, George talking urgently. I heard him mention pay, and indemnity, and the captain, perspiring in the stifling heat, took his hat off, scratched his bald head and said this was not about Cromwell, was it, because as a good Presbyterian he hated Cromwell. Cromwell had nothing to do with it, George assured him. The matter was about a fair deal for the army. Then, unaccountably, there was something about wool, and George called me over and told me that Sam was the son of a London cloth merchant, who had tried, unsuccessfully, to get his soldiers to save a fellow merchant's bales of cloth from a fire.

'Then the ungrateful bastard accused me of stealing them! They were damaged, worthless – had to be dumped,' Sam said indignantly.

I nodded sympathetically, although I imagined, from his agitation, that the cloth had finished up in his father's warehouse as spoils of war. I showed him the indemnity ordinance I had produced at my regiment's muster, pointing out there was no provision for the King's signature. If he did ascend the throne, the ordinance would be invalid.

Sam perspired even more. 'God bless His Majesty, I say with the best of 'em,' he muttered. 'But he ain't too hot on signing – he ain't even signed the Presbyterian covenant yet. What are you waiting for?' he yelled to the soldier with the pike. 'Open the gate!'

He said he would take us to the man in charge of the garrison. We went past statues that were beginning to cast long shadows, down a long avenue lined by trees towards a garden walled by high hedges. From behind it came the chatter of conversation, punctuated by occasional bursts of applause. Soldiers guarded an entrance in the hedge. A tall, greying man with them gave us a long, penetrating stare. George's uniform and mine were torn and dirty from the fight with the mercenary. Scogman had never passed an inspection in his life.

Major-General Richard Browne was in overall charge of guarding the King. He had risen from the ranks, but had never fought in the New Model, and cared not a jot for its petitions, whispered Sam. He had come to revere the King to such an extent that, with his long hair and his carefully trimmed moustache and beard, he was beginning to look like him.

Sam looked about to melt altogether. His courage failed him under Browne's gaze and he began to mumble something about finding us in the grounds.

'Take them to the guard house. I'll deal with them later,' Browne snapped. He was turning away when George stepped forward. He saluted, bringing his heels together with the crack of a musket shot. 'Sir! Cornet George Joyce! At your service, sir.'

Browne turned slowly, giving him a wintry, amused smile. 'And what service would that be, Cornet Joyce?'

'Changing the guard, sir.'

The amusement left Browne's voice. He signalled to two of the soldiers at the hedge, who came forward, muskets drawn. 'Changing the –? I have no knowledge of this. Whose orders are you under?'

If George's salute was exemplary, it was outdone by his about turn. He pointed beyond the lodge gates, towards the rise we had ridden down. At the top was a troop of cavalry, their horses, apart from the occasional tossing head, held in quiet, orderly lines, their spurs, buttons and sword pommels glinting in the late afternoon sun. They flew the flag of Black Tom, the standard of Sir Thomas Fairfax, commander-in-chief of the Parliamentary army. They did so legitimately, for they were from his own cavalry unit, although Sir Thomas, a cautious, correct, man, would have been apoplectic if he had known it was put to this use.

'They are my orders, sir,' George said, pointing to the cavalry on the hill.

Browne looked from the cavalry to the three of us. At that distance, and since they were on the brow of the hill, he had no means of knowing whether we had a hundred horse or five hundred. A burst of laughter came from the gardens behind the hedges. Browne stopped the two soldiers approaching us. They lowered their muskets.

The sun went behind a dark-edged cloud. The air was still and oppressively heavy. Only on the hillside was there a sign of a breeze, fluttering the cavalry's standard. From behind the tall hedges came the click of bowls, followed by a groan of disappointment.

'My orders are that the King is not to be removed from Holdenby.'

'Exactly what we're here to prevent, sir. We had intelligence he was about to be removed.'

Richard appeared at the entrance to the gardens, staring towards the cavalry, then at me. Before anyone could stop me, I darted between the soldiers and through the entrance. A path took me between more hedges. It was like a maze. Chatter on one side of the hedge was followed by an eerie silence, then a burst of laughter.

At the opening to the green I stopped, bemused. It was as though the war had never happened, as though there had been no victory. The whole county had turned out to watch the King playing bowls. They watched him take a bowl, his thin fingers selecting the bias. They were being served iced drinks by a stream of servants. At one end of the green was a table laden with fruit. I could not see my father in the crowd. I went past an ostler holding a white horse being inspected by a man I recognised as Lord Montague, who was placing a bet with the Earl of Pembroke.

'Your Arab horse, against any two in my stable, that the King beats Sir Richard,' said Lord Montague.

My father had discarded the buff jerkin of the soldier for the wine-red doublet of a courtier. The garters on his britches and his shoes were decorated with huge bows in the same colour. As he laughed and joked with the King, he seemed to have been nothing but a courtier all his life. He looked directly at me as he picked up a bowl, smiled and waved.

Automatically, I found myself lifting my hand in return, then pulled it back. Richard smiled again. I cursed myself. Even in that small gesture, he seemed to have out-smarted me.

Until that moment, in my drab uniform I had gone unnoticed, people looking through me, as they did the servants. Now Lord Montague turned to me.

'Know Sir Richard, d'you?'

Before I could answer, the Earl of Pembroke dug Montague in the ribs, tapped his nose and whispered, 'Stonehouse beak.'

My cheeks burned as people stared at me. The chatter died as Richard walked up to bowl. More bets were placed.

A servant pressed an iced drink in my hand. It was laced with sweet white wine. After another glass I was convinced my father was going to win. The game took me over. Curiously, I found myself shouting for him. He had not been playing well and was behind in the last set, but had now caught up. It was neck and neck at the last jack and the King's bowl was close, but my father's looked better.

'Rub, rub, rub!' cried the crowd, the rub being the curve of the bowl towards the jack. It rolled confidently towards a point where it would squeeze snugly between the King's bowl and the jack, but at the last moment the rub of the green, some uneven tussock in the lawn, caused it to roll abjectly away to groans, then an uproar of cheers for the King.

I kept my eye on Richard but, far from slipping away, he beckoned me over. I felt for the comfort of my sword before remembering I had given it up. Then I saw George entering the garden with Sam and some other troopers. He gave me the thumbs-up. I walked across the lawn towards Richard. Browne was talking urgently to the King, who glanced towards the troopers entering the garden, then at me. Conversations began to die as people saw the troopers.

'Had my eye on that damned horse since –'

Lord Montague's bray of triumph stopped abruptly as he realised he was shouting into a growing silence. I lifted my hand to George. It was working in a way I had not dreamed possible. It was Cromwell who had put his finger on the fact that, although the soldiers guarding the King were Presbyterian and George's troopers Independents, they were all from the same regiment; with all their differences, they were comrades. Once again, it was Cromwell's intimate knowledge of his soldiers that had been the deciding factor – not to win a battle this time, but to avoid one. Without fuss, I could draw my father away from the crowd. With some of the troopers, I could take him to Cromwell while George guarded the King.

Richard smiled as I approached him. I felt a wave of cold anger. Anger not just because he had tricked me and made a fool of me, but by the way he had done it. He knew my weakness. It was only at that moment I fully admitted it to myself. Like anyone who does not know his parents, I had been searching not just for him, but for love. He had used that. He was still doing so. He took my breath away as his smile broadened and he opened his arms to me.

'Tom!' he cried.

He could make a bent coin ring true. But not for me. Not any more. Then he did the most obvious, most unexpected thing that took not only my breath away, but the power in my legs. It was, in what I could almost hear him saying in his impeccable French, a *coup de théâtre*.

He gave a deep, sweeping bow and said, 'Your Majesty … may I present my son.'

23

I had inked the King on woodblocks, seen him in the distance, in crowds, processions, in Parliament, in black armour in battle, in austere grief after Edgehill, with the weight of the dead bodies round his standard written into his countenance, seen him on paintings, coins and pamphlets; but I had never met him.

When his eyes met mine, the first shock was that they were so human. The next was that he was amused. It was not just that one usher snatched off my hat and another put me at the correct distance, or that I almost overbalanced as I bowed and was caught by a third. In normal circumstances an upstart bastard like me would never be presented to the King. In fact I was not being presented. I was a turn, an amusement – a *divertissement*, I heard someone say, as I straightened up. My anger flooded back when I saw the smiles. Lord Montague was openly guffawing.

With an act of simple graciousness that, in spite of all his faults, made me realise why people loved him and were prepared to die for him, the King quelled the laughter with a single look and spoke to me as if I was the only other person in the garden.

'Your father plays well.'

'But … but … not as well as you … Your Royal Majesty.' I finished in stuttered confusion, feeling the suppressed mirth around me. I groped for something to say. 'Your backhand draw in the last set was a master stroke.'

His eyebrows went up. 'You play?'

'His reputation is such that few dare play with him at The Pot,' Richard said, giving me the look of a proud father for his son.

'The Pot?'

'A fashionable bowling alley in London, Your Majesty. I have often wished to pit my poor skills against his,' he said wistfully. 'But … with the little differences between us …'

'Then so you shall!' the King said. 'Unless this … changing of the guard …' He looked towards George and the troopers, then at Browne.

George bowed. I bowed. Browne bowed. 'We are all at Your Majesty's pleasure.'

'Then more drinks. Set up the green.'

Lord Montague slapped me on the back, called me a fine fellow, and said his money was on me. He always backed the outsider.

A fine fellow! The wine sang in my head. Tom Neave may have walked across that lawn, but it was Thomas Stonehouse who had bowed to the King. Dizzily, I heard people placing bets. My reputation grew with the bets and the wine. So did that of The Pot, which, as no one wished to be ignorant of it, became the most fashionable bowling alley in London. Anything I said people seemed to find incredibly interesting or hilariously funny. Then I saw the troopers gazing at us: some awed, open-mouthed; others grinning, blank, brutalised, indifferent, waiting for the next order as they had done all their lives. But some faces, like George's and Scogman's, were different. They were not waiting for the next order. Their expressions were like a bucket of cold water. I grabbed my father and pulled him to one side.

'Stop this foolery.'

'Foolery!' The smiling mask slipped from his face. He levelled his finger at the troopers. 'That is foolery. You think you can take away the King with *that* rabble? The country will rise against you.'

I preferred his venom to his charm. I could deal with that. 'We are taking him back to Holdenby, where Parliament will negotiate with him.'

'The King will never do a deal with Parliament.'

I saw the King, smiling and laughing. I remembered the grace with which he had stopped people laughing at me. I suddenly felt, in a giddy surge of optimism, that he could be reached, and I might have a hand in it.

'He will. Once he is away from people like you.'

He smiled. 'Now you have met him, you fancy yourself as a diplomat, do you? You are more like a common constable. What do you plan to do with me?'

'Take you to London.'

'To Cromwell.'

'Yes.'

He smiled and gestured towards the green. 'In that case, you must grant me my dying wish.'

'Save me the mock heroics –'

He turned from the green and gave me a look, stripped of all mannerisms, that cut off my words and dried my mouth. Cromwell would kill him. He would have no compunction – after racking him to get what he could out of him.

'Choose your woods, gentlemen!'

Browne, the jack in his hand, the bowls at his feet, was standing at one end of the green. The guests were jostling into position in a semi-circle round it, their high-pitched chatter dwindling into a buzz of speculation, crowned by the King staring expectantly at us.

That was what finally drew me into the game. Not Richard, nor the wine, the stifling heat, nor the applause, although it was all of those. It was the realisation, as we bowed to the King, that Parliament had to do more than secure the King. It had to secure his goodwill, his mind, his agreement. It was the feeling I might play a tiny part in this which led to me picking up a bowl, weighing it in my hand

and feeling the bias with my fingers. I was drawn into, not playing bowls, simply, but one of the oldest sports in the world: winning the King's favour.

'You're limping,' my father said.

'It doesn't affect my grip.' I had bound up my ankle, so my limp was now slight.

Lowering clouds were edged with black when my father put down the first jack. The game was the best of seven sets. We had three bowls each, and in each set the winner was the one whose bowl came closest to the jack. As soon as the first bowl left my fingers I knew it was bad. So did the audience.

'Short, short, short!'

My next bowl, to great groans, was long and ended in the ditch. My eye had gone, and rust had eaten into my fingers, whereas I could see my father was much better than he had pretended to be with the King. His long fingers seemed to stay with the bowl, curving it, magically slowing it as it approached the jack. He won the first set easily. And the second. I burned with shame when I saw the King, eyebrows lifting, say something to Lord Montague. What a fool I was still to be so full of dreams! Get the King's favour! An agreement for Parliament! From being restless, the audience went to outright derision. I wanted to disappear into the ground.

I had taken off my jerkin and my shirt clung to my back. The low sun came out, heat bouncing from the strip of green grass, blurring my vision.

'Make a show of it,' Richard murmured in my ear.

He had given me an easy shot. Out of sheer pique I would not take it, flinging down the bowl anywhere, just wanting this ridiculous game to be over.

'Come on, sir! Come on, Tom!'

Scogman. Through the sweat dribbling from my eyebrows, I saw that the troopers had moved closer, to form part of the audience behind me. They had been given some beer. The green seemed to vanish, and become the London clay of The Pot. I could almost smell the beer and the Virginia of the pipes as I measured up for my final bowl of the third set. Richard had two bowls close to the jack and one, the easy lay, two feet from it, giving me a safe curve in. But I was unlikely to beat one of his bowls, almost touching the jack. Instead I drove my bowl straight at the pair. I gave it too much. It hit my father's bowls with a resounding thwack, sending them into the ditch. My bowl and the jack teetered on the edge.

'Stop, stop, stop …' yelled the troopers.

My bowl fell back on to the green, taking the jack with it to nestle against it. There was a huge, collective sigh from the crowd. The troopers flung their hats in the air.

'Lucky,' said Richard, but not without the tinge of admiration of the inveterate gambler for someone who takes an outlandish risk which comes off.

'Two sets to one,' said Browne.

In that magical way life has, from having felt an abject failure, I now believed I could do nothing wrong. My head cleared. My eyes were connected to my fingers. The bowls seemed part of me. Richard rose to it. We were evenly matched. Every time one of us picked up a bowl there was complete silence, to be followed, at the finish of a set, by an explosion of sound.

I won the next to level the score, which rattled him. Beyond the hills there was a brief flicker of lightning, followed by a low mutter of thunder. The shadows were lengthening. Deep patches of light and shade crept across the grass, making it difficult to judge some throws. My eye was younger and keener than his. He made up for this with the cunning of his shots, but the concentration was beginning to tell. More and more, he took the handkerchief from his sleeve to wipe his brow and sticky hands. When I went ahead at three-two, the crowd sensed that Richard was beaten. His whole posture suggested it. So did his position in the next set, with his first two bowls wide and my three clustered close, hiding the jack from any direct strike. So did his third bowl, which he sent impossibly wide, to sighs of finality and the beginning babble of conversation, which, however, was abruptly silenced. The bowl was curving in, almost describing a half circle, drawn to the jack like an iron filing to a magnet.

'Rub, rub, rub, rub!' the crowd cried – then held its breath as the bowl wobbled to a stop, before gently completing its journey to kiss the jack.

'Three sets all,' said Browne, in his methodical, pedantic voice.

The crowd roared as my father flung up his arms in an ecstasy of relief and triumph.

I stared at the bowl, still trembling against the jack, with awe and disbelief. 'Not bad for an old man.'

'Better than you can do, you young bastard.'

There was no venom in the word. Quite the opposite. He was grinning all over his flushed face, looking almost boyish as he suddenly laughed. It was infectious. I laughed with him. The applause seemed to die away; the crowd vanished. It was as if we had always been there, in this sort of English garden, on this kind of evening in summer. A note I had never heard before, or expected to hear, crept into his voice: awkwardness, the embarrassment of parental concern.

'Tom … whatever happens … you belong here …' He gestured towards the King and his favourites, who were taking drinks during the break.

Scogman, who, with others, was sitting on the lip of a fountain, where they could dip their heads in the cooling spray, raised his pot to me.

'Not,' I said, 'with those mean fellows.'

'Listen –'

'I'm listening no more to your lies! Tricks –'

'Tricks?'

I laughed with incredulity at his look of injured innocence. 'You tricked me in London to raise an army!'

'Of course I did.' His tone was heated. 'D'you think I would tell you what I was doing and betray my King? Tom –'

'Don't Tom me. You told Challoner to kill me –'

'I wish I had,' he burst out with sudden savagery. 'I told him if he touched you I would kill *him*. You blundered in there, spying. You heard what you wanted to hear, as you always do. His men were throwing you in a cart to take you away and kill you.'

The night when Challoner had drugged me came back to me. What I thought had been the nightmare of the plague cart had been no nightmare.

'I stopped him.' He looked bitterly towards the troopers. 'More fool me.'

'Three sets all,' said Browne, in a flat, neutral tone, as if he had seen or heard none of this. 'Final set.'

We both became abruptly aware that everyone had fallen silent, watching the violent argument as avidly as they followed the game. My father would not meet my eyes. He looked disorientated, hangdog, as if he had confessed to some shameful crime. He had. He had failed in his duty to his King.

'Play,' Browne said.

I felt the first spot of rain on my cheek as my father bowed to the King, then went up to the mark, put down the jack and selected his first bowl. His knee bent, he drew back the bowl, but he never released it. He released himself. I was a second after him. Only a second, but it was enough. He was over the ditch, turning, flinging the bowl over the grass. It caught me between my legs. Somehow I kept my balance on the lawn but tripped over the ditch. My ankle gave way again and I crashed into the table of fruit, which the servants were running to clear as the rain hammered down, pulping a bowl of peaches. My hands were sticky with the crushed fruit as I prised myself up.

My father was untethering the Arab horse. George sent troopers after him but they were impeded by Browne and the courtiers, running across the lawn for shelter. A vivid flash of lightning arrested everyone's movements and lit up my father, already halfway across the park, vaulting across a stream before disappearing into the growing darkness.

'Three all,' Browne said, hair plastered to his inscrutable face. 'Game postponed.'

24

Recriminations began as soon as we took the King back to Holdenby. I was blamed for Richard's escape. A game of bowls! How stupid was that? I had put the whole project at risk! We held the King, but for how long? Nehemiah was open about it. George said nothing, but his silences were just as eloquent. At first I dismissed their fears. We had a considerable force. Richard had only his mercenaries. It would take days for him to put extra Royalist forces together. George's messenger was already halfway to London, telling Cromwell we had the King, and we were awaiting instructions.

The truth was I was only half-listening. I was still thinking of my father. Even though I smarted from the way he had tricked me again, even though he was devious, untrustworthy, dishonest, and my future depended on me taking him back to Cromwell, I could not help admiring his style, his charm, his courage. It was more than that. In those few minutes on the lawn, hadn't he given me the childhood I never had?

'Whatever happens, you belong here …'

He had indicated the King, the court. I went over every look, every word, expanding a few minutes into a might-have-been childhood. And what is a childhood without a hero? And what hero is better than a mounted knight? It was not just me. At a time of signs and portents, for both court and troopers that flash of lightning, burning him briefly into vision on, of all things, a white horse, turned him into an omen.

Holdenby played its part in this trance. It was built for a monarch. Its towers, gables and stately ascent from the vast hall to the great chamber were built by a knight in the hope that Queen Elizabeth would favour him with a visit. She never came. The first royal visitor, King Charles, entered as a prisoner. And Parliament granted him the kind of sumptuous court to which he was accustomed before the war.

Holles, eager to strike a deal, ensured that the Parliamentary Commissioners were people he liked – the Earls of Pembroke and Denbigh and Lord Montague from the Lords, and Browne from the Commons. His gaolers were his most loyal subjects. They spared nothing in restoring the King's household to what it had been.

Even Scogman, who had a discerning eye for such things, was too stunned to put a value on the silver plate. It was all the more dazzling because most houses and palaces, including the King's, had been denuded of it, melted down to pay for the war. Now Parliament had approved the melting down of Communion plate from the King's chapel at Whitehall, so the King could eat from silver.

He was served by cupbearers and waiters, who brought wine and dishes from stewards and cooks running a small army of carvers, turn-bouches, porters, scourers and knaves of the boiling house, larder, poultry, scalding house, pastry, wood-house and scullery. His every need was met by another army of gentleman ushers, pages, grooms, messengers, clerks, barbers, apothecaries and physicians.

'What would have happened if he had won?' said Scogman in awestruck tones.

I marvelled not only at the stupendous luxury, but the King's frugality in the midst of it all. He ate and drank little. A poached egg was brought to him every morning after he had prayed and studied. He walked the green, open terraces in good weather and, endlessly, through chamber after spacious chamber of the east wing in bad. Only then did prison bars become visible; then, and when he refused to attend the service of Presbyterian ministers in the chapel, and at meals insisted on saying his own Anglican blessing.

The price of this relative freedom, and the restoration of his household, was that he had given his word not to escape.

His word. As someone who had only found out who he was through a maze of lies, that to me was the most precious jewel in this glittering palace. I was entranced by this honesty, by the aristocratic code. A man of honour might refuse to swear an oath in court, or to sign a contract. His word was deemed sufficient. To break it was to lose his honour. To lose that was to lose his standing, his life as a gentleman. That was why there were no bars. No close guards. Why George and his troopers melted deferentially into the background. And that was why, on the second day at Holdenby, when I had been so seduced by the court, and the people who lived by this code, I was in a position to hear the word.

Escape.

I had put on my one fine shirt and doublet, somewhat travel-stained, but in that large court, where there were as many gentlemen as the crowd at the 'Change, I passed. On this second day, I sat in the library, not to read, but in the hope of seeing the King, in order to practise my diplomacy.

I had seen the remains of his poached egg – he had left most of the white – on its way back to the kitchen. The wind had changed and there was more rain in the air. Shortly the King would pass the library on his way to the east wing. I was not there to catch a look, or even a favour. I burned with an idea. In the teeth of Presbyterian disapproval, the King read his blessing from the Book of Common Prayer. It was because I left that book out that Mr Tooley had been ejected from his church and, I believed, my daughter Liz had died as a result. Yet half the parish had turned out at night to hear Mr Tooley read from the book at her baptism and funeral. The people wanted it. Cromwell had it on his desk. He talked of nothing else but toleration for 'tender consciences'. The King and Cromwell were closer than they thought. What held them apart was the suspicion of old wounds. If only they could be brought together! So I was musing when I heard voices.

Wanting no distraction, I hid myself in a book. I was in a high-backed chair and they did not see me. I recognised the penetrating bray of Lord Montague. He was talking to the Earl of Denbigh.

'Upstart young bastard! Thought I was betting on *him*! My money's on you, young fellow!'

They choked with laughter. 'The Pot!'

'What and where on earth is it?'

'Some stinking alehouse in the stews. He really believed we thought he was Sir Francis Drake.'

They came into view, their backs towards me. I buried my hot face in the book, peering over the edge of it. Denbigh wiped his eyes. 'Cost you a horse.'

'Cost you your bet Richard wouldn't get away. You owe me that Welsh border land.'

'Damn close,' Denbigh said. 'Richard had to spin it out. Make a game of it. And you were lucky with the weather.'

'Lucky? Part of the plan. Defeating the New Model Army by running not out of, but *into* the rain!'

They mimicked running round in confusion, slapping each other's backs in glee, before Montague put his arm confidentially round Denbigh's shoulder. He dropped his voice, and steered Denbigh towards a door leading to the long gallery where the King walked. 'I'll show you where we'll do it, old friend. Now we've managed Richard's escape we must –'

As he opened the door I craned forward, letting the book slip down. He must have heard the movement, for he whirled round as I put the book up. If my anger had surfaced then I would have confronted them. But it was drowned in humiliation.

I heard them leaving. 'That was him,' Denbigh said.

'No, no,' Montague said. 'Couldn't possibly have been him. He was reading a book.'

There could have been no greater contrast between the palace and our quarters, although they were but a stone's throw away. They stank not only of the servants' privy but of the huge pile of night soil that accumulated from the palace. I flung myself on my bed. What a dupe I was! Presented to the King! I writhed at the thought of the contempt, the laughter, of Montague and the rest.

I must have fallen asleep. Scogman was shaking my shoulder. I heard the word 'messenger' and stumbled after him into the yard, thinking we had heard from Cromwell.

A light rain was falling. George was helping one of his troopers from his horse. A nearby pool was threaded with blood. We took him to my bed as it was the nearest, and attended to his wound, a sabre cut in the arm. It had missed the bone, but he had lost a lot of blood. He was not the messenger from Cromwell we expected, but one of our scouts. Gradually we pieced his story together.

He had lost his bearings in a stretch of forest. Emerging twenty, perhaps as much as thirty miles away, he had come to a large sheep farm, where he was berated by the farmer for stealing sheep. He managed to convince the farmer he was looking for directions, not sheep, and learned that a number of men had 'requisitioned' a dozen sheep 'in the King's name'. On his way back, the trooper had been attacked by a man who sounded like one of Richard's mercenaries. George doubled the guard, complaining that the task, difficult enough because the house was huge and rambling, was made impossible by the troops having to keep their distance.

They began meeting without me. It was growing dark when, crossing the stable yard, I heard voices raised in argument coming from the tack room, which we had taken over as a staff room.

PETER RANSLEY

Standing round a bench, where the ostler normally repaired harnesses and saddles, were George, Nehemiah and Scogman. There was an uneasy silence when I came in, eventually broken by George.

'It's the bloody sheep that worry me,' he muttered.

'Sheep?'

'Why would Richard want a dozen sheep? It's enough to feed a small army.'

'He hasn't got an army.'

'Exactly.'

It was never the facts, always few and mostly inadequate, that decided things. Decisions were made from beliefs, interpretations, stretched nerves. Poyntz's northern army, which Holles controlled, was believed to be a hundred miles to the north, but the distance shrank in our imaginations.

There was another awkward silence. Rain pattered on the roof of the musty tack room. George trimmed a candle.

'It's my fault,' I said. 'I got too close to my father.'

George trimmed the already trimmed candle. Scogman became intensely interested in some horse brasses, rubbing one up with his sleeve. Only Nehemiah looked directly at me, his arms folded, his face expressionless.

'Sometimes … I don't know where I am … which side I'm on,' I went on.

There was the sound of a horse. George went to the door and peered out into the gloom, more from habit now than hope. He returned to pick up the candle. 'Guard change at the lodge.'

Cromwell's messenger was more than a day overdue. Something had happened to him or, worse, to Cromwell.

I pulled the candle away from George, lit it from another and stuck it on the bench. 'You're better off without me,' I said.

* * *

196

I went to my room, half falling on to the bed, before remembering the wounded trooper. I walked round and round, like the King pacing the east wing. No. Not like him at all. He knew where he was. What he stood for. Which side he was on.

I had woken the trooper, who groaned he was thirsty. I went across the yard to get some small beer. The moon was almost full, glittering in pools, etching the gables of the palace against the sky. I tried to put myself into my father's mind. He might be raising an army, but he would not use it to snatch the King. He wanted to avoid a fight, in which the King might be harmed, as much as we did. He would use his elite band of mercenaries to assist the King's escape, then take him to the army.

It might be tonight. Or tomorrow at first light – somewhere like the east wing, where the King walked, the part most difficult to watch and guard.

I got beer from the kitchens, where cooks, stripped to the waist from the heat of roasting a pig, swallowed great jugs of it. One swore at me as I stopped abruptly in his path.

Was the King's escape already arranged from the inside? Was that what Montague and Denbigh were about to discuss when they saw me in the library? I still believed the King would not break his word. But he might be persuaded to if he thought his life was in danger.

I went back into the yard. Candles were still burning in the tack room. I watched George, Scogman and Nehemiah arguing, passing backwards and forwards before the lighted windows. *You're not one of them*, my father had said. *You belong here.* With the nobles, the gentlemen, superior in every way, with their code of honour.

Honour. Was it not the greatest of all confidence tricks? They persuaded everyone else they alone had it. People doffed their hats to it. Sat behind it in church, every man in his place. But was not honour merely a name they stuck on something everyone had? Ever since my printer's runner days, when I had run from Parliament taking Mr Pym's words from Mr Ink to Mr Black, I had been one small link in a chain of people who all had what they called honour. I only knew what it was when I saw from the faces of George and the others that I had lost it. Trust.

My father was wrong. I did not belong to him and his gentlemen. But nor was I with the men in the tack room. I returned to the trooper, propping him up until he had drunk enough, and calming him until he fell into an uneasy, feverish sleep.

I picked up my pack with the intention of placing it as a pillow on the floor, but the movement brought back to me so strongly the times when, with just a pack on my back, I had taken to the road, that I felt an intense urge to do so; an urge to become no one, or anyone I chose to be. I felt this so keenly, that when there was a sound at the door my hand flew to my knife as swiftly as when I was on the run.

It was Scogman. He looked at the pack. Did he think I was going off to join my father? I could not bear that. I threw the pack down. I had walked enough. I would only find answers, if there were any answers, by staying where I was, facing up to what I had done.

'I think they will try to take the King in the next forty-eight hours. They're not going to wait to raise an army.'

Scogman took a clay pipe and slowly filled it while I told him what I had heard in the library. Clattering and shouting floated across the yard from the kitchens. They were clearing the meal. Soon the King would be retiring. Scogman struck a flint. It took several attempts before he lit his clay to his satisfaction.

'Tell the other two.'

'They won't believe me! They think I'm one of them.'

'So you are.' He puffed vigorously at his clay until the tobacco glowed.

'You too,' I said bitterly.

Placidly he watched the sweet-smelling smoke drift up to the ceiling. 'And you're not.'

'Thanks. That's a great help.'

He shrugged. 'Helped me.'

'What do you mean?'

'Wouldn't be here if you weren't both sir and Tom, would I? You wanted me hanged. Until you saw who was going to hang me. Then when the troopers thought you were on their side, you whipped the bloody daylights out of me and some sense into me.' He contemplated the eddying smoke with deep satisfaction. 'Wouldn't be here, Tom, sir, if you'd been on anybody's side, would I? You're your own side. Your own man.'

I stared at him for a long while as he drew contentedly on his clay. It was as if I had been trying key after key in a door, only to discover it had been open all the time. Ever since I had been taken up river from Poplar to Mr Black's I had been searching. For who I was. For my father. Or someone to take his place. Matthew. Mr Black. Mr Pym. Cromwell. And, finally, Richard. Always seeking. Approval. Permission. Who was I? Whose side was I on? I was Tom Neave. I was on my own side.

I went across the yard and into the kitchens. Eating their own meal, the bare-chested cooks turned to stare at me as I stood in front of the fire where the remains of the pig, cut in places to the bone, were still turning. I pulled off the signet ring with such force I scraped the flesh from my finger.

One of the cooks got up as I dropped the ring into the fire. The falcon's wings glowed, spreading as if it was about to fly out of the fire. It must have been a gobbet of fat falling from the pig, but as the ring disappeared into the flames there was a sudden hissing, a spitting of sparks which made the cook jump in fear, and cross himself.

25

They stood round the bench in the tack room staring at me in silence, Nehemiah's and George's faces furrowed in deep suspicion. Scogman pursed his lips, knocking out his pipe against his heel, although the bowl was long empty.

'Take the King?' George said. 'Where?'

'South,' I said. 'Towards a city garrisoned by the New Model. Oxford, possibly.'

They all talked across one another.

'Kidnap the King?'

'You're mad.'

'Take him by force?'

'Cromwell would hang us.'

'He'll hang us if we lose him.'

A dog on a nearby estate farm barked incessantly until someone shouted at it.

'It's just what they want,' Nehemiah said. 'If we take the King by force it gives them every e-excuse to attack us.'

'The same applies to us,' I said. 'We fear for the King's life. *They* have given us every excuse to take the King to a place of safety!'

The dog began barking again. One of the soldiers on guard began barking back, which sent the dog into a frenzy. George rounded on me. 'Cromwell told us we must not hurt a hair of his head. I will not lose my neck for another of your crazy ideas.'

'Nobody will touch him. You will point out the danger. Say it's urgent to move.'

'And he'll come. Just like that, will he?' Nehemiah laughed.

I hesitated. The King said he loved his people. He did not know his people, but he believed he did. He was good at small kindnesses: I still felt a warmth towards him for silencing the crowd when I did my clumsy bow. And there were stories that he treated laundresses and cooks' wives with a concern and consideration he never showed to lords and ladies. He was obstinate. But the converse of that was that he was impulsive. It might work. It just might. It was how we presented it that mattered. It was all about belief, words, as it was at the beginning when I had run with Mr Pym's speech, believing the words were magic that could change the world. They were. They could. Or so I still believed.

'No. He won't come like that,' I said to Nehemiah. 'We offer him advice.'

'And the King is going to accept *your* advice?' George said.

'No. Yours.'

'Mine?'

'I can't do it. I'd be seen as Cromwell's man. Or Lord Stonehouse's. You are the people.'

Nehemiah swept off his hat mockingly. 'Bow the knee, *Ch-Charles*, to George Joyce, Cornet –'

'Shut up, Nehemiah,' George snapped. He gave me a look, half dismissive, half wanting me to go on.

'You tell him he is in great danger. It's true. He knows it. Let me guess. He knows about the plot to "rescue" him. His life for the past five years has been nothing but plots, with conflicting advice, mostly bad. Is Richard's "rescue" any different? He must have doubts about it. Whereas you can speak from the heart, and you have the people with you.'

'The troops.'

'Yes. The troops. The *people*. His people.'

George was still. A tiny drop of sweat oozed from his forehead. I watched it trickle down his cheek and disappear into his small, neat beard. He did not move a muscle. Nehemiah studied his nails. The only movement came from the flickering candles. Even the smoke from Scogman's pipe seemed to hang motionless in the air.

The crack of a musket made us duck instinctively. Nehemiah collided into George. Saddles fell to the floor and candles went over. In the sudden darkness, I grabbed for my pistol. Scogman, drawing his sword, was first outside. Troops were stumbling from their quarters where they had been eating. Cooks emerged from the kitchen. At the distant farm the dog was barking frantically. One of the cooks jeered at our swords and pistols.

'Either the farmer's killed the fox, or he's shot that bloody dog,' he said.

It seemed we had been alarmed over nothing, and we walked back towards the tack room. As we did so, George turned to me.

'I will speak to the King,' he said. 'But only if the soldiers agree.'

But the soldiers, grumbling and jumpy, were returning to finish their meal. 'Only if they agree?' I echoed disbelievingly. 'By the time you have a polite chat with everyone, Richard will have spirited the King away!'

'They're the people,' George replied coldly. 'As you said. We decided to risk our lives together at the very beginning when we snatched the artillery train at Oxford, and we will make this decision together.'

George was scrupulous. He went round everyone, small groups, larger groups, speaking and listening gravely. One minute I was humbled by their reactions, the next fearful that Richard would strike. Humbled, because in Drury Lane, working for Lord Stonehouse, I had not seen what was happening in front of my eyes. Most of the troopers who had come with George were a select group

– not because they had been selected, but because they had selected themselves. They were what peers, magistrates and landowners saw as the biggest threat of all – masterless men. As the men who ruled saw it, first a man obeyed his father, then his master. That was how God the Father had ordained the world. Break that iron law of obedience and the world would collapse.

The New Model, in a way neither the nobles nor the gentry had intended or expected, had become a huge army of masterless men. They thought for themselves. They had been forced to.

I knew now why I had flung the ring in the fire. I had been brought up by a masterless man, in that great festering pool of them, London Without. When Mr Pym had given me his speeches to stir up the crowd, those men had spilled into the City. Once the genie was out of the bottle, no one could put it back.

On the run in Essex, Scogman had become part of another huge pool of masterless men, forced by enclosures to the Without of the parish and the lord. There, they lived on wastes, heaths, commons and forests, where they squatted until driven on – a mixture of tramps, casual labourers, carters, weavers, joiners, travelling craftsmen, cobblers, knife-sharpeners, players, jugglers, gipsies, cunning men, pedlars and mechanic preachers.

Among needles and thread, the pedlars had brought pamphlets. Craftsmen, who had lost their jobs during the war, turned to preaching. Quakers, Baptists, Independents of all kinds, they were religion Without; their churches, for people who never dared to enter or were not allowed inside one, were the wastelands and forests. Pamphlets and preaching had taught them it was the end time. They should prepare for a new world, or the next. The devastation of the war confirmed it.

These pools of masterless men became a great sea in the New Model Army. It had its share of rogues, thieves and cowards, but Cromwell promoted the God-fearing independent from Without, who believed in what he fought for, over a gentleman who was nothing else. The best of these were in the cavalry. And the best of those had joined George Joyce in his ride north.

I looked at them as if I had never seen faces before. Carved by war and weather, they had the texture of tree trunks. I was humbled by their penetrating questions and their trust in one another. Some prayed. Some consulted the Soldier's Bible they carried in their packs. But they made up their minds quickly, as men do when they live from hand to mouth and a delay could be fatal.

'Are you for it, Ben?'

'Aye. The Lord be with us.'

'Joshua?'

'All for one, George.'

Joshua was a carpenter, a forest man, who was always whittling a piece of wood he kept in his pocket. He never could think deep, he said, unless he was 'a-whittling'. He was convinced the wood did the thinking for him, making its own shape. This one came out a soldier, which decided him on the enterprise. When I said he looked like my son, Luke, he declared, 'Luke he be,' and gave me the doll. Thus, by a mixture of thought and faith, religion and magic, everyone reached a decision. There were no dissensions.

It was as if they had all gone there with the specific purpose of taking the King. Where, they did not know. Neither did they know where it would take them.

In his sombre garb, Nehemiah had been roaming the palace. Among the huge staff, he had been taken for a clerk. He had even been given a message to take to the groom of the King's chambers. Before the groom dismissed him, he had caught a snatch of a violent argument between Lord Montague and the Parliamentary Commissioner, Browne.

'Those rebels are planning something!' he heard Montague saying. 'We must act earlier. Give my man the key!'

Cloud drifted over the moon. George put what guard he could round the palace, but the men were thinly spread. The bulk of his force was camped outside the lodge gates. He pinned his hopes on persuasion and did not dare bring in a larger, more threatening number, for fear of overplaying his hand.

There were more than a hundred windows in the palace. Candles burned in most of them as I approached with George and Nehemiah, but the east wing, where I had sat in the library, was plunged in gloom.

I jumped as a figure came out of the darkness of some trees. Joshua.

'Listen!'

We could hear nothing, but he was a man of the forest, who could not only hear the crackle of leaves, but see in the sound the animal who walked on them.

'There.'

For a moment, as the clouds drifted away from the moon, we saw, silhouetted against the sky, someone not entering but leaving. A slim figure in court livery, scarcely more than a boy. We heard him then, running like a hare. No use shouting. He could be desperate to see a girl. Or deliver a message. They must act earlier, Montague had said. The stables were guarded, but the boy could run to Althorp for a horse.

We entered the east wing and approached the King's chambers. Browne saw us and told us we could not go any further. I stared down the long gallery, out into the darkness where the boy had run off. I went through the library and out of the door Montague had used before he saw me that morning. Almost opposite was a door, which should have been locked. It was open. We called Joshua and Ben, the guard on the other side of the gallery. They swore the door had been locked when they tried it.

A grumbling servant went to a board on which hung various keys. The key for the gallery door was missing. Browne was shocked and agitated. He was a stiff, upright man and I thought his agitation genuine. Perhaps the argument with Montague that Nehemiah had witnessed was a disagreement over the escape plan: Browne, cautious, correct, thinking it too dangerous; Montague, much more of a gambler, deciding to go ahead anyway. Speculation was useless. Browne would say nothing except that we could not disturb the King, who was at his devotions.

'Very well,' George said. 'Joshua. I don't want your men in the open. Place them in the library. We'll welcome them from there. And from here, Tom ...' He opened the door to a passage which led to the steward's quarters.

I had stripped off my rank and was dressed as an ordinary redcoat. I pulled out my pistol. 'I can cover the stairs and the gallery.'

Browne's face looked drained of blood. 'You cannot fight here!'

'You give us no option.'

The calmer George became, the higher Browne's voice rose. 'You have no right to be here at all!'

'We have the right to protect our King, sir.'

The sharp tinkling of a bell came from within the royal apartments, followed by a murmur of voices. Browne bit his lip and hurried inside. George put out his boot to stop the door closing. Tapestries of Tudor hunting scenes hung on the wall, no doubt put there when the original owner hoped Elizabeth would stay. A smell of fresh lavender lingered in the air. On a marble table a lantern clock showed the hour of ten. The smell, and the hunters on the tapestries with their raised lances, were an invisible barrier that made it seem sacrilegious to go further. George looked at me. We had no means of knowing whether there was another exit through which the King might have been taken.

George drew his sword and plunged forward, first into one room, then another. He stopped abruptly in a start of terror. A candle or two were barely lit. From the dim shadows a ghost-like figure appeared. Only when a candle burned up did he see the familiar face of the King. Even then, the King's white nightdress, and his face still fixed with sleep, continued the illusion of a spirit until he spoke.

'Who are you?'

'Your Majesty,' George stuttered. 'I-I come to protect you.'

'Protect me. Or kill me?'

George became aware of his sword. He sheathed it. From the hall outside, as another candle was lit, I could now see the servant picking up the silver bell by which he had been summoned. Browne stood stiffly erect in the shadows by the red silk bed.

'You must leave, Your Majesty,' George said.

'Now?'

'First light. This place is not safe. There is a plan to abduct you.'

'Abduct? How do I know *you* are not trying to abduct me?'

George drew himself up. His voice lost its confused tone and became passionate. 'We have no reason to do so. We are not your advisers. We are your people. Every man I have is loyal to you and will protect you with his life.'

The King smiled. Perhaps it was George's youth, his passion, which suddenly made Charles more amused than apprehensive. 'Not my advisers, you say. My bad advisers, you mean?'

George said nothing. He stood unmoving, as if on parade, as the King walked up to him. 'Well, I have had my fill of advice, that is true. Quite true.' He looked at George's uniform, then his face. 'You are a cornet.'

George stood even more stiffly. 'Yes, Your Majesty.'

The King turned to Browne. 'These are your men, General?'

'They are from the same regiment as the previous guard, Your Majesty.'

The King seemed amused by Browne's discomfort, his tortuous choice of words. 'Different bread may be made from the same wheat,' he said drily.

His mood changed again abruptly. He moved restlessly about the room, as if there was no one there but his familiar servant. 'What is the hour, James?'

'Just after ten, Your Majesty.'

'Did I have so little sleep? It felt longer.'

Those stories were right. He treated his servants with a courteous gentility. Perhaps it was because they posed no threats, offered no advice. It was more than that. He had been without the Queen he loved and his children for five years. His servants and companions had become his family. James picked up the Book of Common Prayer from his bedside. No, the King did not want that. James anticipated the King's pacing, moving a chair, placing a cordial where it might be needed. The King's mood switched sharply again. He turned to George.

'I will go on three conditions. One, you promise not to harm me.'

'We will not harm a hair of your head, Your Majesty.'

George spoke with such youthful indignation that the King had felt it necessary to stipulate this, the monarch laughed. 'I doubt you can promise quite that. I have lost a few of those hairs and, no doubt, will lose a few more. My second condition is that you must not ask me to do anything against my conscience.'

George's fervour was as outright as his indignation.

'Your Majesty, you are with men who own their consciences. Your conscience is your own.'

This time the King's broadening smile had no trace of patronage. 'A good answer for a cornet. For a general, perhaps, eh, Browne?'

Browne said nothing.

'Perhaps too good for a general, or a King, for that matter, who has seen too much,' the King muttered. 'But I have a third condition. I must have my household and my Parliamentary Commissioners with me.'

'Readily, Your Majesty,' George said.

The speed with which he agreed seemed to disconcert the King rather than reassure him. He stood stock still, staring into space. It was as if he was seeing the ghosts of similar scenes passing before his eyes.

* * *

Whether the King slept again, I do not know. Few people did as chests were packed and horses checked. There was one alarm during the night. The boy Joshua had seen was caught slipping back over the wall with a message for Montague. It said: 'Plan changed. Have fresh forces and will surround Holdenby.' It was signed Stonehouse.

'We've left it too late,' George muttered.

'The King will ride with us,' I said.

'Are you crazy? He might be killed!'

But to his astonishment, in the grey, early light, when the King was shown a black stallion from the stables his eyes lit up. His favourite painting was of himself in full armour. He loved the activity, the half-darkness, the barely open eyes, the stumbling, the cursing reaching a crescendo of shouting, the thump of chests dropping into wagons and the stamping and neighing of horses. After dreary months of negotiating, of endlessly walking the east wing, to have made a decision, whatever it was, and to be on the move, wherever it was taking him, was exhilarating.

That mood of joviality, almost frivolity, lasted until he rode out to see the troops in the meadow outside, in battle order, flying the flag of Black Tom. It was the flag the King had seen fluttering over Fairfax's regiments at his final defeat at Naseby.

He reined in his horse. 'Where are you taking me?' he asked sharply.

'Oxford,' said George.

George had finally chosen it because it was heavily garrisoned by Cromwell's troops.

The King shook his head. 'Not Oxford. The air is bad.'

The air bad! It would soon be much worse at Holdenby. Scouts returned to report that a regiment supporting Holles was approaching from the direction of Coventry. Richard, with a smaller force, was less than half an hour away.

George suggested Cambridge. That got an even worse reception. The King said it had the miasma of the fens. It was also where Cromwell was MP.

'We could make the royal horse bolt,' Scogman said.

'Take that flag down,' I snapped. 'Where's the royal standard?'

No one could find it. Servants turned one wagon upside down and started on another. The sky was the colour of curdled milk. The last of the mist clinging to the meadows was disappearing, sucked up by the rising sun. Browne was next to the King, as placid as his horse cropping the grass. His face suggested he had known it all the time: we were an incompetent rabble who would disappear at the first shot.

Montague and Denbigh were watching from the lodge. George had refused to allow them to join the King's retinue. They laughed as a drum fell with a hollow echo from the wagon being searched. The urgency that had galvanised the King the previous night was turning into farce.

Montague pointed towards a ridge a mile away. A man, motionless on a horse, was staring down at us. He pulled his horse round and beckoned.

'We must move,' George said.

'We can't force him,' I replied.

'If we stay and fight he could be killed.'

But the King, increasingly agitated, would move only if he had the assurances from the troops that George had given him the previous night. This they gave with such force and one voice that he was reassured; but only to the extent of pressing George to tell him whose orders he was under.

'The orders of the soldiers of the army,' George replied.

Cresting the top of the ridge was a white horse. It was impossible to tell whether my father had fifty men or several hundred behind him. At his side the standard bearer flew the Stonehouse falcon. I felt the pull of it. It was as though the ring had escaped the fire and, like a phoenix, had reformed itself. The King saw it. I felt the longing in his face. To take one last chance. The romance and glory of it, of the Cavalier, the last remnant of the old knights, pitted against the drabness of the new order, with soldiers whose faces must have seemed to him as identical as their redcoats. The King's longing was transmitted to his horse, which pawed restlessly.

'Who has given you this commission?' he said to George. 'Have you no letter? Nothing in writing from your general?'

At a steady trot, Richard, his mercenaries and other troops he had gathered were descending the hill. They looked to be about a hundred. They would not attack against our bigger force, but would shadow and harry us until reinforcements arrived. The sight gave George a fresh urgency. He rode directly up to the King.

'This is my commission!' he yelled, gesturing across the lines of troops.

'The King!' roared the troops, their faces coming alive.

That was another romance. I saw it lighting up the King's face. His people. It was just as much a romance as the Cavalier. He did not know his people. What he did know was that he could not defeat the New Model Army. If it had not been broken up – and here was solid, disciplined proof it had not – what chance did he have? But arid calculations for him were never enough. He needed the music of romance and the roar of the troops provided it. But there was more.

Scogman had found the King's standard. No one was more independent, had less love for the King than Scogman. No loyalist could have lifted it aloft with more fervour than he did.

'The King!' Scogman shouted.

'The King!' the troops roared back.

'The drums!' I yelled. 'Where are the drummers?'

Richard checked his horse and put up his hand to stop his troops. They were about two hundred yards away.

'Newmarket,' the King said. 'I will go to Newmarket.'

Beneath the romance, that was a calculation. Kentford Heath, Newmarket, was where it was rumoured General Fairfax had agreed to meet regiments about their grievances. It was a test of whether George would take him there, or was leading a rebel group.

George lifted his sword. 'Newmarket!'

'Newmarket!' responded the troops.

The thud of the bass drum was followed by a rattle from the snare. The King urged his horse forward, the troops forming round him, lifting his standard above him. High-pitched above the tramp of the horse and the beat of the drums came the shrill skirl of a pipe. It came from a strange instrument that Joshua had carved from elm, somewhere between a fife and a flute. And it was a wild, strange tune he played, one called *Freedom*, which he had piped as a warning when the enclosure men from the lord and the parish were coming and it was time to move on. But few except the forest people, who grinned and whistled it, knew that, certainly not the King. He picked up the tune, and began to hum snatches of it as we moved towards the highway.

Montague had come out of the lodge. 'I thought you were one of us,' he said.

I laughed at the thought of how bitterly wounded I had been when I overheard him in the library. 'An upstart young bastard like me?' I said.

I rode on the outside of the jingling, whistling, drumming column, raising my sword to my father as we passed. After a moment, he lifted his.

Richard followed us, but before his reinforcements came another New Model regiment on its way to Newmarket joined us. People who hated the tramp of soldiers heard the call of the pipe and, sensing something strange and different, came from the fields and the villages to gape at us escorting the King and his retinue. They rang the church bells at Rothwell, picked up by bells at Kettering and Cranford St John, where the villagers threw green boughs and rushes before the King. He loved it. He raised his hands and smiled. Bonfires were lit. A beggar ran alongside, pointing his sore at him. Children joined the procession, stamping their bare feet to the rhythm. Scogman did tricks for them. A coin vanished from his hand to be taken from his nose. In a country desolated by war, depressed by a Puritan gloom which forbade maypoles, songs, dances and players, it was suddenly high summer.

George sent a message ahead to Fairfax, fearful of our reception, since our meeting had been with Cromwell, not him, and we had heard nothing from Cromwell. But I reassured him that it would have been a disaster if the King had been lost. Did not the swelling crowds vouch for that? We had done it! It was a story I would tell my son, Luke, a story every bit as fabulous as those Matthew had told me round the pitch fire in the docks, except this was true. I could picture Luke's round eyes, his open mouth, as I told it.

It lasted until we approached Cambridge, where a hundred bonfires were being prepared to be lit for the King. They were never lit. The story vanished into hard reality.

Reality came in the shape of tough, authoritarian Colonel of the Horse, Edward Whalley, commanding two regiments. He had a commission, in writing. It was from General Fairfax whose anger had scarcely left him able to dictate it when he heard the King had been abducted.

Whalley knew what the pipe meant, and took it from Joshua and broke it. George and I were arrested and told we would be court-martialled.

26

Summer at its peak: blistering heat in London cracked the wood of the houses, dazzling the eyes, cooking the slurry of uncollected rubbish, excrement, decaying food and dead dogs into one unbearable stench. All this was mixed with swarms of flies, of kites feeding on the filth, and of rats swollen with it, baring their teeth at people who tried to kick them away. Furnace heat burned in the mouths of preachers at every corner, warning people that their deeds were even now being counted: the Beast was Without, crawling nearer and nearer, waiting to snatch them up and cast them in the pit of eternal fire.

The Beast was the New Model Army, a great loathsome toad with two swollen heads. One of these was Fairfax, but the voice that came out of his mouth was that of the other, Great Satan himself: Cromwell. So thundered the preacher in St Paul's Churchyard at a growing crowd of militiamen, Presbyterians who had lost their jobs when the New Model was formed, watermen and apprentices. The preacher, long grey hair streaming from the sides of his bald head, on which blazed a livid red scar, urged them to go to Parliament before it was too late.

To Parliament? Why, I did not know. Neither did Scogman. Two months in a Cambridge gaol had reduced everything to whether we would be hanged that day, or the next. Our gaolers had been blank as the walls about our fate, and just as blank about our being thrown out on to the streets. No charges. Why were we being released? The gaolers laughed uproariously. Did we want to go back there? And, look, there was something that had come with the instructions to discharge us. One of the men had thrust into my hand a tattered, sealed piece of paper, stinking of gaol-piss, but when I had opened it, it only increased my confusion. It was an army warrant for ten pounds, five shillings and threepence. It was signed Thos. Fairfax (General) and made out to Tom Neave. Scribbled across it was 'Forre Services Rendered'.

Minds as rotted as our guts, we were so transfixed by the preacher we found ourselves raising our fists and roaring with the crowd.

'Parliament! To Parliament!'

In truth, I was so dizzy with the heat and weary with travel, for a moment I thought myself transported to the time when I was an apprentice, called to protect Parliament from the King. Until the preacher fixed his eye on me and shouted: 'There is one of the beasts. The Devil's child! He put this mark on me.' He pointed to the scar. Even then, it took me a moment to realise it was the wound I had given him when I had escaped from Mr Black's all those years ago. I could scarcely believe it was Gloomy George. The scar glared at me like a third eye. After quoting the Old Testament all these years, he looked as if he had stepped out of it.

'Seize him!'

Before anyone could move, Scogman pointed to a man in a butcher's apron standing next to me.

'I see it!' he yelled, thrusting his finger at the butcher's face. 'I see the mark!'

It was astonishing how many others saw the mark on the unfortunate butcher's face. The mob turned on him. In seconds he was the centre of a seething, fighting turmoil. Before George had howled their mistake at the crowd, we were running down Ludgate Hill. A group of young apprentices pursued us, crying 'Devil's child!'

They had the legs on us and yelled at another group being incited by a preacher outside St Bride's. Both groups closed in on us like the jaws of a pair of pincers. We ran into a white market in Shoe Lane, selling poultry and the like. I cannoned into the stall of a trader, who was in the act of screwing off the head of a chicken. It wriggled from his hands, squawking and fluttering and diverting one group. The other had us trapped against the stall. I slipped on the cobbles, greasy with chicken guts spilling from a pail. The trader grabbed me, demanding payment for his chicken, already despatched by the crowd and disappearing towards someone's pot. And Scogman was disappearing under the press of bodies. Soon I would follow his fate.

But from somewhere among the slimy feel of the cobbles and the putrid stench of the City came the apprentice I had once been, 'living by my wits', elbowing to one side the correct, slow-thinking gentleman I had become.

'Cutpurse!' I cried at the trader, slapping my hand on my belt.

Instinctively, the trader put his hand to his own belt. I pulled out the pail of entrails from under his chopping table and heaved the contents at the crowd. A slithering, disintegrating, evil-smelling yellow and red mess fell on them. Some, literally believing I was the Devil's child and had brought the mess to life, shrieked they were being eaten by the gizzards, craws, beaks, bladders and scraps of liver they clawed from their faces, the blood and scratches they drew only increasing that belief and their panic.

I dragged up Scogman by his belt. As we wriggled under the table some still tried to go after us, only to slip in the pool of grease and crash against the stall, where they were seized by the irate trader.

From another life, I knew the streets, all the short cuts. Wine Court, my feet remembered. Gough Square, Trinity Passage, Pissing Alley, where the sound of the mob faded. Even that alley smelt sweet as we leaned against the wall, holding our sides. Scogman scraped slime from his jerkin and removed a chicken foot. There was more than a trace of admiration in his voice.

'A rogue could have done no better than you, sir.'

Panting for breath, I longed for home, for Anne. To feel her against me. Everything would be healed then. Nothing else mattered, and I forgot that we had parted on such miserable terms. But I was swept with Scogman down The Strand by the mob and, becoming part of that animal, we were forced to move with it. People carried Presbyterian banners and raised clenched fists. In Westminster Hall traders had shut up their stalls for fear of the riots. We were carried towards the Commons, just as it used to be when I was an apprentice, except then we were shouting for Pym and Parliament, and this mob shouted for Holles and the King.

There was another difference. We would have threatened and abused the guards, but would never have breached the lobby. For us, the chamber of the House had the sanctity of a church. But, now, some made an attempt to break through, and were stopped only by the pikes of the guards.

Scogman yelled in my ear. 'Never seen that before. An MP rioting against Parliament.'

I twisted round in the heaving crowd. At first all I could see was Gloomy George. It was as if, with the crowd around him, he had been dropped from Ludgate Hill to that spot outside the Commons. With him, his arm round him, was the Right Honourable Member for Dutton's End, Sir Lewis Challoner. Near them was a small group who had none of the chaotic frenzy of the crowd. They had the trademark bent noses and squashed ears of men who earned a living with their fists. Two were laughing over pails they carried. Each took a drink from a flask before passing it to the next. All had clubs. They nodded to a man giving them instructions, whom I recognised from my army unit in Essex.

'Sergeant Potter,' Scogman said. 'Permission to speak to my old comrade in arms, sir?'

'Don't be a fool.'

But the next moment, as Gloomy George began to incite the crowd, Scogman disappeared into it. My feet left the ground as people surged forward. I was buffeted towards the pikemen who fought to guard the entrance. Among them was my old enemy, the Sergeant-at-Arms, so frail now he could scarce hold his pike. He staggered before a blow from one of the rioters, his pike slipping from him. Another aimed a kick at him. I grabbed the man's leg, upended him, snatched up the pike and drove rioters away with the flat of it. Someone grabbed my arm from behind. I whirled round with my pike, almost driving the butt into a familiar figure.

His fine clothes were torn, his linen stained, his hands splashed with blood. He had reverted from being assistant clerk to the army, who talked loftily of progress and shorthand, and whose name I could never remember, to the old, wild-eyed Mr Ink of my boyhood memory.

In my state of confusion, it seemed that the ink that always streaked his hands had turned into blood, until I saw it came from the forehead of the Sergeant, who had been struck by a stone. The crowd was beginning to draw back, less from our efforts than from the sound that turned their heads: the beat of militia drums coming from Whitehall.

'Thank God,' Mr Ink said. 'The Lord Mayor has sent the Trained Bands.'

The drums had no effect on George, but the rioters around the door slipped away. I could see no sign of Scogman, nor of Sir Lewis and the thugs. We helped the Sergeant into the lobby, where his head was bound by two of the guards. There was one of those sudden, inexplicable silences that fall on a mass of people. The animal was pausing for breath.

The guard who had let us in half opened the door to stare out. Gloomy George had dropped his hectoring tone. He had his audience. He had found his voice. What made it chilling was its note of certainty, its quietness. It forced people to remain still, frightened to miss a word. For he had the Word. The Word was not in there. He pointed towards Parliament, and his finger seemed directed at me.

'It has cast out its true believers who would fully reform the Church. But I tell you – they themselves will be cast out!'

As his voice rose, the murmuring of the crowd rose with it. The guard closed the door. The lobby had the dimness, the gravity of a church, an impression deepened by the mild, unflappable voice of Speaker Lenthall calling for order, followed by the droning of someone, on a point of order, that the question of tithes and the general inequality of taxation had already been discussed and passed to another place. Amidst all the chaos outside, the House was in session, debating, as they seemed to have been doing ever since my childhood, the interminable negotiations with the King.

Outside, there were no hesitations, no uncertainties, no sub-clauses or equivocations in Gloomy George's venomous tones. 'I will prove to you that the devil has taken root in that place – not the Mother but the *Whore* of Parliaments!'

'What is going on?' I cried at Mr Ink. 'What is happening?'

Two months in gaol had made me as ignorant as the child I was when I first smuggled out speeches from him. Mr Ink shook his head in despair. 'Once there was a King and no Parliament. Then there was a Parliament and no King. Now we have half a King –'

'Where?'

'He is held by Cromwell's men, at Hampton Court. So we have half a King and two Parliaments. This one, and the one in Reading.'

'Reading?' I really thought he was mad then, if he believed the nation was ruled, or half-ruled from a downtrodden little town on the road west.

But some of the mist cleared from my mind when he told me that was where the New Model was camped. Holles's attempt to break up the army had failed. The regiments had come together under Fairfax and Cromwell. Cromwell had fled from London the day after I met him in the garden, for fear of being impeached by Holles. Now, wearing his MP's hat, from a tent in Reading, Cromwell had instigated impeachment of Holles and eleven other MPs, including Sir Lewis Challoner. Cromwell's Independents at Westminster duly impeached them and agreed to settle the soldiers' grievances on their terms.

There might be two Parliaments and half a King, but the army was in power.

'Then we succeeded!' I cried. 'We got the King. Saved the army. Not Cromwell. Nor Fairfax. But his soldiers – the people.'

He waved his hands dismissively, as he used to when I was young and bold and passionate, and full of dreams. 'Tom, Tom, this is not a pamphlet.'

'No,' I said bitterly. 'It is not a pamphlet. It is true. What happened to George Joyce?'

'Cromwell denied having anything to do with the army revolt. George Joyce was severely reprimanded. And received a hundred pounds in payment.'

'A hundred pounds!'

'Ssshh.' He put his finger to his lips. 'For extraordinary services.'

'And I only got ten!'

Mr Ink looked increasingly uncomfortable. 'You – er – are an accounting error. Thomas Stonehouse is still in gaol for not fulfilling his mission and bringing back his father. You gave your name as Tom Neave to the gaoler and I ... er, failed to remember that was your original name ... and, er, gave a release notice for General Fairfax to sign, with back pay due from the early days of the war and –'

Fists and boots drummed on the door. 'Repeal, repeal, repeal! Repeal the impeachment of Holles. Repeal the army agreement. Repeal, repeal, repeal!'

Guards rushed in and slid a heavy bolt in place. I knew that door. I had stood outside it long enough when I was a runner, waiting for an opportunity to sneak past it. Its thick, gnarled oak panels looked as if they had grown there. But it began to shiver, to creak and groan at its massive, rusting hinges, as the crowd battered at it. The Sergeant-at-Arms appeared like a ghost, wavering in from the Painted Chamber, where he had been bandaged. Blood was spreading around the dressing on his wound. He had a curious, dazed air of forced calm, his fragile voice quavering with disbelief.

'They have invaded … the Lords … Forced their lordships … to repeal … impeachments.'

'The militia –' I began.

'Gone over to Holles … They are all Presbyterians now … we must take the mace …'

More blows rained on the door. I thought it touchingly absurd that all he could worry about was the mace, his piece of pomp and ceremony, but Mr Ink knew his Parliament better than I did.

'No legislation is lawful without the mace. And the Speaker. Quick!'

There were glimpses of yelling mouths in twisted faces outside as the door bulged inwards, then sank back. Splinters flew from the area around the bolt. The guards fled. Mr Ink took one arm of the Sergeant-at-Arms and I the other. Half lifting him from the floor, we reached the chamber, where the members, despite some looking apprehensive and a few terrified, loudly expressed indignation and outrage. All were held in their seats by the fear of cowardice, the hypnotic atmosphere of that place and, most of all, by the archaic rules of debate and the bonds of tradition.

Even the member leading the debate, Sir Simon D'Ewes, usually absent in the shires at the least sign of trouble, continued speaking, although the papers in his hand shook like leaves in a gale.

'Proposals to make peace with the King. Item: the use of the Book of Common Prayer to be permitted, but not imposed …'

In spite of the tumult outside, tears of joy sprang to my eyes. The use of that book had caused Mr Tooley to be thrown out of his church. He could have his living back!

The Sergeant, shackled by the formality of his role, was making curious genuflections to try to catch the Speaker's attention. I was about to push past him but stopped in amazement when I heard what Sir Simon said next.

'There should be no penalties for not coming to the parish church ...'

The soldiers had achieved this. No, no. The people. This was what we had argued, discussed, debated, in the heady march with the King from Holdenby to Cambridge. This was the music of the pipe.

There was a crack like thunder, followed by a hollow, reverberating boom. The building shook, dust drifting down from the gallery above the chamber. The old door had fallen. The mob, led by Gloomy George and Sir Lewis, poured into the lobby. We retreated into the chamber. Speaker Lenthall turned, peering over his spectacles, as if, up to that moment, he had heard nothing untoward. That movement, that peering, and the members as still as the benches they sat on, expressed the awe that place inspired. The mob stopped at the edge of the chamber, their shrieks and yells dwindling into silence.

'Sergeant,' said Speaker Lenthall to the old man, as if he might not have noticed. 'There are strangers in the House. Please have them removed.'

The Speaker's quiet indifference left Sir Lewis nonplussed. Perhaps for the first time he was struck by the enormity of what he had done. Perhaps he was remembering that even the King had suffered a defeat when he had invaded that chamber, one from which he was never to recover. The Sergeant turned to the crowd, flapping his hands at them as if he was shooing a flock of birds. The feeble absurdity of this gesture was dwarfed by his appearance, his blood-stained livery and bandaged head giving him the look of a martyred apparition. If anyone in that crowd moved, it was a nervous shuffling backwards. A few slunk off. I saw Scogman at the back. He had infiltrated himself among the men with pails and clubs. He gestured upwards, but I could not make out what he was trying to convey.

'Sir Simon,' said Speaker Lenthall.

Sir Simon swallowed and straightened out the papers he had crumpled up in his agitation. 'Errmm … parish churches, no penalties for non-attendance thereof, and no penalties for attending other meetings of worship …'

No penalties for attending other meetings of worship! Eight words. A dry Parliamentary clause, but to me it was the treasure I had dreamed of when I first came to London. Now the chest was opened, I could see it was not gold, but words – not just words that might change the world, but words that *were* changing it. Tolerance. The freedom to say what you believed. Freedom of worship! I felt so uplifted, I was certain others must feel as I did. I turned to find Gloomy George. I would even have shaken hands again with him at that moment. But to George the very same words were poison.

He pushed his way to the front, crying, 'Heresy! This is the Devil's creed. A Babel of different religions? People will fall into error. Thence into the Pit – like this Devil's child!'

He levelled his finger at me. Many believed the war presaged the Second Coming, and with his staring eyes and white streaming hair, George looked like the vengeful Old Testament prophet, predicting the Messiah. He gave authority to the crowd and enabled Sir Lewis to find his voice.

'Mr Speaker, the proposals are not only in error, they are illegal! Forced on this House by the army.'

Lenthall struggled to keep his calm tone above the baying crowd. 'Sir Lewis, you are illegal and in contempt –'

The Speaker's face disappeared in a mass of filth. He jumped from his chair, clawing the evil-smelling stuff from his eyes, spitting it frantically from his mouth. Led by Sergeant Potter, Sir Lewis's thugs scooped more of the night soil in their pails and flung it at the members who came to help Lenthall.

The thugs, like the shit they threw, could be found on any street corner. Gloomy George's followers were different. They had the same burning eyes, the same fanaticism. They seized me and held me against the table where the mace was kept, while Sir Lewis conducted a mock Parliament. He wrenched the papers from Sir Simon and tore them up. Only Bill Stroud, the member who had stubbornly wanted to confront the King when he invaded Parliament, tried to stop them. He was clubbed senseless. There was no more resistance.

'Repeal, repeal, repeal!' the mob chanted.

Sir Lewis forced the members to vote to repeal the impeachments of himself, Holles and the others. With the frightening zeal of the Presbyterian soldiers who had smashed screens and images in Anglican churches, his men seized more papers and burned them. The acrid smell of smoke mingled with the stench of excrement, making me choke and gag. Gloomy George held a lighted taper to my face, burning my mouth and cheek. I jerked my head back, banging it on the mace.

'He will burn. There is hope yet,' he said.

God only knew where his mind had flown to. I had always suspected his beliefs a cloak for worldly gain. But now it seemed there was going to be no world left to gain. It was the end time. I was the task he had been given and he had failed. But there was still time to destroy me and all my brood, he cried in exulted tones. At last he had evidence I was the Devil's child.

'You saw him,' he said to one of the men with him.

'He turned a chicken's entrails into serpents,' the man said.

'One bit me!' cried another, pointing to a cut on his cheek.

I licked at my cracked, stinging mouth where the taper had burned me. 'I saw it!' screamed the man with the cut cheek. 'I saw the snake slither from his mouth.'

The two men holding me slackened their grips in fear. I teetered groggily against the table, on the other side of which the MPs were being prodded into the Ayes lobby to repeal the impeachments.

'Best form of argument,' said one of the thugs, brandishing a club.

'Business as usual,' shrugged another. 'Don't they always do what they're told?'

They laughed uproariously, shoving the terrified men forward. Among them, Mr Ink, who had been mistaken for a member, swam into my dazed vision.

'*Vida supra*,' he muttered.

His utterance seemed part of the general madness. *Vida supra?* It was scribe's language for referring a reader to the text above. *Vida supra* – see above.

I looked up. Dizzy from the blows, the sudden movement sent a wave of sickness through me. I dipped my head back immediately, but not before I saw Scogman in the gallery above. He was carrying one of the pails the thugs had brought in. He lifted his hand and grinned.

Sir Lewis, who was acting as proposer of the motion, as well as teller, shouted, 'For repealing the impeachments: one hundred and twenty-six against –'

'On a point of order, Sir Lewis ...' Scogman shouted.

Sir Lewis looked round, then up. Everyone followed his gaze. There was a moment's silence. Scogman's grin had gone. I felt he was reliving that moment when Sir Lewis had ordered him to be dragged through the hedgerows and country lanes in chains. The shit seemed to hang in the air before descending on Sir Lewis's upturned face in a thick, glutinous, stinking mass, invading his mouth and nose, sliding down his collar, turning him into a jumping, gasping, struggling heap of night soil.

Londoners called it the Sleeper's Revenge, keeping full pots ready for men on night watch with particularly grating, penetrating voices. The thugs, who easily forgot what side they were on, cheered.

'*Vida supra,*' I yelled in triumph to Mr Ink.

'He is calling up the Devil!' cried one of the men holding me.

Like women whose only defence on being accused of witchcraft is to use the very fear they engendered, I poured out a meaningless gabble of Latin tags.

'*Vida supra,*' I jabbered, '*per se ex libris emeritus etiam atque etiam cogito ergo sum …*' As they recoiled in alarm, I pulled away from them.

'Stop his foul mouth!' George shouted.

'*Vice versa,*' I chanted. '*Ad infinitum ad infinit –*'

The man with the cut cheek clamped his hand over my mouth. I bit it.

'The snake bit me!' the man shrieked.

'The mace,' Mr Ink said in my ear.

I picked it up. It was unexpectedly heavy. I lurched forward, almost dropping it. George grabbed me from behind by my hair. It was an old form of cruelty of his, which he used to inflict on me when I was an apprentice. My hair had grown longer in prison and he yanked my head back. His supporters, gaining courage from him, surrounded me, raining blows on me. Two seized the mace. A shape flashed in front of me, knocking them to the ground. Scogman had jumped from the gallery.

'Palm your pike!' he yelled.

Mindless hours of numbly boring drill instructions have their reward when you are too battered and shocked to think. Long before it became a ceremonial symbol, the mace was a club, shattering breastplates and bones, only going out of fashion when heavy armour was developed. It must have been two centuries ago, around the time of Richard the Third, when that five foot silver club had last been used for its original purpose. I swung it round. Once I gained momentum it became a frightening weapon. The man with a cut cheek tried to duck under it to grab my arm. It caught his skull with a crack like rotten wood and swept on to shatter the thigh of another. He went down screaming. The others scattered.

'Mr Pym's passage,' said Mr Ink. 'Mr Scogman is getting a boat.'

It was the way Mr Ink had escaped with Mr Pym and the other members after the King's invasion of Parliament. The cellars of Parliament were supposed to have been made more secure since the Gunpowder Plot, but it was still a rabbit warren with a passage to the river.

I was staggering, head still spinning from wielding the mace. Mr Ink found the Speaker and led us both to the river end of the chamber. A nightmare figure stopped us. His stink almost asphyxiated us. Sir Lewis would have been comical but for his eyes glaring venomously from his darkened skin, and the knife in his hand. At close quarters the mace was useless. The knife flashed towards me, but before it struck home Bill Stroud brought a volume of Hansard down on Sir Lewis's head. The MPs were fighting back.

We threaded our way, as Mr Pym had done five years earlier, through cellars of mouldering papers and stacked furniture, the Speaker protesting that it was useless; members had ordered the passage to be blocked during the Civil War. At first it looked as though he was right, but then, guided by a draught carrying the smell of the river, Mr Ink shifted some crates and there it was. I wrapped the mace in some old sacking and followed the others into the passage. It was narrow and low, forcing us to bend our heads and scrape our backs as the damp, mildewed passage rose closer to the river. At the top of a flight of stairs was a heavy door, barred and locked. The Speaker's despair was alleviated with the gloomy satisfaction of being right after all: the security of the House had not been compromised.

Silently, Mr Ink ran his fingers down the wall until he found a brick looser than its fellows. From the cavity behind it he took a key, one which spoke to me of years of smuggling out banned speeches in ways known only to scribes and runners. The Speaker said nothing more.

Scogman was standing by Westminster Stairs, a shadowy blur wavering against the bright sun. The tide was running strongly upstream. The Speaker got into the boat, followed by Mr Ink, who confessed he had rarely left Parliament, let alone London, but he must follow and record the speeches wherever they were made. He stared at the old building, where the clamour was beginning to die down, and I realised that, for him, it was like leaving home.

With the water lapping round my feet on the steps, I gingerly passed down the sack-wrapped mace.

'What have you got there?' the waterman said. 'I charges extra for corpses.'

Hoping he would show every care, I said, 'The mace Richard the Third used.'

'And I'm Oliver Cromwell,' he said. 'Where to, guv?'

'Parliament,' the Speaker said.

The waterman closed his eyes in disbelief before stabbing a finger towards the building. 'You're there. That's Parliament.'

'Reading,' Speaker Lenthall said.

The waterman cast off, the sun behind him glinting on the waves thrown up by the boat and, as the sacking slipped from it, on the silver mace.

27

Evening. Bread could have been baked on the cobbles. The crowds were thinning out, cramming into the nearest alehouses.

I was walking rapidly, so deep in thoughts of Anne and Luke, that when I turned up St Martin's Lane it was a moment before I realised Scogman was continuing down The Strand.

'Where are you going?'

'Home.'

'Where's that?'

He smiled, and waved vaguely in the direction of the City. I told him not to be a fool. He was coming home with me. He smiled again and said he could see I was already at home. I put my arm round him and practically dragged him through Covent Garden where he grew more and more uneasy. He broke away in Long Acre, stopped, shook his head, and said it was all too neat for him. It was like the enclosures, pruned and controlled. He felt at home only in the deep forest of Without, where the buildings were squashed together, gables almost touching and streets as winding and narrow as forest tracks. These buildings were as severe and straight as hanging judges. They brought home to him, not to mince any more meat to make a pie, that he was a rogue and I was a gentleman.

'What nonsense!' I cried.

I forgot I had ever had similar thoughts myself. I told him the days of rogues and gentlemen were over. We had been together, we had seen great things and done great things, and we would stay together. Holles's mobs might have control of the City and Westminster, but Parliament was being carried up river towards the army. And the army was the people.

'Oh, Tom,' he said, very quietly.

That was all. He turned away, back towards The Strand, but almost immediately spun back, clutching at my arm. Still full of dreams, I thought he had changed his mind, until I followed his pointing finger. People were running up Drury Lane. Some were carrying red pails. Even as I ran, I prayed it would not be our house. Please God not my house. Not my wife and child. But I knew it was. I knew it. I should have foreseen it. But I was so full of my wretched dreams! Why, oh why, did I not foresee it? Why had I not been there to protect them?

All this while Scogman and I were running, smelling first the fire that I feared, then seeing the thick smoke billowing from our house. We collided into people filling pails from a pump, then into others walking aimlessly up the street to stare. The houses were brick and stone, but might have been wood with all the smoke that was pouring out. Servants from surrounding houses had given up trying to stop the fire in mine and were throwing water on their own. It was being sucked up by the heat as soon as it was thrown. I gabbled to one I recognised, a serving-maid from Cromwell's house.

'My wife … son …'

Her frightened face was stained with smoke. 'They were here … I don't know, sir …'

I snatched the pail from her, upended it over my head and kicked open the door. The explosion was like a cannon going off. Flames shot upwards, driving me back. The fire had been slumbering. Now it began hungrily to eat the timber of the floor, the beams of the ceiling.

'Anne!' I kept crying. 'Luke!'

I grabbed another pail and flung it into the room. It hissed almost instantly into steam, but momentarily doused a narrow pathway through the flames. Before the flames leapt back, I ran through. The yelling of people was snuffed out by the roar of the fire in my ears. It followed me into the hall, consuming my papers, my Bible.

'Anne – Lu –'

They were choking screams, not words. It was the hot acrid smoke that was engulfing me now, charring my lungs, stopping my breath. I put a foot on the stairs but there was a crash above me and a burning piece of timber narrowly missed me, driving me through the hall towards the back of the house. Here the walls were of stone and there was less wood for the fire to feed on. I almost fell over the body. Scarcely able to see, I recognised Jed more from his wooden arm, which was beginning to smoulder. I dragged him over on his back, seeing the blood soaking his chest. He had died not from the smoke, but from a knife wound. I tried to pull him away but the smoke defeated me.

Coughing and retching, stumbling down the stairs leading to the kitchen I saw Anne's shoe. Or what was left of it. A tiny brocaded fragment whose pattern I recognised. Somehow that pattern, bleached like bone, was Anne. I could see her foot in it, as small as mine was gross; see her movement, as delicate as mine was clumsy. I had always loved watching her. I could not believe I would never see those movements again. And, as my hand reached out towards it, I saw something else – the wooden horse that the old ostler had made for Luke. The shape was perfect, even down to the curls of the mane, but it crumbled into ash as I touched it, leaving only the piece of chain that Jed had put on it as a bridle.

A piece of timber hit me. I almost welcomed it. I wanted to die with them, wanted the house to fall on me, to be consumed with them. From being a choking enemy, the smoke became a friend, filling my nose, stopping my lungs, sending me into a deep pit, not the plague pit I had always been destined for but a kinder pit where there was no lime, only silence and blackness.

But, for some reason, I was being pulled out of that pit of silence. There was a stabbing pain in my head. I was destined for the pit after all, the eternal pit of fire. There was a voice in my head telling me so. I began to struggle. The pain in my head increased. There was a draught of air. Air? It was too strong for me, sending me into a paroxysm of coughing. I was going back up the stairs. Up? No. Not going up – being dragged up. The heat was increasing.

I heard his muttering. Saw above me his white hair and beard. Only his cruelty kept me alive: he was dragging me up the steps by my hair. The pain brought me reluctantly back to life, to hear his ravings. Even then I was curiously detached, interested not in living any more but in how my life was coming to an end. It began – I saw this with a strange clarity – with jealousy. Gloomy George was Mr Black's successor. I supplanted him. When I married the woman he had chosen, jealousy became hatred. Hatred found an explanation, a meaning, authority, in his religion of violence and intolerance, which made me into a devil.

We reached the top of the steps. There the heat was more intense but the smoke less. Only then, when my head began to clear and I heard what he said, did I come to my senses.

'The last one. Then it's done. Then it's finished. He must go into the heart of the fire, to burn with the rest of his brood …'

Come to my senses? I came to my rage, my own hatred. I wrenched my head away, yelling as hairs tore from it. Taken by surprise, he fell down the steps. I levered myself up, moved to throw myself after him, but my body stayed where it was. He drew his knife.

'Would you. Would you.' He seemed almost pleased I had come round. 'Remember this?' He pointed to the scar I had inflicted as an apprentice, glowing red on his forehead. 'The Lord has promised. It will disappear when you are dead.'

He lunged with his knife. It ripped my jerkin as I stumbled backwards. The knife was at my throat. He could have killed me then. What stopped him was habit. He was that journeyman again, and I the apprentice. He never simply inflicted his punishments. He savoured them. Now he forced me away from the stone hall towards the heart of the fire. He drove me backwards with his knife, step by stumbling step. The knife went through my jerkin and pricked my flesh. He would not be satisfied until he saw me not merely burning, but charred to ash.

The fire seemed to be reaching out for me, scorching my hair, my neck. I fell over something. There was a stench of burning flesh. Jed. His wooden arm had gone but the hook remained. As George brought his knife back for the final thrust, I snatched up the hook, the hot metal searing my hand. This time there was no one to stop me when I drove the hook up into George's face again and again.

I heard their voices through the roar and crackle of the fire. It was as if their spirits had been released by George's death. Anne would be where the threadbare pattern of her shoe was left. If I could only find that, I would be with them for ever. But my lungs were on fire and my eyes half-blinded by the stifling smoke, and their voices, their billowing shapes, were like the will o' the wisps of my childhood, who enticed people on to the marsh, from where they were never seen again.

28

Breathing was like drawing in thorns, so I breathed as little as possible. Which meant I moved as little as possible. I did not know where I was. I did not want to know. My soul was detached from my body, in the inferno with Anne and Luke. Why did people not leave me alone, to burn with those I loved? Only when I was lifted on to a pot, or had the bandage stripped from the raw burned flesh of my hand, did I become a screaming body again, my lungs torn by the thorns.

Eventually, they forced me back into that body, but still I did not want to hear or see. Most of all I did not want to think. The way to avoid that was to count the stitches in the sampler on the wall. But the stitches became letters and the letters words: *Two things there are that will not come back.*

I looked wildly away. The words seemed to have formed themselves as I looked, burned into the wall as they were for Belshazzar. I got up to try to sweep them away. Only then did I realise it was a familiar Puritan aphorism. *Two things there are that will not come back: the appointed hour that could not wait and the helpful word that was spoke too late.* Neatly, and probably thankfully after the months it had taken to sew, it was signed *Elizabeth Bourchier 1608*.

I fell back on the bed, knocking against a table next to it. Something fell on the floor with a metallic tinkle. I picked up a small, twisted piece of metal, staring uncomprehendingly at it for a moment before I realised it was the bridle from Luke's toy horse. There was a tiny trace of soot on it, which came away with the sweat of my finger. I could hear him. *I can ride! I can ride! Watch me, sir.* But where was the other shoe? Where was Anne? The door opened, but I did not look up until I heard Jane's voice.

'You are awake, sir.'

'It seems so.' The only thing I wanted to ask I could not bear to. Instead, nothing but empty trivia came out of my mouth. 'Who is Elizabeth Bourchier?'

'Why ... Mrs Cromwell, sir. Bourchier was her maiden name.'

'Cromwell is about to put me into prison again, is he?'

Jane stared at me blankly. 'Mr Cromwell is with the army. His wife is in the country. We heard you shouting through the smoke –'

'We?'

She described Scogman, who, she said, had been fighting the fire from the stables. They heard me crying out for Anne and Luke. Scogman kicked open the kitchen door. The air fed the flames but cleared some of the smoke. They saw me on the floor, holding the piece of bridle, and managed to pull me clear.

'Where's Scogman?'

He had gone. Where, she did not know. 'He left you this.' She gave me a leaf. It was a dry, flaking laurel leaf, which he had carried in his hat during the march with the King. She seemed reluctant to part with it, and when I caught her eye, she blushed. Life was going on as normal, then. I wanted to cry out, *Why should it? How could it?* I dropped the leaf, picked up the twisted piece of toy bridle, and forced out the words.

'Where are Anne and Luke?'

'I – I do not know, sir,' she said falteringly.

'What? There was nothing left – nothing?' She stared at me as if I was crazy, as twisted and misshaped as the tiny piece of metal I turned round in my fingers. 'Nothing but this? No shoe?'

'Shoe? She lost her shoes when Luke went back for his horse. That man –'

'George?'

'Was waiting for them but Jed saved them and –'

'Saved them? Jed saved them? Their bodies?'

She stared at me as if I was mad. 'Bodies? They escaped. They are alive, sir.'

'A-live?' I stuttered. 'But they – I thought – you said – what did you say? You said you didn't know where they were and I thought – alive?' I seized her by the shoulders. 'You are sure? Alive?'

She began laughing at my craziness. 'Yes, sir.'

I kissed her. Then for some reason I went over and kissed Elizabeth Bourchier's sampler. It was not too late. Not too late. I noticed that she had skimped some of the cross-stitching on the border. It made the child who had done it less perfect but more alive. Alive! I began to smell the lavender Jane had placed near my bed, and heard the sounds through the window I had not realised was open, the rattle of wheels, the clank of a milkmaid's pail.

I gripped Jane by the shoulders again, savouring the pain in my bandaged hand. 'Where are they?'

She looked away. I had to shake her before she answered. 'With the Countess.'

'I see.' I walked gravely round the room, my hands folded behind my back. 'After I expressly forbade her to go there?'

'She – she told me not to tell you, sir.'

'Told you not to tell me?'

That meant nothing to me then. Nothing mattered but that they were alive. I could not keep up my charade. To Jane's astonishment, I danced her half round the room, before dropping back on the bed, wheezing with exhaustion.

'Never fall in love, Jane. It is the sweetest, but the most painful thing in the world.'

'I have no intention of doing so, sir.'

'Good. I may keep this then?' I held up the laurel leaf.

'He left it for you, sir.'

'Are you sure?' I dropped it in her hand. A small smile trembled round her lips.

I shook my head. 'He is a rogue and a thief, Jane.' The smile went. 'But reformed,' I assured her, closing her hand round the leaf.

The Countess was not at home to Tom Neave. Mrs Stonehouse was indisposed. Indisposed! Well, she could be anything she liked, so long as she was alive. I told my old enemy the footman to tell her that I too was indisposed, and to suggest that we might be indisposed together. He looked askance at the cast-off steward's clothes Jane had found for me, his expression as severe as Cromwell's frown, and did so reluctantly. When he eventually returned, he told me he had been unable to deliver the message because her ladyship was asleep.

Her ladyship! I pushed past him, up the stairs into the salon. It was empty. Another servant looked up at me, startled. He appeared to be putting a picture on the wall. The Countess had kept up her habit of having Royalist pictures on one side, dominated by a Van Dyke of Charles, and Parliamentary pictures on the other. The portrait the servant had in his hands was a rather florid one of Holles.

I heard voices from an adjoining room and opened the door. The Countess rose from a chair without speaking. Anne, her feet bandaged, was stretched out on a chaise longue.

'I thought even you would not break in …'

'Not break in? I thought you were dead!'

'I wish I were.'

She spoke so tonelessly that I went to her in alarm. 'What is it? Your feet?'

'My feet will heal.'

'Is it Luke?'

She looked away.

'Where is he?'

'Asleep.'

'Where is he?'

'Don't wake him. He has bad nights.'

'Is he all right?' I became frantic when they evaded my questions, and went towards the door. The Countess stopped me with something I never expected from her. Gentleness. 'He needs his sleep.'

'Thank you,' I said awkwardly to Lucy, 'for taking them in.'

'Is that all?' Anne said savagely. 'You forbade us to come here. You insulted her. Or have you forgotten?'

I thought of the picture of Holles being put up. What I had said the night I left to ride to Holdenby seemed only too true. She had gone over to Holles, even if she was not actually warming his bed. I turned to the Countess and managed to get the words out.

'The … the manner in which I spoke to you was unpardonable. I am deeply sorry.'

'Manner? Deeply sorry? You are mincing words, sir. You are taking back nothing you said?'

'Enough, Anne,' the Countess said. 'Please. I'll leave you –'

She moved to go, but Anne gripped her hand and practically forced her to sit in the chair next to her. Her anger flushed her cheeks and tightened her skin. She would not release Lucy's hand. My gratitude to Lucy for sheltering my family began to slip away.

'I am sorry, but I cannot take back what seems to be true. Now Holles is in control of London, I see you are putting up his rather florid portrait.'

There was a silence. Anne swung her feet from the chaise longue and tested them gingerly on the ground. I thought she was going to fly at me. Then they looked at one another and began to laugh. Lucy poured out some cordial, which she refreshed with white wine. When I refused it she gave it to Anne, who looked over the edge of it at me, one of Lucy's mannerisms. She was even beginning to sound like her.

'For a pamphleteer – is that what you are again? – you are singu-larly ill-informed.'

'Holles's portrait is not florid,' Lucy said. 'It is gross. And it is being taken down, not put up.'

She told me that the riots had been a futile gesture from the City, who feared and hated the prospect of the army taking control. They were misled by people like Sir Lewis, who puffed up the numbers ready to fight for the Presbyterians. Cromwell played a clever hand, showing force but never using it. As soon as the Presbyterians heard Cromwell was twelve miles away, they melted like snow in spring. While I was recovering, news came that authority had been added to force, with Cromwell being joined by the Speaker and a number of fugitive peers. In a few days the army was expected to march in and restore Parliament.

'I hope you have commissioned a portrait of Cromwell by a better painter,' I said to the Countess.

'Cromwell?' Lucy said, as if the name left a bad taste in her mouth. 'I have an old one of him. More importantly, I have my Van Dyke of Charles. The talks with Parliament are going well and he will be back on his throne in the autumn. Long live the King!'

She raised her glass. Anne stared into hers. Her enjoyment seemed to have been short-lived. For the first time she looked at me straight in the eyes with that old look of contempt, which I did not mind, but indeed welcomed, for it was mixed with hunger and need.

'What on earth are you wearing?'

Anne's eyes were wild. Her hand shook, spilling her drink. I took it from her. 'What is it, my love?'

I sensed, rather than saw, Lucy with her glass still upraised, then she became no more than a piece of furniture as I watched the movements of Anne's throat, still thin and delicate as she tried to speak. And words almost came, but each time she tried to say them she swallowed them back and tears came to her eyes, and I held her to me, shaking and gasping, and kissed her until we lapsed into silence. When she eventually stirred, and I again asked her what was the matter, and she shook her head, I could no more keep my words back than a river can keep to its banks at flood time.

'Oh, Anne, I have been on such a journey. I have seen wonderful things. You know the treasure we talked about as children? I have found it. It is not in a chest, as we always thought, held by big rusty hasps, locked by a key that must be found. It is in ordinary people. They have brought King and Parliament together. They have begun to speak.'

'Speak?' she whispered, half crying, half laughing.

'Aye. The dumb have found their voice.'

She was as we were when children, half rubbishing me, half eager to hear more. I told her about Scogman, oh, a desperate rogue, who now talked of a better world. About the masterless men and the pipe of freedom. Even the King had sung to its tune! In spite of slaughtering half of them, the King had always said how much he loved his people – now he had ridden among them, his standard flying with that of Black Tom. I told her that the prophets were wrong; every doom-saying, nay-saying one of them. The war was not the end of the world. It was the beginning – a world in which King and Parliament would have to answer to the people.

There was a small rap as Lucy set her glass down on the table.

I got up, still clasping Anne's hands. 'Come. Let us go home.'

It was just an ordinary phrase, the most comforting in the world, so well-worn it slipped out without thought. It was like setting a match to a train of gunpowder. She snatched her hands away.

'Home? Where is that? Tell me. Go on. Tell me.'

'We can go to your father's while we rebuild –'

'Rebuild? What with?'

Without waiting for an answer, she rounded on Lucy who seemed as frightened of her explosion of anger as I was. 'Tell him. You tell him. I can't.'

She flung herself back on the chaise longue and turned away from me.

For once, Lucy told me without preamble. 'Both Lord Stonehouse and Cromwell have disowned you as a dangerous radical for kidnapping the King.'

'Kidnapping? We saved the King from Richard!'

'He has denied it.'

'Denied? He was there!'

I groped for the wine and poured myself a drink.

'It's going round the 'Change that anything might have happened with such a dangerous band. The King is using that as a bargaining point. Cromwell denies having anything to do with Cornet Joyce and the rest of you.'

'He – he paid them!' I stuttered, fumbling in my pockets to take out the army warrant I was given.

'Of course he paid them. They will keep their mouths shut.'

'I will not.'

'No doubt that is why you were thrown into prison.' She took the warrant. 'It looks genuine. That is curious, I admit. That you were released and paid.'

I could say nothing without giving Mr Ink away. I took back the warrant. 'Cromwell's blessing,' I said bitterly. 'You can trust none of them. Richard is welcome to what he gets from his father. If he gets anything. The last time I was in Queen Street I saw the woman he intends to marry.'

'Lord Stonehouse?' Lucy cried.

I took a savage satisfaction from, for once, telling her something she did not know. 'It seems so, madam. I saw her leaving in his carriage.'

'A tall woman,' Lucy said. 'Handsome rather than beautiful, with greenish eyes?'

'You know her?'

'I know who she is.'

'Her name is Geraldine,' Anne said. 'She is the daughter of the Duc de Honfleur and a close confidante of Charles's Queen Henrietta.'

'Even more important for Lord Stonehouse,' said Lucy, 'is that she has given birth to a son.'

'Lord Stonehouse has another son?' I cried.

'The woman is Richard's wife.'

Anne spat the words out. I groped for my drink, but put it down immediately. I could take nothing more in that place, not even the drink I badly needed. I turned to Anne. 'Come. We are better off without them.'

It was another unfortunate choice of words. The Countess's eyebrows lifted. Anne sprang at me. 'Better off? Is that meant to be a joke? If you had shown your father's lying letter to Cromwell –'

'Betrayed him. Acted like he does, you mean.'

'Oh, you are too good for this world, sir. I would not have married you if I had thought you were only a printer.'

I laughed. 'Come, come, that is not true. You are a printer's daughter, madam, masquerading as a lady, as I ape the gentleman from time to time. It is all nonsense, all play. We have been through this many times before. Come. Let us get away from these people.'

She walked towards me. She scarcely came past my shoulder, but seemed to stretch up as tall as me. Her borrowed clothes were more sumptuous than we could ever afford. Her silk gown crackled as she walked, its deep blue matching her eyes, which never left me. Behind her, her mentor the Countess watched approvingly. Anne's voice was unnervingly quiet.

'And Luke, what is he?'

Lucy half rose but, in the exchange of glances between them, sat down again abruptly. I could not understand the look they shared, and said nothing.

'I am a lady, sir, and you a gentleman,' Anne said.

'Well then,' I said equally quietly, 'you must get used to your new station in life.'

Why was she always at her most desirable when she was so angry? Her voice remained low, but her fists were clenched and her cheeks a dull red. 'That estate is yours, sir. You have been promised it, you have earned it and you have been cheated of it. And I will see that you get it.'

'You will?'

Her voice rose. 'One way or another. Yes.'

Lucy had coached her well. I had had enough of this nonsense. 'Come,' I said abruptly.

'Where? To your forest people?'

I would not be goaded. 'Anne. It's happening. We must be part of it. Together.'

Her lips trembled. Her eyes filmed over. I could feel the old magic between us. Once we were away from Lucy it would be all right. 'Come,' I said more gently.

'You talk of masterless men,' she said.

'Yes.'

'Is there any talk of masterless women?'

I smiled. 'Not that I have heard of.'

She dropped her head and went to the door. 'Very well.' Her voice began to break. 'I will obey you, just as I did before you went away. I pleaded to come here, but you would not let me and I obeyed you.' Her voice became charged with bitter regret. 'You care for your forest people more than you care for us.'

Lucy sprang up. 'Anne! Don't disturb him.'

'What is it?' I cried. 'What has happened?'

But Lucy had gone after Anne. I followed her across the gallery where the servant, who was putting up a picture on the wall, gaped down at us from his ladder. Lucy went down a dimly lit corridor leading to a withdrawing room. I called out after Anne. Lucy stopped and turned, putting a frantic finger to her lips. I collided into her, knocking a table from which a vase fell, shattering on the floor.

I had never seen Lucy so distressed, but when I mumbled an apology she kept saying, 'The vase doesn't matter. The vase doesn't matter.'

There was a high-pitched scream. I could not believe it was Luke. It was like the cry of some animal caught in a trap. I blundered into the withdrawing room. He was on a couch, made up as a bed. One side of his face was practically untouched. The other was burned raw. It had been treated with one of those bandages that Ben and others had developed during the war, consisting of more ointment than bandage. The most painful business was getting it off. Part of it had come away from the skin. He screamed even more when he saw me.

'It's him! It's him!'

'Not him, Luke, not him. It's your father.'

He ducked away to bury his face in his mother's breast, but flinched back, afraid of the pain it would cause his inflamed skin.

'It hurts, it hurts!'

'This will make it better.'

'Doesn't, doesn't!'

'It will, it will.'

With infinite gentleness, she adjusted the bandage until it was secure. She fed him small sips of cordial until he began to be drowsy. I sat on the end of the couch and stroked him quietly.

'You said you would kill him,' Luke murmured.

'I have.'

'He will not come back?'

'He will not come back.'

Eventually he fell asleep in Anne's arms. I continued to sit there, her words ringing in my head. *You care for your forest people more than you care for us.* If I had betrayed my father, or at least not written to him, I would have brought the medicine back to Liz. She might have lived. No, no. That was ridiculous. But the thought would not go away. I should have been there. And now this! If I had not forbidden Anne and Luke to come here, this would never have happened.

I had to stay. I had to stay with them. But to stay, I must be Thomas Stonehouse. She wanted nothing less. She had said so: *I would not have married a printer*. Ah, that was just nonsense, said in the heat of the moment. But it carried in it the hint of another voice, one I had never heard, but was always there, somewhere inside me, that of my mother. There was an echo of that voice when Anne said: *that estate is yours. I will see that you get it. One way or another.* I shivered.

It was not only that I believed in the forest people and that the world was about to change. *I* had changed. She had not made that journey. Until she did, had I any right to tell her what to do? Masterless women. I smiled at it, but was it so ridiculous? Was that not what made me fall in love with her in the first place? And still loved about her.

So my thoughts spun uselessly, endlessly round and round, as the light went and shadows crept into the room.

Luke had his thumb in his mouth. Soothed by the bandage, his burned cheek rested on his mother's breast. Miraculously, in that position, he looked whole again. All our breathing was in concert. Then Luke shifted, his face twisting in protest at being dragged from sleep by the pain, and she turned him on his good cheek and rocked him gently.

I got up. 'You must stay. I cannot.'

'Cannot?'

'I will find a place for us.'

'Where?'

'I will find somewhere.'

She looked up. We stared at one another wordlessly, more in shock, bewilderment and disbelief that we were parting than anything else. My legs were shaking. She moved to put Luke back on the couch but he gave a wailing cry, and she drew him back to her. I went out into the corridor, walked away, then back to the door of the room, then back again. Lucy appeared at the door to the salon.

'Ah. I thought I heard you. What do you think?'

The servant was picking up his ladder. The picture he had hung in place of Holles was one of Cromwell I had seen before. It had been retouched so that the nose was less prominent and the warts scarcely visible.

'I'm afraid I don't find it very ... characteristic.'

'I should hope not. The painter has done what he can, but the raw material has defeated him.'

I held out my hand. 'Thank you for taking care of them.'

She took it, smiling warmly. For a moment there was a glimpse of a different person, before she had lost her only child and realised she could have no more, a glimpse of why she had such a close relationship with Anne.

'There is a suite I have prepared for you, Tom.' She picked up a bell. 'I will get the servant to show –'

'I am not staying.'

She mouthed, rather than said, 'Ah.' That was all.

As I went down the stairs, I heard the resigned thump of the servant putting his ladder against the wall again and the Countess saying, 'I think a little more to the left. Away from the light.'

PART THREE

Without

Autumn 1647

29

Lucy hung up her picture with her usual impeccable timing. The day after, Fairfax and Cromwell entered London. Twenty regiments marched down Cheapside, colours flying and drums beating. The City went from Presbyterian – at least politically – to Independent in a day. It was not just the muskets that were persuasive. The City wanted only one thing: business as usual. They had been told by the Presbyterians that Cromwell's army was a drunken rabble. They were amazed at how orderly and obedient they were: above all, that there was no looting.

'They took not so much as an apple,' marvelled one alderman.

Cromwell and Ireton would have thrown me back into prison if they could. But, while the army was in control of the country, Cromwell was not in control of the army. Not completely. I joined in the march with George, with Levellers like Nehemiah, and a small number of MPs who feared that Cromwell's negotiations, like those of Holles, would give too much away to the King. What had started as a rebellion in the army was on the verge of becoming a wider revolution: above the heavy martial beat of the drums and the blare of the trumpets floated the defiant skirl of Joshua's freedom pipe.

After the march, I went to Mr Black to see if Anne and Luke could stay at Half Moon Court.

'You mean when they return from the country?' he said.

'Country?'

'Did you not know?'

Anne and Luke had left London to go with the Countess to a house she had at Maidenhead. Anne had evidently told her parents nothing of the difference between us and I struggled to keep up the pretence. The pewterer who lived opposite Mr Black had died, leaving the house empty. I cashed my army warrant and took out a lease. The house was in a bad state and while work was done I slept above the shop of Gun Press, in Spitall Fields, close to the apothecary's where Matthew worked. He loaned his kitchen maid, Ellie, to keep it in some kind of order. There I worked night and day with Scogman and Nehemiah on what Mr Ink, who had been carried back in triumph to Westminster with Speaker Lenthall, called The Great Opportunity.

But opportunity for what?

Lucy was wrong in one thing. The King rejected the army's proposals. Ominously some, like Nehemiah, said 'there should be no further addresses to the King.' Did he think we could rule without the King? We nearly came to blows. I said vehemently that we had seen from the crowds leaving Holdenby how the people loved the King. Nehemiah argued that the King was using the crowds to get his Royalists back into Parliament.

God was prayed to endlessly for a solution to the stalemate. From St Katharine's in the east to St Dunstan in the west, people knelt for hour after hour for an answer. None came.

So many words dried so many throats in the Leveller alehouses that The Windmill in Lothbury and The Bull and Mouth in Aldersgate both ran out of beer.

The King played bowls in Hampton Court. A Royalist pamphlet reported him as saying, 'You cannot be without me – you will fall to ruin if you do not sustain me.'

Not a day, scarcely an hour, passed, without my picturing Luke in his mother's arms, hearing again that terrible scream. I stopped in the middle of composing a pamphlet, or wiping my hands, to go over that last scene with Anne. I was angry at her for leaving without a word – then more angry at myself, for how could she write when she did not know where I was?

I wrote to her and, miraculously, because I was writing as Tom Neave, poetry flooded back to me. I told her I had leased the house in Half Moon Court. I had planted a new apple tree there, to replace the one where we had fallen in love. It gave me the most intense longing for her and for days I was full of hope. I had no illusions about her reaction. She would obey me, but she would hate it. I could hear her objections, feel her silent contempt for the place. Even that was preferable to not being with her at all. And, gradually, as the first leaves formed and then buds opened, we would come together again. I believed more than anything else that, whatever happened, neither of us could live without the other.

A week passed. There was no reply. I wrote again by 'hanging man', which gave the letter the urgency of a pardon. Nothing. I was short with everybody, particularly Matthew's kitchen maid Ellie, who was always at my elbow. She had become less interested in cleaning than in running pamphlets to the Levellers' groups, or copy to Mr Black's when our press broke down. She was, I think, fourteen – fifteen, she claimed. Like a plant that shoots up too quickly, she was always overbalancing in her pattens and kicking them off to run through the streets, her dress pinned up against the mud.

One day she gave me a letter from Maidenhead, which had been posted eight days previously. As she always collected the post, I rounded on her, thinking she had forgotten about the letter. She fled in tears. Scogman remonstrated with me, pointing out it had been wrongly addressed, and gone backwards and forwards to Maidenhead.

I was known by everybody now as Tom Neave. Anne had written to Thomas Stonehouse. She had closed the letter with the falcon seal.

I flew into a rage. I would not open it. It was not to me. I would return it, scribbling over it: 'not known at this address'. My childish tantrum lasted all of five seconds. I tore it in my eagerness to see her sprawling impetuous hand. I stared in bewilderment at the neat, upright lines, stiff as a regiment standing to attention. She had dictated it to a scrivener. She addressed me as her dear husband. She had taken Luke to the country because she feared he would suffer even more distress when a looting army took over London (as she expected Cromwell's troops to be). Had she known where I was, she would, of course, have asked for my permission. Not a day passed when Luke did not ask after his father. She begged to be excused from making any judgement about Half Moon Court until the good country air had led, hopefully, to Luke's recovery. She remained my affectionate wife, etc., etc. She signed it Anne Olivia Stonehouse.

Anne Olivia! She never used the second name. She hated it. Wait, wait! I paced the press room, ignoring people who questioned me. It was how she had signed the marriage deed. The whole letter bore the hand of Lucy, and probably some lawyer. Hopelessly, Anne was still pursuing the Stonehouse estate. Well, that would burn itself out. It would have to. It was fruitless. I wrote to her in cold anger that she must now address me as Tom Neave and take that as her name. She wrote back immediately, and perfectly civilly, that, although she would obey me in most things, it was superseded by obedience to her Church and her God, who had made her Mrs Stonehouse.

What made it worse was that she was right. Or, I suspected, the hidden hand of her lawyer was. As September darkened into October, my cold anger persisted. The house at Half Moon Court was ready, but I did not occupy it. I was in exactly the same state as when I first met her. Half the time I hated her. The other half I longed for her with such passionate intensity I could neither eat nor sleep. Then my work took an astonishing turn, which allowed me to put her in the back of my mind, at least for a few hours.

A sometime lawyer, who now styled himself Major Wildman (although there was no record of him ever fighting), had put his finger on what Mr Ink called the Great Opportunity.

It was breathtakingly simple. He turned the soldiers' case, their pay and grievances, into the people's case, the soldiers' rights into the rights of the people. To win those rights, Parliament had to be reformed. Until Parliament had been reformed – this was Wildman's key point – it was futile to negotiate with the King.

With other pamphleteers I worked eagerly to turn the ideas into a pamphlet called *The Case of the Army Truly Stated*. It was ready to print, but our press broke down. My relationship with Mr Black was now stiff and awkward, and I told Ellie to take the copy to him. I could not stop myself from asking her to find out if he had heard from Anne in Maidenhead. She looked at Scogman, who was struggling to repair the press. He started to say something but, irritated by the delay, I told him to wait until I had done a last minute correction.

I gave it to Ellie. Through a placket in her skirt she was in the act of putting the copy in her pocket and dropped a couple of sheets. I picked them up and saw she had flushed a deep red. 'What is it?'

'I did not know whether to tell you, sir.'

'Tell me? Tell me what? Has something happened to my wife and son?'

'I saw them.'

I was incredulous. 'When? Where?'

'Two days ago. At Mr Black's.'

'Were they all right?'

One moment she was as nervous as a kitten, the next sullen and indifferent. She shrugged. 'Your wife?' Her indifference abruptly left her and she gave me a coquettish smile. For a moment she was Anne. It was unnerving. She caught some of Anne's mannerisms exactly. She lifted her chin. Her snub nose quivered slightly, as if she was detecting a bad smell. She teetered on her clacking pattens, lifting her skirts, like a lady fearing they would be fouled.

'Enough. Stop that!'

'Stop what, sir?' she said innocently.

I caught a grin on Scogman's face. I told Ellie sharply to take the pamphlet. She gave me a surly flounce of a curtsey, pinned up her dress and, once outside, dropped her airs and was whooping halfway down the street before I called after her and asked how Luke was.

'Nothing wrong with curds face,' she scowled, 'that a good thrashing won't cure.'

Curds. The lumpy, cheesy residue when milk separates conjured up such an agonisingly vivid picture of how Luke's face must have healed that I could not speak for a moment. Then I raced up to her and shook her so that she overbalanced from her pattens and fell against the wall. 'Don't you ever call him that again!'

She scrambled up just as violently. 'Well, I raced him round the apple tree and I won, and he called me Spitall slut. I knew I shouldn't have told you, I knew it.' She burst into tears. She fumbled through the petticoats she had taken to wearing, which she sowed together from varicoloured dorneck linen off-cuts, begged or stolen from the market, took the copy from her pocket and flung the sheets at me. 'Here! Take them yourself!'

Before I could stop her, or say a word, she ran off.

The papers scattered in the wind. I caught some; Scogman chased after others. 'I was going to tell you,' he said. 'She asked me to, but none of us wanted to. We were afraid you'd leave.'

'Leave? Here? I'll never do that. Not until we've convinced Cromwell Parliament must be reformed.'

He said nothing, but gave me the sheets he'd collected. My hands shook as I put them together, muttering that I would take them to Mr Black myself. I could not get the image Ellie had conjured up of Luke's face out of my mind.

'Don't take it out on Ellie,' Scogman said quietly.

'She deserves thrashing.'

'She'd love that,' he grinned. 'Anything rather than you ignoring her. You know what she feels about you.' He gave me a wink, but it was tempered with a strange kind of concern.

I stared at him with astonishment. 'She's a child.'

Scogman returned my look with interest. 'She's a bitch on heat,' he said shortly, and turned away.

30

Anne and Luke had been back not just for a few days, but almost two weeks. Mr Black told me all this in a strained, spasmodic conversation, most of which was on the setting up of the job to be printed. All he would say about them was that Anne was 'better, better' and Luke was 'oh, lively, very lively, in the circumstances, very lively'. He told me Mrs Black was out, but from his frequent glances upstairs I knew she did not wish to see me. Only Sarah was normal.

'Well. Tha's back. It's Tom again, is it, my lord?'

'It is.'

She nodded towards the house I had leased. 'I gave it a once over.' My heart gave a little jump. It was not Drury Lane, but it was one of those autumn days when summer seemed reluctant to leave and the place looked at its best. Sun sparkled on the open windows. The jetty leaned over the courtyard. From the windows of the garret you could see over to St Paul's and beyond, for the City was not yet covered with its shroud of winter smoke. It was the best place in the world, I thought, for a child to hide and dream, and for me to tell stories to him, as Matthew once did to me. Across the courtyard, I could see Mr Black's journeyman picking up his composing stick to set my copy.

'Did Anne look at the house?' I asked Sarah.

'Glanced. Nights are getting chilly. Do you want me to light a fire?'

'Lay it.'

'Aye. Waste not, want not,' she said drily.

I had got so used to rolling out of bed in Spitall and clambering down the ladder into the press shop that I had forgotten how dirty I was. I washed in the pail in the yard as I used to, but the ink was ingrained in my hands again. I had no desire to see Anne's nose wrinkle at my appearance.

I saw Anne alone in her small apartment at Lucy's. I went to kiss her. It was not that she recoiled, it was much subtler than that: a slight quivering of her lips, a tightening of her perfectly groomed hands, a glancing flicker at my ink-stained ones. She made me so conscious I had the stink of Spitall about me that my anger boiled over.

'Two weeks you have been back. Two weeks – and not a word.'

'I wanted to prepare Luke.'

'For what? For his father? Does he not know me? If he is well enough to chase round Half Moon Court he is well enough to see me.'

There was more of this until my rage simmered down and I saw beyond her fashionable light blue dress with its bows and cobweb-lawn trimmings; saw with shock her thinness, emphasised by the tight lacing of the bodice, and the papery fragility of her white face.

'Oh, Anne, you are not well.'

'Well enough. I do not sleep much. That is all.' Every word seemed an effort, as pale and ghost-like as her face.

'All!' I knelt by her. 'We must stop this. It has not done you any good. Nor me. I have leased a house.'

'A house. Yes.' I told her that her dreams of becoming Lady Stonehouse were pure fantasy.

She smiled faintly. 'And your dreams of changing the world are not?'

'No. The world has changed. Cromwell is the most powerful man in England.'

'And the King?'

'Is playing bowls.'

She understood. That was the joy of being with her. When we connected we entered each other's head. One word could convey a book of meaning. She was obsessed with the Stonehouse estate, but it was not only riches that infatuated her. It was power. We had that in common.

'Until Parliament disbands it, Cromwell must listen to the army. And, before Parliament disbands it, the army will first disband Parliament.'

She was quite still, except for her eyes, larger and more liquid than usual in her pale face, in which I could see tiny reflections of myself, even down to my scar and the stains in my army jerkin. I told her the army had seen enough in five long years to know that Parliament was rotten. Not just the junior officers but colonels were determined it would be reformed.

'Forget the estate. Lord Stonehouse is in disfavour.'

'And you are in Cromwell's favour?'

'No. But there will be a new Parliament. And I intend to stand for it. With your help, I believe I stand a chance.'

I more than half expected her to laugh, to belittle me, but she said quietly, 'Yes. I think you do.'

She spoke with such conviction I grasped her hands eagerly. 'Mr Tooley is being reinstated. You can return to our old church …'

'As Mrs Neave? When I married someone else?'

'I have seen a lawyer. It can be easily arranged.' It was true. Wildman had said it was possible. I did not tell her he had also said it was easier to reform a Parliament than a wife.

'The house is not suitable.'

'Not suitable! It is what I can afford and suitable or not, it is where we will live, madam. Pack your things.'

'Will you give us a little more time? Please?' She almost never pleaded, and she had such a wild, desperate air that I was on the verge of giving in. But I was afraid of her falling even more deeply under Lucy's influence.

'No. You have had enough time. More than enough. You will go to the country again. I do not know what you will do. I will give you an hour. I will order a coach.'

She lowered her head resignedly. 'Will you explain to Luke where we are going?'

'Of course I will. I will be glad to. Where is he?'

She picked up a bell on the table by her side.

I had seen it so often in the army, so I was prepared, yet not prepared. I knew, but did not know. It was the way Luke came into the room. Sidled. He had adapted, as all people do, to what had happened to him. He knew where the light was and instinctively turned the good side of his face towards me. I instantly rebuked myself – 'good side'? All of him should be good to me!

Jane came in with him and gave him a little push towards me. He turned angrily towards her and I saw the burned side of his face. It had not healed well. Curds was a generous description. It had a red, lumpy rawness, as if scraped by a farrow. I learned later that some fool of a surgeon, claiming an infallible cure for burns, had made things worse.

Almost instantly, he turned back so the scarred cheek was in shadow. I tried to prevent it, but he saw the instinctive beginnings of my look of anguish and tilted his chin defiantly, dismissively. I wanted to take him in my arms but that, of course, is not what fathers do. In fact, in a curious way, the meeting so disorientated me it was as if he was the father. He was a little Stonehouse. His hooked nose was a perfect replica of his grandfather's. The eye that I could see had an arrogant gleam. When I had last seen him he had been in skirts. He was now in britches, fashionably wide over red silk hose. We stood there like strangers, him defiantly staring up at me, robbing me of speech.

'Why … you are a man, Luke,' I managed at last.

'I should hope so, sir. Mama wanted to keep me in skirts,' he said with disgust.

'Well, you are a little young for britches –' Anne began.

'Older than my years, Aunty Lucy says!' Paradoxically, he plunged his head in his mother's skirts.

'Well, perhaps, perhaps,' Anne murmured indulgently, caressing the love-lock that was growing from his dark curly hair, in which there was not a trace of red. All the while Jane was gazing fondly at him. When he dropped his handkerchief from his cuff, she picked it up and tucked it back. I could see that, in a household of three women, Luke ruled the roost.

I coughed and cleared my throat. I suppose that sounded gratifyingly like a father, for he sprang up and pushed his mother away, as if she had entwined him, rather than the reverse.

'Did you ride in the country, sir?' I asked.

'A little.' He scowled. 'The stable boy insulted me.'

'Insult –' I stopped when I saw Anne, behind Luke, frantically patting her cheek. Jane's alarmed face and clenched fists were an equal warning.

'But I got rid of him,' Luke said.

'Did you,' I said faintly. 'Did you.'

'I did,' he said with satisfaction. 'He went above his station.'

Emboldened by this, and seeming less conscious of his scarred face, he came up to me to give me a closer scrutiny, his eyes travelling wonderingly up my battered boots to my stained jerkin and grubby shirt.

'You have been fighting, sir?'

'Fighting?'

'In some battlefield.'

'No, no, no. In some printing field.'

He frowned, suddenly looking quite old as he struggled with this, suspicious I was making game of him. I could not bear the distance between us and knelt and put out my arms to him and smiled. 'I am come to take you home, Luke.'

He backed away. 'Home? Home? I am home.'

'This is Lucy's home, isn't it?'

He said nothing, but darted a glance to his mother, who smiled encouragingly.

'I have taken a house opposite Grandfather Black's, in Half Moon Court. You like that, don't you?'

He grew very still. He put his thumb in his mouth. Jane took a step towards him but was stopped by a look from Anne.

'Does it have a cellar?' Luke brought out each word in odd jerks.

'It does. You can hide in there. And a garret, where I can tell you stories about battle –'

He ran to his mother to hide in her skirts again, but she stopped him and tried to calm him, telling him he must listen to what I had to say. Then he ran to Jane and when she said the same began hitting her until she caught him by the hands.

'Stop that!' I yelled at him.

I suppose that is what he expected from a father because he stopped immediately. His voice was curiously high-pitched, like that of a child in a choir. 'Is this to punish me?'

'Punish you?'

'For my face?'

I was too appalled to speak for a moment, and he ran to Jane who picked him up. 'No, no, no, Luke. I am to blame, Luke, not you. Listen to me.' But his back was towards me, his face buried in Jane's bodice. 'What have you been saying to him?' I flung at Anne.

'Saying to him? How can you think that? You suppose I got him to say that? Is that what you mean? Now you know what we have been doing, why we went to the country, why –' She took Luke gently from Jane, and rocked him until he took his thumb from his mouth. He whispered in her ear with a sidelong glance at me. She told him 'no whispers', but they murmured together with remonstrances from her to 'be a soldier' and, from him, 'well, why doesn't he come and live here?'

Finally, when he had quietened, she became firmer and said he would have to ask his father those questions. She set him down on the carpet in front of me and he stared up at me, questioning me like a little lawyer.

'Did the man who burned my face live in Grandfather Black's house, sir?'

'He did once. Yes.'

'Did he lock you in the cellar?'

I gave Anne a bewildered glance. She was twisting her hands in anguish. 'That was a story, Luke ...'

'It was not true?'

'Well, yes, but ...' I squatted down in front of him. 'Luke, he is dead. I killed him.'

'You said that before,' he cried, in a rising panic. 'When he killed my sister –'

'No, no, no, I said I *would* kill him – and he did not kill Liz, not, not exactly –'

The more I tried to get through to him, the worse it got. He seemed to believe that, even if George was dead, his spirit was waiting for him in the cellar at Half Moon Court. It was as if I had somehow transferred my childhood terrors to him. The more I struggled to reassure him, the more he seemed to pick up that troubled part of myself, until sweat broke out on his forehead and his scarred cheek took on a livid aspect.

It struck me, with a bitter irony, that our one point in common was this fear. Thinking, at least, that I might use this, I put out my arms to him. 'Come, Luke. We will fight him together.'

'You said he was dead!'

'I mean –'

I tried to hold him. He struck out at me, screaming. I caught his flailing fists, then snatched him up, holding him tightly to me, but he thrashed and kicked in increasing distress. Anne held out her arms and took him. He slipped from her, still screaming, and Jane tried to quieten him. I stood impotently until I saw Anne's mute appeal for me to go.

I stood outside, unable to leave until, mercifully, exhaustion turned Luke's screaming into crying, then sobbing, then silence, then the first coherent words.

'Has he gone?' he said.

Whether he meant me, or George, or whether I had become George to him, I did not know. The footman, who must have been standing there all the time, seemed to come out of the wall.

'The Countess would like to see you, sir.'

I scarcely heard him. All I wanted to do was to get out of that place, but as I stumbled down the stairs, Lucy came out of the gallery. Her face bore the signs of something I never expected to see there: age. She was not made up, and her skin was like crazed porcelain.

'Tom … You must go back to her.'

'I have not left her! I came to fetch her. You heard …' She waited but I could not go on.

'You must come back here. For her sake, as well as Luke's.'

'Luke's? He only calmed down when I was gone. He is terrified of me!'

'He is terrified of where you might take him. It will pass. He needs to get to know you. Do you realise how little he has seen you? I mean not just now, but all his life. And you need them. Look at yourself.'

She drew me to Cromwell's picture. It was so dark the glass acted as a mirror. I was shocked when I saw myself. I was used to a youthful, impish face looking back at me. My cheeks were just starting to slacken. Tiny frown lines were sketched in above the aquiline nose. Aquiline? Yes, it really did look eagle-like in this weathered, more austere face. Previously, saying I was a Stonehouse was a prediction. Now it was a fact. Only my flaring red hair was a gesture of defiance.

I turned away. Anne's grief and concern were genuine. But I could not stop the thought creeping into my mind that she and Lucy were using it to draw me back. And if I came back here, it would be as a Stonehouse.

Lucy was sitting, as usual enjoying the impact she had made. Or so I thought.

'You seem suddenly very concerned about my welfare, madam.'

Her words came out raw and bitter, without the usual conversational preamble. 'You think I have no heart for anything but politics. It never seems to occur to you that, after my child and my husband died, I had no heart left for anything else. I do not want to see that happening to you.'

She spoke with genuine feeling, but I could not entirely dismiss the feeling I was being manipulated. I walked restlessly about the gallery.

'I suppose I owe you for things. That dress must have cost –'

'She pays for everything with her own money,' Lucy said coldly.

'Her own money? She has none. She returned the money from my army warrant. Her own money? Where does she get it from?'

'I have no idea,' Lucy said with increasing coldness.

I went halfway up the stairs to Anne's apartment from which came a murmur of voices. Then came a sound I did not expect to hear. Luke was laughing. Anne wanted him to give her something, and he wouldn't. I almost had my hand on the doorknob when he said, 'I heard him.'

'Luke … he's your father. There's nothing to be frightened of.'

'I heard him!'

His voice took on that note of rising panic that had led to his previous attack. I could not bear putting him through that again and returned to Lucy.

'What is happening?' She shook her head. 'You don't know? You seem to know as little about what is going on as I do, madam.'

She leaned forward urgently. 'That is why you must come back here. I cannot reach her.'

I stood irresolutely, looking up the stairs. There was another peal of laughter. This time it was from Anne.

'Well, I certainly cannot reach her,' I said.

31

I became impossible. I shut myself off from everyone, unless it was to do with work, which I pursued with a ferocious zeal. From thinking about Anne constantly, I never thought about her at all. Nor about Luke, although he invaded my dreams, in which I became George trying to thrust him into the fire. I would awake sweating, burning hot, although winter cold had clamped hard on the attic. Then I would wander downstairs and correct a proof, or oil the press. Several times I nearly trod on Ellie, sleeping like a dog at the foot of the ladder. I kicked her out, yelling at her to go back to Matthew, but she would always return, always under my feet, ready to run with a pamphlet, or putting a pie on my desk, which I would take a bite from then forget.

The Case of the Army, the pamphlet arguing for Parliamentary reform, had sold out in the bookstalls and we were doing a second printing when Wildman came in, full of excitement. Cromwell had agreed to call a meeting of the Army Council to discuss it at the end of the month. The Army Council did not consist only of senior officers like Cromwell, Fairfax and Ireton. Two officers and two soldiers from each regiment sat on it. Many soldiers and a few officers supported our arguments. Wildman was to present the case for these arguments at the meeting.

I helped prepare his speech. Because Wildman would not reject the King, Nehemiah, who called Wildman 'a smooth-talking cove', was always trying to discover what we were planning. He would wander into the press room on some pretext, with Bennet, the marksman from my old regiment. Now there was no fighting to be done Bennet had gone to seed, drinking with the watermen with whom he used to work, contributing little but listening to Nehemiah and agreeing with him.

One day I had to go out urgently. Ellie swore she would keep an eye on the press room until I returned. When I did, she was not there but Bennet was. He claimed to be looking for Nehemiah. He seemed to have taken nothing, but when he left I searched through my chest and could not find notes of a meeting with Wildman. When Ellie came in from the privy outside I was frantic.

'Couldn't you wait?'

'No! Do you want me to soil myself?'

'You're coarse as well as stupid. Now he knows what we're planning. You've ruined everything!'

'I *will* ruin everything!' she screamed at me. She picked up some quoins, blocks of wood that held type in place, and flung them at me. For good measure she added the inkwell, spraying my jerkin with ink. Then she burst into tears and fled.

I was picking up the quoins and retrieving papers not ruined with ink when I remembered. I searched a shelf where galleys were stored. Underneath a pile of them I found the notes I had convinced myself Bennet had taken. I had worked such long hours the previous night that, dizzy with fatigue, I had forgotten I had put them there.

Ellie was not at Matthew's. Nor was she at the market, where he thought she was doing the shopping. On my way back I passed the house where Scogman had a room. We were in and out of each other's places so often I did not bother to knock. I had seen Scogman charm women with words often enough, but I had never seen him at it. His britches were off and his hairy arse was about to come down on someone. I began to mutter an apology, then recognised the multi-coloured underskirts of the woman he was on top of. Ellie's frightened face appeared. She yelled, kicked and bit Scogman. I pulled him from her and threw him against the wall.

'Can't you leave any woman alone? You really have no feelings, have you?'

Sobbing and crying, Ellie pulled a sheet over herself.

'Cover yourself up, man.' I threw his britches at him.

He yanked them on, bringing out his words in savage bursts, as he hooked the britches on to metal rings under his shirt. 'It is *you* who have no feelings for people – only paper people.' He kicked at a pamphlet on the floor. 'I'm human. Unlike you. She came at me. Didn't you?'

She screamed as he pulled the sheet from her.

'She doesn't want me. She wants you, you pious prig. God knows why. Don't you? Don't you? She couldn't stand it any more. Could you?'

I stared at her, waiting for an answer, but she shrank back, sobbing.

'Well, go on. Tell him. Tell him.'

She looked like a broken doll. Some red ochre paint that could be bought at the market for a penny was smeared over her face. The stitching on a tattered patch of her underskirt had come apart. She pulled her skirt down, looking wildly about her, then darted to the door. I grabbed her by the wrists. She kicked and struggled but at last went limp, panting, her head bowed. She had twisted her hair into a fashionable bun that had come awry. The ribbon holding it was on the point of falling. I took it and held it out to her, telling her I had found the notes and was sorry I had wrongly accused her. She stared at me, warily and suspiciously, snatched the ribbon and ran.

She was on her hands and knees in the press room when I got there, covered in soapy ink from hands to elbows.

'You must go home to Matthew, Ellie.'

'I told him what I had done and he said I must clean it up. Every spot of it.'

I replied it was my fault, but she would have none of it. I had some press work to do which I was late with. She wanted to help me, saying she had learned from Nehemiah. Again I told her to go home, but press work is tediously slow for one person and, after I had inked the type and she had inserted the paper, I no longer tried to stop her. While the ink was drying I went to the market and got a loaf and some herrings, of which I knew she was fond. She sniffed when she saw them, wiping her nose on the back of her hand. She had put coal on the banked-up fire. The light from it and the candles gleamed on the polished floor. She had removed the ingrained dirt of months with great effect, but this drew more attention to the ink spots. I began to say so, but she looked so stricken and was for getting out the pail again that I hastily said I was joking, and swore I could not see where the ink had fallen.

I always ate where I happened to be, but now she spread her apron out on the floor and we sat leaning against the press. We ate in silence. The only sound was from the shifting coals or the rustle of her skirts as she bent to pick up another herring. She ate delicately, picking every shred of fish from the bone, from head to tail. She had kicked off her pattens, and when a piece of coal fell from the fire she scuttered in her bare feet to fling it back.

Gradually the warmth of the fire stole over us. I had not eaten like this, with someone, without feeling the need to talk, since I had left Anne. I could understand why Scogman thought I had no feelings. The only way I could cope was by shutting them out. Now they flooded back I had such a devastating ache for Anne I must have given a little groan, for Ellie looked at me with alarm.

'What is it? Is it the fish?'

I laughed and shook my head. She looked aggrieved at my laughter and said, as if to tell me she was quite aware all pains were not physical, 'Is it –' And she did her imitation of Anne, lifting her chin and pointing a contemptuous toe at an ink spot. I turned away sharply. Immediately she ran to me, contrite, and dropped on her knees beside me.

'She makes you unhappy?'

I smiled at her instant concern. Her cheeks were flushed and her tattered underskirt splayed out in a fan of different colours. 'No, no.'

'She makes you happy?'

I was silent.

'What then?'

She was so full of life, so full of that moment, in which she cared not a jot about the past or the future, it was impossible not to share that joy, to laugh again, not at her, but with her. To talk. She listened with a sudden graveness. Her liquid brown eyes took on a greenish tinge in the eddying light of the fire, like a cat's eyes. All her movements had the exquisite economy of a cat's, darting, abruptly stopping, listening, every sense alert.

I tried to say that love was not just love, but a fight, sometimes even hate. That sounded crass, so to illustrate it I said that, unlike Anne, who would not do anything I wanted, Ellie would do anything for me. That sounded so arrogant I winced. But, far from being offended, she leaned forward and said she would. What did I want her to do?

It was said with such eagerness, such childlike innocence, it snatched any risible laughter from me. But, at the same time, it was knowing, predatory. Her bodice was so tight-laced round her already thin waist it pushed up her emerging breasts. Between them was a pad exuding a strong smell of musk. A vivid picture came to me of her sprawled out on the bed, skirts thrown up. Scogman was wrong. I was as human as he was.

'Go home, Ellie,' I said. 'Go home.'

Quietly, submissively, she rose, cleared up the mess of fish bones, put the remains of the loaf on the press where she knew I had breakfast, if I had breakfast at all, rolled up her apron, thanked me very civilly for the herring, which she assured me was the best she had ever tasted, and walked away.

She was closing the door when the words came from me. It was as if there was another person inside me, letting out a cry, almost a scream of despair. I hammered my hands on the stone floor where I was still sitting.

'Oh, Ellie! What am I going to do!'

She ran to me, flinging her arms round me. I never even kissed her. I went for her like a starving man swallowing food. It was more of a savage attack on Anne than making love to Ellie. She responded with a hungry, violent desperation akin to mine. It was fiendishly uncomfortable, on the floor, or moving against the hard edges of the press. But our instincts told us nothing would happen if we did not do it there and then. I could not get her bodice unlaced. I pulled up her skirts. She cried out and rolled away. Still sticking to her arse was the skeleton of a herring she had picked clean. I peeled it off, kissed the slowly disappearing image on her flesh, then solemnly held up the skeleton.

We broke into fits of laughter. We could not stop. We kissed the skeleton. We kissed each other. I undid her bodice. From being so knowing, so assured, with her musk and her rainbow underskirts, she suddenly became clumsy, shy. Her eyes seemed to grow larger, more fearful. At first I thought it all part of her act, her pretended innocence. It was only when I was going in her that I realised. I drew back.

'Go on,' she choked ferociously. 'Go *on!*'

She was not expecting the pain. Her face crumpled, distorted. I held her close, then I came. It meant more pain for her but I did not care. I stayed in her, wanting to go in her as far as possible until I was finished. I rolled away; dozed; I may even have slept until sounds began to creep back: the fall of a coal, the bark of a dog, the clank of a pail. The pail was level with my half-open eyes. She was cleaning up the blood from the floor.

'Leave it.'

She ignored me, rinsing the rag, staring at the mark the blood would leave among the archipelago of stains on the floor.

'I didn't realise –' I began.

'Like your son, you thought I was a Spitall whore.'

She took the pail outside. I heard her emptying it and pumping it full for morning. Returning, she wet some slack in the coal bucket and banked up the fire so it would smoulder through the night. Once, I glimpsed her furtively drawing her sleeve over her eyes.

'Ellie, leave it! Go home. Matthew will be worried –'

She rounded on me ferociously. 'Matthew? Matthew worried? Matthew would be worried if I came back. Matthew knows.'

'Knows? Knows what?'

'Don't you realise? … You don't, do you? You don't realise anything that's happening around you, do you? You think you want to come back here and live among the people, but you don't, you don't. You want to tell us what to do. What to be. I don't know. You're just like –'

She tried to mimic Anne with a few mincing steps, but tripped over her pattens and would have fallen if I had not caught her. She burst into tears. I held her to me.

'Let me go, let me go, let me go!'

She caught me in the face with her fist and when I held her wrists kicked out at me with her patten. I gripped her tightly until, in another avalanche of tears, she finally went limp.

'What does Matthew know?'

She looked up at me, her face criss-crossed with tear-stained rivulets of red ochre and ink. I kissed her gently. Her lips tasted of salty fish. In fits and starts, with gulps as tears threatened again, she said Matthew had told her I was in great danger from an evil spirit. I sighed, and said Matthew told stories, very tall stories, as tall as St Paul's. But this one was true, she cried vehemently. There was a pendant in which an evil bird lived. It had snatched Anne and now it wanted me.

I began to laugh, then I felt her shivering. I remembered the pictures Matthew had painted in my childish mind: the will o' the wisps on the marsh, the man with a scar. There was a pendant, she asked. There was. Matthew warned me it was a source of evil? He did but … I tried to tell her it was the Stonehouse estate, and greed that was the evil. How much she understood I did not know. What mattered was that she believed in evil, in Matthew's story, not my literal version. And, as usual, Matthew's story was a mixture of nonsense cunningly wrapped round a kernel of common sense.

She pulled away from me, sniffing. 'Anyway,' she scowled, 'he knows. I'm fed up with the two of you being miserable, he said. Why don't you sod off and be miserable together?'

I laughed outright. There was no doubting the truth of that. She caught Matthew's tone perfectly. I could see now what had been building up between them. Matthew had never liked Anne. He had refused to go to our wedding. He had a fear of the Stonehouses and a regret for stealing the pendant, which had been the seed for everything that followed. And, I felt with a pang, he wanted me back. In the way that most mattered, in bringing me up, I was his son.

Ellie thought I was laughing at her, snatched up her pattens and ran for the door. I caught up with her as she opened it. She screamed. On the roof opposite, silhouetted against the moon, was a bird.

'The falcon!'

She hid in my arms. I tensed and my hand went for my dagger for a different reason. From one of the doorways opposite I saw the shadow of a man before he slipped away towards an alley.

'It's a kite,' I muttered. 'Not a falcon.'

She refused to look in case she caught its evil eye. The kite, disturbed by the scream, flapped upwards, then almost lazily dropped, tail forking to steer it towards a rat darting from a pile of rubbish. Ellie shuddered and pressed herself tightly against me as the kite rose so close to us we caught the draught from its wings. I glimpsed the tiny spikes of blood where its talons gripped the mewling rat. The echoing sounds of the man running down the alley dwindled into silence. I pushed her inside and locked the door.

'It was the falcon!' she said, shaking with terror.

'It was a red kite. Catching its supper.'

'Then why are you holding that?'

I was still gripping the dagger. I sheathed it, barred the door, which I did not normally do, picked up my pack to act as a pillow on the floor and told her to sleep upstairs.

'Not alone,' she said. 'Please! Not alone.'

I sighed, and dropped the pack back where it was. She scurried up the ladder like an arrow from a bow and by the time I was in the sloping room all I could see of her was a sight of her large eyes peering from the edge of the blankets. Her teeth did not stop chattering until she felt the warmth of my body. She pleaded with me not to blow out the candle. I did not do so even when I felt her regular breathing, but lay watching the shadows, tensing when I heard the sound of some drunk in the street. Her fear brought back all my youthful fears, when I was hunted and did not know why. The man watching could not be anything to do with my father. He must know I had rejected the estate – even his name.

I dreamed I was with Anne. Liz was still alive, giving out her stuttering cry. We continued making love, trying to ignore her. I awoke to find the candle guttering fitfully and Ellie rousing me. I shoved her away.

'Ellie, we can't, we musn't – you know I'm married –'

'Are you?' she said, eyes round with mock horror.

'Ellie, stop that. Listen. I can't love you –'

'Love?' she spat scornfully. 'Ain't none of that in Spitall. Love? This is what we have. This is what I want. This.'

When we had finished and I was falling back to sleep, she stroked the scar on my cheek. 'You pious prig.'

The candle finally blinked and went out. In the darkness she whispered, 'It didn't hurt as much. It does get better ... don't it?'

32

It did get better. Not only in bed. Ellie knew Spitall, knew the Levellers, and with her quick wit opened many doors to me. From being suspicious, from tapping their noses when they saw me, a warning of the Stonehouse within, the people accepted me as one of them. And I began to accept myself.

When I signed my name, Tom Neave began to flow naturally from my quill. So, astonishingly enough, did pamphlets. One, on the freedom ride from Holdenby, sold so well that I began to save, determined to show that Tom Neave did not need Thomas Stonehouse's money.

Best of all was supper with Matthew. We had eels and pike and cold rabbit pie, washed down with strong beer. Matthew demanded Scogman told his story of being caught with his britches down. Ellie tried to leave the room, but I stopped her, saying I had never seen her blush before, and she blushed so prettily.

She struck out at me angrily. "Course I blush! I'm a woman, ain't I?'

The men howled with laughter and beat the table. She ran to the kitchen. I followed her and she burst out that she knew I didn't love her, but she was a woman, she had her feelings and, and … Then she gave a great gulp. She was ready to hit me again, but looked so vulnerable I held her and could have made love to her there and then, but Matthew came in and said, 'You say none of my potions ever work, Tom. What about this one, eh?'

He stroked Ellie's heaving shoulders gently until they quietened.

On those days it was like coming home to Poplar. I could almost smell the tang of the salt wind across the marsh and hear the hammer of great ships being built to sail into Matthew's stories.

I never saw anyone watching the house again at night, but I felt it. Sometimes, in a crowd, or an alehouse, I thought I recognised someone following me, but I always lost him, or it turned out to be no one I knew. It was on one of those black days, when Ellie said I had got out of the wrong side of the bed, that I had the idea.

I was at the goldsmith's on London Bridge, where I deposited my money. I determined to lease a better house than the one at Half Moon Court, with no cellar, well away from any ghost that Luke might fear. I hired a horse and went to the Countess's house. Once there, my spirits deserted me. I heard again Luke's cries of terror. A clumsy, unannounced visit could destroy everything. Both Anne and I were being stupid. I would write asking the Countess to act as an intermediary. I was turning to go when Luke came out, running down the steps, chased by Jane.

I was preparing to mount my horse to follow them, when a Hackney hell-cart drew up. A woman came down the steps, curtly dismissing the footman. I say woman, for at first I did not recognise Anne. She wore a half-mask and hood and a long, flowing cassock, for it was very cold.

She was in the Hackney before I could so much as shout. I followed it past St Giles's Fields, along Holborn and into Gray's Inn. There I lost her, but I had seen enough. There were no bread-and-cheese lawyers there. They dealt with great estates, family disputes and divorce. Milton, whose wife had deserted him, just as, by slow degrees, Anne seemed to be deserting me, had written a pamphlet that railed against divorce that was not a divorce, for there was no nullity, no remarriage, only separation of bed and board. And money.

'That's your game, is it?' I kept saying to myself as I rode furiously, anywhere, just to keep riding.

Was Anne's visit to Maidenhead just to take the country air? Luke was well enough now to skip down those steps. She was putting him up to his nightmare about me, I was convinced of it. I rode back to the Countess's house to confront Anne, but again my conviction vanished. Nobody could invent Luke's cries of terror. I rode the horse into exhaustion but could not exhaust my mind.

What hurt me most was that I no longer knew her. What had been pretence, practice before, had become part of her. She was more elegant, more distant than ever. And that was not the worst thing. The worst thing was that I wanted her. I wanted her so badly that dark October evening that I gazed into the oily blackness of the Thames at London Bridge until some drunk lurched into me and told me to get on with it, as there were others wanting my space.

The shops along the bridge were putting up their shutters and I stopped the goldsmith putting up his. I told him I was no longer interested in leasing a property. I pointed to a necklace, which took a good deal of the money I had saved.

'It's gold, innit?' Ellie whispered.

'Enamelled gold,' I said. 'You're gold to me.'

She looked at me levelly. 'You're a bloody liar, Tom.' Then she burst into tears. 'You're leaving me, ain't you?'

Nothing I said would convince her that exactly the opposite was true. She pointed to the mouldering herring skeleton, which she had pinned to the side of the press. That was all she needed, she said.

'Your *memento mori*,' I said softly. When she looked at me blankly I told her it was an object that reminded people of death.

'You're a cheerful bugger, ain't you, Tom?' she said. 'But you're bloody right.' And she buried her head in my chest and we held each other tightly, before she looked up with a sniff and a grin. 'I could never wear that in Spitall – I'd get nubbed!' Her grin broadened. 'But I could wear it at night.'

It was a week before the Army Council was due to discuss Wildman's *Case of the Army*. The Bull and Mouth was a ferment of argument at the Levellers' meeting in the upstairs room. Nehemiah put down a motion that 'Wee should urge the meeting that no further addresses be made to the King.'

This was Leveller talk for a republic. It was insane and I said so. Cromwell would never accept it.

'Why should we accept Cromwell?' Nehemiah flung back at me. 'He is not the meeting.'

My relationship with Nehemiah grew even worse when Will, whose father was seriously ill, proposed me as a representative in his place for our old regiment.

'Point of order,' said Nehemiah. He had the army lists in front of him. 'There is no Tom N-Neave on this list.'

If he had kept his mouth shut, I would never have gone. Even though I was still Major Stonehouse on the army list, I hated the name too much to use it. But if my longing to be there when the words I had run with as a boy might finally be heard was not enough, his rancour tipped the scales.

'I will go as Tom Neave,' I said. 'Disguised as Major Stonehouse.'

Everyone except Nehemiah thumped the table at that and the meeting broke up as all such meetings do, late at night, with a bundle of jumbled decisions that John Wildman, in presenting the case for the soldiers, was instructed to 'lick into shape'.

He came back to Gun Press for a late supper. While Ellie spitted herrings over the fire and Scogman fetched strong ale, Wildman took me down to the depths of despair. He looked at the pamphlet not from the point of view of the radicals, who all agreed with one another, when they were not cutting each other's throats, but from the point of view that mattered, that of Adam, the ordinary, cautious, middle-of-the-road soldier.

Wildman stroked his silky moustache. 'Adam don't want to get rid of the King. His Majesty robs him and kills half the Adams in the country, but the remainder still loves His Majesty, like a beaten wife loves her husband. He knows Parliament is rotten, but better the devil, eh? Cromwell's rigged it. He's got enough Adams on the Army Council to –' He threw the pamphlet in the bin.

'We're fucked then,' said Scogman.

'Unless we rig it different.' He beamed at Ellie. 'You grill the most delicious herring, my dear! Look at the roe on this one.'

He swallowed it whole.

It was in the air that late October morning. Mixed with the stink of coal dust and sewers, the whiff of hot bread from the ovens was the smell of excitement. Many people believed it was something like the mysterious force of magnetism charging the air, for it moved a normally stingy baker, who had fought at Naseby, to give free bread to a couple of soldiers and wish them good luck. It was in the sound of the carts rattling to the river, carrying soldiers in tattered uniforms, waving when they recognised old comrades, only to fight with them for boats at the riverside. Above all it was in the boats. From Iron Gate Stairs, Puddle Wharf, Queenhithe, Milford and further west, boats were in constant demand. At the Fulham ferry to Putney, you could scarce see the water for boats.

From a small, sleepy village of watermen and farmers, with a number of grand houses where rich merchants retreated from the stink of the City during summer, that season Putney had become a miniature city overflowing with the stench and struggle of people the rich normally escaped from. They were awoken not by a crowing cock, but by the beat of a drum. Since August, Putney had had the doubtful privilege of being the army HQ.

The best houses, with river views, were occupied by the grandees, Fairfax, Cromwell and Ireton. Officers billeted in the High Street. Soldiers pitched their tents in the fields of bickering farmers, although they and the shopkeepers stood to make a small fortune from the soldiers – at least on paper.

Overlooking the river, at the centre of it all, was the medieval church of St Mary's. There the army held its meetings, partly because it was the only place big enough, but mostly because it was hoped God would give guidance.

As people went into church, Scogman and I distributed the new pamphlet that came from Wildman, 'licking the old one into shape'. It had been agreed in hurried meetings and printed the day before. Every one of the hundred people squeezing into that dark, damp church for the prayers that preceded every meeting had the pamphlet.

'Put it among the prayer books,' Wildman said. 'God needs to read it too.'

Mr Ink was very grand again, with replaceable paper cuffs to catch the splashes of ink, and an ink boy who scuttled to the Communion table in the chancel with horn and paper. He pulled me round a pillar.

'Ireton found out how I released you from gaol. But I was not reprimanded – I was told I should have paid you more.'

'Why?'

He shook his head. 'Something is up.'

'What?'

'You are, it seems.'

In fact, as I rose to my feet from prayers, Cromwell came up to me. He was distant, but I was amazed he was speaking to me at all.

'I am glad to see you are a Stonehouse again.'

Ireton must have seen the muddle of feelings in my face, for he gripped my arm and drew me away.

'I should stick to Stonehouse,' he said. 'Unless you want to find yourself in prison like your father.'

'You have him?'

'He has been seen near the Exchange. Do you know where he is?'

'No. I did not even know he was still in the country.'

'Oh, he's in the country all right. He wouldn't be anywhere else at the moment, would he?'

'What do you mean?'

'You know what I mean. I know why you're a Stonehouse again.'

There was almost a wink in his black, sloe-like eyes. I found his sudden friendliness not only puzzling, but more unnerving than his enmity.

'I did my best to persuade Cromwell you did not help your father to escape from Holdenby. You're not such a fool. I know this is just a charade.' He tapped the pamphlet we had just printed.

'I believe in it totally!' I said hotly.

He gave me a sceptical look and glanced at Cromwell, who was gathering his papers. He looked brooding, lost in another world.

'He's indecisive again. Waiting for God to tell him what to do. Everything's coming to the boil,' Ireton muttered. His manner changed and he became almost pleading. 'If you know anything, for the Lord's sake tell me. Cromwell has redoubled the guards but he won't have the King kept in close custody. It is his royal prerogative. Royal prerogative! He has been seeing anyone he likes at Hampton Court … including Scottish ministers. Has he reached an agreement with them to fight another war? I don't know – but I know he has withdrawn his parole not to escape.'

I almost felt sorry for Ireton. He did the bulk of the drafting and planning. With Cromwell, he ferried between Putney and Westminster, struggling to reach an agreement between Parliament and an increasingly recalcitrant King. The last thing he wanted to do was debate soldiers' rights. But a split in the army would be ruthlessly exploited by the King. Perhaps his and Cromwell's conciliatory attitude towards me was because of that. No, no, it was more than that. Something

to do with my father. With the Stonehouses. I jumped at the sudden
flutter of a trapped bird in the roof of the church. Just as Ellie had
done that night, I felt the eyes of the falcon watching me. Absurd!
Nevertheless, I whirled round. Nehemiah was looking at me steadily,
broodingly. He did not look away, but did something he rarely did,
least of all with me. He smiled.

It was extraordinary. People on both sides who had previously
hated me seemed to be taking a liking to me. I expected him to
loathe the pamphlet because it said nothing about getting rid of the
King. But he shook me by the hand.

'Makes everything so simple,' he said.

It did.

Cromwell, the master of tactics and ambushes, had been outma-
noeuvred by Wildman. Expecting an onslaught on the King and the
grievances of soldiers, he got neither.

Instead he got a pamphlet that broadened, yet simplified, *The
Case of the Army*. It went to first principles. It asked where the power
of the rulers came from in the first place. What, or who, gave them
the right to such power? It was no longer a case for the army. That
word was not even in the title. The pamphlet was called *An Agreement
of the People*.

People were crammed in the pews, craning round the pillars to
see Cromwell's frown growing deeper as Wildman presented the
case. Perched on a sill, I could see Mr Ink's quill flying over the page.
Miraculously, the trapped bird had found a way out, as, it seemed
to me, *An Agreement* found a way through the impasse between
King and Parliament.

It turned the soldiers' case, their pay and grievances, into the
people's case, their rights into the people's rights. But how could
those rights be determined by a Parliament that had already rejected
them? Parliament itself must be reformed.

The pamphlet was as astute and significant in what it did not say
as much as in what it did. Cromwell had prepared his arguments

as a rebuttal of criticisms of his case against the King. But the pamphlet said nothing about the King. Nothing about the House of Lords. It was as if they did not exist – as, at the beginning of time, it was argued, they did not.

The pamphlet proposed a written Constitution. It held that power belonged to the people, who alone could elect a party in Parliament.

Again, there was no mention of the King.

By negotiating with the King, Cromwell was attempting to put new wine into old bottles. Those bottles were cracked and broken. Before any negotiations with the King, the people had earned their right, through the blood they had spilled, to say what those rights and liberties were.

'Sovereignty of the people?' Cromwell retorted. 'The people *themselves* will not go along with it!'

'No negotiations?' put in Ireton. 'We are halfway through negotiations with the King. We have made declarations we cannot break!'

There was an uproar at that. The soldiers' friends had been killed and they had all risked their lives, yet were not to be allowed a say in those declarations? They were not a mercenary army!

People who had never spoken, never even thought they had a voice, shot up their hands clamouring to speak. What did they fight for? To enslave themselves all over again? Mr Ink darted up and down, struggling to identify them, in the end recording them simply as 'Bedfordshire man' or 'Suffolk trooper'.

When it became too dark to see, Ireton grudgingly gave way and said the declarations with the King would be reviewed in the light of the agreement. But it was during the second day that I felt God had spoken.

The words came from the mouth of an officer, Colonel Rainborough. 'I do believe that the poorest he in England hath a life to live as the greatest he … Every man that is to live under a government ought first – by his own consent – to put himself under that government.'

By the time we left the church, the moon was up and the stars out. Scogman, Mr Ink and I were drunk on words. Ireton had argued about property as the basis for votes, but the meeting had agreed that 'all but beggars and servants would have the vote'. Cromwell said he would put it to Parliament.

Parliament? We felt we were Parliament! We stood on the river bank relieving ourselves. Nobody had dared to leave for fear of missing the final vote. With a sigh of relief, Scogman arced a line of piss, shimmering in the moonlight, into the Thames.

'There's my message for Westminster.'

We laughed at anything. Beer was passed round. Camp fires were crackling near the tents in the fields. The rumour that the King had been talking to the Scots caused some to cry that the 'man of blood' should be brought to trial, but most were euphoric.

'The King will be no more than icing on the cake,' Mr Ink declared solemnly. 'And that cake was baked today.'

I stared down the river, which was eddying this way and that, for the tide was on the turn. The City was a great pall of smoke, pierced only by the moonlit St Paul's and church spires. It seemed like yesterday that I had come up river to seek my fortune. I felt as if I was that small boy again, who had been given smeared, smuggled words from Parliament, to run with through the streets. Even my voice sounded smaller, like a child asking questions.

'It was true then,' I said to Mr Ink, 'when you said the words would change the world.'

Mr Ink wagged his finger at me, correcting me, exactly as he used to. 'Have, Tom,' he said. 'Have.'

'Here!' Scogman said suddenly. He fished in his pockets, where he found sixpence and two groats. 'Does this mean I have a vote?'

'With your capacity to find money,' Mr Ink said, 'I wouldn't be surprised if they made you Chancellor.'

Many felt they had votes that evening. More than that. They looked at the torn, muddy ground and thought they had reclaimed a piece of England. Although it was cold, and a light drizzle was falling, one man prayed, alternately looking up to the heavens, then kissing the grass. A group sat huddled round a fire. They talked about a hill in Surrey one knew. It was barren, but might be dug. Animals would fertilise it. Thy Kingdom come, on earth as it is in heaven. Did that not mean that God had given this soil, this grass, to everyone?

I heard the soft skirl of Joshua's pipe, but it was not martial, it was a jig. Puritans dancing? They were godly men, but that night there was a maypole in them all.

Scogman and I were looking for a boat to take us back to Spitall when we smelt it. Duck. Roast duck. It made us realise how hungry we were. We were drawn by the smell to the edge of a field, a little apart from the other tents. Gobbets of fat from the duck dropped into the fire, throwing up flares of light on Nehemiah's face. He was having an argument with someone. It did not seem politic to interfere, but when we realised the other man was what we were looking for – a waterman – we stopped.

'Evening better for poaching – if that's what you're after,' the waterman said.

'Morning. It's got be morning. Upstream.'

'Upstream?'

'Beyond Richmond. Stag Island.'

'Stag Island? Have to be early. Tide turns. Goes downstream, eight, nine o'clock, thereabouts …'

Nehemiah took out his purse. From the rattle, he was not short of money. Firelight flickered on a double crown. The waterman stretched out his hand. Nehemiah drew the coin back and resumed his negotiations, but I heard no more, for there was the click of a gun being cocked in my ear and the barrel of it was pressed into my cheek. Scogman pulled out his knife.

'I wouldn't,' Bennet said.

There was a steady, unchanging blankness in his face, which was in stark contrast to the distant sound of the pipe playing the jig, and the murmur of psalms from another group. Nehemiah shaded his eyes against the light of the fire. In one sharp movement, Bennet shoved me staggering forwards towards the fire and brought the gun round on Scogman.

'Caught them spying,' he said.

I almost collided with the waterman, who prevented me from falling.

'Why! He's not a spy. It's Tom. And Scoggy. We're all brothers tonight, aren't we, Tom?'

I rubbed my bruised cheek. 'I would hope so.'

Bennet looked anything but brotherly. He took Nehemiah to one side and there was a hurried, whispered conversation, which ended with Nehemiah snapping at him not to be a fool and to lock his gun. The waterman said this was a bad business, and he wanted nothing to do with poaching.

'Poaching?' Nehemiah looked amazed as he pointed to the sizzling duck. 'That ain't poaching, is it, Scoggy?'

Scogman looked puzzled. His mouth was watering so much the words came out as a mumble. 'Poaching? No such thing as poaching after today, is there?'

Nehemiah laughed and clapped him on the shoulder. 'Good old Scoggy! And God said: let there be winged things … and God found them good …' He hacked off a piece of breast, the burned skin shrivelled round the dark meat, with bubbles of fat winking from it, and held it out to me. 'After today, everything belongs to everyone, right, Tom?'

I mumbled between mouthfuls that I did not think that was quite in the agreement, but the roast duck was certainly a powerful argument for it. Nehemiah's laughter redoubled, as beyond the camp fire came the sound of horses. Cromwell, Ireton and the other grandees were riding to the village for their supper. I caught Ireton's eye as Nehemiah put his arm round me, declaring I had a way with words.

'You taught me everything I know ... Well, not quite everything ...' He was never one to show his feelings but his voice caught. 'We have had our disagreements, Tom, but I think we share the right e-e-end?'

I embraced him. 'We do, we do.'

During this Bennet squatted, taking a cloth to his gun, although it had not been used. It was a curious instrument, with a tubular sight, an exposed spring and a decorated plate, which he polished assiduously.

'Oh, put it away, put it away, Bennet!' cried Nehemiah. 'We're all brothers today!'

Ellie had fallen asleep by the dying fire. I could not stop talking about that momentous day, even in the moment when we were undressing for bed in the shivering cold upstairs.

'... and then Colonel Rainborough said ... The poorest he in England hath a right to live –'

'What about the poorest she?' she said.

She turned round. She was stark naked, except for the gold neck-lace I had bought her. I never answered the question, but blew out the candle, and we made love which made her cry out with joy, for she said it did not hurt any more, and I said brotherly love was a very great thing but it was not to be compared with the love of a man and a woman.

'Tom ...' she whispered in a trembling voice. 'You said you loved me.'

I did not think I quite said that, but I kissed her gently and said nothing. She curled up tightly, with me still partly inside her, and I fell into the deepest of deep sleeps – until the knocking started.

It was part of a dream. At first it was the hammering of the soldiers on the pews in Putney church. Then it became something darker, more sinister, my hammering on the cellar door when I was locked in as a child. Finally, it was real. The whole building shook with the blows. Muttering that it was the falcon, Ellie clung to me in terror.

The knocking stopped and a voice shouted. 'Tom Stonehouse!' There was another voice I did not catch, then the first voice yelled, 'Stonehouse or Neave or whoever you are.'

Ellie lit a candle while I scrambled into britches and shirt, picked up my dagger and stumbled my way downstairs.

33

The knocking began again when I reached the press room. I could hear windows being flung open down the street. People were cursing. A dog barked incessantly. Through the cracks in the door I could see the shape of a Hackney coach. The driver, a surly-looking figure in a heavy overcoat, was about to raise his fist again.

I slid back the bolt, but left the chain on. 'Who is it?'

'I'm looking for a party called Stoneneave.'

'Neave! Tom Neave. Who wants me?'

'A lady.'

'A lady!' There were whistles from a nearby window. 'You can give my door a knock, sweetheart.'

Another voice yelled, 'Let's have a look inside your placket.'

I took the chain off the door. The first real fog of the winter was building up. It took a moment for me to see a cloaked and veiled figure descending from the coach. There were more whistles but, from a window opposite, came a volley of epithets, followed by what looked like the Sleeper's Revenge sailing through the air. The coachman ducked. The woman almost fell in her haste to avoid the object, which shattered near her. Fortunately, it was not a chamber pot, but a bowl of cold pottage that splashed her skirts. Her veil blew back as I caught her, and saw it was Anne. The abuse and the catcalls continued as I pulled her inside.

'What is it, Anne? What is it?'

She was staring beyond me. Halfway down the ladder, still holding the candle, was Ellie, a blanket wrapped round her. I had only one thought. One terrible fear that turned my stomach to water.

'It's Luke, isn't it.'

Anne did not answer. Her breath came and went in little jerks. Beneath her thrown-back veil her face was dead white, her eyes fixed on Ellie.

Ellie gave one movement, a small tilt of her chin, a ghost of her imitation of Anne. The blanket slipped, exposing the glint of the gold necklace hanging between her small breasts. She pulled the blanket round her more tightly, turned and went back up the ladder.

I shook Anne violently so that the veil flopped over her face. I tore it half off. 'Answer me. It's Luke, isn't it?'

'It's your grandfather. He's dying. He wants to see you.'

I had been so convinced it was Luke I had been unable to breathe. Shutting my eyes in relief, I sucked in great gulps of air. Now she shook me, spots of red flaring up in her cheeks.

'Don't you understand? Lord Stonehouse is dying.'

I feared some kind of retribution if I did not answer a dying man's request. And, although there was no love lost between us, at the dead of night, in the Hackney rattling through the empty streets, Lord Stonehouse felt for the first time like my own flesh and blood.

He had been dying for so long, I never thought he would. The first time I met him, I heard him tell his son he had a year to live. That was five years ago. He had survived the stone, and countless other ailments, real and imagined. Long before I met him in the flesh, he had been a strange figure of the imagination, pulling me on invisible strings. Such figures do not die.

The thought crossed my mind that it was a trick to get me back. I gripped her arm. 'Are you telling me the truth? He's really dying? Lord Stonehouse?'

Her taut face gave me the answer. 'I pray we are not too late.'

'He asked for me?'

'For Tom Neave.'

'Tom Neave? Not Stonehouse?'

'Yes. Tom —' She swallowed and her lips tightened. It was as if she could not bring herself to utter my birth name again. 'He has moments when he's as clear as day. Then he gutters like a candle. He rambles.' She turned to the coachman. 'Can't you go any faster?'

'In this?'

He waved his hand at the thick, dirty yellow fog creeping up from the river, reducing the moon to a pale ghost, softening buildings, swirling up alleys, inserting clammy soot-smelling fingers into the coach.

'A man is dying.'

'Won't get there by killing my horses, will we, ma'am?'

The fog grew even thicker, the coach lurching more slowly over the cobbles. I could hear but not see the horses, and the coachman was just a dim shape.

'Ropemaker Street,' he muttered. 'I tell a lie. Silk Street. Scarce see the horses' heads in this.'

'Did he send for you? What happened?' I asked Anne.

She stared outside, although she could see nothing but the wall of fog. 'I have been going to Queen Street. Day after day.'

It came out, in fits and starts. She had gone there begging, even though he would never see her. Then one day, about a month ago, he had an attack. His heart was failing and it looked as though he would die. In the general confusion she had gone upstairs, helping Mr Cole and comforting Lord Stonehouse. With an enormous effort, he had rallied, but only she, Mr Cole and a few of the closest servants knew his condition.

'That is where your money has been coming from.'

'I earned it,' she said bitterly. 'Every groat. As a servant. A nursemaid.'

Convinced, as always, he would recover, Lord Stonehouse was more terrified of those in power learning how ill he was than of death itself. Then, one day, Ireton came, unexpectedly …

Of course! Ireton's sudden friendliness. *I know why you're a Stonehouse again.* Hadn't he almost winked? They needed the power, the influence of the Stonehouse name. They needed me. For some reason that, more than anything else, told me that Lord Stonehouse was going to die – or was already dead.

It was Anne's expression that made me ask the question. 'Did you tell Ireton how ill Lord Stonehouse was?'

'He did not get it from me,' Anne retorted. She shrugged. 'Jane may have been indiscreet to Betsy Cromwell's maid. They are very close.'

In other words, she used the servants to tell them.

'What have you been saying to Lord Stonehouse about me?'

'I have been trying to help him put his soul in order.'

'His soul – or his affairs?' She continued to stare at the blank wall of fog. I gripped her arm. 'Anne! What have you been saying –'

Another coach loomed out of the fog, heading straight towards us. Although both were travelling slowly, the horses reared in panic. The coach tilted and Anne was thrown against me. Only the wall against which it grated saved the coach from going right over. Among the jolting and rocking, the whinnying of the horses, the shouts of the coachmen to calm them and their yells of abuse, I held Anne tightly. Among all the subtler odours of her perfumes was the sharp, simple smell of rosemary I used to catch when I was an apprentice and she was distant, unattainable. God knew how much I had tried not to want her. I gently stroked her trembling thinness.

She pulled away violently. 'You stink of that whore.'

I pushed at the door, which scraped open reluctantly, and jumped out of the coach. Fog eddied round me. 'Call her that again and I will leave you and not come back.'

She bit her lip. 'There is no time to argue!'

'What have you been saying to Lord Stonehouse about me?'

'Get in. Please!'

The horses had been quietened, and both coachmen turned from their argument to listen, open-mouthed, to ours. Neither of us cared. When I did not move, she spoke in a violent rush of words.

'I have been saying what you should have been saying. That he has done you a great wrong. He tried to kill you when you were born. More than that. No one has done more for him, for the estate, than you. No one has done more to destroy it than Richard.'

It was impossible not to be drawn in by her vehemence, by the hypnotic glow in her eyes. A new fear ran through me. She had always been the realistic one, pricking my dreams, or at least channelling them to a more practical course. But her obsession with the estate seemed to have gone beyond sense.

'Anne, Anne, listen. The estate is entailed. It must go to the eldest son, from one generation to the next. To Richard. Lord Stonehouse has no power to break the entail.'

'In normal times. Cromwell will break it.'

'Cromwell must do a deal with the King. Richard is one of the King's favourites – Cromwell will not upset an agreement just to change the ownership of Highpoint!'

'It is possible.'

'It is *not* possible!'

'I have seen Roger Hanmer, Lord Stonehouse's lawyer. He has assured me it *is* possible.'

I remembered following her to Gray's Inn. It was not a separation from me she had been seeking – far from it. She needed me to secure the estate that she was determined, by any means, to possess. Her manner had changed. Her tone was matter-of-fact. There was even a faint smile on her face at my stunned reaction.

'Do you want me to take you or not?'

The coachman stood scowling. The coach he had collided with was driving off. Anne beckoned to the man, her voice low and husky.

'My husband is desperate to say farewell to his grandfather before he dies. Please, please could you hurry.'

I was her husband again, even if I was Tom Neave. The coachman tipped his hat and looked dubiously at the fog, yellow as newly shorn wool. 'I'll do my best, ma'am.'

'I'll double your fare if you get there before he dies.'

The coachman slammed my door shut after me, scrambled into his seat, shook the reins and careered off, throwing us back. He drove by pure instinct. I shut my eyes as he plunged through the fog, or grabbed at the door, which had been damaged and kept flying open.

As we bounced and struggled to hold on to something, I yelled at Anne in jerky snatches. 'I am going there to pray for him. Do you understand? Even if it was possible to break the entail, I would not do it. I don't *want* the estate. The world has changed! Land – belongs to the people!'

'I have done all this for you. I have not slept –'

The strap she was clinging to slipped from her hand. She was flung against me. 'You did it for yourself!' I said.

'I know what you want better than you do. You no sooner get one thing than you want another.'

The coachman struggled to yank the horses clear from a mound of rubbish. The coach ploughed through it, the stench of rotting meat filling the cab. Smithfield. A dog howled as one of the horse's hooves caught it, its whimpers gradually fading as the coachman urged the horse blindly on. I held the door shut while Anne clung to me.

The foul reek of tanning and the tarry tang of the coal barges meant we were going over the Fleet. In Holborn the fog was more spasmodic and the coach picked up speed. Anne alighted almost before it had come to a stop in Queen Street. I began to hurry after her but the coachman blocked my way. I pulled out some money.

'The lady promised double if ...' I gave him all I had. 'Why, thank you, sir. Good luck, sir.'

Through shreds of mist the stone falcon peered down at us as if we were interlopers. I always had that feeling and usually gave him the apprentice's finger, but that night I bowed my head and slipped up the steps like a thief. The hall was so ill-lit that the house seemed already in mourning. Mr Cole appeared out of the gloom. Anne lifted her veil, her eyes shining with tears.

'Oh, Mr Cole, is he ...'

'Still with us, ma'am, but barely ... The minister is confessing him. You cannot see him now –' he began, but she pushed past him and grabbed me by the hand. There was such a force driving her, it seemed I had lost my own will. Mr Cole shouted something but we were already at the top of the stairs, passing the study that had marked so many of the climatic stages of my life. The door was open and it was silent and empty. The fire, which burned winter and summer, was out. I glimpsed the strip of carpet where I had stood so many times. The desk had been cleared of papers; only the seal, with which he had made so many orders, including that condemning me to death as a plague child, rested on the leather top.

Anne pulled me away, down corridors where I had never been, towards Lord Stonehouse's private chambers. Two servants came forward, but she scarcely checked her pace, her tone and look dismissing any idea of dissension.

'Mr Cole sent for us. Lord Stonehouse wishes to see his grandson.'

Before they could properly take in my crumpled shirt, my britches, which, I was suddenly acutely conscious of, had the buttons stuffed in the wrong holes, and a tattered jacket I had snatched up from the floor, we were in the bedroom.

Bedroom?

It smelt and sounded like a church. There was an overpowering smell of incense, under which lingered an insistent odour of urine and decay. It was so dark we stopped, feeling our way with our hands in front of us. The enormous bed loomed like a chancel, emphasised by the screen-like curtains from which came the only source of light and the intoning of the minister.

'... give him repentance for all the errors of his life past.'

The shifting light of the candles played on Lord Stonehouse's pallid face, his wax-like hands folded on the sheets, as if he was already an effigy. Anne stared at the image in a mixture of disbelief and terror, then fell on her knees, covering her face in her hands.

'God forgive me for what I have done, God forgive me!' she repeated over and over again.

For the first time, from the shadowy movements turning in our direction, I realised there were other people in the room, but could not distinguish who they were.

'... if thou wilt, even now, thou canst raise him up,' the minister went on.

Anne was shaking in such distress that I dropped on my knees to comfort her. Only then, as she continued to beg for forgiveness, and was shaking with such fear, did the truth strike me.

'Did he really ask for me?'

The minister glanced round, the light catching his outraged expression, before he continued. 'Yet, as in appearance it seems his dissolution draweth near, prepare him, we beseech thee, against the hour of death ...'

I shook her, then rammed my lips against her ear, whispering, 'Answer me. Did he ask for me?'

She lifted her head. She was shaking, her eyes running with tears. 'No,' she cried out. 'He should have done – he rambled about Tom Neave often enough. After all I did for him!'

Scandalised, the minister drew back the curtains, spilling light into the room. I sensed rather than saw the people on the other side of the room staring. 'Get up,' I said to Anne. When she did not respond, I dragged her to her feet. She went submissively, passively, head bowed, as I guided her towards the darkness of the hall, desperate for it to swallow us up, away from the battery of accusing eyes. We were almost into that comforting oblivion, where the shadow of Mr Cole was there to escort us out, when she stopped abruptly, staring back into the room at the people there. I tugged her one more step to the door but, like a horse that refuses a fence, she would go no further. Her knuckles gripping the door jamb were bone-white, her gaze rigid.

Among the group of people watching our departure, dressed in dark grey silk, sombre but not morbid, with an expression that managed to be both censorious and amused, was Richard.

34

It was no more than a second, but the tableau was as still as if it had been painted: the minister, eyes bulging, cheeks flushed to the point of apoplexy; Dr Latchford, glasses threatening to fall from his nose; a man with a wart on his chin, his face half turned away as if trying to conceal himself; a young woman in a gold-embroidered silk dress craning avidly forward. I guessed she was Richard's wife from the locket I had seen, and knew it as soon as she opened her mouth.

'Dégoutant! Est-ce la femme diabolique?'

'Laisse-moi m'occuper de la salope, Geraldine,' muttered Richard. He raised his voice. 'Mr Cole. The lady is not well.'

Only Richard, by putting the slightest of hesitations before 'lady', could reduce the word to something from the gutter. Anne tore away from me, her voice like ice. 'The lady is perfectly well!'

Richard ignored her. 'Tom. I must see you.'

Treating her as if she was not there infuriated Anne more than any verbal insult. She lost control completely, whirling round on me. 'Don't listen to him. Haven't you had enough of his tricks? He tried to kill you. Have you forgotten?' She turned on Richard. 'Ignore me. Go on. Ignore me. You should be in the Tower. I'll have you put there.'

'Elle est une gamine des rues … une folle,' muttered Geraldine, stepping back hastily as Anne glared at her, treading on the foot of the man with the wart, who let out a yell of pain.

With pretended sympathy, Anne rounded on him, instead of Geraldine. 'Your gouty foot, Mr Hanmer?'

Hanmer, I remembered her telling me in the coach, was Lord Stonehouse's lawyer who had given her the assurances about breaking the entail and, it seemed, from her scarcely veiled anger, the impression he was on her side. I stood like the others, hypnotised and appalled, unable to stop her, as Dr Latchford caught Hanmer, hopping on one foot, and helped him to a chair. During the process, Dr Latchford's spectacles fell from his nose, Hanmer's skipping foot coming down on them with a crunch.

Anne rounded on Geraldine. 'You speak English?'

Geraldine was tall and had a Norman arrogance about her. Her green eyes had a flinty, contemptuous glitter in them. 'Bett-er than you, I zink?'

'You zink.'

Anne advanced on her. I should have moved then, but my urge to do so was overwhelmed by a desire that Anne would say something to wipe the supercilious smile from the face of this woman, whom, I realised with a shock, was my stepmother. It was more than that. It was impossible not to admire Anne's dogged singlemindedness in the face of these people. It had never struck me before but, just as I tried to challenge their arrogant assumption of power through freedom for the people, in her own way and for very different reasons, was Anne not trying to do exactly the same thing?

The smile left Geraldine's face when Anne was a step away. Just as it dawned on everyone that, for Anne, it had gone beyond words and she might physically attack Geraldine, a voice rang out.

'Enough.' It was the minister. He seemed to realise how disturbed Anne was, for his tone was more gently reproving than hectoring. 'You seem to have forgotten we are praying for a soul to depart this life in peace.'

Anne stared around her as if waking from a dream. Her gaze rested on the still figure of Lord Stonehouse. She shook with terror, clasping her hands so tightly I thought they would snap. I put my arm gently round her. She blundered into a chair as I began guiding her from the room. Richard began to follow me, saying again he must speak to me, but I gestured him violently away.

A cry rang out, demonic and chilling. It seemed to come from the air itself. Anne screamed and buried her face in my chest. There was a movement, a quivering white shape in the dim, shifting light at the head of the bed, to one side of Lord Stonehouse's body. Everyone shrank back except Hanmer, who got up to flee, forgetting his gouty foot. He fell back in his chair with an agonised grunt. I was convinced I was seeing, literally, the departure of Lord Stonehouse's soul from his body. So, it appeared, did Dr Latchford for, losing his fear in the interests of natural philosophy, he scrabbled for his spectacles, squinting excitedly through one cracked lens.

'We are witnessing,' he whispered in awe, 'the transfer of the corporeal to the spiritual.'

The shape sank back, struggled to rise again, then in a sudden blur of movement, shot up. Everyone gasped, ducking their heads away. Peering back, we saw the draught from the movement had swelled the light from the candles. This revealed the spirit was a sheet in which Lord Stonehouse's hands had been trapped and were thrashing about frantically. His right hand jerked up, knocking the prayer book from the minister's hands.

'Horseborne!' he cried, in a feeble remnant of his old voice.

His eyes remained closed. A servant scrambled to rescue a candle that had been knocked over. There was silence except for Lord Stonehouse's laboured breathing, like the crackle of dead leaves.

'Dead child,' he muttered. He brought up his hand again so abruptly the minister had to duck back. 'Plague order.' On his clenched fist I saw the glint of the falcon signet ring before he brought it down, pressing it into the sheets as though he was making an impression in molten wax. His eyes struggled to open, being gummed with some kind of discharge. The servant darted over and wiped them free. Lord Stonehouse pushed him away. His eyes jerked open, fastening accusingly on the minister.

'No peace ... I saw him. A moment ago. The boy. Just now ... over there. You promised ... he'd go ... You'd get rid of him.' He levered himself from his pillows with a sudden burst of words which echoed his old strength and irritability. 'The bastard's still there! What are you people paid for, eh? Your tithes, your rich livings, and you can't get rid of a wretched *boy*?'

Spent, he sank back, his eyes closing. The minister put his hand over the still clenched fist of the dying man. 'Oh Lord, we beg thee to strengthen the inner man, so that before he goes hence –'

He stepped back hastily as the hand thrashed up again, pointing a shaking finger at me. 'Look! There he is. Look. Throw your words at him!'

'My lord, he is real.'

'A real spirit?' Lord Stonehouse groaned. 'Then I'm done for, done for.'

I ran forward, past the scandalised minister, and flung my arms round the old man. The stench of putrefying flesh and sweat mingled with the sickly sweet smell of incense and almost overpowered me. 'I'm here. I'm real ... I'm ... I'm ...' Threatening tears took me unawares.

'Real?' His voice was touched with his old scorn. 'I want no bastards in this family. Throw him out!'

Richard was touching my arm, Mr Cole hovering on one side and the servant on the other. They hesitated as Lord Stonehouse began speaking again.

'Real?' His hand, hot as fire, the skin rustling like parchment, moved over my face, stopping at my hooked nose. 'Boy's a Stonehouse,' he muttered. 'No doubt. No doubt about that.'

He sat up in a sudden moment of clarity, his eyes shrewd as ever, brooding, as if he had lifted his head from papers on his desk. 'All here, are you?' His rusty, faltering breath belied the sharpness in his eyes. 'Son, daughter-in-law, doctor, lawyer, minister – anyone would think I was dying.' He choked with laughter at the minister's shocked expression. An old servant with a bent back held out a potion. His hand was as shaky as his master's.

'You should come and join me, Joseph,' Lord Stonehouse said. He laughed again and took a sip before turning to me. 'And you. You, sir. Who let you in? Coneyed your way in, did you?' I could almost swear that his right hand, fumbling in the sheets, was automatically feeling for the third drawer down in his desk, my drawer. 'You get nothing, do you know that? Nothing.'

I jumped up. 'I don't want anything. I never did. However many times I tell you, or anyone else, no one *ever* believes me!'

He gave a short, disbelieving laugh. 'Nothing?'

'You gave me everything I ever wanted when you picked me up in the docks. You gave me a chance.' I turned to go.

'Wait.' A note of incredulity crept into his voice. 'You mean … you just came … to see *me*?'

I said nothing. What could I say? How could I destroy that look in his eyes? It was exactly like the first look he ever gave me. The potion he was holding was dribbling on to the sheets. I took it from him. 'London Treacle,' he said suddenly. 'Remember?'

I nodded. London Treacle was the cordial he had given me when he first saw me as a young boy, after I had been burned by pitch at the docks. Everyone else in the room disappeared beyond the soft light of the candles. For an instant we were alone in the Poplar of my childhood, in the shipwright's cabin, me not knowing whether I was asleep or awake, his eyes troubled one moment and shrewd the next.

'London Treacle.' His eyes glistened. 'Now …' He began to laugh. He tried to speak but the words were drowned in splutters of laughter. He shook with it so that the whole bed trembled. He began to cough again. I held out the cordial. He took a swallow, spraying most of it on to me. 'London Treacle. Now you're giving it to me.' He pushed the cordial away. 'Enough!' He wiped his eyes and blew his nose on a corner of the sheet.

'Minister! Where is that wretched minister?'

'Here, my lord.'

'Did Jesus not say: the first shall be last and the last first?'

'He did, my lord, but –'

'Never understood that before, never.' Colour was seeping back into his pallid cheeks. He heaved himself further up in the bed, wincing, but the pain seemed only to infuriate him into fresh energy. 'Hanmer. Hanmer! Where is that cozening lawyer?'

The minister bent beseechingly over him. 'My lord, you are not yourself. You must forsake all earthly things –'

'Forsake them to the Church, you mean? I was far too generous there. Not myself? I have never been more myself in all my life! More light, more light!' he shouted to the servant.

The room was in a kind of hushed uproar, Hanmer hobbling to his feet, servants rushing for candles, and Dr Latchford staring through his cracked spectacles.

The fresh candles drove back the shadows, picking up the sweat shining on Lord Stonehouse's face, the feverish exultant gleam in his eyes. 'Move, Hanmer. We all have gout. We don't make other people suffer for it. Hurry!'

The minister wrung his hands repeatedly. 'This is most irregular, illegal, at this time, in front of the family!'

'On this side of the world, I am the law.'

The minister's voice hardened. 'My lord, you are close to your maker.'

'You prayed for him to raise me up, didn't you?'

'Yes, my lord, but –'

'He has answered your prayer. Mr Cole! Pen. Paper. Move, man! Hanmer!' His eyes abruptly squeezed together in a spasm of pain, his skin wrinkling up like a decaying apple. Dr Latchford scuttled forward but was stopped by an angry gesture. Nobody moved. The only sound was the laboured rasp of the old man's breathing. When it had become more regular, he continued as if nothing had happened. 'Hanmer, that piece of sharp practice ...'

Hanmer coughed reprovingly, shooting a nervous glance towards Richard. 'If you are referring, my lord, to the Parliamentary Ordinance on seized Royalist property, which may be interpreted to mean –'

'Yes, yes. That one. Dictate.'

One servant placed a small table before Mr Cole, another a quill in his hand, while a third put paper in front of him. Inured to his master's moods, indeed seeming happy that his employment had not yet been terminated, Mr Cole dipped in the quill and waited expectantly while Hanmer cleared his throat and people inched closer, faces craning, eyes staring.

'Oh, Tom, Tom,' Anne softly breathed in my ear. 'You've done it. I knew you would, I knew it!'

'I –'

I stopped. Nothing I said would make any difference. Nobody would believe I did not want the estate. Nobody. Was it more than that? Of course it was. Colour was returning to Anne's cheeks. Her eyes were brightening. She was so much the old Anne then, the woman I had fallen in love with, that I gripped her hand impulsively. She returned the pressure.

Even so, when I saw Lord Stonehouse twisting his signet ring, the ring with which he had sealed the plague order and would shortly seal the new will, and caught the flash of the falcon's eye in the candlelight, I shuddered. I might have stepped forward then and stopped it, but for the word I caught.

Diable.

I knew little French, but I knew that word. Devil. I had had that word flung at me often enough in my time with Mr Black. That, and bastard. Geraldine managed both. She had been throwing up her hands in bewilderment, firing puzzled questions at Richard, which he was too distraught to answer. Half a dozen times Richard looked as if he was about to come over and rip the quill from Mr Cole's hands. Every time, his father's cold look stopped him. Hanmer said all previous wills and codicils were revoked.

'Que veut dire "revoked"?' Geraldine asked.

'Révoquer.'

Up to that moment, Geraldine had either not understood, or not believed, what was happening. Her voice was shrill. 'Incroyable! Ce diable va hériter? Ce *bâtard*? Il faut l'en empêcher.'

Richard took a couple of steps towards his father. Hanmer stopped dictating. Lord Stonehouse looked up. This time it was not a cold look. Rather it was a weary, ineffably tired look he gave Richard, not without warmth, even love, in so far as Lord Stonehouse had ever been able to express it. He had so often told his son Richard he was not fit to inherit, and there was now a resignation in the father's gaze, a final lucidity, that suggested he knew exactly what he was doing.

Between Richard and the bed was a strip of carpet, patterned much like that of the worn strip on which we had both stood before him many times. Richard was fearless in war, but that carpet, with that look, was a barrier he could not cross.

'Seul Dieu,' he muttered to Geraldine, 'peut arrêter mon père.'

I managed that French, too. *Only God can stop my father.* Lord Stonehouse stared not just at me, but into me. It was not merely as if he was scrutinising every part, it was as though he was transferring his very feelings, his burden, to me. Burden. He gave a little nod, as if I had actually spoken the word. In that moment I understood. He knew I did not want the estate. It was for that very reason he was passing it to me. It was not out of perversity. It was because, in the scene played out to him, he had seen that I would not enjoy it, but treat it as a duty, a burden, as he had done.

He seemed to read my thoughts, for he smiled at me. It was one of the very few smiles I ever remember him giving me. I bowed my head. When I lifted it, he was in the act of signalling to Hanmer to continue. His hand froze in mid-gesture. His face crumpled and cracked like parchment, but the cry of pain was soundless. It increased in severity. Richard reached him first, taking one hand, while I took the other. The creases finally eased from his face and his eyes opened.

'Family gathering ... at last,' he managed with a ghost of a smile. 'You know ... my wishes ...'

He gasped. It was as though a great vice had seized him. His body hammered against me as he thrashed up and down like a panic-stricken horse. We caught him as he almost slipped from the bed in his violent movements. His hand with the signet ring clenched repeatedly, then, very slowly, closed. His eyes stared.

Dr Latchford bent over him, then nodded to the minister.

'Almighty God, now he is delivered from his earthly prison ... we humbly commend his soul ...'

I was numb, scarcely hearing him, convinced the doctor had made a mistake, that I could see an ironic gleam in those staring eyes. Suddenly I was full of the things that I might say to him that would bring us closer. I still felt the grip, the feverish heat, of his hand in mine, and the nearness of Richard. Family gathering. He had brought us together and that would revive him, I was sure of it. It was his last subterfuge, his final trick.

'Teach us who survive,' the minister went on, 'the lesson of mortality, to see how frail and uncertain we are, so we may forget earthly desires and steadfastly apply our hearts to heavenly things ...'

The pages of the will Mr Cole had written fluttered from the table unheeded as the minister stood and bent in prayer. The servants followed him. I felt the closeness of Anne, moving next to me, the closeness of everyone circling the bed. Even Hanmer stood motion-less, his gout forgotten. Shadows thrown by the candles flickered over awestruck faces. Geraldine's fervent 'Amen' rang out above the rest. Only when Dr Latchford closed Lord Stonehouse's eyes did I realise there was no subterfuge, no trick; I would never say the things I meant to say to him, which had a clarity I could never find when he was alive. I flung myself on him, weeping bitterly, uncontrollably. I forgot all the things he had done to me. All I could see was his face when he had picked me up at the docks, his troubled expression. I buried my head in his body, overpowered not by his stench, but by the sweet, syrupy smell of London Treacle. Hands tried to remove me. I clung to him until two servants pulled me away.

The minister gave me a look of distaste. 'I know what you must feel, my son. But you must reconcile yourself to what you have lost.'

He was looking at the pages of the half-finished will, which Mr Cole was picking up. He thought that was the source of my grief.

Hanmer, whose gouty hobble had returned, shrugged and muttered, 'Waste paper. Unfinished. Unsigned. Not valid.'

Forgetting all sense of propriety in her eagerness to understand, Geraldine leaned over the corpse to pick up the men's whispers. 'C'est quoi "not valid"?'

'Non valable,' Richard replied.

Geraldine clasped her hands together exultantly and raised her eyes to the ceiling. 'Dieu est Catholique!'

'Here God is a Protestant, madam,' the minister cried.

Anne was arguing with Hanmer. 'I heard him! We all heard him say what his wishes were!' Hanmer told her that, even if it had been signed, Lord Stonehouse's mind had gone. I tried to draw her away. She was so frantic she would not listen. Over and over again she kept on telling me to do something. In her desperation she tried to seize the uncompleted will from Mr Cole. Only the old servant, Joseph, remained with his master, straightening the sheets, removing the signet ring, drawing the curtains round the bed with an unsteady hand, motioning another servant to do the same on the other side. Even now Lord Stonehouse seemed not to be at peace, his lower lip jutting out and his forehead creased, as if he was frowning over some piece of paper on his desk. Again, I saw none of the brutality, the deviousness, the secretiveness in that troubled face. All I saw was the burden: the chaos he had steered a course through, the arguments, the decisions, the recriminations, the time of hope when his wife had been alive and his children young, the time of despair in war and the family feud. As the curtains closed, seeming to draw him into that other world, the quarrels in this one were still going on around me. I could stand it no longer, told Anne I would wait for her outside and hurried from the room.

'Tom!'

My father was the last person I wanted to see. I knew exactly what he would say. Like the minister, he would believe my grief was over losing my fortune, offering me some paltry consolation I did not want. I redoubled my speed, half-jumping down the next flight of stairs.

'Tom – I must see you!'

I ran along the gallery towards the grand staircase, desperate to be out of that suffocating place. But my pace faltered when I reached Lord Stonehouse's study. A single candle was burning on his desk. By its light a servant was preparing to hang black drapes at the window. There were shouts and curses outside from the stables.

'Open the gate for the messenger!'

A single horseman clattered over the cobbles. By morning London would know that one of the great officers of state, who had helped steer Parliament to victory, and who knew more of its secrets than any other living soul, was dead. Only then did the enormity of what had happened strike me. It shrank our petty quarrels into insignificance. At the top of the staircase my father caught up with me, putting his hand on my arm. I pulled away. He grabbed me and shoved me against the wall.

'Who is planning to kill the King?'

The question was so unexpected and so bizarre I began to laugh, stopping only when I realised how frantic Richard's manner was, how unlike him, how out of control, as much pleading as threatening. Still I dismissed his questions, shaking my head in bewilderment, making my way down the stairs, until, as the servant opened the door for me, a thought stopped me. Like a drop of water striking a pool, it sent a chilling ripple through me.

35

It was nonsense, of course, the sort of conspiracy nonsense that seemed to infect the very air of that house. But I stood stock still, feeling the bruise on my cheek where Bennet had pressed the barrel of his gun.

'Caught them spying,' he had said.

I had a vivid picture of Bennet, in the firelight, polishing his gun, with its exposed spring and tubular sight. Mechanically, I followed my father into the reception room, where, as Lord Stonehouse had just described my last appearance, I had first coneyed myself in, five years before. The mourning was already up. It was dimly lit, the satyrs chasing nymphs across the oval ceiling looking like pale ghosts. Richard closed the door.

'You know something,' he said.

'I know nothing.'

'I saw it in your face! Tom, I believe it will happen soon. Tell me what you know.'

I hesitated. Nehemiah was a hothead and Bennet a killer, but I could not believe they would try to kill the King, an act that would plunge the country into an even more disastrous war. How would they get the opportunity? It was absurd. They were poaching, that was all. That was why Bennet had overreacted when we stumbled on them.

'Is Cromwell involved? Ireton?'

'Cromwell?' I laughed. 'It is the last thing he wants. He would be the first suspect. And he knows more than anybody how much the people want their King.'

'Do you believe that?'

I remembered the cheering crowds during the freedom march, the rushes and green boughs strewn before him in villages, the hundreds of bonfires laid round Cambridge, before the Parliamentary force had stopped us. 'Yes,' I said shortly. 'I do.'

Although there was a damp, clinging cold in that room, his forehead gleamed with sweat. First he had tried to kill me. Then he had used me. Now, for the first time, if what he was saying was true, he needed me. There must be some trick, some unexpected card he would play, but I could not think what it would be. He had got what he wanted. He had Highpoint, with its power and riches.

'Tell me what you know,' I said.

Now he hesitated, striding agitatedly round the room before, reluctantly, telling me about the Royalist network of spies. He gave no names, but disclosed enough to show he had infiltrated meetings at The Bull and Mouth. He knew about the shadowy, breakaway group that argued there was no point in negotiating with the man of blood, and that he should be brought to trial. I remembered the man watching Gun Press on the night Ellie and I first slept together, the feeling of being followed afterwards.

'You've been spying on me?'

'Of course.'

'That's progress of a kind, I suppose. You spy on me not to kill me, but for information.'

I heard Anne's voice in the hall, asking where I was, and got up. He pulled a piece of paper from his pocket. I took it to the light from a candle. It was addressed to the King at Hampton Court and marked 'most urgent'. It was dated two days earlier and warned him that eight or nine agitators had resolved to kill him. It was signed 'E.R.'

'This is a copy.'

'The original has information I cannot show you.'

Each of us was giving away as little as possible. He had inherited distrust from Lord Stonehouse. I shrugged and gave him back the paper. 'Is that all?'

'Isn't it enough? Why do you think the King has withdrawn his parole? They cannot keep him safe there! Or will not.'

'Cromwell has redoubled his guards.'

'Is he safe from his guards?'

I could not talk to him. Cromwell had put his most trusted men at Hampton Court, who would guard him with their lives. I went to the door, hearing Geraldine say 'Au voir' and some horses draw up.

'It is during the debates they plan to do it.'

I stopped with my hand on the door knob. 'Putney?'

'Yes. My informer heard one of them say Putney would be perfect.'

'Why?'

'I suppose because the top officers would be there. Distracted.'

'When was this? Where?'

He described the meeting at The Bull and Mouth, the arguments. Much of it was lies, written to supply the Royalists with what they wanted to hear. It painted the Levellers' sole aim as seeking to foment a rebellion in the army, rather trying to reform a rotten Parliament. The informer had clearly never been at the meeting. But he had picked up the angry explosions in the alehouse afterwards from people who disagreed with Wildman's measured approach; the empty, violent threats fuelled by drink. There was one group, however, where the men were quieter, more purposeful. The informer heard them whispering about Hampton Court. The palace.

'When they broke up one of them said that proverb "Time and ..."'

'Time and tide wait for no man?'

'That's it.'

I sat down and put my head in my hands, remembering Nehemiah's negotiations with the boatman. A double crown? For a boat trip or a bit of poaching? He had suddenly become friendly. Because that was the mood that day? Or because he had decided what to do – the euphoria that comes from taking a decision? What had he said – we all want the same end? I broke into a sweat. Ireton had ridden past. He had seen me eating duck with Nehemiah.

'What is it, Tom? Tom?'

My knowledge of places outside London was hazy, confined mainly to places I had fought over. 'Where is Hampton Court?'

'Just beyond Richmond. Half an hour's ride and ferry from Ham House.'

'Near the river?'

'On the river.'

The lantern clock struck one. I jumped and stared at the tulips on the face of the clock, struggling to remember what I had heard by the camp fire. 'Upstream?'

'Of course it's upstream! Are you involved with this?'

'If you think that, to hell with you!'

'I'm sorry, I'm sorry, but if you know something for God's sake tell me!'

I almost spilled out what I had heard. But suppose I was wrong? It could be another of his tricks to get me to betray the Levellers to the Royalists.

'I cannot. But I will ride with you to Hampton.'

'No. No.'

There was something he was not telling me. There always was. Always. 'That or nothing, Father. We go there together.'

'Impossible.'

He went impetuously to the door, half-opening it, but stopped when he saw me staring at the clock. It had barely crept a few minutes past one, but it felt as if half an hour had passed. One o'clock. I struggled to remember the times they had mentioned, what the boatman had said about the tide. It turned downstream at eight, nine o'clock in the morning, was that it? The coming morning. They had to be there before it turned, in seven, eight hours' time. Richard slammed the door shut and came over to me. I could not take my eyes off the clock, although it had only an hour hand, and was not visibly moving at all.

'It's tonight, isn't it?'

'I don't know.'

'A matter of hours?'

'It might be. I tell you I do not know!'

'All right, all right. We go together.'

'I'll see to the horses.'

'Better if we go by boat.'

'At this time of night?'

'There's my father's boatman. At Milford Stairs. The tide is with us.' He held out his hand. 'Ab imo pectore.'

I almost laughed out loud. The Stonehouse motto: *Ab imo pectore*. From the heart. I had seen precious little heart in him, but at that moment he stood so stiffly, and his grip when I took his hand was so warm and strong, I could not help wondering what life would have been like if we had been on the same side. I meant to say the words ironically, but could scarcely trust my voice when I muttered: 'Ab imo pectore.'

Richard's wife was in the hall, but not Anne. I had expected her to be there, full of recriminations, trying to seize the lawyer again and make a last-ditch fight for Highpoint. But Mr Cole told me she was incensed to find I was closeted with my father and had ordered a Hackney. While Richard talked to Geraldine, I went to the stable to get horses. Riding to the street, the thought struck me. It was a wild guess, but after believing I would inherit one moment, only to have it snatched away the next, Anne was crazy enough to do it.

'Mr Cole. Where did my wife go in the Hackney?'

He shook his head. I remembered hearing Geraldine mockingly say 'au voir', and asked her the same question. She gave a disdainful shrug, as if it was beneath her to register such things.

'Répondez-lui!' Richard snapped.

Geraldine muttered something about never understanding the English and said, 'Drury Lane.'

Richard looked at me. 'Your house is rebuilt?'

I shook my head and turned my horse round. 'She has gone to tell Cromwell you are here.'

The name shook Geraldine out of her complacency. She poured out a stream of agitated French as Richard scrambled on to his horse. 'I'll stop her.'

'You will make things worse. Leave it to me. I'll see you at Milford Stairs.'

'Pouvez-vous vous fier à lui?' Geraldine cried.

Richard laughed. 'She wants to know if I can trust you.'

'Tell her you can trust me as much as I trust you,' I said as I rode off down the street, past the house, which was now fully draped so that not a glimmer of light showed. Only the head of the falcon, peering through the shreds of fog, was visible.

At the bottom of Queen Street I jumped as a figure rode out of the gloom. It was Scogman.

'Ellie thought you might need me.'

My suspicions about Nehemiah and Bennet grew real as I related them to Scogman on our way to Drury Lane. I had avoided the place since the fire. A superstitious dread filled me as I saw the burned-out shell. For the first time I fully understood Luke's terror of George's malignant spirit. The place had been boarded up, but vagrants had broken in and there was a heap of festering rubbish where my study had been.

We galloped down to Cromwell's house, where the Hackney was standing, and I told Scogman to wait. The driver of the Hackney was dozing.

'My wife's inside?'

'She raised them at the back.'

Anne was in the kitchen, where a kitchen maid was stirring the fire back into life. The maid gaped at me, knuckling sleep out of her eyes, struggling to catch the shawl she had wrapped round the underskirts she slept in. Somewhere in the house there was knocking and then a murmur of voices. From the rooms above, I recognised the deep, rising tones of Cromwell's steward, Hugh Marshall, threatening to throw the servant out on the streets if he did not go away.

'You've seen sense then,' Anne said.

'Sense? What the hell are you trying to do?'

'What you should have done in the first place. Have him arrested.'

'Are you mad?'

'I have never been saner in my life. Lord Stonehouse wanted you to have Highpoint and you shall have it.'

'By having my father killed?'

'He deserves it.'

'Do you want me killed as well?'

The kitchen maid was staring open-mouthed, no longer pretending to build up the fire. Even in her present state, Anne forced me think clearly. Telling her brought home, with sickening clarity, the dilemma I was in. I groaned out loud as I drew Anne away from the maid, knocking over a pile of dirty pans. I whispered incoherently how Ireton had seen me with the people I suspected. Anne stared at me as my disjointed gabble, like the rocking of a pan lid, came to a stop.

There was a moment's silence before a thunderous roar came from Marshall upstairs. 'What the devil is going on down there?'

The maid gave a whimper of fear and scuttled to pick up the pans.

'Richard Stonehouse? Why didn't you tell me?'

There were two thumps above us as Marshall levered his massive frame from the bed. The ceiling creaked and there was the sound of doors opening and more voices. I could not think, speak or even stand, lowering myself to a bench at the table, the maid darting between my legs to pick up the pans.

I heard Betsy Cromwell's questioning tones, then: 'Richard Stonehouse! Oliver needs good news. Quick, man!'

I closed my eyes. Once Anne had told them, that would be the end of it. All I wanted to do was sleep. I felt that strange kind of relief that comes when one realises there is nothing more one can do and, in a moment of lucidity that came with it, saw again Nehemiah and I embracing over the camp fire.

'You taught me everything I know ... Well, not quite everything,' he had said.

I dropped my head in my hands. Not quite everything. I saw the gun, the polished barrel, the tubular sight. I was as certain then, as I have ever been certain of anything, that he was on a boat somewhere on the Thames with Bennet, being carried by the tide to kill the King.

'Tom ... I gather you have a prize for us.'

At another time Marshall, who still had his nightcap on, and whose nightgown barely closed round his fat belly, would have looked ludicrous. But from hurrying downstairs, he breathed heavily and his eyes gleamed, like a rider in a hunt close on his quarry. Resignedly, I opened my mouth to tell him. Perhaps there would be some way of warning the King – if they believed me.

'I'm sorry ... I'm sorry ...' Anne was weeping. It was the first time I had seen her cry since the fire. I jumped up and held her. She tried to speak, but her tears only redoubled.

'My dear,' Betsy Cromwell said, 'I know Richard Stonehouse is your father-in-law, but Tom is doing the right thing.'

'It was not Tom who saw him. It was me – thought I saw him,' Anne said with a sudden ferocity.

'Thought?'

'I, I was upset at Lord Stonehouse's death and –'

'Lord Stonehouse dead?'

'I left. Without Tom and, and … in the coach I must have fallen asleep. I had such a nightmare I thought I saw Richard …'

There was more. Her whole body shook against me. Although it was damp and cold, she was feverishly hot. I began to believe what she was saying, let alone Betsy Cromwell, who murmured to the disgruntled Marshall that Anne had not been the same since the fire. It was true. It was as if all that had happened since then had been wiped away and we were together again. She clung to me as I helped her out to the coach. Betsy Cromwell stood in the porch, anxiously offering us a bed. I thanked her, but said it would be better if I took Anne home. Home! I held her tightly and she buried her head into me.

Only when the door closed behind Betsy Cromwell did she pull away, her body taut, her eyes blazing. 'It is true? You are involved in a plot to kill the King?'

'No! Not involved. Not knowingly. But people might think so.'

'Not knowingly. God help us, that is you, Tom, that is *you*.' She leaned forward and kissed me.

36

It was all part of Anne's feigned madness, an act. Of course it was. But the soft pressure of her lips, the trembling of her body, stayed with me as I rode with Scogman to Temple Bar. I exulted in the sanity of her madness, in her quick wit. Even though it was an act, it brought back to me everything we had been to one another.

'I thought you were over it,' Scogman said.

'What?'

'Love.'

'I am,' I said curtly.

'Ellie thought you might need this.'

Scogman threw me a leather jacket.

Ellie. The jacket smelt of her, a weird mixture of herrings and printer's ink. My life seemed like the muddle of mean streets we were edging through, which, in the fog, seemed to lead endlessly back into themselves. We only found our way by stopping the horses and listening for the lapping of water. No bells sounded. The weather was too bad for boats. A sudden burst of laughter made us both jump and control our horses as cobbles suddenly gave way to a muddy bank.

I slipped from my horse, signalled to Scogman to tether it with the others, then squelched through the mud and on to the cobbled go-down that ran from a warehouse. Through the sooty smell of the fog I caught a pungent odour of tobacco. Across a yard were the lights of a boathouse where the laughter came from. The oiled paper it had for windows was too greasy and misted to see much more than the edge of my father's cloak.

'It's a damnable thing this has happened,' someone said. He spoke with an accent I thought I recognised.

'Not at all,' my father replied. 'Couldn't be better.'

A pebble I had dislodged flew from my boot toe and skidded along the ground. I froze.

'How so?' the man asked.

My father disappeared from the window. 'I can do something I have wanted to do for a long time.'

'What's that?'

'Go into action with my son, not against him.' The door was pulled open abruptly, blinding me with a yellow light. For a moment I could see nothing and it was all I could do to keep my hand away from my dagger.

'Hello, Tom.' My father gave me such a warm smile, I was ashamed of my suspicions. 'I thought I heard you.'

He held out his hand. I shook it while my eyes adjusted to the light. On a small table, a bottle of Dutch brandy weighed down some charts of the river fluttering in the breeze. A waterman whose enormous hand dwarfed the pot he was holding leaned against the wall, weighing me with his eyes, as he sniffed and took a swallow of brandy.

Huddled over the table, in a thick jump jacket that had seen much of war and weather, was the Dutchman I had first seen with my father's mercenaries at Sir Lewis Challoner's. He was cleaning a pair of pistols.

'This is Jan,' my father said.

'You were at Challoner's,' I said.

The Dutchman squinted up, then gave me a broad smile from which most of the teeth were missing. 'Of course. I remember,' he said, in guttural but perfect English, as if it had been a social occasion, and began loading the pistols.

'I thought we might need an extra body to –' My father's expression changed as he saw Scogman approaching in the light of the door.

I smiled at him. 'I had exactly the same thought, Father.'

Scogman's eyes gleamed as he saw the fine metalwork of the pistols. He stretched out a hand to pick one up. Jan slammed his hand down on it, pointed the pistol he was holding at Scogman and cocked it. The brandy stopped halfway to the waterman's lips and there was a moment's silence, except for the steady lapping from the surging tide.

'Come, gentlemen,' my father said. 'We are working together.'

Scogman stared down the barrel. 'Italian, isn't it? Like the people – all decoration and no firepower.'

'Enough to blow your head off.'

'Snaphaunce lock?' Scogman shook his head disparagingly.

Jan gave him his toothless smile. 'More efficient than the English dog lock.'

In a blur of movement, Scogman twisted away, pulling his pistol from his coat. 'You think so?'

I brought my hand down on Scogman's pistol. 'We won't get very far if we shoot one another.'

'Well said, Tom.'

My father was as taut as I was. He looked a military man again, in bucket boots over his knees and a jump jacket of oiled leather. He was good with men, I had to admit it. He questioned Jake, the boatman, listening carefully to him, deferring to his knowledge of the river. But when Jake said it would take him five hours to get to Hampton in this weather, he laughed, felt the boatman's rippling muscles and said: five for an ordinary boatman, four for you, Jake. Jake shook his head, but pinked with pleasure. By the time my father sent him to check the boat and the weather, he was convinced he was the best of the six thousand watermen on the Thames.

'What does he think we're doing?'

'He doesn't know. He doesn't ask. Except about the money'

He poured brandy in one glass, tossed it down, filled it and passed it to me. I took a small swallow and was about to hand it to Scogman when my father stopped me.

'Cold on the river. You'll need a drop more warmth than that, Tom.'

I needed to keep my senses, but it was impossible not to return his smile, not to begin to feel that, now he had Highpoint, had what he had always wanted, our relationship had changed. I gulped down the rest. It burned my throat and stung my eyes. My father poured a brandy for Scogman.

'I can see you're a man who knows his guns, Scoggy. What are these prigs carrying?'

'One is a sharp cove.'

'Good?'

'The best.'

'Apart from Jan,' my father put in.

The Dutchman gave him his toothless smile. I could feel even the cynical Scogman falling under my father's spell. 'He has a wheel-lock I've not seen before,' he said. 'The spring hangs out of the stock.'

Jan leaned forward. 'Tschinke. Silesian. Backsight?'

'Yes. How accurate is it?'

'Five, six hundred yards.'

My father spread out the charts on the table. We crowded round him, watching his finger follow the snaking loops of the Thames. For the first time I appreciated how far we had to go. I saw the sprawl of Hampton Court Palace. It was surrounded by a moat.

'They'll never get over the moat,' I said.

'They won't have to,' my father said. 'They can't keep him cooped up like a common criminal. When the weather is good, the King rides in his park.'

I stared at the huge area, including a forest, surrounding the palace. 'Where?'

'It varies.' It was a fleeting moment, but I thought I saw a quick exchange of glances with Jan. 'Do you know where the prigs are heading?'

It was seeing the shape of the island on the map that jerked out of my memory another piece of Nehemiah's conversation with the boatman. Beyond Richmond … Stag Island …

My father was waiting for an answer. I shook my head, determined to give him as little information as possible until it was necessary. After all, it might be only a duck shoot.

'What do they look like, Scoggy?'

'We'll know them,' I said.

My father sighed, giving me a tight little smile. The oiled paper over the windows flapped suddenly. A candle went out and another threatened to do so as Jake opened the door. He told us the good news was that the fog was beginning to clear. The bad was that it was an easterly wind that was sweeping it away, and if that got worse we would be in trouble in the treacherous parts up river.

The wherry had a canopy that gave us some protection, but I was glad of the warmth of the brandy. Jake pushed off and the streams of fog seemed to slide away from us down river. The tide was strong, and the strengthening wind was with us.

There was not a star in sight. Earth and sky were merged into a tunnel of impenetrable blackness, except when a pale, guttering moon filtered through, picked up in the oily ripples of our wake. Moored boats loomed up and vanished. Drops dribbled from the oars before Jake dipped them again. Fires lit up the shapes of tents and the tower of St Mary's Church. Putney. Nehemiah and Bennet would be in position by now. I remembered how neat, well-organised and methodical Nehemiah was. Meticulous. I had helped to train him.

'What time does the King ride?'

'Early.'

Charles, too, was a man of methodical habits. A poached egg every morning, a glass of fair water, a stroll on the terrace to decide whether to ride or walk the endless corridors. Curious that he and Nehemiah were similar in many ways – stubborn, rigid. Each never questioning whether he was right. Soon Nehemiah would be in place. Somewhere near Stag Island. With Bennet. Waiting. Two or three hours later Charles would finish his poached egg, then wander out on to the terrace to see if the weather was fit to ride.

That was why, when I heard the first patter of rain on the canopy, I had such a sense of relief. I had been dozing. I came round not only to the sound of rain but to a different landscape. The sky was as black as pitch. We had just passed through Richmond. A sudden flurry of wind hit the boat, making us cling on to the pillars over which the canopy was stretched. One of the ropes holding it snapped and it flapped like a sail.

I had never been this far up the river and was totally unaware of the danger. Jake looked carved into the woodwork of the stern of the boat. The howling air filled out my clothes and cleared my head. I yelled into the wind, a boy again, doing what I had always dreamed of doing with Matthew, going to sea in one of the boats we had made, in search of treasure.

Jake's mouth moved, but I heard nothing, admiring what I took to be his calmness, his strength, as the boat sped on. In truth, he was not rowing but steering, the boat driven by wind and tide. I only realised what speed we were going when a bank veered towards us, the dark silhouettes of wind-bent trees whipping away from us. Even then it merely exhilarated me more until I saw another boat, adrift from its moorings, careering towards us. Jake rowed desperately. The gale flung the rogue boat away from us. We were almost past it when it lurched back, striking our stern. The wherry slewed round, water cascading over us. Jake struggled to keep his oars, his deep voice booming frantically.

I caught two words: 'Weir ... canopy.'

I understood the latter. Stretched like a sail, the torn canopy made it impossible to control the boat. My childhood came back to me again, this time not as dreams but reality. As pitch boys we climbed the rigging of ships as a dare. I stood up, slipping on the wet deck. My father grabbed my legs. I kicked off my boots, not just to get a better grip, but because bare feet know the surface in a way boots never can. Even in that moment I remembered how much I had hated boots when I first wore them.

I waited for a lull in the wind, scrambled up, found a precarious purchase and, holding on to the pillar with one hand, stretched across to cut the ropes holding the canopy. Jake was rowing frantically again, struggling to steer the boat back into the centre of the river. He shouted something about 'currents', which I did not understand. I pulled the knife out of my belt, almost dropping it as another burst of wind caught me, a corner of the flapping canopy lashing my cheek. I cut partly through one rope, then started on the other. Scogman seized me by the belt to steady me. Abruptly, one rope snapped, then another, the canopy fluttering away like a demented bird, flinging me backwards into the water.

I seemed to go down for ever, the wind cut off in a world silent but for the bubbling rush of water. If I had worn my heavy boots, I would have stayed there. The wind was back, pounding my ears. I gulped in more river than air, glimpsing the blur of the hull above me, a hand, an oar, before I went down again. Odd what came back to me – plunging into the Thames as a child, yelling: *I can swim, I can swim!* It had been a dog paddle at most. But perhaps the memory got me to claw off my coat, to kick frantically. The wind buffeted me. Through the water streaming from my eyes, a hand appeared. I clutched at it. Another hand. Voices torn by the wind. The swell took the boat away, the hands slipping away from me. I grabbed at the oar being held out to me and clung on.

'The weir, Tom ... I must row!'

I understood, more from the driftwood that collided with me than the words. Whole branches ripped from trees were being carried towards a weir, whose roar I could hear even above the wind. A hand was being held out to me, but I could not reach it.

'I must …'

Jake pulled his oar away. I grabbed for the hand. Held it. The boat tipped over towards me. There was a confusion of yelling and shouting. I saw Scogman and Jan almost in the water as they threw their weight on the other side of the boat. My hand was slipping but another hand was on my arm. It felt as if it was being wrenched out of its socket. The river was thundering in my ears, sucking me down its throat towards the weir. I felt I must snap in two until, like a fish jerked from the sea, I landed in the boat, thrashing, coughing, spluttering, retching out water, gasping for air. I was dimly aware of Jake's straining arms and legs above me, of the others bailing out with a pan, or their hats, of my father taking off my shirt, wrapping his coat round me and forcing the neck of a brandy flask between my chattering teeth.

'Couldn't lose you, Tom,' he said. 'Need you to take us to those fellows.'

'Stag Island,' I said, and saw Jan and my father exchange glances before I closed my eyes.

Two promontories jutted out from the island like the antlers of a stag. The wind had dropped but rain was falling steadily. I now understood the timing that Nehemiah had talked about. The tide was on the turn and on the last stretch Jake had to pull strongly.

'Let's not give them an easy shot at us,' my father muttered. 'We must seem to be poachers like them.'

We huddled down in the boat, peering into a scene of unredeemed grey. There was no sign of a moored boat. The rain seemed to have washed the colour from everything, the drab river merging into a sky of beaten pewter. Clumps of trees on the island were dark shadows.

Jan had a pistol cocked, staring with a marksman's eye as the creeks and inlets of the small, uninhabited island gradually took shape. In his thick, guttural Dutch accent, he said, 'They'd have to be on one of those peninsulas to reach it.'

'Reach what?' I asked.

Jan looked at my father, who replied, 'It's called King Henry's Ride. He used to go hunting there. The forest was much bigger then.'

'You're sure he's a marksman?' Jan asked.

'The best,' Scogman said.

'He's only got one angle, one chance there. A sideshot,' Jan grunted.

'All he needs. And he can escape from this side of the island without anyone knowing where the shot has come from.'

The rocking of the boat, the amount of water I had swallowed and their macabre argument over the finer points of assassination, made me feel nauseous and I was glad when my father snapped at them to be quiet. The rain slackened a little, but had a steady, remorseless feel as we crept slowly round the island. I jumped as a duck whirred upwards.

'He won't ride out in this,' I murmured.

My father didn't reply. As we rounded the island he took out a spyglass and put it to his eye. Jan muttered that it had been invented by a Dutchman, Lippershey, starting yet another whispered argument with Scogman when he said the English couldn't paint, make printing machines or glass. All they could do was rear sheep. Again my father motioned them angrily to silence.

As we navigated the island he stared, not at the banks, but towards the palace, whose towers and twisted chimneys came and went between dripping trees. I had never used a spyglass before and, like a child, begged him to let me see through it. He did not seem to hear me, putting it back in his pocket.

'Oh, do let me, Father – please!'

I believe it was the first time he had ever really registered me calling him that. He flushed and gave it to me without a word. I stared eagerly through it, jerking the glass backwards when the banks leapt at me, afraid they were going to hit me. Disappointment filled me. I could see nothing but a leaden blur. I thought the glass was smeared, but no; then that it must be my eyes. I swung the spyglass upwards and shivered, awestruck. This was truly magic, the sort Matthew often claimed, but never produced.

I was a field away from the palace. I took the glass from my eye to make sure I had not been transported there. My father grinned at my enchantment. I could pick out the slime on the moat, the bricks on the walls, giddily sweeping up to land among the twisted chimneys before slithering down, coming to rest on some kind of terrace. It was further away, and the picture blurred, as it did when objects were too close. I was about to sweep back on to the roof when a figure appeared. He looked up at the sky, then walked towards me, becoming a little sharper. Frustratingly, he stopped, dipping away, becoming hazy again. He had dropped something. When he picked it up, all I could see was a smear of red, but, for a moment, his face became more distinct and I glimpsed his pointed beard and long hair.

'The King! I can see the King.'

My father snatched the glass from me and stared through it, quite still. He shook his head. 'It's one of the Grooms of the Bedchamber. They all ape his beard.' He put the glass back in his pocket. By this time we had scanned the island, becoming bolder as we saw no sign of life except a herd of forlorn-looking deer huddled in a copse.

My father grew suddenly agitated. 'We must find them.' Abruptly he darted a suspicious look at me. 'That's if they are here.'

I shrugged. In spite of my father's coat, I was beginning to shiver again. 'Perhaps they really have gone duck shooting.'

He seized me by the collar. 'Are you telling me the truth? You heard them? You know them?'

'Why would I lie?'

He released me. 'Yes. Why would you?'

There was an exchange of glances between him and Jan. He pulled out the brandy flask, then offered it to me. I shook my head. The energy seemed to have drained out of him. He stared down river, flicking away drops of rain that had gathered in his bushy eyebrows. The boat creaked and swayed gently, Jake dipping the oars in just enough to keep it in the same position. Twigs, whole branches, torn off by the recent storm and rubbish from the palace flowed past us.

'I'll go up to the palace and warn them,' I said.

'And send them after me?'

'Do you think I'd do that?'

Jake motioned us to be quiet. He pointed with a dripping oar towards a willow trailing its branches into the water. It had shed its leaves, but the branches were so thickly entangled and the light so bad I could not see what Jake was pointing at. He rowed closer to the shore. Now I saw it. Among the willow branches was a jumble of dark green ivy, which, at a casual glance, looked as if it was growing up the tree. It had taken a boatman's eye to detect that the edges of the leaves had begun to brown and wither. They were concealing the prow of a boat.

While we moored, Richard told me to investigate the other boat and Jan and Scogman to scout the approach to King Henry's Ride. He seemed to know the area intimately: before the war, he whispered, he had hunted here. He pointed out where Jake would conceal our boat. I took one of the pistols from Scogman and made my way through the bushes to the hidden boat. It was empty, but had not been so for long. On the bank were fresh boot prints in the mud, already being filled and washed away by the tide. I scratched my head, as if merely puzzled by the boat's presence, shrugged as if it was no consequence to me and wandered off the way I had come. And slipped into the bushes. And waited.

It did not take long. The boatman was desperate to escape. He made so much noise he did not hear me approach behind him. I waited until he crouched down to untie the boat. He was trembling so much and the rope was so wet, he could not loose the knot and took a knife to it.

'Poaching is a hanging offence,' I said.

He whirled round, coming at me with the knife. I ducked back, the knife ripping into my father's coat. Absurdly, I felt that as keenly as if he had cut me. It was the only thing my father had ever given me, or at least lent me. I kicked the knife from the boatman's hand and threw myself at him. He went down, striking his head against the base of the willow tree. I lashed his hands behind his back with his own belt.

At first I could not get him round, or he was pretending to be in a daze. Then, although I snatched up his knife and put it to his throat, he muttered with a sullen sneer that he knew nothing about the men, where they had gone or what they were doing. He was only a waterman, doing his job.

Scogman appeared, beckoning urgently. I followed him through the thinning bushes and trees to the edge of the parkland, where Jan was standing with my father. They were staring towards the distant palace.

In spite of the weather, the King was taking his morning ride, a column of Cromwell's soldiers round him. They were about a mile or so away, far enough to seem scarcely to be moving. The rain, if anything, had increased, softening the riders to a blur. The path they were on led across open parkland to King Henry's Ride which, my father pointed out, skirted the beginnings of a forest, stretching almost down to the river.

'We must stop them,' I said.

'He'll get his shot in before you reach them,' Jan said, matter-of-factly.

'Or Cromwell's soldiers will shoot you,' my father said. He got out his glass and scanned the forest. There was mile after mile of it.

'Proverbial needle in a haystack,' Scogman said.

Rain dripped steadily from the end of the spyglass, from our hats and the tree we sheltered under. It pockmarked pools in the muddy path going back to the river and drove even the deer to huddle under copses where they gazed warily at the slowly approaching column of riders. I could just distinguish the King's cloaked figure on a black horse. My father muttered that the marksman could not be too far from the boat. Jan argued we should circle round into the forest.

'Blunder about?' my father snapped. 'We'll see nothing from there.'

It was true. Jan and Scogman took up positions so that at least when the first shot was fired they could retaliate, in the hope that the first shot missed. It was a forlorn hope. I took the glass. All but a few tattered brown leaves had fallen, though the mass of thickly intertwined branches might well have been a wall for all I could see through it. In my mind's eye I could see clearly Bennet's cold gaze, his absolute calm as he stared at the riders through that tubular sight. He knew he had one shot. For him it was all he needed. I wasn't the only one who would be implicated in the murder. Cromwell would be, too. No one would believe he had not instigated it. One shot, and England would be plunged into chaos again, even bloodier than before.

I wiped the glass and swung it round to the column. Through the smeared lens I could see the King's spade-like beard. He was gesturing at the rain-soaked landscape, smiling and chatting to the man riding next to him. From his insignia, the man was a colonel. He dipped his helmeted head deferentially. The column was going at a leisurely trot. It would take them about ten minutes to reach King Henry's Ride, bringing them within range of a marksman.

As I gave the glass back to my father he saw the slash in my coat. It was completely trivial in the light of what was about to happen, but his tetchy snarl betrayed how near the edge he was.

'How did you do that?'

'Waterman.'

Waterman. Without another word, I scrambled down the path towards the river. The waterman had almost got one hand free. I put the knife to his throat and swore I would kill him if he did not tell me where they had gone. Either I did not have Gloomy George's enjoyment of cruelty, or the taste for it Nehemiah found when he made the mercenary talk, or the waterman did not know.

I drew the knife back in despair. It was the gleam in the waterman's eyes: contempt at my weakness, perhaps, or triumph that he had read me right that made me do it. I let the blackness in, that violent, uncontrollable rage that, after lashing Scogman, I swore I would never succumb to again, pulling him down the bank, dragging him through the mud until the water was lapping over his face.

'Tell me!'

His splutter that he did not know where they were was cut off by a mouthful of mud. The incoming tide washed over his head, his legs flailing wildly as I held him down. I yanked him back on to the bank. He gasped, retched water, spat and screamed he was just a waterman. He knew nothing. I glimpsed my father watching from the top of the path.

I dragged him down again, the mud almost sucking off my boots, and immersed him, this time holding his head down until the thrashing of his legs grew weaker and his body went limp. The tide was growing stronger and when I began hauling him out I lost my grip and he was almost swept away. When I finally got him out he was quite still. One of my boots came off as I shook the waterman, slapping his cheeks and hammering at his back. There was no movement. My father gave me a futile gesture of despair and began walking up the path.

I retrieved my boot, preparing to follow him, when I was suddenly overwhelmed by what I had done. The waterman had been part of Putney, part of all those ideals. I heard again the words ringing round the church: the poorest he had rights as much as the richest he. The biggest right of all was the right to live and I had taken it. Why was this waterman's life worth less than that of the King's?

I fell down on my knees, clawing mud from his face, washing it with the lapping water, sucking it with my mouth from his mouth and nostrils. I put my ear to his nose, but in the driving rain could feel nothing. Then I saw it: a small, lead-coloured membrane quivering across one nostril. I knelt over him, pumping frantically at his chest. The membrane distended, lost colour, became a small balloon, burst. Another began to form. His body twitched, went into spasm, then water exploded from him. I held him as he coughed and gasped back into life. The tide washed round us. I lifted him to drag him up on to the bank. Did he realise what I had done? Or did he fear I was going to immerse him again?

'Five –' he spluttered.

'Five?'

'– Oaks.'

'Five Oaks?'

He nodded and his head fell back on his chest. I scrambled up the bank. My father was on the edge of the forest with Scogman and Jan. When I told him, without a word he went down a path. I stopped Scogman from following him and told him what I wanted him to do.

'But your father said –'

'Never mind what my father said. There's no time. Do what I tell you. Give me your pistol.'

He did so and I ran along the path after my father.

'Where's Scogman?'

'His ankle went.'

The rain and the thick carpet of sodden leaves helped conceal the sound of our approach. Between the trees I could see, blurred like a charcoal sketch, the column of riders turning. The Five Oaks were enormous trees, their branches spreading into a huge interlacing network. The three of us scanned them, but could see nothing. The same thought must have occurred to all of us: the man was lying. He would say anything not to be thrown into the river again. My father whispered to Jan to fire across the line of riders. He raised his pistol as I saw it: a bootmark squashing an acorn into the loam.

Another and another. We followed the track formed by them, round the biggest of the trees, but could still see nothing. Wildly, we stared about us. I could hear the horses, their voices, the King laughing.

I gripped my father's arm. We were looking in the wrong place. On the ground, not up. Even then I would not have picked out the russet brown of his jerkin against the tree, were it not for the vanity of the decorated plate, the glint of the polished barrel resting on a fork. We had perhaps a minute, which seemed an eternity – until the riders broke into a canter. The King's face was flushed. He was ahead of the soldiers, laughing as if he was playing some kind of game with them, turning towards the forest. Breaking free from the column made him an even easier target.

After all his boasting, Jan seemed slow and clumsy. I took out my pistol to aim at Bennet. My father made a violent gesture to stop me. The King was almost at the oak trees. I turned my head away, unable to look – and found myself staring into the eyes of Nehemiah. He was emerging from one of the other trees, pointing a pistol at Jan. I fired. Half deafened by the explosion in that confined space, blinded by the smoke, for a moment I could see or hear nothing. Sound rushed back: the neighing of the horses, confused yelling of the soldiers.

'The King! The King!'

Numbly, I stared upwards to see Bennet's boot moving to descend from the tree. We had failed. Then the boot slipped, branches snapping as it twisted round, hesitating before being followed by an elbow, the decorated stock of the musket and a face, half of which was like chopped meat on a butcher's slab, half untouched, the milky blue eye arrested in the act of sighting the gun.

'Where is the King?'

Through the trees, among the milling, shouting soldiers, I could see no sign of the King.

A soldier grabbed me. 'Here he is!'

'We shot him, you fool.'

'We?'

'And the other one.'

'The –'

He gaped at the shattered face, the musket, then at Nehemiah sprawled against the next tree, his face as contentious as it had been in life, his mouth slightly open, as if he was about to start an argument. There was no sign of my father or Jan. Or of the King. More soldiers were crashing into the bushes. The soldier moved to seize me again. I lashed out, sending him spinning into two of his approaching companions.

'Ride!' I yelled at their stupefied faces. 'The King is heading downstream!'

I ran through the forest, half jumping, half scrambling down the bank towards the river. The boatman had been further revived by Scogman and was at the oars. His head was bent. There was little strength in him, but the tide was running strongly for us. I clambered in after Scogman and the boatman pushed off.

'You saw Jake leave?'

'As soon as you went to Five Oaks,' Scogman said.

'He moored further downstream?'

'I couldn't see. He went out of sight round the bend.' Scogman reloaded the pistol. 'How did you know?'

'I know my father. He might have been able to raise Jake at that time of night – after all, he was Lord Stonehouse's waterman. But Jan? Then, through the glass, I saw the King hanging a pennant on the terrace ...'

Richard must have had it all planned. Then the King received the letter warning him that agitators had resolved to kill him.

'Why didn't he call it off?'

'It was the perfect opportunity. I caught him saying that to Jan at Milford Stairs, although I didn't know what he meant at the time. The King will claim Cromwell tried to murder him – that's why he had to escape. If the King gets away, the people will rise up for him.'

Stag Island was falling behind us. The rain was slackening, a pale sun flickering in patches on the river. There was no sign of another boat. I was convinced my father would ride with the King to pick up the boat further downstream. They could then make it to the other bank where Cromwell's soldiers would be unable to reach them. That conviction began to ebb gradually away as we rounded another bend and there was no sign of the boat or Richard. I began to feel they must have completed the escape on this side. Perhaps Richard had men and horses waiting for them up river.

Spongy grey clouds shut out the sun. We were now approaching Teddington. The river widened, the boatman keeping close to the bank as we felt the drag of the weir. Apart from the steady, oily dip of the oars, it was eerily silent. We slipped under overhanging trees where drops of rain gathered and shivered before falling in large splashes.

Cows stared at us, still as the trees they stood under. Scogman gripped my arm. He pointed across a huddle of farm buildings. At first I could see nothing but, as the clouds parted, in a transient patch of light I saw a movement between some trees. Although the tide was pulling us strongly, I urged the boatman to go faster.

From a distance it looked a huge man on a horse. Only as we got closer did the gap between the two men riding on it become visible. My father looked towards us and leaned forward. The King had chosen his horse well. In spite of the load, it responded, galloping downhill towards the river.

We could now see the boat, moored in an inlet just beyond the farm buildings. Jake was standing ready to cast off. I could see the King's flushed face. He had been painted endlessly as a man of action;

for the first time, as he reined in his horse in the narrow bay, I saw him living it.

Richard twisted round on the horse. I saw too late the pistol in his hand. It echoed like a cannon in the confines of the inlet. The boatman fell, the boat lurching round. One oar slipped into the water but I managed to grab the other. We were close enough to the shore for me to touch bottom. I stood in the crazily rocking boat, struggling to control it like a punt, ramming the oar into the mud. The current swept us towards the inlet. My father and Jake were in their boat, helping the King to board. What happened next was due partly to the clumsy structure from which I had ripped the canopy, partly to Jake pointing at an approaching troop of Cromwell's soldiers. The King slipped, floundered. Jake had cast off and was holding the boat to the mooring. He let go to grab the King, missed, and the boat drifted away.

The same current that had driven us into the inlet threatened to carry the King out. Scogman grabbed a branch to pull the boat in as I plunged out, losing my balance, half wading, half swimming towards the King. I got my arms under his, felt the tide pulling us out, kicked frantically until I found bottom and, painfully slowly, drew him to the shore. At first he could barely stand. I held him until he gave me a freezing look. I released him. He stood unsteadily, dripping, until he found his feet and his dignity.

'Thank you,' he said, as though I was his gentleman-of-chamber with his poached egg.

His change of expression made me whirl round. Scogman was bringing his pistol to bear on the boat. I brought my hand down on it.

My father stood, holding on to the canopy structure, an easy target, the very model of aristocratic honour. It was as if, having failed, he wished to die. It was both absurd, and curiously moving. He raised his hand and, as he disappeared from sight, I raised mine.

'Your father is a fine man,' the King said. 'I wish you had his loyalty.'

The soldiers encircled us. The Colonel dismounted and, as if nothing had happened, gave the usual deferential bow to his soaked and shivering sovereign. But neither he, nor anyone else, was getting any more deference from me.

'Your Majesty,' I said, 'a man can be loyal only to someone he trusts.'

PART FOUR

The Signature

1649–1659

37

Who could trust Charles Stuart? He escaped again later that year, this time getting as far as the Isle of Wight before being recaptured. In captivity, he made a secret deal with the Scots, plunging the country into another year of war before being defeated a second time and brought to trial.

By then, January 1649, I no longer cared what happened to Charles Stuart. Or the country. I returned from the last battle, in Preston, to find Anne fighting for her life.

She was still in Lucy Hay's house, although the Countess was no longer there. Cromwell had arrested her for her part with Holles in the Presbyterian uprising. Jane told me Anne's illness began the day after she had visited Lucy in the Tower. Dr Latchford said Anne had caught gaol fever there. She ate little and could scarcely keep that down. Jane whispered that Anne had brought back more than fever from the Tower – she had carried with her the conviction I was dead.

It was a common symptom among women in London. During the fighting they did not hear from their men for months, sometimes years. Astrologers were more likely to pronounce the men alive or dead than the army. But not only did my presence not cure the disease; my being there seemed to exacerbate it.

Anne did not recognise me, pushing me away, crying, 'No more doctors!'

'Is she going to die, sir?' whispered Luke.

It was a house of whispers, of drawn curtains, and of fires built up, even though the fever was burning her. At least her illness seemed to drive Luke's fear away and he no longer hid his scarred face. He kept Anne alive, not me. She rallied when he came into the room. He read to her, not from the Bible that Mr Tooley had placed at her bedside, but from the only thing that gained her fragmentary attention – old chap books, of knights and love, and wrongs being righted. In one tale there was a knight called Thomas. She rose with an unexpected burst of energy.

'Not that one. Thomas is dead.'

Luke broke down and protested that I was alive. I tried to hold her but she pushed me away. I fell on my knees, weeping, trying to bring back her memory, recalling the days we first met when I had walked bare-footed into Half Moon Court.

'Monkey,' she said.

I had a great burst of hope then, but she remembered Tom even less than Thomas. If Thomas was dead, Tom had barely existed. All she remembered was the sight of bare feet, picking up a quill or a piece of type between the toes, and that I had been some kind of messenger. Once I mentioned kissing her under the apple tree. She became so agitated and her fever ran so high that Dr Latchford sent me from the room.

I sat outside her room so at least I could hear her voice, her cries, or open the door to listen to her troubled sleep. Dr Latchford thought her mad and wanted to send for a doctor from Bedlam, but I refused. Anne's state of mind made perfect sense to me. It was my fault, for I should never have left her. I had killed myself in her mind. She was my life, and I could not live without her. The real madness had been my own, leaving her for a world of hopeless dreams, and for Ellie.

It was at the height of this, when I scarcely knew whether I was asleep or awake, that Ireton came. If I had been thinking with any kind of clarity I would not have seen him. He and Cromwell had destroyed the last of my dreams. They had suppressed a Leveller demonstration by trapping the group in a church. Three were sentenced and shot on the spot. Cromwell's men broke Joshua's flute, and broke the Levellers, although the movement continued underground, in a desultory way. Jane, however, had showed Ireton in, and I had no option but to see him, half-expecting, as I always had, ever since coming up river from Poplar with Mr Black and Gloomy George, that I would be sentenced to death myself.

My dark thoughts could not have been further from the truth. It was the King who was to be executed.

Of course I knew about the King's trial. But since I never left the house, I knew little else. Nor cared. I vaguely assumed that, whatever the findings of the court, the proceedings would end with the King's abdication.

We met in Lucy's salon, with her glittering Van Dyck of Charles on one side of the room, and, on the other, the rather scruffy portrait of Cromwell by the follower of an artist whose name Lucy always forgot. When I entered, Ireton was viewing the contrast with his pale smile, but made no comment. He was courteous to a fault. I had never seen him more nervous.

He said the King had refused to plead. He had laughed at his judges. He had argued that a small fraction of the *Lower* House – I could almost hear Charles's contempt in the emphasis – elected eight years before, had no mandate to try him. How could the people try the King? *Rex est Lex* – the King *is* the Law. I wondered, fleetingly, why I admired the courage and style of the King's convictions, while hating those convictions; and why, although Ireton's beliefs were broadly mine, I loathed his manner of expressing them, like a small-town lawyer calling in a debt.

Ireton had expected the King to do what he would have done: to accept the court's jurisdiction to save his life. The trial could have proceeded and Charles would have abdicated. The refusal to plead meant yet another stalemate. I could hear Cromwell's harsh, irate tones, when Ireton told me of his reaction in private. Was there to be no end to it? The King would not compromise. Could not be trusted. God had judged him by his defeat in war. Twice. God would not be so patient with his people a third time. Charles Stuart must go to the block.

I had no idea why Ireton was telling me this, or why he now paced the gallery, sliding glances at me, and why, never at a loss for words, he said nothing for some time. It was only when I heard Jane calling me and said I must go that he twisted his hands together, cleared his throat and said that he would appreciate my signature.

I stared at him, bewildered. 'My … my signature?'

'On the King's death warrant.'

I laughed in his face. 'Tom Neave's signature? On the death warrant of the King of England?'

'Of course not,' he said tartly. 'Lord Stonehouse's signature.'

I grew even more confused. 'Lord Stonehouse is dead.'

'I mean you.'

'Me? I am not Lord Stonehouse.'

'You could be.'

Gradually it dawned on me that he was not making some macabre joke, but was deadly serious. When it became known that Cromwell was determined to prosecute the King and a brief had been prepared, the Inns of Court emptied overnight. Barristers fell ill, were away, or on other business. Only one barrister was found prepared to take the brief. I gathered from Ireton that ailments, and other problems, were creating similar difficulties in amassing the number and, above all, the quality of signatures on the death warrant.

I cut him short. I told him that even if I wished to be Lord Stonehouse, which I did not, it was impossible. The estate and the title were my father's.

'He is in France. If the King is executed, he has no one to support his claim.'

'He has my grandfather's will.'

'There is another will.'

That took my breath away. As usual, Ireton's intelligence was impeccable, even if his judgement on how I would react was not. He had seen Roger Hanmer, the solicitor present at my grandfather's death. By a thorough, diligent search of precedence, he had found a case for breaking the entail that left the estate to the eldest son.

'That other will was not signed,' I said.

Ireton looked puzzled. 'I am told it was signed and witnessed before he died.'

I looked at Ireton with contempt. I believed that Charles Stuart, who had laughed at his judges and shown no remorse for the thousands killed and families destroyed, deserved to die. But I had no love for Cromwell and Ireton after their crushing of the Levellers. I told Ireton I would not do it. He thought I was bargaining. While he was offering me some preferment as an additional inducement, there was a confused argument outside and the door opened.

Anne was standing in the doorway, swaying slightly. Her nightdress hung about her wasted figure. Her long hair, prematurely streaked with grey, drifted about her shoulders. Her voice was thin and halting, but this only gave it a curious kind of majesty, which her mentor, Lucy, could not have bettered.

'Mr Ireton ... it is good of you to come at last.'

Jane, hovering behind her, tried to stop her, but Anne shook her off and came forward towards me.

'Thomas ... is Mr Ireton being attended to?'

Her legs gave way, and I just managed to catch her before she struck the floor.

38

I signed. I joined the other fifty-nine names on the death warrant; some men of political conviction like the lawyer Roger Bradshaw, who presided over the trial; some lecherous rogues like Henry Marten; some radical hotheads like the young Lord Grey of Gorby, the only peer on the list; some pious men like Edward Whalley, who believed that God guided his pen, and some like me, whose motives were known only to themselves.

At least, when I dipped the quill in the ink, I finally knew – or determined – who I was when I signed my name: Sir Thomas Stonehouse. I had refused the peerage so I could enter the Commons where I had once run with the words that I thought would change the world, although now I could scarce remember them. Anne would have objected if she had been aware of it, but she was aware of little, except that I was Thomas again. I believe she clung on to life because of Ireton's visit, and because, once more, I had a good tailor.

I had arranged alterations for the suit I had ordered from Mr Pepys two years before, but been unable to pay for when Lord Stonehouse withdrew my allowance. Mr Pepys had looked askance at the dark green cloth which he said was not fitted for a funeral, let alone the King's execution, but I had no time for such niceties. Cromwell wanted the axe to fall as soon as the ink and the seals dried on the warrant and the sentence was passed. A scaffold was hurriedly knocked up in Whitehall and the execution scheduled for noon on 30th January 1649.

Waking up that morning, I was already writing the pamphlet in my head – a disreputable and grisly habit it would take years to expunge – when the thought struck me. If a King died, his successor was always proclaimed immediately. King Charles's son, who had fled to Holland, would certainly declare himself King, but it would be a disaster if anyone made such a proclamation in London. I told myself Cromwell must have thought of this, but when I mentioned it to Ireton he went white. Tragedy became farce. The proceedings were delayed while enough compliant MPs were found and shuttled to Westminster to pass an Act making any such proclamation of a successor illegal.

Assuming the execution would go ahead despite the delay, I went to collect my suit from Mr Pepys, as previously agreed. Anne would not forgive me if I failed to look presentable at such an occasion.

'Will it go wrong, sir?' said a voice in my ear.

It was young Samuel Pepys, my tailor's son. The money Pepys had earned from his scissors had enabled him to send Samuel to St Paul's.

'Should you not be at school?' I said sternly.

'We were sent home,' he said evasively, then, with increasing anxiety, 'Is it not going to happen?'

'Do you want it to?'

'Indeed I do, sir!' He must have been about fifteen, his voice scarcely broken. He stood there, his hands clenched and his cheeks flushed. 'If I had to deliver a sermon on him, the text would be: "The memory of the wicked shall rot".'

I laughed at his enthusiasm, but there was little else to laugh at that morning. I paid Mr Pepys for the suit and took some comfort from possessing the means to do so. I was relieved, too, by the knowledge that a good tailor will gain a man admittance to places that would otherwise be closed to him.

One of those places was a prominent position at the King's execution. Ireton as usual sat silent and composed, only just a little paler than usual.

There was a very sharp wind that day, cutting across the Thames from the east, and the King wore an extra shirt, so his shivering could not be mistaken for fear. He said his prayers, wished his children goodbye and walked through the banqueting hall of the Palace of Whitehall, under the Rubens ceiling panel of Solomon, portraying the divine power of Kings.

On the scaffold, added to his natural nobility was a sense of purpose he had never found on the throne. It was fuelled by the same stubborn inflexibility that had brought him there. The few words I heard that were not scattered by that biting east wind were that he was not an enemy of the people, but a martyr for them. He had governed to protect the people's lives and goods – but government itself, or a share in that government, was not a matter for them.

When the axe fell, a horrified groan spread through the crowd. Young Samuel, in spite of his radical bluster, went pale and clutched at my hand. Many groaned because they felt God's laws had been desecrated. I groaned for all the lives lost and at how the King's stupidity became martyrdom in one moment of theatre. Cromwell was not there. He detested theatre. As inflexible in his own way as the King, he was at prayers. I groaned for the past, for all my old fellow-pamphleteers like Crop-Eared-Jack, on the edge of the crowd as I had once been, for, as the executioner held the head aloft, I knew that the King, now he could no longer speak, had all the best lines, the most compelling stories, and could do no wrong.

Mr Ink was really too grand for it these days, with a corpulent belly and clean collar and cuffs, but he was kind enough to take down my maiden speech in the House, which was on the subject of censorship. Now I sat in Lord Stonehouse's chair in Queen Street,

I saw an urgent need for censorship as I had never done on the other side. We were the pariah state Europe, horrified at the execution of an anointed King. We had enemies not only without, but within, in Ireland and Scotland. I was Secretary for Intelligence and Special Affairs – in short, as Lord Stonehouse had once been, spymaster.

I asked Mr Ink if he remembered the words which he once told me would change the world. He was silent for a while, his hands linked over his belly, before saying, 'Well, Sir Thomas, I do believe now that it is the words that change. The world never changes.'

My main concern was Anne. She was physically better, but had a strange vacancy about her, staring at people as if she was always on the point of remembering something. I took her, for the first time, to Highpoint, in the hope that the country air would revive her. It was a mistake, driving her even further into her shell. It was as if she had expended all her energy in her desire for the place, and had not a shred left to enjoy it. I hated the place. It was half a ruin, pillars pitted by musket balls, the park overgrown, and the fountains choked. Black drapes still hung in one neglected wing, marking Lord Stonehouse's death. Anne stared at it in bewildered dismay. A dream that had sustained her all those years had turned out to be a nightmare.

I had taken her to Highpoint on impulse and without warning Mr Fawcett, the house steward, who continued to regard me as a usurper. His frog-like eyes gaped at me before he silently summoned the servants to stand in line and greet us. Anne shrank away. She was wearing the dress she had worn the night Lord Stonehouse died, which she refused to be parted with. It was threadbare and the servants looked better dressed than she was. I put my arm round her. My heart ached for her as she clung to me. She meant more to me than anything I strived for and I was glad to turn my back on that cursed place. If she was rid of her obsession with it, it could go to rack and ruin for all I cared. I led her back to the carriage, intending to stay at the Stonehouse Arms before returning to London.

But we could not find Luke.

He had been seen climbing a tree. A servant had chased him along the gallery. Eventually we found him in the stables, entranced by the ostler, who had lost an eye at Dunbar and who greeted him by saying, 'I see we have another wounded warrior. Let me look at thy badge of courage.'

From that instant, Luke stopped hiding his face. He refused to leave Highpoint. He loved the ruin of it.

'Is this ours? And this? What? All of it?'

The servants came alive. With his natural arrogance, they accepted Luke as a Stonehouse, in a way they never accepted me. I made Jane housekeeper, as her mother had been, and Scogman steward. He learned to write. His hand was execrable but he knew his rogues, the cheats who had leeched the estate to decay. Gradually, the place recovered and, as it did, so did Anne. I was rarely there. While Cromwell subjugated first Ireland, then Scotland, I protected his back. Every nation plotted against the Protectorate, as we had become. From Queen Street, reporting to Secretary of State John Thurloe, I ran the most formidable network of double agents and informers in Europe. By the mid-1650s, we were the most feared nation in Europe.

Each time I returned to Highpoint, my heart beat faster. It was as if our love was being rebuilt along with the house and Anne's health. She planned everything. The servants and the tenants began to respect her, then, to my astonishment, to love her.

Lady Stonehouse was said to be a lady and not a lady. She had the perfect manners inculcated in her by Lucy, who came to stay after I had secured her release from the Tower. Yet she could talk to the architect about the giant pilastered centrepiece of the rebuilt wing and to a tenant about a stillbirth, or a sick cow. I was immensely proud of her and, if possible, more in love with her than ever.

I longed for another child. We had not slept together since her illness, and I approached her with the same diffidence I had displayed when I first met her. She wished for a little more time. Her health was still fragile. Then, although she had always scorned her mother, who would not leave her bed if her astrologer warned her the signs were inauspicious, she consulted with one, who invariably found, on the week of my visit, that Saturn was in opposition to Venus.

When the restored wing was opened, the county was invited. It was a great success and, flushed with that and too much wine, I went to Anne's room when she was preparing for bed. As awkward as the callow apprentice I once was, I read the first poem I ever wrote her, ending, 'I hope that my love for thee may make your eyes see me.'

She gave me a wicked smile, just as she used to, and asked me if I ever realised when she had first fallen in love with me. My heart pounded and, as she seemed to regret saying it, I begged her to tell me. As fired by the evening and the wine as I was, she said it was when she first discovered the accounts book in her father's office, marked with a letter 'T', and realised there was more to me than my ugly feet.

She told it as a joke, but it took root. I remembered her choking tears when she had told me she would not marry me, because she stood in the way of my inheritance. Did that not show she loved me? But then, by what I no longer saw as a coincidence, Lucy had appeared to take her to the party where she would be introduced to Lord Stonehouse. Just as in the accounts book, did Anne not make her own calculations?

When I raised it, she laughed and kissed me, and I dismissed it. What did it matter? She made no more excuses, and, in the following months, never refused me her bed, but it felt dutiful, a masquerade. The child never came. I suspected she took something to prevent it, but could never prove it.

In spite of – perhaps because of – the fact that we rarely saw one another, we were judged the perfect married couple. Cromwell never disbanded the army and in the county, where all the junior officers were in love with her, Anne glittered like an exquisitely cut jewel. In London she impressed Cromwell with her sober mien and godliness, which, like her high-crowned Puritan hat, she took off with a sigh of relief on returning to Highpoint.

All this time, I worked harder than ever. In late autumn – it was always late autumn, when the candles were lit early and cold crept into old wounds, that I became first edgy, then unbearable – I would tell Mr Cole I must on no account be disturbed. From a room no servant was allowed to enter, I would change into a drab suit, such as a low-grade clerk might wear. Putting on a cloak and wide-brimmed hat, I would slip out the back way, like a tenant who has been begging unsuccesfully for time to pay. Secrecy seemed an essential part of it, although, in any case, it was a wise precaution in Puritan England.

My limbs always creaked at first, for although I was but thirty, I carried a good belly and, at other times, walked little. My pace would quicken as I went past Lincoln's Inn, and my pulse would beat faster as I approached Smithfield, breathing in the stink as if it was fine perfume. In Half Moon Court the printer's sign was still there: RB with a yellow half-moon, although Mr Black and his wife were long dead, buried where they wished to be, in St Mark's. Cromwell had kept his promise. Barring Catholics, there was more religious toleration in England than there had ever been.

After the funeral I had told Anne I would sell or rent the place. But when it came to it I always found the tenant unsuitable, or the price too cheap. There was some reason behind this. The place went with the Dutch printing machine that Mr Black bought after making me his apprentice. The bottom had dropped out of the market. Political pamphlets were banned. There were plays, with some popularity in printed form since the theatres had all been closed, but it was a thin business. One day, I always told myself as I gazed through the dusty window at the gauze of cobwebs shrouding the platen, the market would return.

The house opposite, now a tailor's, was bursting with life, full of children who believed I was a ghost and ran shrieking inside when I turned to the apple tree I had planted. They had picked most of them but there was usually one they could not reach, or a windfall. I would take a bite or two, perfectly calmly, not believing it would happen again. Abruptly, as the sourness cut my tongue, the tears came. They blinded me and racked me. Each time I thought they had stopped they began again, until they drove me from the court.

The exhaustion that followed them was the beginning of relief, and I would go to the address Scogman had found for me. He always said he knew what I was looking for. For a time it was the widow of a baronet, but she grew too attached and talked of love, and I had had enough of that. Whores were easier. That was the real relief, the pretence of love on both sides, and a few hours of wild freedom. Afterwards I would slink back to Queen Street, change back to Sir Thomas, sometimes picking up a draft report I had left in mid-sentence, and work through the night.

Some years are etched in the memory. The very numbers have an aura, a sense of magic about them. The most notable was 1655: for many it was the year we took Jamaica from the Spanish, and were on the road to becoming a colonial power. For me, it left a memory of the damp, clinging fog in the court and the apple I bit that had a worm in it, and a reminder of Scogman, directing me over London Bridge, deep into Southwark. The morality merchants, as he called them, were having one of their sporadic purges. Brothels had been closed and alehouses strictly licensed.

On the most memorable evening for me of that year, the place I went to was as black as pitch outside. The brightness and the stench of musk as I entered made my senses reel. It was done not only to excite me, but so the woman who ran it could size me up and take my name.

'Tom Neave.'

It was compulsive. There was a degree of risk, but it was small and only added to the excitement. I could see from her reaction she took it as false, for it was the name of a well-known scurrilous pamphleteer during the war, who had not written for years, and was believed to be long dead.

She directed me down a hallway, which plunged me into darkness again. Overwhelmed by the changing light, the pungent smells, the murmurs from one room, and a burst of laughter from another, I was full of the most delicious sensations.

A boy took my hat and cloak, showed me upstairs and opened a door. The girl who rose to greet me was young enough to be the virgin she was supposed to be. Her trembling, awkward smile suggested it might even be true.

I was so set on my purpose that it was only when I closed the door that I took in the retreating boy. It was not just that his hair was red – it was that shade of bright, fiery red that had always been a curse to me.

'Wait.'

He turned with slow insolence. He was about eight or nine. He wore some servant's discarded livery, picked up at a rag stall. In the feeble yellow light of the tallows guttering on the wall, I could not see his face.

'Come here.'

He did not move. His voice was loaded with mock deference. 'If she ain't what you want, sir, see her ladyship.'

He bowed, and began to make his way downstairs. I hurried after him and caught him in the dark well of the stairs. 'Do as you're told! Come here.'

I began to pull him into the light, but he caught me a vicious kick on the shin and yelled: 'Trouble!'

Seeing there was no one at the desk, he ran upstairs where I cornered him again. He gave the most ear-splitting scream, more animal than human. A door flew open. Ellie was barely recognisable. The paint on her face glittered but could not completely hide her cratered skin. She was pulling a robe over her slack breasts and belly.

'How many times have I fucking told you –'

I might have slunk away, but she stopped yelling at the boy to stare at me.

The shock in her face transmitted to the boy, who, with the unerring instinct of a child foreseeing some disaster, lost his cocky manner and ran to her. Against her robe, I saw his face. There was no doubt about it. He had the Stonehouse nose, but instead of the falcon-like arrogance of Luke had the predatoriness of the kite, the City scavenger. He had a knife and, emboldened by the protective arm of his mother, his expression showed he was prepared to use it. Both of them were abruptly shoved aside as Ellie's irate customer blundered out of her room.

'Who do you think you are, sir –'

He stopped abruptly. He knew who I was, and I vaguely knew him as some minor official in the navy. The bluster went out of him, like air from a punctured bladder. Not only was I far above him in station, I had my britches on.

'Get out.'

He began to stumble away, remembered his britches and returned, almost knocking over a piss-pot in his hurry to find them. The boy let out a peal of laughter, cut off when Ellie gave him a stinging clip on the ear. The navy official gave me a curious half-genuflection in deference to my rank, then scurried down the corridor. By now the woman at the desk had appeared. There were lowered, panic-stricken voices and doors opening and closing, as people feared a raid by the morality merchants. Ellie made some signal to the woman, who told me to go. I told her if I went I would have the place closed down. Having crept in as Tom Neave, my voice had taken on the sharp tones of someone who expects to be obeyed.

Ellie bundled the boy into the room she had been in. My manner had driven all the bravado out of him, and he shrank into a dark corner. The room was much like many others I had been in; shadowy, cheap-coloured drapes, heavy cloying smells, all of which normally drove me into a frenzy but now filled me with disgust.

'I will take him.'

'Take him?'

'Give me an address.'

Her robe fell open but she did not notice or care. I looked away. 'Take him where?'

'Off your hands.' I could not bear the sight of her a moment longer. 'The address. My man will collect him. Come on. You want to be rid of him, don't you?'

She nodded in a vague, fuddled way, clutched her robe to her and muttered, 'Never known one of you claim a bastard, that's all. Always the other way about.'

I snapped my fingers at her. 'The address!'

She shrugged indifferently. 'Bankside. At the sign of –'

'Don't you tell the cove,' said the boy. Up to now he had seemed as indifferent and acquiescent as she was, but his look of truculent insolence returned. 'I ain't going with no arse-cove.'

'Sam, Sam. It ain't that, I promise you. He ain't all gentleman. He knows us. Him and me – well, never mind that.' She knelt down and smiled. 'This is something to your advantage.'

There was something mechanical about her smile, but he rushed to her and flung himself into her arms, which drew a real response from her. She kissed him, her voice catching as she repeated, 'Something to your advantage.'

'Don't want something to my whatever it is. I ain't going.'

'You will do as you're told,' I said sharply.

Ellie drew away from him and turned to me. Without warning, Sam flew at me, knocking his mother to one side and attacking me with flailing fists. He was big for his age and it was a long time since I had been in any kind of fight. He landed a blow in the stomach and another in the face. I saw a boot coming towards me and upended him, but not before he had sent me staggering against the wall. He scrambled up and I saw the glint of a knife. It was what I had feared would happen some day. It was part of the excitement. But I was alert to the pad in the alley, not this. I was slow, far too slow. It was Ellie who caught him by the neck of his livery, dragging him to one side, so that the blade slashed into the doublet, grazing my skin. I fell back into a chair in a daze.

She wrenched the knife from him and proceeded to thrash him. He took it without a murmur, lips bit closed, not even raising his hands to his head, as if the blows were a kind of love. She did not stop until her chest was heaving, and turned to me.

'Are you all right? Look what you've done to the gentleman's clothes!'

She turned to inflict more punishment, but I told her to desist. She offered me some sickly sweet posset, telling me it had brandy in it. I shook my head. During this, he stood mutely, a thin line of blood trickling down from his forehead where a ring on her hand had cut him.

'Wait until I tell your father! He'll break every bone in your body.'

Father. The word wounded me as no blade had ever done. 'You have a husband?'

'I call him that.'

'Has he a trade?'

'He makes candles,' the boy said. Something in his tone suggested that, far from breaking every bone in his body, his father never touched him. 'Good candles, not tallow.' He stared at me defiantly, fists clenched, lips curled, his hair burning like a beacon, as mine had done at his age, although now the fire was banked down, a dull glow sprinkled with ash. From that moment, a pain began which I knew would never go.

Ellie told me how Alfred's business had failed, how the army had not paid him for his disability – the usual story, the usual excuses. I was only half listening. I said I would be in touch, would help them if I could, then left the place with my senses dazed and feeling in no state to make decisions.

I left it to Scogman. He found there was sufficient truth in the story, and sufficient temptation in a new life in Half Moon Court to drag them out of the mire. Alfred was one of those people thrown on the scrap heap by the army. He was a bit hapless, dragging his crippled leg after him, but kind, a combination that led him to accept someone else's child and Ellie's trade. I never met him, nor did I see Ellie or Sam again. Alfred believed he owed his good fortune to some disabled soldiers' charity. I do not know what Sam believed, or suspected.

Every three-month Scogman sent a report to Queen Street, as Mr Black had sent on me. I had the boy tutored by Mr Ink. Nothing fancy, I told him. He was to be no gentleman. Give him his letters and his numbers. For the rest, he would have to make do with common sense. He had plenty of that. Oh, he was sharp! Candles being a seasonal trade, in the summer he persuaded Alfred first to sell then to make pewter candlesticks. Vicious and unruly at first, Sam became softened by Alfred's increasing reliance on him and they began to build up a good business, of which, to tell the truth, I was as proud as they were.

Each autumn, as the first fogs began to roll up the river, I was consumed by the same restlessness and, clad in my clerk's suit, would slip out of the back door. But now I had only one destination.

From the opening of Half Moon Court I would watch them at supper, or Sam and Alfred still in the workshop, building up stock for winter. Sam had my old room at the top. He sat there pondering over a new candlestick, or staring out of the window full of dreams, as I had once done. He was the last to blow out his candle. I gazed until he did so, and the house went dark, and, feeling a strange kind of peace, I would return to my desk at Queen Street.

So it went on, year after year, until the news came that part of me had been longing for, and part dreading.

39

Cromwell was dying. Like King Charles before the war, he had run out of money and friends. I hated him because he had never called a properly elected Parliament, relying to the last upon the army. Now the soldiers were beginning to desert him. I loved him because he had not only made England into Britain, but had turned it into an overseas power – but mostly because, from coast to coast, the killing had stopped. And most of all, I loved him because Sam, and all the other Sams, had been given time to have their dreams.

Cromwell's son Richard succeeded him. He was an affable fellow, who could make an effective speech, when the words were written for him. But he had never been a soldier and, fatally, lost control of the army. There was growing unrest against military rule – even talk of the return of Charles's son from Holland.

On a bleak day in December 1659, I stepped from my carriage in Queen Street to find consternation round my front door.

Mr Cole, rarely disturbed by anything, was on the steps, anxious and apologetic. He had no idea how it had happened. The servants in charge of the entrance had been dismissed. With pails of soapy water, scullions were attempting to clean the front door. Crudely lettered in black was the word REGICIDE. King Killer. Slashed through the word was a red plague cross.

I told Mr Cole to find a letter that had arrived that morning. Such letters arrived at irregular intervals, from various parts of Europe that had not signed a treaty with us. After the first, I tore them up unread. Most of the pieces of that morning's letter were retrieved from the night soil and brought to me. It resonated with a sincerity missing when my father had first written to me. He blamed himself for not killing me. It had contributed towards the death of the King whom he worshipped and he would not rest until I was dead.

He went into some detail on how the Regicides who signed the death warrant would die. I would be 'hanged until half-dead, dragged to the Scaffold where my foule prick and balls would be cut offe'. I would watch 'that devil witch Anne Black (I wille not soil my family's name with hers)', saved from the same punishment 'onlie for decency's sake', burned at the stake before my bowels would be 'scouped out and throwne on the same fire'.

I studied it closely, not for its content, which I had seen before, but for the style of the scrivener who had written it. Dutch, I thought. A plain hand without flourishes, used to composing merchants' letters. Probably Amsterdam.

I had been careless. At first I had kept track of Richard as the self-proclaimed Charles II begged his way through Europe. I had lost the trail and must find it again. I selected a few fragments, with distinctive ways of writing 's' and crossing the 't', and dictated a letter to a merchant in Amsterdam, ostensibly about the purchase of Flemish tapestries. He was one of our best agents in Europe and, within a month, with a bit of luck, I would know where Richard was. Within three months, and a little more luck, he would be dead. It would not be true to say I had no concern. But it was passing. Similar decisions crowded it out and it was easier, indeed necessary, to make them dispassionately, with the stroke of a pen, and a seal.

I put the remaining pieces of the letter in the drawer in which Lord Stonehouse had kept Richard's correspondence or, more accurately, his bills and debts. I had not opened it for years. The candlelight caught a glint of metal in the crevice.

'Mr Cole. What is this key?'

He took me to an upstairs room where various personal goods and papers of Lord Stonehouse were kept. At times I had vaguely thought of going through them, but more pressing matters always intervened. Mr Cole pulled out a casket. Intrigued, I opened it. I started back so suddenly I would have fallen if Mr Cole had not caught me. It was as though the falcon, flying up abruptly from its jewelled nest, had pushed back the lid. The rubies that were its eyes hypnotised me. My mother had stolen it shortly before my birth and Matthew, the man I once thought was my father, had told me that everything that happened came from that. Well, he was a fine storyteller, but I was long past such childish things. A promise I had made came back to me. I laughed at myself, my young self.

I was a Stonehouse, as cold and dispassionate as my grandfather, a rational man, with a bent towards natural philosophy. I dismissed the promise I had made as silly, irrational superstition. Yet still I sat there, on a box of mouldering papers in that musty room, staring into the bird's red, flickering eyes until the candle went out.

I went to Highpoint next day, not by carriage with guards, as prudence and position dictated. I rode with Scogman, bearing his banter and my stiff, aching legs. The plague cross on my door had triggered old, long-buried instincts. Look for the unexpected. Never do the expected yourself. We went the green way, the old drover's road. To Scogman's amazement, I insisted on sleeping rough. I would not even stay at the Stonehouse Arms in Oxford, although I owned it. It had been a favourite haunt of Richard's and, throughout the Cromwell years, Oxford had remained stubbornly, subversively, Royalist.

Scogman was as out of condition as I was. We both got colds and grumbled and swore at one another like crotchety old men, but by the time we had emerged from the Great Forest one morning our senses were singing.

Below us, silencing us, were the parklands, the fountains, and Highpoint itself, which had taken years to restore, the gleaming projected portico over the entrance guarded by a crouching falcon.

There were so many things I ought to be doing. I should be in Queen Street, attending meetings, plotting, making contingency plans. Why was I here to fulfil this obscure promise, a promise I had made only to myself, and so many years ago?

I told Scogman to tell Lady Stonehouse where I was going, reflecting that now I never called her anything else. It struck me, with a smile, that ever since we were children, she had always been that to me.

While Scogman rode down to the house, I forded the river, taking the hill road to Shadwell. The landscape was as bleak as ever, fit only for sheep, whose bells tinkled tinnily as they raised their heads to stare at me.

Shadwell church was much the same. It could have been yesterday that I came up here, trying to trace my father, believing my mother had been married here to Lord Stonehouse's son Edward, who had the living. Edward had denied it, denouncing the obscure spot where she was buried as evil. *Origo mali* – the source of the evil.

I had cried, 'I will put a fresh stone there!'

Where? That was the problem. I searched around the drystone wall at the north of the church, where the grass and weeds were thickest. What stones there were had no names, or names eaten away by the wind and rain. There was a step behind me. As if it was the ghost of one of the Stonehouses, I whirled round, feeling for my knife. Whirled? My movements were so clumsy and rusty, if it had been a Stonehouse I would have been dead.

A fat, jovial man was blinking at me. He introduced himself as Travers, the present incumbent. He knew the stone very well, he said, for my mother, Margaret Pearce, was a legend in the village. I thought he was seeking to add to his frugal living, but he went immediately to a stone that had become part of the roughly built wall. Tearing away grass, I saw a fading red mark, and I remembered some long-forgotten obscenity scrawled on my mother's stone.

Travers pointed to the village and to the moor where it became even wilder. 'Some people claim to have seen her. Some are afraid, but some see her as a free spirit. She goes with the land, some say. Poor as it is, this is all common land. Stonehouse Without, some call it.'

Then it came back to me. Strange how one forgets, but I had signed so many papers, sealed so many documents. And many of those documents had concerned this land. When I could, with Scogman's help, I had turned back the relentless tide of half a century of Stonehouse enclosures. It was not easy, because the legal entail only left the estate to me in trust. There had been a wood, no, two woods, marshland, a stream, fishing rights, this moor. I could almost hear the ghost of Joshua's flute playing. That I had done, at least.

I came to with a start. Travers was talking about mutton. The land might be poor, but it produced the finest mutton in the country. And some of that very mutton was turning on the spit at his house. My mouth watered at the thought and I accepted his invitation to eat.

The mutton fell off the bone. As we washed it down with wine, the stone grew into a monument. I tried to keep it within bounds, but I could not resist Travers's suggestion that it should bear the Pearce coat of arms, a wildcat with a raised paw and the motto *Tantum Teneo*. Only persist. My mother would have liked that. 'I will have one of them,' she had said, in her determination to marry one of the Stonehouses and take over their estate, as they had swallowed up her father's. 'I will have one of them …' *Tantum Teneo*. Only persist.

I had never known her. All I knew about her was in Matthew and Kate's stories. But, that afternoon, I felt I had known her all my life.

I told Travers I would definitely add the Pearce coat of arms for my mother. Then, thanking him for the mutton, I said I must be on my way. But, on leaving him, I found myself drawn to look again at the stone. It was late, the light going, but I was reluctant to leave. A north wind drove spatters of rain against me as I stared at the stone. Stories: that, in the end, was what we all became. Now I might need to earn an honest living again, perhaps I should write this one. The thought brought back Half Moon Court and my son Sam. If we had to flee, what would happen to him?

I had observed him secretly, more greedily than ever, that autumn. He was thirteen and big for his age. A real Neave, cocky, streetwise, full of dreams – not of poetry, but natural philosophy. He had developed from making pewter candlesticks to experimenting with laboratory equipment for natural philosophers – even instruments which were said to see new worlds in drops of water. I had given him his start in life. No one knew of his existence except Scogman and me. Sam, I thought, could take care of himself.

In spite of all the advantages lavished on him, I was more concerned about Luke. He was a Stonehouse from his beaked nose to his fashionable, baggy-topped boots. He displayed rather than shrank from his scarred face, which made him look much older than his sixteen years. Since I was rarely at Hightpoint, he considered it his seat, and would not give it up easily.

My two sons knew nothing of one another. It struck me that they were the two sides of my nature, sure of themselves in a way I never could be. For years, I had worn the ruling arrogance of the Stonehouses until I had almost become one. Almost. Now I could feel what I thought had been long dead and buried, the radical stirrings of Tom Neave, creeping back.

It was now quite dark. I had scarcely noticed the rain increasing and was soaked to the skin. It must have been a night like this that

Matthew was told to pick up a plague child. I could hear his cart. See his whip lashing. No, it was not a cart but a carriage. Out of it came my mother.

I swear it. There she was as I had always pictured her, running through the driving rain between the gravestones, half-torn cloak billowing, held together by the glittering pendant, red hair flaring. Too petrified to move, it was only when she was in my arms that I saw the red had faded from her hair.

'I thought something had happened,' Anne cried.

'Happened?'

'There's been a riot in Oxford.'

She told me REGICIDE, with a red plague cross, had been daubed on the Stonehouse Arms.

She was trembling. It was a long time since I had felt her heart beating next to mine. Perhaps it was fear, or need. I did not care. I no longer wanted to analyse our feelings. I just wanted to hold her – hold Anne, not Lady Stonehouse.

'Anne … Anne …'

I whispered her name continuously as I pulled her cloak round her and fastened the clasp. On our way to the carriage we were silent, one of those old silences, when neither of us needed or wanted to speak.

It was only when the carriage forded the river, water splashing up to the windows, that she broke the silence.

'You're back.'

'I'm back.'

We held each other tightly as the candle-lit windows of Highpoint swept into view. First I had been in awe of it, then I had hated it. Only now, with the threat of losing it, did I realise how much it meant to me. I dismissed my fears. Who was Charles II? Few knew him. Few wanted a King back on the throne.

Luke greeted us to say, with a typical shrug, that he had 'dealt with the little local difficulty at Oxford'.

I felt closer to him than I had been for years. I pretended not to have eaten to join them in a meal that turned into a feast. It was as if we had just moved in. The great house, which had torn us apart, that December evening brought us together, and we celebrated far into the night.

Historical Note

The Stonehouses are fictional, but what happened to them in 1647 is shaped by real events. The King surrendered not to the English, but to the Scots, from whom he hoped for a better deal. For coming to the aid of Parliament in the Civil War, the Scots presented a bill for £1,300,000, but were knocked down to £400,000, for which they returned to Scotland and gave up the King. Charles himself accused them of selling him.

Once Charles was in England, under house arrest, there was public pressure to reduce the size of the New Model Army. A fanatical Presbyterian divine, Thomas Edwards, produced three huge books called *Gangraena*, one of which accused the army of spreading not only false doctrine but dangerous radical views, such as that supreme authority belonged to the Commons.

In fact, all that most of the army wanted was to be paid (arrears ran to forty-three weeks in the cavalry), with indemnity against prosecution for acts committed during the war, and not to be compelled to go to Ireland. In short, unsurprisingly, most wanted to go home.

There is no greater example in history of unintended con-sequences in what happened next. Public opinion, whipped up by people like Edwards with *Gangraena* – the tabloid press of its day – and combined with overreacting, inept politicians, created the exact opposite of what they wanted. They politicised the army.

Presbyterians, led by Denzil Holles, were prepared to have the King back on minimal terms. Independents, a coalition led by Cromwell, wanted to bind Charles with strict limitations on his powers before the army was disbanded. At the critical time, Cromwell was ill.

When Holles forced through the Commons an immediate disbandment of the New Model foot soldiers, and was clearly building up his own forces, revolt began to spread through the New Model Army. Sir Lewis Challoner is a fiction, but there was a conviction in the army that the Presbyterians were plotting to transfer the King to Scotland.

This was the trigger for George Joyce, very much a real figure, to carry out one of the most stunningly audacious acts of this, or any other, war. He did meet Cromwell in his garden in Drury Lane on the night of 31st May when Mrs Cromwell served bread and butter and small beer. He outlined a plan to march to Holdenby and secure the King under guards loyal to Cromwell.

By this time Cromwell knew that his efforts to keep army and Parliament together were in tatters. He had to choose between one or the other. He gave George Joyce, tailor and cornet – the lowest rank in the army – his blessing. Exactly what that meant gave rise to bitter disputes.

The King was playing bowls at Althorp when Joyce arrived with his men. Holdenby House, where the King was held, was the largest private house in England and was much as described. Richard is fiction, but his escape mirrors that of Colonel Graves, who had been in charge of the Presbyterian guard on the King. Having had no word from Cromwell, Joyce feared Graves would return 'with a party' and snatch back the King. He entered the royal bedchamber at ten that night and warned the King to be ready to leave at first light.

Fairfax, the army commander, and senior officers swore that Joyce had acted 'without their privity, knowledge or consent'. Cromwell called Joyce a rascal for saying he was only carrying out his instructions. On 10th July, Joyce was issued with a warrant in Fairfax's name for £100 for 'extraordinary services'.

There was another 'Parliament' in Reading – here the army proposed and framed impeachments on Holles and ten other MPs. By mid-July, Westminster was virtually under the control of the army which instigated the extraordinarily generous peace terms Tom hears read out in the Commons: promising religious tolerance, and that the King would be restored to his regal powers, including his legislative veto.

The attempted Presbyterian counter-revolution which led to the riots in the Commons, when excrement was thrown, was incited by Presbyterian clergymen, prominent members of the City government and almost certainly by some of the MPs impeached with Holles, who, when it failed, went into exile and obscurity. When the mob left, the Speaker did flee to the army, taking the mace and fifty other MPs with him.

I have taken a large amount of liberties with Mr Ink, who is based on a real, rather more prosaic figure, William Clarke, a Londoner of poor origins who became secretary to the Army Council. He used the same shorthand system as Pepys, based on Shelton's *Tachygraphy*, which broke letters into smaller units to be joined together. The notes he made of the Putney debates, which really did contain words which would change the world, with the beginning of what would become universal franchise, were buried for almost two and a half centuries.

They were left to an Oxford College by Clarke's son, and their importance was only recognised in the 1890s.

John Wildman, who adroitly presented *An Agreement of the People* before Cromwell and Ireton at Putney, was described by Disraeli as one of the most remarkable men nobody had ever heard of. His goal was the establishment of a democratic English republic. For fifty years he conspired to achieve it, plotting (as his biographer Maurice Ashley puts it) with admirable lack of discrimination the murders of both Cromwell and Charles II. After spending much of his political life in prison, he ended up as Postmaster General and one of the richest Aldermen in London.

Nehemiah's attempt to assassinate the King is fiction, but it is based on a plot among some Leveller agents to seize him at Hampton Court. They may have intended to abduct him rather than kill him, but he feared for his life after receiving an anonymous letter warning him that 'eight or nine agitators were resolved to kill him'. He escaped for the last time on 11th November and was recaptured on the Isle of Wight.

From Queen Street, Tom would have reported to John Thurloe, Cromwell's Secretary of State, who established an intelligence system unrivalled in Europe. Pepys wrote: 'Cromwell carried the secrets of all the princes of Europe at his girdle.'

If history is nothing more than the story of unintended consequences, then 1647 ought to be ranked with iconic years like 1066 and 1815.

The army had no intention of revolting. It had little political consciousness at the year's beginning. Cromwell had no desire for political power. Like Tom with the Stonehouses, he saw it as a burden. The army grandees bent over backwards to reach agreement with the King. Originally, they had said he could not have control of the army for twenty years. They cut that down to ten. Charles treated the army generals with disdain. With each concession he expected more. When Charles made his final escape attempt towards the end of 1647, Cromwell washed his hands of him. He would have to go on trial. Abdication was the expected outcome; but the unintended consequence was execution.

The final unintended consequence was that while Cromwell's domestic policy ended in failure (after 1647 he never felt he could disband the army and trust Parliament), he came to be held in awe by Europe, where he increased Britain's power and status; and his foreign policies, far ahead of their time, laid the seeds of the British Empire.